/17

Izzy White?

By

Barry E. Wolfe

Copyright @ 2015 by Barry E. Wolfe

All rights reserved. Published in the United States by The Wolfe Forest Publishers.
Sarasota, Florida, USA

Title Page illustration by Kristen Petrie.

ISBN: 978-0-692-45254-7

Table of Contents

Dedication:
For Annette Forever

Chapter 1.
Crazy Man Crazy

My name is Isadore White, but everyone calls me Izzy. I hate that name with a passion. Always did, but can't seem to escape it. Early in my life the name became a source of ridicule. Kids in my neighborhood made fun of the pronounced nasality of my speech. They would hold their noses and honk out "Iiizzy". I remember vividly when I was ten, after I had endured my eighth operation to close my palate, I had been encircled by a group of my so-called friends in the middle of Roxboro Place. I was trying to break off their laughable, demeaning imitations of my broken speech. I burned with humiliation as each took his turn in producing a lacerating parody of my speech. Sobbing heavily I screeched at them "STOP DOING THAT!!" Each of my tormentors mimicked my plea, only it sounded like "SFNOP SFNOING SFNAT!" Everyone laughed so hard they held their stomachs. This made me cry harder and screech louder. They responded with more taunts and laughter. I became so enraged that I lunged at each one swinging my fists wildly; and each managed to easily dodge me. I finally gave up and ran home barely able to see because of the flood of tears pouring from my eyes.

I was born incomplete, which makes me human. I was born incompletely formed, which for years made me think I was something less. Strangers to the malady would say I was "deformed". In 1942, most people were strangers to the malady. I had clefts. My lip was notched like a hare's. Since I was unable to suck, I was fed with a turkey baster. I had a second cleft in my palate. The roof of my mouth was like a pink vacuum sucking away air meant for plosive speech. Whenever I spoke, air would perversely escape through my nose into the faces of ridiculing kids. For the first decade of my life I struggled to be understood, even after I had endured the first eight of my ten surgeries attempting to repair these clefts. When I was eleven, my palate was successfully repaired. Now my loud and long monologues were no longer able to bust the stitches holding my palate together. Only then did my speech improve enormously. Only then was I understood.

The early repair of my cleft lip, however, left a hideous scar. This sickeningly ugly lip was still there for all to see. When I looked in the mirror I saw a wrinkled and thick mass of flesh that began at the left side of my face and progressively thinned as it stretched across my mug. The thickness at the left was hoisted into full view by a scar that looked like a centipede crawling up inside my nose. Rather gross don't you think? I hated to look at myself in the mirror. What I saw convinced me that I was strange, a different sort of human. And the truth of my differentness was revealed to me in so many ways. There were the frequent trips to the hospital, my hotel of fear; the funny sounds my peers would make in our conversations, resembling steam escaping from radiators; the mysterious explanations by teachers for my rejection from speaking parts in school plays; the long lonely walks from my classroom to the speech therapy room where I met so many others whose speech had been corrupted by a panoply of physical maladies. I felt like I was in an asylum for damaged humans.

The pain became unbearable when at the age of 15 I "fell in love". My friends Peter Kaplan and Bobby Levine dragged me to a birthday party for a girl of their acquaintance. The party was held at the Villa Rosa Restaurant in Silver Spring, Maryland, just beyond the northern Washington, DC line. This was new terrain for me. We entered the party room and I was immediately overcome with the intermingled smells of pizza, perfume, and bubble gum. About ten couples were dancing to Andy Williams' "I Like Your Kind of Love". Laughter gathered overhead like smoke.

We entered. The three of us decked out in our own personal variant of mid-1950's coolness. My hair roughly mimicked the current style of Tony Curtis; a curl of hair slithered seductively down the middle of my forehead and ducktails were coerced in the back of my head by pomade. I thought all my coolness was in my hair. My friends displayed it in their clothes. In Peter's case that meant tapered pants and black loafers, a plaid sport shirt with rolled sleeves and a lifted collar. Bobby put all of his coolness in his Marlon Brando motorcycle jacket. We stood there like three marble statues waiting to be acknowledged. After much scanning of the gyrating crowd, my friends discovered the birthday girl and introduced her to me. There she was, Dara Levenson, a vision in a poodle skirt and ponytail. I fell in love with her smile. She kept on dancing, her ponytail flopping every time Andy Williams sang "honey babe". Dara kept smiling straight into her partner's eyes, then at me, and then at the crowd. Her smile felt like a community welcome and I was grateful. I had then the rare experience of the joy of living. I struggled with myself to acknowledge the possibility that I could belong to that radiant smile. Instead of becoming her boyfriend, I became Dara's dear friend and confidant; but she would never kiss me. Her refusals brought back all the painful memories and doubts. The painful aftermath of the plastic surgery on my lip the year before had eliminated the physical scar, but left the emotional one intact. Dara's refusal to consider me boyfriend material made me wonder if the surgery was worth it. All that physical pain could only be extinguished by a highly controlled regimen of morphine shots every four hours.

It frustrates the hell out of me that every girl I like likes me as a friend. Agh, the curse of friendship! Girls like to confide in me. I guess I'm a good listener and I rarely criticize. But while I'm listening to a girl I like, I'm also dreaming that we are deep in liplock and exploring each other's erogenous zones. Girls! I desire them! Fear them! Hate them! Love them! I was now 15 years old and in love and equally in pain. For years I searched desperately for remedies for both.

The first remedy that I found for the bitter stings of cruelty, ridicule, and unrequited love was music.
But not just any music.
It's the rhythmic and bluesy sound of Black singers and vocal harmony groups that never fails to soothe my soul. My introduction to Rhythm n' Blues came when my best childhood chum Eddie Charles and I would listen to his older brother

Ethan's cool records. Eddie and I listened over and over to the Clovers, the Drifters, the Moonglows, and Hank Ballard and the Midnighters. This music was so different, so moving, and, at the age of 12, so in tune with my spanking new sexy feelings. When I listened, I was gone, man. I couldn't—and still can't-- get enough of this music. One day Eddie and I were listening to the Midnighters' first big hit, "Work With Me Annie". We played this record over and over while we sang along with the moaning background voices. This record possesses the hard-on producing- refrain "Let's get it while the getting is good". When the Midnighters followed this with "Annie Had a Baby", we are treated to the following refrain "And that's what happens when the getting gets good." About two days after we first listened to the second "Annie" song, Mrs. Charles came down to the basement and confiscated both Midnighter records, and we were hereafter forbidden to listen to these dirty songs. Nor is she the only one to disapprove. The song was banned from the radio as too suggestive, and The Midnighters therefore remake Work With Me Annie as Dance With Me Henry, and Annie Had a Baby (Can't Work No More) as Henry's Got Flat Feet (Can't Dance No More). Well, these remakes eliminated everything that was good and exciting about the originals, and neither Eddie nor I gave them the time of day. When Little Richard appeared on the scene in 1955 with his first hit, "Tutti Frutti", I was so taken by the wild excitement of the music that it always lifted my spirits. The staccato piano chords, Little Richard's screams, and the honking sax of Lee Allen filled me with such energy that I was convinced I could do and achieve anything I wanted. The doo-wop harmonies of dozens of wonderful Black vocal groups, beginning for me with the Heartbeats' "Crazy For You" also in 1955, perfectly resonated with the perpetual longing I'm beginning to feel at the tender age of 13 for a special girl—any girl-- who would love me.

In early 1956 a classmate of mine, Frank Baucom, and I discover that we share a taste for Rhythm N' Blues. We often took a streetcar down to Waxie Maxie's Quality Music Store on 7th Street between S and T Streets to listen to some of the latest doo-wop hits. Never have I heard such beautiful music in all my 14 years. On one hot summer day, we are sitting in a booth in Waxie Maxie's listening to a Black singing group in a Black part of town. We are listening to the Solitaires' "The Angels Sang". Listening for free. What a gift to be able to hear this music before deciding to shell out 98 cents for a 78 rpm platter, 98 cents that neither one of us can afford. When I ask if we could hear the "Ship Of Love", the Nutmegs' latest hit, the tall, mocha-colored manager peers down at us and looks as if I have just blasphemed. After he reaches for the top shelf of the store's wall-to-wall record collection and retrieves the requested platter, he turns to us and with his bug eyes ablaze he grouses, "Boys, don't make me reach again. You make my nose bleed!" We quickly make our way to the booth, remove the desired record from its brown sleeve, place the record on the turntable, put on the headphones, and enter a new and safer world. We listen to "Ship Of Love" followed by "Crazy For You", eyes closed, harmonies washing over us, before we see the same aggravated store manager knocking on the booth window. Because of the headphones, neither Frank nor I can hear the knocking or the ominous words that are surely firing out from the manager's rapidly flapping lips. But we get the message—buy or fly. We hastily remove our headphones, replace the record into its paper cover, leave it on the table, and nonchalantly head for the other end of the store. As soon as we think we are out of the manager's field of vision, we dash to the door, yank it open and take off. We make such a racket yanking open the door that the manager sees us and we hear him yelling something about our white behinds not ever returning to Waxie Maxie's without money to buy. We laugh the nervous laugh of would-be criminals. Though we take nothing, we are excited and relieved to have escaped the manager's scary fulminations.

After taking a few deep breathes, we head to U Street, turn left and head west toward 11th street. We eventually arrive at the headquarters of WUST (W U Street) and there in the window we see the man we are seeking—Lord Fauntleroy, the number one DJ in DC for doo-wop and rhythm and blues. We stop to say hello and he asks us where we go to school. We tell him that we have just graduated from Paul Jr. High School. John Bandy, who in a delicious Jamaican accent loves to speak in rhymes when he is on the air, says for the sake of his listening audience, "Hello, you all from Paul. What pound of sound from out of the ground would you like to hear?"

"You mean you'll play our request?" I ask incredulously. "Of course," he replies with a brilliant smile that increases the luster of his smooth brown skin. "I'm the host with the most. What rhythm and blues treasure is your pleasure?" I look at Frank and he at me. We nod to each other and I sheepishly ask, "Can you play Little Richard's "Slippin' and Slidin'"?" Still grinning, Lord Fauntleroy Bandy laughs and announces, "We play what you say. Here's Little Richard and "Slippin' and Slidin'."" An explosion of syncopation breaks upon our ears. Frank and I start dancing. I try to reproduce the moves that I have seen Black teenagers perform on the Milt Grant Show. The sight of us dancing charms Lord Fauntleroy. "You should see these white boys dance," he exclaims to his radio audience, "Like they have ants in their pants." He waves us into the studio and he comes out to shake our hands. We are astonished to find that John Bandy is at least 6'6" tall and can't have weighed more than 180 lbs. We look up at amazement at this animated brown string bean who moves with such looseness and grace. He asks us about our plans and what high school we will be going to in the fall. I can barely hear the words I am so captivated by the musicality of his Jamaican accent.

Doo-wop is the glue that binds me to Frank. We are the odd couple of Black rhythm & blues, first at Paul Jr. High and then beginning in the fall of 1956 at Coolidge High School. While our white contemporaries are making the slow transition from the music featured on the Hit Parade to rock n' roll, we have become connoisseurs of the rare vocal harmonies of Black singing groups that can only be heard on Black music stations such as WOOK and WUST. Since we first heard Marvin & Jonny's "Cherry Pie" and "A Sunday Kind of Love" by Willie Winfield and the Harptones, we have been glued to our transistor radios eager to hear the latest Black sounds on the Cliff Holland show on WOOK and Lord Fauntleroy 's show on WUST.

It's not just the music. It's also the dancing.

I love to watch black teenagers dance on the Milt Grant Show during "Black Tuesday", the only day they are allowed to appear. No whites are on the show at the same time, of course. I'm in awe of their rhythm, and their nimble swaying moves. It's unlike anything I have ever seen. Whenever I watch Negroes dancing on Milt Grant, I stand in my living room tethered to the front door knob and attempt to imitate these wonderful jitterbug moves. And as the succession of specialty dances become popular among Black teenagers, I learn these as well—The Birdland, The Slop, the Snap, the Chicken, and the Mashed Potato.

Before I ever saw the jitterbug performed by Black Teenagers, I was encouraged to go the conventional route. Most pre-teen and teenage kids I knew went to Groggy's dance studio, but I refused. So it was left to my mother to teach me the basics of slow-slow-quick-quick. But I am not fond of the way white kids dance, not after I have seen what the Black kids can do. On many an afternoon, I practiced my jitterbugging in Rachel Sandow's basement where impromptu parties were usually held. There I would slowly introduce my Black-inspired style of jitterbugging to see if it would be accepted, admired, or even imitated. Too often, however, my would-be audience is too busy making out to pay much attention.

And there is basketball!

My love affair with basketball began before I ever played the game. The games of kindergarten included one called "Put the Ball in the Basket". A mesh-covered trash basket was placed in the middle of our room. Two teams were formed. Each team lined up on either side of the basket about seven feet away. The kid at the front of each line would loft the ball underhanded at the basket, each team alternating turns. After one's turn, the shooter goes to the end of his or her team's line. I rarely missed.

I loved the skill I showed, the sound and sight of the ball entering the basket. I also loved the attention I received, and the fact that all my classmates wanted me on their team. I was popular. I was wanted.

By the time I was in junior high school, I had developed a two-handed set shot that was accurate to 22 feet. I tried out and made our school's basketball team even though I was not even 5 feet tall. I was the second leading scorer on Paul's varsity team. In addition to my set shot, I had a high court IQ, what many called savvy. My opponents often say, "That White, he's got savvy." Savvy? I call it survival skills. Always playing with bigger, stronger guys, I learn ways to survive my opponents' efforts to beat me down or take advantage of my limited physical gifts. I know where I learned these skills too. During my junior high and high school years, there was something called "Canteen Night" at the Coolidge High Gymnasium. Two nights a week kids could go play ping-pong, listen to records, and play basketball. This will help stop "juvenile delinquency," so the authorities would say.

Basketball is now an obsession that compels me to religiously show up on Canteen Night and try and get into the games with the bigger boys. As the Washington D.C. schools begin to desegregate, so do the Canteen Night basketball games. As time goes by, more and more Negro ballplayers show up and fewer and fewer whites, until finally, by the time I'm a junior in high school, I am the last white ballplayer at Canteen Night.

I love Canteen Night and I love the Coolidge High gymnasium. It's always well lit, and I appreciate the cream-colored wooden backboards. Other gyms are getting the new, fashionable glass backboards that often skew the light into a weird shot-distorting glare. I love the sound of the bouncing basketballs and the swishing sound of the shot that is so true that it touches nothing but net as it goes through the hoop. Despite my Negrophobia, I relish Canteen Night and the opportunity to play with gifted basketball players. What is

Negrophobia you might ask? Well, it's when white people get the heebie jeebies around black people. That's what would happen to me. I would get around Negroes and I would immediately start feeling the heebie-jeebies. I'd get so nervous that I didn't know what to say or do.

My Negrophobia takes a holiday on those transporting nights of teenage joy. During the games you might hear, in the next room, the sounds of Gene Vincent singing Bee-Bop-a-Lula or Mary Lee by the Rainbows playing on the portable 45-RPM record player marred only by the popping sounds of ping-pong balls.

Canteen night is always crowded with would-be ballplayers. Those who are not currently playing sit on the fold-up bleachers, which, when opened, fan out into six or seven rows. With them sit the many fewer spectators who come to see the latest talent. Your team has to win in order for you to stay on the court.

During Canteen Night there are few full-court games. Instead there are two simultaneous half-court games with 3 guys against 3 others or occasionally 4 on 4. Negroes play the half-court game differently than whites, at least in my part of the world. In white games, when a shooter misses a shot and a member of the other team rebounds the ball, he has to either dribble it back beyond the free throw line or pass the ball back to another teammate beyond that line before any member of that team can launch a shot at the basket. This is known as "taking the ball back". Many an argument breaks out over the precise distance a player has advanced the ball back to or beyond the foul line. "You're not BACK!" is the perennial cry of the aggrieved.

When Negroes play half-court, there's no such thing as taking the ball back. If a shot is missed, members of both teams battle under the basket for the rebound and whoever gets the ball can shoot it right back up. To succeed under these conditions one has to either be able to out-jump his opponent or learn how to use his body, particularly his ass, to block other players out of any position to get the rebound. I'm in shock the first time I play in a no take-back game; because at 5' 4" and 130 lbs I can neither jump very high nor push people around.

And my teammates cut me no slack! I would try with all my might to battle for a rebound, and my taller and stronger opponents would out-jump me or push my featherweight body out of contention for the rebound. Needless to say, it is the player I'm defending who is scoring regularly against me, particularly under the basket. Then I hear, "White, get your white ass stuck on him and play some "D"! "Grab his nuts if you have too, but don't let him score!" Or I hear, "Come on White stop his ass! Push his ass out of there!" My ass, however, is about half the size of my opponents'. I wonder if that's where the phrase "half-assed" comes from. In addition to being bounced around like a ragdoll, I receive many an elbow to the head during my pitiable efforts to get a rebound. It's positively Darwinian out there.

Over time, however, I learn to use speed and trickery to obtain position under the basket before my opponent. I become skillful in tapping the ball back up into the basket rather than wasting precious seconds in coming down with the rebound and going back up with another shot. If I try the latter, it usually results in my opponent pinning the ball to my face or slapping it with such force that it ricochets off the top of my head. I also learn how to quickly and accurately judge where an errant shot is likely to land and beat my opponent to that spot.

I eagerly apply all of the skills I have learned during Canteen Night to my basketball games as a member of the Paul Jr. High varsity. Our first game is against Banneker Jr. High School. Banneker is the first Black junior high school I have ever entered in my life. The gymnasium is bigger than the one we have at Paul, and it's filled with fans rocking to rhythmic cheers. As we are warming up, I take a moment to watch their lay-up drills. Their lay-up line keeps shifting its starting position until everyone is driving down the center of the court from the free throw line to the basket. A much fancier routine than we have. Their star player, Grant Lawson, however, is putting on a show. Instead of driving all the way to the basket, he takes off from the free throw line and literally flies the rest of the way in for a perfect lay-up. And each time he takes off, the crowd roars its approval. After one of his baskets, I overhear one girl in the crowd yelling to another, "Ooooh wee, Carlita, what did you do to that boy? You must have given him some last night". The howling laughter that follows drowns out Carlita's response, but it is apparently an affirmation of the claim.

Grant is as pleasant a human being as he is talented on the basketball court. He wears his talent lightly and never engages in any attempt to verbally humiliate his less talented opponents. In fact, this phenomenon of verbally mocking or humiliating your opponent during a game is called "talking trash". It is introduced to me by Grant's teammate, LeDroit Parks. Both LeDroit and his trash talking are a shock to my system. He's an inch taller than I am, but he looks 20 years old. He's in the 9th grade, but he possesses a mustache and is built like someone who spends most of his time at Muscle Beach. LeDroit is a non-stop trash-talker. This is a very handsome well-built brown man playing on a junior high school basketball team. "Come on Hammer Nose, do your stuff! How did you get such a hammer nose? You truly ugly, man. You look like you been hit wit an ugly stick." LeDroit's taunt about my nose made reference to the misshapen lump that developed as a result of my cleft palate and lip. Somehow he intuits that this taunt will infuriate me more than any other that he might conjure up.

On and on, he chatters. Laugh and chatter. Chatter and laugh. The entire game! The more he talks, the angrier I get until I want to punch him out. But I check the size of his biceps again and think better of the idea. After he steals the ball from me on a couple of occasions and blocks one of my shots, I learn to ignore his taunts and to stay focused on my game. Then I begin to score on him regularly and often. The taunts get nastier. "You got lucky, Hammer Nose! Maybe I'll break that nose for you and we can make it right? What d'ya think about that?" After the game, LeDroit comes toward me and I'm terrified. I think he's about to kick my ass in retribution for my finally besting him on the court. As he gets closer, he suddenly flashes me a huge grin. "Great game, Hammer Nose," he says, giving me a friendly slap on the back. And then to no one in particular he says, "This white boy can PLAY!" Still grinning he adds, "My trash-talking almost fucked you up, didn't it?" I nod uncomfortably as it finally dawns on me that there's no malice in the trash talk. It's just a tactic.

In the showers LeDroit engages me in an extended conversation about our origins. I ask him how he came by the name LeDroit and he tells me that he is named after the neighborhood in which he lives. LeDroit Park, situated just to the south and east of Howard University, was once home for the black social elite, including many of the University's faculty members. By naming him after the neighborhood, LeDroit's parents believed he was marked for greatness.

We compare notes about growing up in different parts of Northwest Washington, he in LeDroit Park and I in Brightwood. His tone throughout seems to be a strange mixture of defiance and ingratiation. I think I'm missing something in what he is saying but, in any event, my focus mainly is on whether he likes me.

Basketball provides me with my first real exposure to Negro people. This inauguration is the beginning of my education. During these games, I feel some lessening of the hold that my phobia has on me. Perhaps, this is where I first get the idea that if I spend more time with Negroes, my phobia will be cured. Although our association is limited to the confines of the basketball court, a question forms in the back of my mind. Why should these decent guys be the subject of such hatred and fear? It's disturbing to me to feel their friendship and yet think such awful thoughts about their supposed violent tendencies and lack of smarts, cleanliness, work ethic, and sense of responsibility.

I wonder how I acquired such shabby ideas about people that I not only admire but for whom I feel great warmth. Then the memory comes. During the Eisenhower vs Stevenson presidential campaign back in 1952, all my peers were freaking out and shrieking to the heavens that if Eisenhower were elected, he would allow "niggers' into the Takoma Park Municipal pool. My ten-year imagination began to conjure up some dark miasma that would emanate into the pool water contaminating us with God knows what. What am I so afraid of? What do I fear will so contaminate me? Perhaps there were earlier conjurings, but I date the beginnings of my own Negrophobia to this imagined aquatic pollution. But when I'm playing basketball, I somehow forget this fearful sense of otherness and want only acceptance and validation of my growing talent. That validation comes one night when my Canteen Night teammates make me an "Honorary Nigga". I kid you not, that's what they called me. That's what I would hear whenever I beat my opponent to a spot, retrieve a rebound and score. "Good going, White! You, our Honorary Nigga".

And being an Honorary Nigga saved my ass on more than one occasion. There is one night when I'm hanging out with my best friend, Eddie, in the alley near his house, when a group of about ten Negroes about our age approaches us with menace in their eyes. They are dressed in green raincoats, pork pie hats or grey fedoras, and pointy-toed shoes. They are known as "Block Boys" and they are equal opportunity shit-kickers. A person's color does not matter. They seem to always be looking to kick somebody's ass, Black or white. My first response is to myself, "Holy shit, we're gonna get our asses kicked now". My friend and I just freeze. Their leader, who oddly is one of the smallest members of the gang, approaches me and asks, "You got a match?" As the rest of the gang moves closer to us, my friend and I frantically search ourselves for a match as if our lives depended on it. In fact, we think our lives do depend on finding a match. While we continue to fumble around our clothes, resembling nothing more than dancers doing the "mashed potato," a young black man in his early twenties walks close by. He sees the gathering and quickly deduces what is about to happen. I recognize him to be one of the regulars at Canteen Night. More importantly, he recognizes me and begins conversing with several of the Block Boys. I strain to hear what he's saying. And what I hear is salvation itself. "Hey that's Little White. I know him; he's okay. Leave 'em alone". Suddenly, there is room to breathe as the Block Boys disperse. Fresh spacious air fills my lungs, and I have never been so happy to be an Honorary Nigga.

My Canteen Night experiences taught me a great deal about the game of basketball. But there is one skill I develop that fires my dreams of becoming a member of my high school's varsity basketball team-The Jump Shot! As my opponents become bigger, faster, and stronger, my two-handed set shot is rendered obsolete. Basketball burns appear regularly on my forehead from the numerous blocked set shots that land there. While I attempt the set shot, everyone else is shooting the jump shot. It's embarrassing to watch my already taller opponent soar even higher over my head to loft a soft jumper. Even when I maintain perfect defensive position and time my jump to be perfectly congruent with my opponent's rise, my outstretched arm is pitiably below where the ball leaves my opponent's fingertips. Now my defensive deficiencies are even more apparent, much to the great chagrin of the members of my team. I want to be able to shoot a jump shot. Again, survival skills! If I want to survive in this game that I love so much, I'm going to have to learn how to shoot "a sweet J".

So I study everyone's idiosyncratic way of shooting the jumper. I study the form, the spread fingers, the way most shooters instinctively position the grooves of the ball perpendicular to their shooting hand, the flick of the wrist, the beautiful back spin that softens the shot as it approaches the rim of the basket. I practice and practice my own version of the jump shot, and I'm gratified to see that because of my quick rise into the air and my quicker release, even much taller defenders cannot block my shots.

As my accuracy improves, I become emboldened to try out for the varsity. Few of my friends hold out any hope that I can make the team. But I'm selected along with a few other 10th graders to be nominally on the varsity. Most of our playing time, however, is with the junior varsity team. My junior year is also spent mostly playing on the JV, but now I'm averaging 20 points per game mainly on the strength of my jump shot.

Music, dancing, and basketball—my holy trinity-- fills me with warmth and admiration for Negroes that perfectly balances my Negrophobia. I admire them and yet I fear them. But I fear even more what my white peers, pals, and parents will say if I get too close to Negroes; if I become too much like them. That's part of Negrophobia too, worrying about what your white friends and family members will think; even white people you don't know. I don't know why. I feel so humiliated if and when they accuse me of Negrophilia, although they wouldn't put it so nicely. Whenever I'm called a "nigger-lover," I feel like I will soon die -- unwanted, despised, and alone. This love-fear feeling makes no sense to me.

Chapter 2.

What's The Reason I'm Not Pleasing You?

I'm a senior in High school. Wow! Hard to fathom that I'm that old. One more year of boring classes and pompous teachers, Ugh! The school year is just beginning, and I already have senioritis. Besides the fact that I have little motivation for my classes, there is another reason why I can't focus on my studies. Basketball! Yes, I'm still banging that teapot. Basketball. I will make the team—come hell or high water. I have grown all the way up to five feet six and a half inches. Still small, but not shrimp size anymore. Every morning now I get up at 7 am and ride my bike to the outside basketball courts at Paul Junior High School and work on my shooting, moves, and fundamentals for 45 minutes. Then I ride home, take a quick shower, and wolf down a hurried breakfast and run the two blocks to Coolidge High School. Of course I tend to doze off during Solid Geometry my first class of the day.

I can't wait for basketball tryouts, which begin in the middle of October. While I'm asleep I dream about the pending scrimmages and how I will impress the coaches with my dribbling, shooting and –what else—my savvy. In one dream I am guarded by a 6 ft 1 inch opponent who keeps telling me I'm too short to play this game. I respond by dropping a soft "J" over his head and into the basket. I have no girlfriend, no likely candidate for a senior prom date, and am clueless about what I will do after I graduate. But all that seems insignificant compared to my all-important goal of making the team.

Well, make the team I do although it looks like I won't see much playing time. Our coach is so excited because the two best guards in the city are living within the Coolidge geographical boundary. Grant Lawson, by the way, is one of them. The other is Bobby Spackle who played with me at Paul and was our leading scorer. Both Grant and Bobby have All-Met written all over them. Coach then learns that both of them have been recruited away to Catholic schools, Bobby to DeMatha High and Grant to John Carroll. Our coach is furious. He can't stop talking to us underlings about those two. I think he visualizes a dismal season without these stellar players. And the previous year Coolidge only won three out of 18 games. He had hopes of turning that record around—until now. At the beginning of the season, I find myself sitting on the bench, a 2nd string guard. We travel to Baltimore to open our season against Patterson Park High. We lost! I don't play until near the end of the game and manage to score six points. During the second game of the season against High Point, however, I find my confidence and my accuracy. The coach put me in during the second quarter, and I ended up leading the team with 17 points to our first victory. I am first string after that.

Many, if not most, of the high schools we play against feature all black or mostly black teams. A few others are integrated. Wilson—our arch-rival—is the only all-white basketball team in the City Interhigh League. Our team is only slightly integrated. We have three black ballplayers on the varsity. As the season wears on, my confidence grows until I begin to believe that I can play well against some of the best Black basketball players in the city. The more I feel the equal of these talented Black players, the better I play. And the more I chastise myself for my racist feelings.

Coolidge's basketball season is an up and down affair but, surprisingly, we end up on the brink of becoming a playoff team for the first time in years. In order to qualify for the Interhigh Playoffs, we have to play our rival, Wilson, for the third time. We split two games during the regular season and our identical records force the rubber match. The game goes into overtime. The game is decided by a tactic I had learned all those years ago at Coolidge's Canteen Night playing those no take-back half-court games with bigger and stronger black players. Our sharpshooting forward launches a rainbow jump shot from the corner. Because he rushed it, both the 6' 3" Wilson forward and I could tell that the shot is too strong and will careen off the far rim of the basket where we both await the rebound. The Wilson player has inside position on me; but as we both go up for the careening ball, I use my ass to nudge him underneath the basket. I catch the errant shot in midair and in the same motion twirl around and softly guide the ball into the basket. Just as the ball goes through the net the buzzer sounds the end of the overtime period and the game. I'm carried off in the arms of my teammates and even our Principal, with whom I have regularly battled about the quality of my daily school garb, comes up and with a great smile on his face congratulates me and joins the others in chanting my name, "White! White! White! White!

In the DC Public High School Tournament, we play against a highly talented and heavily favored team from McKinley Tech. We surprise them early on. By the third quarter we are leading by 15 points. Then their superior conditioning takes over. Our fatigue lets them back into the game. With 5 seconds left in the game Tech is leading by 2 points. We have to foul a Tech player so we can get the ball back. He misses the foul shot. Our center rebounds it and throws a pass to me. I drive across midcourt and continue driving as if I'm going in for a lay-up. Instead I pull up for a jump shot from 22 feet that goes through the net as the buzzer sounds. We trade baskets throughout the overtime period; and in an ironic twist, we are faced with the identical situation as the end of regulation. With 5 seconds left in over-time and Tech leading by 2 points, we foul the same Tech forward as before. Again he misses the shot and again our center rebounds and sends a hard pass to me. I drive across midcourt just as I did before, and once again I pull up in almost the identical spot for a 20-plus foot jumper. This time the ball rolls around the rim three times before it goes off to the side, ending the game and our hopes to go into the semifinals for the city championship. I am inconsolable.

For the entire following week, I am in full-bore moping. I keep replaying that last shot over and over in my mind. As far as I'm concerned, my high school year ended with that shot. My mind is in a fog in class and out, weekdays and weekends. It's hard for me to focus on schoolwork or fun. Outside of school I spend most of my time lying in bed listening to doo-wop, which in my befogged state of mind sounds like it's coming to me from another planet. One day my mother finally breaks through the fog. She implores me to think about what I'm going to do after I graduate from high school. "Izzy, I don't care what you do, but you have to do something. Izzy? Izzy, are you listening to me? You can't just lie around forever."

"I know, Ma. I guess I'll go to college, but I don't know where I want to go. I know you and dad don't have any money to send me away and even GW seems to be beyond our reach. The U of Maryland is too far from here to commute and we can't afford for me to live in a dorm. So what else is there?" My mother gathers herself together—all 5 feet of her—to tell me something difficult. "Well, we might be moving soon..."
"WHAT!"
"Now don't get your bowels in an uproar. It's nothing definite, but your father seems eager to move, and we heard about this brand new apartment complex in Langley Park, Maryland." In fact, we'll be very close to the University of Maryland."

"Moving? Langley Park? Are you people crazy?" My mother holds out her hands with palms up as if she is trying to hold back a flood.

"Nothing is going to happen until after you graduate." She hesitates before giving me the real reason for the move. "Look Izzy, you know a Black family is moving in next door. Now I got nothing against Black people, but their presence is going to make it harder to sell this house. And if any more Black people move in, we're not going to get any money for it. So we have to sell soon."

"Mom, how can you do this? You know what real estate agents are doing now. They buy a house in an all-white neighborhood and then "bust" the wholly white block by selling to a Black family. Once that happens, everybody else on the block panics and sells as quickly as they can. This ain't right and you know it."

"It's the way the world is. I can't change it. You know we don't have much money so we have to get as much as we can for the house. You can understand that, can't you?"

"I understand perfectly. You're gonna succumb to the shitty tactics of these Block-busters and fly out of town like everybody else. I can't believe this is happening. You know those sons of bitches are gonna turn around and sell this house to a Black family for twice the amount that you're getting for it. They're making money off your fear!"

My mother doesn't want to pursue this conversation any further and therefore changes the subject. "So which college do you think?" I'm still reeling with shock and anger. "I think I'll go to Howard like Jason." My mother gives me this funny look she gets when she is pushing down anger. She thinks I am trying to get her goat. She smiles brightly and says, "Whatever you think is best, dear." She quickly turns around and leaves my room.

I'm angry with myself for this exchange and sad because my mother for many years has been my confidant. Not that her answers were always helpful. Because my father was often too embarrassed to answer my questions about the facts of life, I would go to my mother. Her answers, however, were often so vague that they were subject to grave misinterpretations. When I was in the 7th grade, I had finally mastered the facts of reproduction. But a new question had dawned on me: How does one stop the process? The exchange with my mother went as follows:

"Mom, if someone doesn't want to have a baby, but wants to have sex, is there any way to prevent a girl from getting pregnant?" A look of horror comes over my mother's face.

"My God, Izzy, why are you asking me this question? What have you done?"

"Ma, this is school work, not funny business. I am trying to understand the facts of life."

Still looking at me suspiciously, she breathlessly replies, "Yes, you can prevent pregnancy."

After a long pause, and it's clear that she's not going to elaborate, I asked,

"Well, what?" And where do you get it?"

"Er, it's called protection," she answers cautiously. Exasperated, I ask,

"Where do you get it?"

"You get it at the drug store. It comes in bottles," she replies. Actually, I can't swear that she said it came in bottles or whether I drew that conclusion from the fact that you could purchase this protection at our local Peoples Drug Store. In any case I'm satisfied for the moment and also extremely tired from my efforts to extract the "blood" of knowledge from this very reluctant "stone".

Well, the next day, I'm sitting with my buddies at the lunch table at Paul Junior High and they are engaged in a frantic sharing of whispered intelligence.

"What gives," I ask. My buddy, Frank, says, "Haven't you heard? Bobby Bangheart has been going around the whole school selling protection." "Ah," I say triumphantly, and loud enough that the entire cafeteria can hear, "I KNOW WHAT THAT IS. IT COMES IN BOTTLES AND YOU CAN GET IT AT PEOPLES DRUG STORE. The entire lunch table stares at me as if I'm a Martian. They then begin laughing and laughing. It's hold-your stomach laughter that rings in my ears. I am flummoxed by a confusion of feelings, embarrassment, anger, and incomprehension. When it is explained to me the kind of protection Bobby is selling, I turn beet red with mortification.

I always thought my mother was a beautiful woman. She didn't think so however. "People used to think I was cute," she would say. "People would say 'That Pearl, she has a nice shape.'" She would never say she had a nice figure. It was always shape. I didn't know if this was something just she would say or a word that people in her social circle employed to describe the physical appeal of females. On the surface she seems so pleasant and friendly, but underneath she is a very private person. To those who do not know her well, she is all warmth and caring. But in my experience, her pool of warmth was not very deep.

From my Jewish mother I learned the pros and cons of Christian charity. I learned tolerance and its decay into bum pity…"He's had a rough life." "He didn't mean anything by it." "He couldn't help himself." She tried to teach me how to tolerate insults, but I also learned to deny that I had been insulted. "Don't let it worry you." It's nothing." I learned compassion for others, but I also learned to unwisely let them off the hook. She tried too hard to be loving, forgiving, and tolerant. And now I do the same.

If I do harbor prejudicial thoughts against Blacks, it's not because of anything my mother said. She tried to teach me to treat all people with respect and I never heard from her any bitter or derogatory remarks about Black people. But in a confusing qualification to her apparent "love for all kinds of different people", she would often suggest with words of discomfort or a curious facial expression that social mixing was somehow inappropriate. It just wasn't done.

Even though I told my mother in anger that I was applying to Howard University, the idea has increasing appeal to me. It seems affordable, and it would certainly help me to learn much more about Negroes and maybe why so many white people seem to hate them. And maybe cure my Negrophobia. I have heard many people say that knowledge is power. I hope knowledge is also good health. I know that I will have a humongous battle selling the idea of going to Howard to my father. So in preparation I decide to talk to my brother whose intellect I enormously respect.

My brother, Adam, was six when I was born. When I came into the world with my needs as evident as potholes, his reign over the affections and attention of our parents came to an abrupt end. Needless to say, he did not take kindly to this change. He became private, inaccessible, tending a garden of hatred for me. For years he would invite me to see it. I would wander with deference and fear in his garden, begging at times to water it, to tend it myself hoping to plant some loving growths. Occasionally, I would succeed. Yet he felt a responsibility toward me even as his dislike for me grew. And in the early years I felt his protection almost as much as his displeasure. I eventually came to view him with awe, as some walking encyclopedia with something to say on every subject. I wanted to be like him. He was my model: intellectual, cultured, disdainful, a champion of polysyllabic words, a cornucopia of knowledge—these became my aspirations.

Adam has recently completed a B.A. degree in English Literature at GW and is currently working for the Feds at the Department of Health, Education, and Welfare. I find Adam in his room reading Jude the Obscure by Thomas Hardy. He's now a little shorter than I am; but because of his intellect, I still think of myself as the smaller brother. "Adam, you got a minute? I see faint annoyance on his face for the interruption, but it quickly dissipates. "What's on your mind little brother?"

"I'm trying to decide which colleges to apply to and I'm stuck. We don't have the money for me to go to GW like you and Uncle Sol, and Maryland is too far. What do you think about my going to Howard, you know, where Jason is going?"

"To be honest, Izzy, I don't know enough about Howard to be able to advise you. You'd be better off talking to Jason who actually has some experience there. What is this his second year?"

"Yeah, that's right, and thanks for the idea. I think it's a good one." It really is a good idea and I'm surprised I didn't think of it. Adam is one of the few people I know who can tell me when he doesn't know something. Before I leave I ask him, "Have you heard the rumor that the folks are planning to sell the house and get an apartment in Langley Park?"

"Yes and I'm pissed. All they're doing is increasing the length and difficulty of my commute to work. It could be a blessing in disguise because it motivates me to get my own place closer to the HEW building." I'm surprised to hear that he will be leaving the nest. Although I know it's time, I feel abandoned by my long-time adversary and friend.

Jason Davidoff is my first cousin. Because he is a commuter student at Howard, he is still living with his parents on the next street over from us. Jason is about 30 months older than I am. We are more like brothers than cousins and growing up did almost everything together. We played on the same Walter Johnson League's 12-and-under baseball team and early on he was a faithful attendee at Canteen Night. Jason is two years ahead of me in school. His sports in high school were football and baseball, and in 1957, he was part of the formidable battery, along with "fireballer" Barney Repsac, that led Coolidge to a DC high school championship. I was in awe of the fact that they got to play for the title at Griffiths Stadium. Jason's high school grades were not the best so his brother-in-law suggested that Howard's pharmacy program might be a good fit. Jason not only got in, but also seems to have found his niche. His grades soared dramatically during his first year at Howard, and this past year he integrated the football team. At his father's behest, Jason is cleaning up his backyard after a recent windstorm.

When I enter his yard, he is throwing debris into a large trashcan. He has two inches and 30 pounds on me. This somewhat obscures the already faint resemblance between us.

"Hey Jason, how would you like company?"

"Sure, I could use the help in cleaning up this shit."

"That's not what I meant. What I'm saying is how would you like company at Howard?"

Jason gives me a quizzical look. "You thinking of applying there?"

"Yeah. The price is right at Howard." Jason stops his yard-work and points to the backyard steps for us to sit. "But Izzy, with your grades and your smarts you can get into a much better school."

"I'm not sure you're right about that, but (I add with rhythm in my voice) I ain't got the *dough* so I don't get to *go...* to a better school. What I want to ask you is what do you think about your experience at Howard?"

"Let me put it this way. If you go, then we're both crazy." We both chuckle at his joke. "But you're right we don't have much choice. I have to admit I like the pharmacy program at Howard, and I have met some neat people. But don't plan on having much of a social life. You know the taboo on interracial dating goes two ways. I know a lot of Negro women who are about as eager to date a white boy as I am to date a Black girl. You know most, but not all, of the racial animosity in this country is on us white folks. I learned just how crazy this country is about race when I traveled with the football team. Did you know that when we traveled south, I had to get food for the entire team because restaurants would not serve Schwartzehs? The guys on the bus used to joke with me. I would bring the food and everybody on the bus complained that I was a lousy waitress because I got their orders mixed up. And I would kid back. I'd tell 'em everybody but me has to sit in the back of the bus."

"But it sounds like it's working for you." Jason gets up and does some stretches. "Here's what I think. If you have a career plan and you keep your focus on your plan, I think it can work for you."

I get up to go and hold out my hand to shake his. "Thanks, Jason. I appreciate your talking with me. You know, when you were 14, I thought you were dumb. Look how smart you've become in seven years." He punches me in the arm and says with a laugh,

"Kiss my ass, Schwartzeh-lover."

OK, in all honesty I think it's a little crazy to choose to go to Howard. Well-meaning friends inquire, "What kind of social life will you have there?" I really have no answer for them because I don't know what I'll do, nor do I know whether the students at Howard will accept me. My father thinks I'm crazy too. He can't fathom why I would do such a stupid thing. It seems like we have the same conversation every night.

"Look Dad, whether you like it or not, I'm gonna go to Howard."

"No you're not! Don't you realize what a foolish mistake that would be?" What kind of job will you get with a degree from Howard? People just won't accept you."

"What people? How do you know this? Are you some expert on racial job trends? I don't know where you get this stuff. After all, Dad, it's 1959 and times are changing". We just stare at each other in mutual incomprehension. I'm truly puzzled. Where do these attitudes come from? I could not understand this man or the world he came from. His father had left his family behind in Lithuania and came to this country seeking a better life. After three years my grandfather saved enough money to bring his family over. My father was six years old in 1912 when he, the baby of the family, his mother, and his four siblings arrived. He managed to finish the 8th grade when he was finally required to go to work in order to supplement the family's meager income. I suspect though that he was also not fond of school. After trying several different lines of work, he eventually became a butcher. Growing up I rarely saw the man because he worked long hours and would arrive home around my bedtime. When I did see him, it wasn't love or joy I felt. It was fear, awe, and a distant admiration. In those days, there were a few things we did together like going to ballgames, playing catch in the side yard, or going to the kosher butcher, Marinoff and Pritt's, on Sunday morning for bagels, lox, chubs and whitefish. There were even infrequent showers of affection. Much more often, though, there was criticism. I remember more clearly his impatience with my fumbling attempts at skilled labor. His explanations were hurried, full of urgency; my imitations barely begun before, "No! Not that way! Do it this way!" The shame and loneliness would overtake me and my mind would zone out.

I stand there staring at this man who I resemble so strikingly. He is now an inch or two shorter than I and by now he has developed a sizeable paunch. In the past, we might have been mistaken for brothers, the same brown hair, the same hazel green eyes, and the same moody expression. But he was always much more muscular in build. Yet looking at his face, I have the odd sensation that I'm yelling at myself in the mirror.

My father finally breaks the silent staring stalemate. "Look Boychik, I've been on this earth a lot longer than you have and I know what I'm talkin' about. You can barely wipe your ass and you're gonna tell me?"

"Why do you have to be so prejudiced? Of course, I'll be able to get a job. I'll have a Bachelor's degree."

"Yeah, a Bachelor's degree from Howard."
"Dad, many prominent people have graduated from Howard," I continue. "In fact, people refer to it as the Harvard of Negro Education."

My father, however, keeps coming up with endless reasons against my going. With each volley, he ratchets up the severity of the threat to my well-being.

"Don't you know that Howard is filled with Communists and queers?"

"Oh come on, Dad, how would you know that? You're digging in the bottom of the barrel now. Why do you make this stuff up? I can't believe you."

"And I can't believe you want to go to school with Schwartzehs."

"That's the real reason, isn't it? You're not thinking about what's good for me. You just can't stand the thought that I might choose to go to school with people that you consider to be inferior. When you say, 'Schwartzeh,' that says it all."

"What?" He protests with feigned innocence. "Schwartzeh means black, that's all."

"No, Dad, it's the Yiddish equivalent of nigger and you know it. So does the rest of this damn family. All the time, "Schwartzeh this, Schwartzeh that. How many times have I heard one of your sisters complain, 'You just can't find a good Schwartzeh anymore to clean the house.' I hate that word. They're people, Dad, just like you and me!"

"No, Boychik, that's where you're wrong. They'll never be like you and me!"

At this point, the fencing match begins. He "thrusts" with a story that proves to him beyond the shadow of a doubt that black people are dumb, ignorant, unreliable and untrustworthy. I then "parry" with a tale of a bright, accomplished Negro who is without doubt a paragon of middle class virtues. Neither one of us can sell the other on our particular vision of Negroes.

I hated the constant arguing with my dad. I longed so desperately for the rare good times we had together. Sunday brunch is the only time of the week that the four of us have a meal together, and it's the only time we bond. My father makes his crude jokes and my brother Adam and I laugh hysterically. I think we laugh more at seeing our father in a light-hearted mood than at his crummy jokes. My mother gives him a stern look, "Oh Mort," and then giggles uncontrollably. Soon, all four of us laugh until it hurts. We do this over a breakfast of unmatchable fried potatoes that my father prepares, bagels, lox, cream cheese, white fish, Revelation fish or Sable fish as it is otherwise known. Adam proclaims, "I love this Jew food," and we all respond with raucous laughter.

None of us is high on religion, but we clearly know we are Jewish. After my brother had suffered through six years of Hebrew school with one crazy melamed after another, and was finally bar mitzvahed, my parents decided not to burden me with this requirement. Instead, to get me prepared for my own bar mitzvah, I had a private teacher for nine months. My teacher was a single, depressed melamed, who had survived the Nazi concentration camps in order to teach recalcitrant learners like me. We used to get into strange philosophical discussions. He once suggested that modern medicine with all its shots and medicines was making mankind weaker. I rolled my eyes and asked,

"How do you figure that?" He answered me with another question. "How old do people live today?"
"I don't know, 70, maybe 80 years."

"Ah ha," he said triumphantly, "Methuselah lived to be 969 years old." I muttered to myself, Oy Veh! With the help of his tutelage, I sang my Haftorah with such passion and with "a tear in the voice" (as was said of the best Cantors), even though I didn't understand a word I said.

My father is convinced that the men who run the synagogues are all hypocrites. My mother, who knows no Hebrew, is content to go to services only on the High Holidays and to Bar Mitzvahs. I announce one Sunday morning that we are at the very least, "gastronomical Jews," and there is unspoken agreement.

On this particular February Sunday, my father turns serious and reopens the painful topic of my choice of college.

"Look, Izzy, I'm happy to borrow the $1,000 a year that you will need to go to George Washington University, like your brother and your uncle." Shocked by the utter recklessness of this idea, I reply with a great deal of frustration in my voice, "Where are you gonna get that much money?"

"I'll get it," my father answers defensively.

"Yeah, I hear you, but I'm askin' where?"

"Look, haven't I always taken care of you, provided for you? I'll get the money, don't you worry."

"Dad, I appreciate the offer, but I'm set on going to Howard."

I do appreciate the offer, but I'm more repulsed by the thought that he would put the family finances in some jeopardy in a desperate attempt to dissuade me from going to a mostly Black university. I can see his fear but I'm unable to grasp its source. What awful experiences has he had with Black people? Or is there some deeper psychological reason for his hostility and sense of superiority over them? Is there some wisdom in his cautionary protests? I know he's very frightened for me, frightened of my idealism. "You can't take the whole world on your shoulders." This is his patented closing statement on virtually every meaningful disagreement that we ever have. But it's impossible for me to give any credence to his concerns. He's on the other side of a fence that is forming in my mind between the bigots and the open-minded; the sophisticated versus the ignorant. And to prove that I clearly fall on the right side of this divide, I am going to Howard whether my father can accept it or not.

Chapter 3.

Maybe

My father and I argue about my college choice throughout
the entire winter. We argue in the morning as soon as we both
are awake. We argue when he returns from work in the evening.
We argue at Sunday brunch, which had been our most joyous
time together. We argue when I am in the bathroom and he
would shout from the other side of the closed door. He would
start the argument again when he was on the throne and I on the
other side of the bathroom door. I submitted my application to
Howard anyway and only to Howard. And when my acceptance
letter arrives, still he argues. "Of course they accepted you," he
said, "You're white."

Up to this point of my life I really have not been a
rebellious teenager. Yes, I had engaged in some risky behavior,
but these are acts of conformity to whatever group I crave
acceptance —the jocks, the semi-delinquents, or the popular
kids. But when it comes to choosing my college, I somehow
develop some backbone. I am terrified of my father's anger, but
on this I cannot yield. By the middle of April, my father throws in
the towel, but not without a parting shot:

"OK, so I guess you are really gonna go to that Schwartzeh
school. I can't stop you, but I don't have to pay for it. You're on
your own. You find a way to pay for your education."

This was an unexpected blow. Through all our arguing, I
never gave a thought to who might be paying for my education. I
just assumed he would. In fact, I thought I was doing him a
favor. Howard's tuition for the fall of 1959 is $213 per year, a
fifth of what it would cost to go to GW. Two hundred and
thirteen dollars is a great deal of money and I haven't a clue how
I am going to come up with such a sum. I guess I'll have to get a
job. Work? Exactly! I will have to find a job. And find a job I do—
as a playground director. I become the director of Shepherd Park
Playground where I coach 12 and under baseball, run arts and
crafts programs, and offer profound philosophical bon mots to

teenagers, such as treat people the way you want to be treated. Except, it is done in teen-speak. "Like, do him like you want him to do you, man." And, of course, I teach anyone who is interested how to shoot a basketball.

I love the job and I am actually saving money for the first time in my life. I am not sure though whether I will have enough money for even my first semester at Howard. Then the oddest thing happens, one of those "out- of- the- blue" events that can transform your life. On a rainy day in April of 1959, I am trapped in the Shepherd schoolhouse with about 20 pre-pubescent kids screaming out their creative ideas for projects, when Andy Klein, a Coolidge classmate who lives in the neighborhood shows up. We are friendly but not close.

"Hey, Izzy, rumor has it that you're going to Howard in the fall. Is that true?" Oh God, here comes another critic about to tell me what a fool I'm being. "That's right," I say, bracing for the verbal onslaught. "Well, I am too."

"Really? I'm blown away. Why?"

"Well, the price is right and my family has no money to pay for college," he offered. "Me too," I say enthusiastically as if I had found a landsman from the old country.

"Listen, do you know that Howard is having a scholarship exam in two weeks? If you win one, they will pay you $500 a year for all four years. That's more than enough money for your entire college education. Why don't you come with me and we'll both take it. Apparently, they have plenty of money. I think we both can win one."

"Andy, I can't thank you enough for telling me. I had no idea that they were having a scholarship exam. I didn't think they had any financial aid. Count me in. I desperately need the money." Whatever trepidation I feel about going to Howard immediately evaporates with the knowledge that I will have a high school classmate join me in this fearful adventure.

When the day of the test comes, I am so nervous I feel as though I am going to hurl my breakfast. The nausea follows me into the exam room. But once I see the questions, I am shocked at how easy the test seems to me. Andy and I both win scholarships. When I show my father the award letter, he begrudgingly congratulates me with a downcast look.

With news of my scholarship, my mood soars and my feet spontaneously began to perform an effortless "Pony". I kick up my heels and try to coax from my motor memory the 'blackest" version of the dance that I know. I am rehearsing for the Saturday Night Social that is being held that night at the Tifereth Israel Synagogue at 16th and Juniper Streets. I love nothing more than to show off the dances that I have learned watching Black Tuesday on the Milt Grant show: The Birdland, the Slop, the Snap, and the Pony. To my white peers these dances seem so exotic, but they are impressed nonetheless. There will be another dance contest and I hope to win. No, I know I will win…. again.

The beautiful early May evening gives me such a strong sense of the changing season. In the fragrant evening air, I can barely contain the feeling of well-being. I now have a college to go to and money to pay for my education. I am getting ready for my new, more exciting life. I see in my decision to attend Howard a romantic journey into the unknown, which both exhilarates and terrifies me. I imagine myself a courageous explorer who is embarking on an expansion of his social boundaries that have felt so confining. Privately, I torture myself with questions. Depending on the time and my mood, I think myself crazy, rebellious, naïve, foolish, odd, or a disturbed goofball. But not this night! This night I entertain only good thoughts about my decision. It is not only bravely different but the right decision for me.

The Three Miscreants show up late as usual. Peter Kaplan, Bobby Levine, and James Feder are the truest friends I have despite the fact that each is psychologically wounded in his own unique way. Peter's insecurity borders on paranoia. To say he has a thin skin is to state the easily observed. Until I met Peter, I held the mistaken opinion that only women were vain. He literally could spend 30 minutes in front of a mirror combing his hair. He would shriek in panic if he thought he was losing a hair.

And he is a fastidious dresser, if you can call fastidious an obsessive attempt to dress in the late 1950's version of the truly cool--pegged pants, black loafers, shirt sleeves meticulously rolled up, a pack of Lucky Strikes tucked underneath. The final touch, a collar majestically turned up. We are about the same height, but he has black hair and eyes, compared to my brown. But he dresses way cooler than I do.

Bobby Levine has a mother who has always wanted a girl child; and when he was a toddler would occasionally dress Bobby in feminine attire. His features in fact are delicate and he is more pretty than handsome. Needless to say, his looks and his upbringing produce some serious doubts in him about his masculinity. He thought if he could just be Marlon Brando, these masculinity issues would not haunt him. After seeing Brando a few years back in "The Wild One", Bobby had to have a motorcycle. As soon as he turned 16, he bought a 1950 Triumph Thunderbird 6T, the same brand that Brando rode in "The Wild One". Bobby is never seen without his Harley Davidson Black Motorcycle Jacket, which is the standard garb of teenage rebellion.

James Feder comes from a family run riot. He is the second of six children ranging in age from 5 years to 20. The sibling rivalries are so intense and the resulting chaos so traumatic that James literally became a man of few words. He doesn't see the point of speaking up. Instead, he communicates through stares. He has a bucket load of stares that attempt to communicate different and sometimes subtle shades of meaning.

One stare says, "You know and I know that you are not my equal." Another intimates, "Can't you see that I have had a rough life and I need you to take care of me?" A third challenges the recipient of his stare, "Tell me why I should think you matter." Very few people pick up on his ocular lingo and typically think he is just odd.

James honks the horn of his 1956 Chevy Impala while Peter and Bobby call out my name in derisive hooting noises. Peter bellows, "Iii zzy, it's time to go. Bobby, imitating the voice of an ogre yells, "I'm going to crush your skull if your ass is not out here in 10 seconds." I pretend to be petrified and fly out of my house and into the car. James peels away with the clear intent of showing off the wonderfully low, thudding sound of his fiberglass mufflers. We all genuflect in praise in James' direction. His response is to announce in a seductive but barely audible whisper, "You can't catch me. If you get too close, you know I'm gone like a cool breeze." When James does speak, it is often in a song title, particularly Chuck Berry's titles which are his favorite. If he doesn't want to do something or to deal with a difficult issue, he says, "Too much monkey business for me to be involved in." If he's feeling particularly insecure, as he is now, he says, "I'm a brown-eyed handsome man."

Miraculously, we make it to the synagogue biologically intact and free of any traffic citations. As we pull into the parking lot, we hear the sounds of a saxophone stuttering into the cool night air. Just below the infectious rhythm of Lee Allen's sax, I hear and almost visualize Little Richard banging out his signature, repetitive high chords on the piano which are interwoven with a very rhythmic guitar riff.

We enter the social hall and all four of us are immediately caught up in the excitement of the moment. The scene is bright and loud, bright with possibility and loud with so many beautiful young girls singing along with the Shirelles' new hit, "Dedicated to the one I love". So many hungry teenage boys are dancing with them, holding them close and hoping to be the young lovers to whom these glowing girls will be dedicated. Many of the girls are wearing poodle skirts and ponytails and look like models of their age, class and gender. As the DJ plays the next song, "Please Say You Want Me" by the Schoolboys, with 14-year-old Leslie Martin's Doo Woperatic vocal plea that always creates such longing in my heart, I search the room for her. When I don't immediately see her, my mood sinks. I begin to feel sorry for myself and indifferent to the music and high spirits that surround me. Bobby picks up on my mood and knows exactly what I am thinking. After a few moments, he grabs me and excitedly says, "There she is, Izzy! There's Sophia." In the far corner of the social hall, Sophia Schreiber is dancing with Sonny Hanson, one of the few gentile boys who regularly shows up at Jewish socials. They are dancing a new form of the jitterbug that came out of Prince Georges County, Maryland, known as "The Queenstown". This style substitutes smoothness for rhythm little rhythm and a lot of smoothness. As they move toward one another, couples hold both hands and double pump them; and as they move away, both dancers put one arm behind their backs. Throughout the dance, they seem to be engaged in a effortless promenade.

As we drift toward the center of the hall, I see her more clearly; see her look lovingly into Sonny's eyes. As I move closer, I can see those almond shaped green eyes that rob me of any sense of power. I am frozen in place whenever I look into her eyes. She finally notices me looking at her, gives me a pleading, sheepish smile, and then buries her face in Sonny's shoulder. I feel briefly welcomed by her tentative smile, but my momentary joy quickly turns to shame and anger. I continue to look at them slow dancing to Two People in the World by Little Anthony and the Imperials, and once again feel like a third wheel at their private party. My mind immediately goes to memories of the New Year Eve's disaster.

Sophia has always viewed me as a friend, a very good friend and a wonderful dance partner. I'm her friend, but she is my true love. Throughout the fall and early winter, she seems to increasingly desire my company, and she even kisses me goodbye one day after I spontaneously drop over her house after school. That kiss gives rise to the most optimistic fantasies of connection, closeness and warmth. I imagine long, languid make-out sessions on Valley Street, on Hayrides, in her basement and on her bed. I imagine that in her love for me, she invites me to explore the heavenly curves, crevices and youthful swellings of her bare body. I imagine that I experience the Heaven on Earth promised by the Platters. Perhaps I have a chance with her after all, I begin to think. When she invites me over for New Year's Eve, I am ecstatic and convinced that all my worrying and self-doubting is foolish.

My friend Peter is going steady with Charlene Kessler who is not only best friends with Sophia but who also lives up the street. At 7 pm, Peter stops by my house to pick me up and we begin the two-mile trek to Riggs Park where so many Jewish families are migrating as part of a large "white flight" from the integrating neighborhoods of Northwest DC. Charlene lives at the top of the hill on Chillum Place and Peter leaves me and goes up to the door of Charlene's house.

I look down the long hill of Chillum Place and try to gather my nerves. As I walk down to Sophia's house, my mind is awhirl with images of me dancing, holding, kissing and touching her. Then the fear takes hold. I imagine my doing it all wrong and her being appalled at my incompetence and lack of experience. Worse yet, I see myself completely exposed and emasculated by her derisive laughter. Diffidence and lust continue their epic struggle within me until I ring her doorbell.

Sophia answers the door wearing black pedal pushers and a tight red sweater that accentuates the rapid development of her "secondary sexual characteristics". It's difficult to remove my eyes from her chest and my mind flashes on a memory of my father's comment when he met her at lunch the summer before. She had come to lunch dressed in cut-off shorts and a halter-top.

After she left I asked my father what he thought of her. "Nice tits," was all he said.

"Hi Izzy," she says in a seductive voice. "Why don't you come in?" I can't read the meaning of her smile. I hope for joyful, but fear it's malicious. The living room is small but cozy. To the right of the front door is a violet plushy sofa framed by two La Z Boy recliners. To the left is a Philco radio-record player console that also serves as a buffet. The top of the buffet is completely covered with family pictures of Sophia, her parents and her younger sister Marsha: The four of them on vacation at the Nevele, the two girls playing on the beach; Sophia's parents smiling happily at the camera as they dance; several of family members I do not know; Sophia alone in a skimpy two-piece bathing suit that sets my heart to thumping once again. I can't believe she's just 15 years old. From within the console emanates the beautiful sound of the Chantel's biggest hit, "Maybe".

"Come on, Izzy, let's dance." Sophia grabs me and pulls me to the center of the living room and I can barely catch my breath. I hold her tentatively. "No, Izzy," she complains, "Hold me closer!" I feel her soft ample breasts on my chest and my legs go rubbery. Here, one of my fantasies is coming true and I'm so nervous I can barely remain upright. I almost topple over backwards pulling her on to me. I'm able to keep the both of us from falling; but in my effort to achieve equilibrium, I overshoot the mark and lean too far over in the other direction. Now she almost topples over backwards. Again, I'm able to keep her from falling. We eventually right ourselves and she looks at me puzzled and asks, "Is that a new dance step, Izzy? I've never seen that before."

"Why yes," I say, my mind racing around for an answer. "It's, it's called the Birdland. You see, I lean back and pull you toward me, do a half-stop with my right heel and then I lean forward as you lean back. You see how smooth and rhythmic it is?" I explain, gaining confidence in my story. "Yes," she says, "I love it. Where did you learn it?"

"I learned it from the Black kids dancing on the Milt Grant Show," I say with great pride. "I try and imitate their moves as closely as I can." A look of recognition comes over her face. "So that's why you look Black when you dance.".

"Do I?" I answer with feigned innocence and inner glee that my impersonations are so successful.

"Oh Izzy, everyone says that. Half the world thinks you're part-nigger." The word sounds strange coming from the mouth of this angel. After a moment's disorientation, I opine. "Well, I don't want to be Black, but they do dance better. It's so much cooler than the way white kids dance." I show her the Pony the way white kids do it and the way Black kids do it so she can see the contrast. In between these up-tempo dances, I sneak on a few slow tunes, which gives me the opportunity to hold her close to me. The more slow dances we do, the more confidence I gain. Finally, I move in to kiss her lips and she turns away. She sees the look of devastation on my face and quickly pecks my cheek and pulls away from me. "Let's eat," she suggests a little too enthusiastically, "I'm starving." So am I, I think to myself, but for a different kind of sustenance.

As we eat, she gossips about her friends. She details the breaking hearts, the blossoming love affairs, and planned treacheries of her core group of girl friends. She follows this monologue with frank and detailed analyses of Peter, Bobby, and James. She's in the middle of a scathingly accurate delineation of the meaning of James' portfolio of stares when the doorbell rings. She gets up to answer the door. The seductive, flowing movement of her gorgeous behind automatically yokes me in her direction and I follow her to the door. She opens the door and in the same seductive voice with which she greeted me says, "Come in, Sonny." Sonny Hanson steps inside and we both look at each other with astonished incomprehension. Almost as if we rehearsed it, we simultaneously turned toward Sophia and ask in unison, "What's he doing here?" Sonny just glares at me with his Bible-black eyes. His black flat-top looks a bit incongruous atop his overly large head which sits on a very slender six foot frame. He keeps on with his menacing stare and looks as if he's ready to mark his territory with a spray of saliva. I stand there completely befuddled trying to figure out what is going on.

"I invited you both to see in the New Year," Sophia finally says. "Sonny, can I speak to you in private? Izzy, we'll be right back." They disappear into the kitchen. My confusion only grows. About five minutes later, they both return with linked arms and huge smiles. Sonny's attitude has done a "180" and now begins to act in a very chummy manner towards me as if we we're dear old friends.

"So Izzy, how's it hanging?" he asks. Resisting his oily chumminess, I reply, "Long as ever."

That ends his phony overtures. Sophia puts on "The Twelfth of Never" by Johnny Mathis and grabs Sonny out of his chair and pulls him close to her. She then puts her tiny feet onto his huge box-toed bombers and they continue to dance. As the music swells, they begin to kiss. They kiss and dance their way over to the deep violet couch. He lands on top of her and they commence a serious and prolonged make-out session. I sit there looking on in horror. The humiliation and the tears well up inside me. But I can't believe what I'm seeing. I am frozen to the La Z Boy for about ten minutes watching their lips glued together and listening to their heavy breathing. Finally I rise up from the chair and with as much disdain as I can muster I say, "I think I'm gonna go now." Unbelievably, Sophia whines, "Aw Izzy, don't go. We're supposed to see the New Year in together. I want to be with my boyfriend and my best friend."

"WHAT!!! Listen, I wish you both a very happy 1959," I utter, my voice dripping with sarcasm. I storm out of the house, slam the door, and immediately burst into tears. I can't fathom what has just happened, but the humiliation that I feel is the worst I have ever felt. I walk slowly and dejectedly up the hill and replay the entire evening over in my mind. Several times I replay the evening until I finally put Sophia's diabolical plan together. I remembered that Sophia's parents had forbidden her to see Sonny Hanson because he's not Jewish. Her parents and sister are out for the evening and she needed a decoy. She told her parents that she had invited me over for the evening. The parents know me and know that I am Jewish. Then Sophia told Sonny to come by around 11 pm, but she didn't bother to mention that I would be there. She figured she could mollify both of us. "Best friend, indeed," I scoff aloud. "Best patsy, you mean." The pain of being used in such a manner is damn near unbearable. As I walk up Chillum Place toward Riggs Road, I'm drowning in despair. "Where is that Black gang now, I cry aloud? I want you to come and beat my ass to a pulp. I want to die!"

As you go through life, remember this rule. Everybody's somebody's fool.

All this comes back to me as I watch them dance at the synagogue social.

I search for my premiere dance partner, Cookie Zelner, who is all rhythm and bounce. She's one of the few girls who can follow the stylistic changes I make in my fast dancing. I even show her some of the different moves that Black dancers employ in their jitterbug. Because of the unique style that we have created, a style that is a fusion of black and white, we stand out. We won the dance contest last year and are looking to repeat.

"Hi Izzy," Cookie chirps with the same enthusiasm that she puts into her dancing.

"Hi Cookie, are you ready to win again this year?" I ask in the mode of a coach trying to motivate his team before a big game.

"You best believe it," she answers. We clasp hands and spontaneously move into our dance routine to the sound of Bobby Darin's "Queen of the Hop". We bounce around to the frolicking rhythm of the song and Cookie's short, dark hair flips and flops in time with the music. People begin to form a circle around us. They watch and clap and cheer. But occasionally a voice in the back of the crowd rises above its cheering and clapping, "Look at that nigger dance. I can't believe he's white. He moves just like a jigaboo."

I hear the epithets but pretend I don't. My anger pours out into my dance moves. The moves become so aggressive that I lose the beat. The smooth, rhythmic, swaying moves degenerate into a spastic parody of their graceful predecessors. Cookie looks confused, and as the crowd begins to murmur its concern, she is increasingly embarrassed. "What are you doing, Izzy?" she whispers frantically. Without replying, I break away from her and begin to do a very aggressive version of "the Snap". This dance involves the sharp snapping of the knees as one's legs alternately bend and lock up. Every beat of the music elicits a snapping movement from my legs. The crowd begins to cheer again. They've never seen this dance before or certainly never have seen a white person performing it. I welcome the praise of the crowd, which enhances my confidence. Cookie is able to pick up what I'm doing because of its similarities to "the Slop". The crowd's cheers grow even louder and there are no more epithets. The dance ends to great applause.

The announcement that the dance contest is about to begin brings twenty couples to the floor. I know that our main competition involves two couples, Ben Fox and Maxine Weinkof who have been dancing together for several years, and my best friend Peter Kaplan and his girlfriend, Charlene. Peter and Charlene are excellent dancers, smooth, precise in their steps, and inspired by the choreographed routine that Peter has developed. I fear Peter the most because he is so bent on beating me. I fear for our relationship if Cookie and I win again. He and Charlene had been a close second in last year's dance contest.

He resents me for it because he thinks –with some justification— that they are better dancers than we were. But where we have the edge is in the Negroid movements that we have been able to master. We lack their precision, but they can't approach the expressiveness of our moves. After two rounds, there are three couples remaining, Ben and Maxine, Peter and Charlene, and us. The DJ plays "Little Star" by The Elegants and I immediately begin to panic. The song has a relaxed, smooth sound that seems to favor the Queenstown style that Peter and Charlene love and excel in. As we start to dance my fear melts away and I let the music dictate our moves. To be honest, I see no real differences in quality among the three couples. At the end, however, Ben and Maxine are eliminated. The four of us stand close together while waiting for the final song. Peter leans over and in a loud whisper implores, "Hey Izzy, why don't you dance like a white man for a change. Leave that black shit at home." "I dance the way I feel, Peter. The music and the beat pull the moves out of me. I don't plan anything and that's the God's honest truth," I add.

The DJ plays the brand new release by Ray Charles, "What'd I say". As soon as the piano begins a low driving blues beat that evolves into a Latin riff, my body is on fire. Cookie and I start as a jitterbug twosome but within seconds break off into a very rhythmic and expressive version of the slop and the snap. Cookie anticipates the quick spontaneous changes in dance style that I make and matches me step for step as if we had created a choreographed routine. After a minute of solo dancing we reconnect and begin a series of complex turns accompanied by some fancy footwork. Then we break off again into the snap and the slop. Out of the corner of my eye I see Peter frowning at me while he and Charlene perform a series of precise turns in their speeded-up version of the Queenstown. In Part 2 of "What'd I say", Ray and his back-up singing group, the Raelettes, begin their signature response call of grunts and groans. Their erotic siren call draws me further into the song. I feel an almost mystic connection to the music. New steps spontaneously rise out of me and Cookie mimics them perfectly. Although I can hear clapping and cheers from the crowd, they seem far away. Only Cookie, the music and I exist as the song eventually comes to an end. I hug Cookie when we are pronounced the winners, but I'm still in a trance-like state. Nothing feels real. People keep coming up to congratulate us and I can see myself shaking hands and laughing while I hold Cookie close to me. Yet everything seems to happen in slow motion, in a dream-like reverie. Every person in the social hall approaches us to offer words of praise—all except Peter.

As we leave the synagogue, people still are coming up to Cookie and me to offer their congratulations. The night air is sweet with the smell of spring and the sound of praise. The crowd eventually thins out. I give Cookie a hug and we leave for our respective rides home. The three Miscreants and I have just reached James' car when I hear someone call me. I turn around and see Stanley Sobel standing in front of me with arms akimbo and a perpetual mocking smile on his face. He's a little less than 6 feet tall with a perfectly even flattop, which gives the top of his head the appearance of a well-carpeted brown lawn.

"Hey Izzy, I hear you're gonna go to a nigger school," Stanley hissed.

"Well, I'm going to Howard University, if that's what you mean, Stanley." He blanches at the sound of his hated name. His given name is to him such a mortifying moniker that he has gone on a single-minded campaign to convince every friend and acquaintance he encounters to call him Stan. For his trouble, he now has to listen to just about everyone call him Stanley to his face.

"Well Iz, after watching you dance tonight, I can see that you'll fit in perfectly," he sneers. "You move just like all the rest of those jungle bunnies."

"OK Stanley, why do you have to be such a prick? What do you got against Black people anyway?"

"I don't know, Izzy, I just don't like 'em. Besides, I wouldn't want to be known as a nigger-lover."

I wince every time I hear that phrase but I don't know why. I find it repulsive but at the same time I feel so degraded to be called that. It makes me extremely anxious to imagine that I might be one. What the hell did it mean to be a "nigger-lover"? And what's wrong with love anyway? It seems to me to be preferable to being a hater. How does a phrase that trumpets love take on such an insulting connotation? These questions make me so irritable that I want to either punch Stan or get the hell out of his sight. "Well. Stanley, why don't you crawl back into whatever hole you came from?" With that, my friends and I get into James' car. As he peels out of the parking lot, James makes sure to glare menacingly at Stanley Sobel, which is his way of saying you're lucky we let you live.

As we speed down 16th Street, the four of us are oddly silent. I look at my friends, my best friends, and think about what a strange quartet we are. The glue that seems to hold us together is not so much a commonality of interests, but a shared acceptance of our psychological wounds. We are a community of the mentally maimed: gender-whipped Bobby, image-obsessed Peter, the linguistically challenged James, and me who fears the catastrophe of not being liked. There had been so many times when three of us would have to come to the rescue of the fourth who had just been hurt in the hardest place for him to bear.

Peter sits sulking in the back seat behind James, as far away from me as possible. I realize it was my turn to apply the balm of sweet words to his wounds.

"Come on, Peter, don't be like that," I say as sweetly as possible. "It's only a dance contest."

"Yeah, it's only a dance contest," he fires back mockingly. That's why you work your ass off to beat me. I'm sick of losing to you. You know I'm a better all around dancer than you. The only reason you and Cookie win is because of those nigger moves of yours. All I know is that we got hosed.

"Yes, Peter, you're an excellent dancer." I hate it when I try to kiss his ass. "But why do you have to take it so hard?"

Peter refuses to be consoled. He pulls out a Lucky Strike from under his shirtsleeve and tries to light it in great haste. Five tries later he begins cussing out the matches. Once he finally gets his cigarette lit, he begins to wax philosophical. "You know, maybe Stan Sobel is right. Maybe you are part black." I look at him as if he had just eaten a cockroach. "Yes, a black, Ashkenazic Jew. Come on, Peter, you know my father's people are from Lithuania and my mom's relatives are from Russia." Peter stares at me and takes a drag from his cigarette. He knows his idea is preposterous, but he's not ready to let it go. After a long pause he spits out, half in anger, half in jest, "Well, nobody really knows where the 10 lost tribes of Israel ended up."

Chapter 4.

One Summer Night

You might have thought that after winning the dance contest I would fall into a "sleep of kings". But instead my sleep is intermittently disturbed by dreams of Peter's resentful, sulky face and his recurring harangue that somehow I had betrayed him. In my dream I see an enlarged version of his face screaming at me over and over, "I GOT HOSED!" I know I will be the one to call first thing in the morning and be the peacemaker. I'll have to apologize for "stealing the dance contest" from him and Charlene. When I call him at 10 am, I begin by offering him a totally insincere apology. It takes me 15 minutes to mollify his anger. When he finally "forgives" me, it is with his patented line, "You know, Izzy, you really have to stop being jealous of me." I bite my tongue until it starts to bleed. I tell Peter that James is picking me up shortly to go to the Silver Spring Pool Hall, and, with some reluctance, I ask him if he wants to go. "I guess," he says in his annoyingly sulky tone of voice. I wanted to say, "Don't do me any favors you whiny putz," but instead I practically beg him to come along. "OK," he replies with an air of noblesse oblige that leads me to nearly sever my tongue in two.

The burbling sound of fiberglass mufflers announces James' arrival. I inform Peter that we're leaving now and will be at his place in 10 minutes. James' lowered red and white Bel Air Convertible is gleaming after one of James' too frequent wash and wax jobs. James is as fastidious about grooming his car as Peter is in his personal grooming. I get in and notice that James is donned in all black: black tee shirt, pants and loafers. He looks like a beatnik, but with his own kind of poetry. I recount to him my phone exchange with Peter and how he reluctantly agreed to go with us to the pool hall. James' response is, "Too much monkey business for me to be involved in." We drive in silence the rest of the way to the apartment house that Peter lives in with his parents. We drive past the large stately houses on Rittenhouse Street, cross Georgia Avenue and continue past Fort Stevens. This Civil War relic was an alternate playground for us in our childhoods. None of us were aware that the major battle fought here in July of 1864 stopped the furthest advance into Washington by the Confederate army. This was the first and last Confederate attack on the District of Columbia. As kids, we used to jump across the parapets where cannons were once placed. I counted it a major achievement of my childhood when my short legs were able to carry me successfully across one parapet to another.

Just as we pull up, Peter comes dashing out of the apartment yelling cuss words at the top of his voice. "I hate that man! He doesn't get a word I'm saying." Peter looks back toward his apartment and yells "Well, Fuck you, Pop!" Peter is in tears by the time he reaches the car. James looks at him with pity and as pitiful at the same time. Peter throws himself into the backseat and continues bawling. "What's going on?" I ask solicitously. "My old man don't understand shit." "What don't he understand?" I inquire in my sympathetic voice. "He knows how much I need a car. Charlene's always bitching at me about having to rely on others for wheels. I need a car man or I'm gonna lose Charlene."

"When you told him that, what did he say?"

"Get a job! Get a job! Get a job! That's all he ever says. I have a job. It don't pay me enough bread. I asked him for a loan; a little loan that I can pay him back over time. No, he says. Get a better job, he says." As stressed as he is, Peter still takes time to look into James' rear view mirror and comb his hair.

"How much of a loan?" I ask.
"All I want is $300. I've already saved about $400. I have my eye on a hot '55 Mainline Ford 2-door sedan. It's a two-toned beauty, baby blue and white, separated by a cool chrome strip. It's a V-8 with 110 horses. I saw one advertised for $700. Boy, what I couldn't do to soup up that baby."

I pause for a moment and see that we're approaching the pool hall. From the outside the building seems old and decrepit.

Inside is another story. The space is cavernous, well lit, and surprisingly clean. The room is filled with 20 pool tables arranged in five rows of four. Even though it was a little after 11 in the morning, the place is packed. We are lucky to find a table being vacated just as we enter. As James racks the balls, Peter starts in again with his diatribe against his father and his girlfriend. "My father's such a putz," Peter grouses as James and I barely listening, carefully eye the available cues.

"And Charlene; I know she's gonna leave me. My life is shit," Peter continues. "Peter, you know you've been saying the same thing over and over about Charlene the entire time you've been dating her and she hasn't left you yet. Why can't you see that?" I ask with great exasperation. Peter is offended by the implication that he reads into my question; namely that he's dumb. "Well, what do you know, asshole, you can't even get a girlfriend." James sees that I'm stung by Peter's attack. He looks at Peter sternly, and chastises him with an Elvis Presley line. "Don't be cruel/to a heart that's true!" After a pause, James starts blasting balls into the various pockets. He makes six in a row. Before each shot he lines up the cue, and when he's ready, he wiggles his ass and talk/sings "I'm in love; I'm all shook up." That line becomes his signature prelude to every shot.

James easily wins the first three games and then begins to tire. Peter and I split the next two games. During the 6th game we're interrupted by a loud conversation, taking place at a nearby pool table. Two guys almost identically dressed in black motorcycle jackets and pants and identically coiffed with perfectly formed duck tails in the back of their heads are commiserating over a developing sociological phenomenon not to their liking. The fellow with the blond ducktail is loud in his complaint: "You know the niggers are gonna take over Silver Spring soon. They keep moving north up Georgia Avenue. They already are taking over Jewlidge High School. Only niggers and Jews go there now and a few Greeks." Brown ducktail nods in vociferous agreement. "Yeah, the coons are gonna come after our white girls soon and somebody's gotta do something about it."

"You best believe it," Blond Ducktail agrees. "We've got to rumble those nigs and let 'em know that Silver Spring is still white man's land." Their fulminations are interfering with Peter's concentration as he's lining up a shot. He stops and yells over to the ducktail boys, "Would you guys keep it down? I can't hear myself think with all your jabbering." Blond ducktail takes umbrage at Peter's rebuke and says in a menacing tone, "How about we come over there and kick your ass?" James, the only member of our trio who even approached the size of the ducktail duo, steps forward and says, "We're not looking for a fight. But we can't hear ourselves playing pool with all your 'Yakety Yak, don't talk back." And as for kicking our asses; that'll be the day when you say goodbye," James sang in a sneering tone. That is one insulting song title too many for the ducktail boys, and they begin to move toward us. "Hey Don, I see some pansy asses cruising for a bruising," says brown ducktails to blond ducktails. Rack'em Harry, the owner of the pool hall, sees what is about to happen and gets between us. "If you guys want to fight, he says, "take it outside. Otherwise, shut up and play pool." "My point precisely," Peter agrees triumphantly. Brown ducktail waves his hand and says, "Aw you guys ain't worth bruising my knuckles on. Come on, Don," he says to his blond companion, "Let's blow this joint. It's filled with nigger-lovers anyway."

After the ducktail boys leave, Peter starts in on me. "You see how everyone is worrying about the niggers..." He sees my frown and says, "OK, Negroes. Everyone is scared to death that Negroes are taking over our neighborhoods."

"A few blacks move into a neighborhood and the entire block panics and begins to put up "For Sale" signs. I wouldn't call that taking over the neighborhood," I rebut. "I'd call it a cowardly retreat by white home owners."

"Well, all I'm saying is that if you get too cozy with Negroes, you're gonna end up in big trouble. I want to say, "Peter, you're full of shit." Instead I seethe in silence. I feel like a harness is strapped across my chest, which prevents me from offering Peter an offensive rebuke to his racist prattle.

"Well, you know what, Izzy, you go to Howard and be with your nigger friends. Those hard asses that almost beat the crap out of us just now were right about one of us at this table." James, who had obviously tired of Peter's nattering, finally says, "We gotta go, fellas, I've got the rockin' pneumonia and I need a shot of rhythm and blues. Roll over Beethoven and tell Tchaikovsky the news."

We drive down Georgia Avenue, past the Hot Shoppes and cross the District Line. James veers right onto Alaska Avenue, which was one of the most attractive streets in the city. He drives past the flower streets, Holly, Geranium, Floral and Fern, past Walter Reed Hospital and turns left onto 16th street. I sit fuming in the shotgun seat. I am pissed—at Peter, certainly, but more so at myself for allowing him to trigger my Negrophobia. But what if Peter's right, and I'm rejected by white people? Or what if I'm changed by saturating myself with Negro contacts? Will I become Negro-like? The fear inside me keeps rising until this whole train of thought seems to suddenly implode. And then a moment of peace comes over me when I finally ask myself the only rational question of the day – What the hell am I talking about?

After James drops me off, I flop my pissed-off self onto my bed. I loathe myself for being unable to tell Peter what I really think. I hate the way I always act nice to Peter when I'm actually appalled by his whining and his paranoia. It's all I can do to gently challenge his absurd and fearful fretting about Charlene. It is obvious to everyone but Peter that she is nuts about him. I hate even more that I let his attitudes toward Negroes fill me with fearful questions.

My only antidote to my self-loathing is music-- Rock n' Roll music and Rhythm and Blues. I put on Little Richard's "True Fine Mama" and pure joy rises in me and obliterates my self-loathing. I grab on to the nearest doorknob and start dancing. I rock and sway trying my best to make some cool Black moves. I can't stand the spastic movements of my clumsy, rhythm-deprived peers. It's not that I want to become a Negro, but I want to move with the same expressiveness, freedom, and pure uninhibited joy that I see in the dancing of black teenagers. Heads shaking in rhythm, graceful swaying arm movements going in one direction while legs and hips seem to move in another. Bodies moving in smooth undulations to a rocking beat. But I want to create my own moves that are neither black nor white. I just want to be cool. OK, I'm not being completely honest. Black is cool!

Then the voice takes up residence in my head...again. "Look at you dancing like a jigaboo, trying to be a Schwartzeh. What's the matter with you? You are odd. You want to step over the line that's been there for centuries? For what?" And the eternal debate commences-- Izzy the Conformist vs. Izzy the Rebel.

Izzy the Rebel: "But the line makes no sense. I don't understand all these barriers."
Izzy the Conformist: "I don't know where they come from either, but it feels very dangerous to cross it."
Izzy the Rebel: "It's outrageous to have such an irrational barrier separating people. It's stupid!"
Izzy the Conformist: "Yes, but are you willing to risk ostracism, ridicule, maybe even violence for associating with Schwartzehs."
Izzy the Rebel: "Well, I am going to Howard."
Izzy the Conformist: (Mockingly) "Well, you are insane."
Izzy the Rebel: "Look, I've already been through this with my father."
Izzy the Conformist: "Ah, but now you have me to deal with."
To escape this internal chattering, I call my friend, Henry Prescott. Henry is light-skinned and is among the first wave of Negroes that integrated Coolidge High School. He's bright,

pleasant, and easy to talk to, and we have fallen into a comfortable friendship. For some reason he does not trigger my Negrophobia. Maybe it's because he's so light-skinned that whenever I'm with him, I never self-consciously think of him as a Negro. When we're together, he brings out in me whatever latent intellectual tendencies lurk in the muddle of my brain. We have many wonderful conversations; and like a crowbar slowly opening a heavy crate, he opens my eyes to larger issues in the world, issues that go beyond my current obsession with dancing, doo-wop, basketball, and Negrophobia.

Henry and his family have spent most of their life in Northeast Washington. When the DC schools began to integrate, they were able to move into a beautiful, spacious house off Kansas Avenue in the northwest quadrant of Washington, DC. This allowed Henry to be eligible to attend Coolidge, which at that time was generally considered to be the second best high school in the city after Wilson.

Here I am in the house of a Negro family; and not only is it twice as large as my house, but it is filled with the most beautiful works of art I have ever seen. So many sculptures and masks from Africa adorn the shelves, along with more books than I have ever seen in any house. I'm astonished because I had been told that Negroes had neither the education nor the money to live in such elegant surroundings. And there are flowers and exotic plants everywhere. I could not make sense of the barrage of feelings overtaking me, feelings of surprise, jealousy, and finally comfort and tranquility.

When I find him in the downstairs study, Henry has his nose in a book. He is reading about Thurgood Marshall who is his most recent role model. Until Henry informs me, I have no idea who Thurgood Marshall is. But Henry likes to say that if Marshall doesn't make it, he hopes to be the first Negro appointed to the U.S. Supreme Court.

"Hey Henry, let's go play some ball," I say, oblivious to his obvious absorption in the book.

"In a minute, Izzy. I just want to finish this chapter," he says without looking up.

"Why hello, Izzy," I hear a sweet voice say as Mrs. Prescott enters the study. "I thought I heard your voice," she adds.

When I first met Mrs. Caroline Prescott, I was immediately taken by her dignity and elegance. This would have been off-putting if it weren't for the fact that she was so friendly and warmly welcoming. She's so light-skinned that I wonder how anyone, including herself, could think she's a Negro. In fact, her entire family is so light that she has several siblings who pass as white.

Mrs. Prescott and I have many conversations that clearly demonstrate to me just how crazy the racial attitudes are in the United States and how psychotic the Jim Crow Laws are. On this day we discuss the meaning of race and how the term is used to hold down the Negro.

"You know, Izzy, I am quite convinced that there is no biological basis for the concept of race. Human similarities far outweigh their differences. Race, I believe, is a term that was made up by white people to separate them from people of color in terms of a hierarchy of value. Beyond all of the fancy academic terminology, what race really means is that white people are better than everyone else. It is a socially constructed reality. The problem is that if you get enough people to believe in it, a socially constructed reality becomes reality. I hope that this "reality" will eventually become clear to you."

I 'm not quite clear what she means by a socially constructed reality, but I do catch the gist that there might be other, better ways for people to think about people who are different. She pauses for a moment as she looks at a portrait of her husband, a prominent physician in DC.

"Let me tell you a story that illustrates the point," she continues. "Not too long ago I met a good friend for lunch. She happens to be a Jewish woman who had just returned from Florida. She was, in fact, deeply tanned. We entered the restaurant and without waiting to be seated, we sat ourselves down at the nearest empty table. When the waitress finally came to our table after a terribly long wait, she had a look of dismay on her face. After eyeing us both, she said to me; "I'm sorry, I can't serve your friend here." Feigning innocence, I asked, 'And why not?' "Because we don't serve Negroes," the waitress replied. With great indignation, I began chastising that waitress for her rude and insulting behavior toward my friend. Without waiting for a reply, we both got up and stormed out of the restaurant. Once out of the waitress's line of vision, we began to double over with laughter. But our amusement soon turned to sadness, however, when we both began to reflect on the fact that people are actually turned away because of the color of their skin. You see, Izzy, it is reality; a stupid one, but reality nonetheless."

"I know! I know," I said excitedly, "but what can be done? What can we do?

Mrs. Prescott looks at me with such sternness. "We have to fight, Izzy. We have to push back against the long, painful history of Jim Crow."

"Enough lecturing, mother," Henry says as he enters the room. "Izzy and I are going to play some baseball." As we make our way to Rudolph Playground at 2nd and Hamilton Streets, I am so struck by Mrs. Prescott's words that I can barely pay attention to what Henry is saying. I know he is complaining again about the dismal play of the Washington Senators, but I am trying to figure what I can do to bring about the end of Jim Crow. What can one person do to change the world? But another question begins to insinuate itself into my mind. If someone as light-skinned as Mrs. Prescott chooses to think of herself as

Negro, then what does Negro really mean? And how can it be a choice?

I am awakened from a deep sleep by a phone call from, of all people, Shannon Creamer. Shannon is a beautiful blond-haired, blue-eyed "shiksa" who rocks my boat in every direction. I've lusted after her since my first wet dream. Shannon is every Jewish boy's forbidden fruit. Those Jewish boys who do not know her, and whom she does not want to know, call her in their sour grapes manner, the Grave Virgin. Many of these guys actually believe that she really isn't saving herself for marriage, but is in fact planning to take her charms with her to the grave. The odd thing about our relationship is that however much I want us to be boyfriend and girlfriend, she considers me only her best friend. Why that is not enough for me has to do with the weird way in which teenagers categorize relationships. For a teenage boy intimate knowledge of the soul of a girl is no comparison to intimate knowledge of her body. Hormones Ueber Alles, I guess. But we can and do talk about anything. Neither one of us is afraid to reveal any shameful thought nor any action we aren't proud of. And we talk often about the meaning of life and of our plans for the future.

Now don't get me wrong, ours is not an affection-free relationship. In fact, we frequently go to Valley Street in Silver Spring, Maryland, 'the most popular lovers' lane in my neck of the woods to make-out. But I am not allowed with mouth or hands to venture any further than her neck. Kissing or touching her below the neck is verboten. Shannon is only the second girl I've ever kissed. It still amazes me how something so pleasurable had been something so feared. When I was 14, Barbara Goldberg, a girl who lived around the corner from me, invited me to a New Year's Eve party that also happened to be the eve of her 13th birthday. Babs knows very well how hung up I am about my lip. When the clock strikes midnight, she wants me to kiss her Happy New Year and Happy Birthday. I think she is trying to humiliate me. When I refuse, she steals my hat and says she won't return it until I kiss her. I become so enraged and feel so humiliated that I leave hatless. A year later, I had plastic surgery on my lip that totally eradicated my ugly scar. Still it is difficult for me to believe that any girl would be willing to kiss me. One day Babs and some other kids in the neighborhood are over my house and we are engaged in forbidden play. No, not that! We are playing my brother Adam's High Fidelity record player, which he forbade me to touch. As we are dancing, Babs starts up with me. "Now, Izzy, you have no excuse. You are going to kiss me with your brand new lip. Sensing humiliation, I back away. She keeps coming toward me and I keep backing away until I bounce off the wall and into her arms. She is kissing me passionately. Thinking is no longer possible for me—not even thoughts of humiliation. I kiss her back just as passionately. I enjoy it immensely. Afterwards, everyone there applauds. That kiss gives birth to a brand new way of seeing myself.

When Shannon and I make out, I invariably cream my pants, but it is never clear to my inexperienced eye whether Shannon has joined me in orgasmic ecstasy. We often tell each other that our make-out sessions do not mean we are in love, but that we are just taking care of our mutual sexual frustrations. On other occasions she likes to tease me sexually. When we were horsing around one day, she let me touch her knee and then she rolls her skirt back inch by inch. With each inch she would allow me a little more access to her thighs and then she would laugh. But when I reached the middle of her inner thigh, her hands would clamp down on mine. She laughed every time. If I tried to push my hand—now manacled by hers—any further up her thigh, she would become indignant. "Stop it, Izzy," she would cry out. "No means no! "I understand that," I would reply, "but it had been 'yes, yes, yes' and then no. That's a little harder to deal with."

About six months ago, Shannon started seeing this hard ass named Nick Karpas, a Greek god with all the height and looks I could ever want. He is a definite delinquent and he has approximately half of Shannon's brains. They both agree, however, that he is God's gift to her. But he forgets to mention that he believes he is God's gift to all women. From what I could see, he never treated her very well, but the worse he treats her, the more infatuated she becomes. I could not fathom this logic at all. The worst part of it for me, though, was that since she started going with Nick, Shannon and I have had zero make-out sessions.

When I'm fully awake, I hear her sobbing over the phone. "Shannon? What's wrong?"

"Oh Izzy, I'm so unhappy. Nick told me he is seeing another girl and he wants to cool our relationship. How could he do this to me, Izzy, I love him so much."

"Shannon," I reply, "I told you he wouldn't stay true to you. His philosophy is to get as far as he can with every girl he meets. He just wants to get in your pants."

"How do you know this, Izzy?" she asks with great exasperation.

"Because he blabs his conquests all over the place," I reply, matching her exasperation. "He can't keep his mouth shut if his life depended on it."

"Oh Izzy, I can't believe it. You wouldn't believe the things he said to me. He told me he loved me.

"You and everything else in skirts. Come on, Shannon, I'm sorry you're hurting but you've got to wake up and see him for what he is."

"I can't take this. Izzy, let's go to Valley Street." Although I know she is only trying to soften her pain, I have no objection being her salve, if not her salvation. In fact, I jump at the chance.

"Let's do it," I say a little too eagerly. "I'm sure I can get my father's car. I'll pick you up after dinner. How's 7:30?"

"That's fine," Shannon says tearfully. I think I hear a tinge of regret in her voice that she has so hastily decided she wants to see me.

I'm so excited (and let's face it horny) that I arrive in front of her house 10 minutes early. I sit in the car staring at my watch and listening to Doo Wop on WOOK. Ironically, the song playing is "Been So Long" by the Pastels, a Doo Wop vocal group with one of the smoothest sounds around. I have to sit in the car because I'm not allowed in the house. Shannon's father is a prominent physician and just as prominently an anti-Semite. Her mother is also a social snob, but for some reason she likes me and makes allowances. Often she serves as a buffer to protect Shannon's friendship with me from her husband. They live in a beautiful house in the North Portal section of upper northwest Washington. I think of North Portal as the Land of Mansions. I have never seen houses that big. It is a mystery to me why Shannon's father bought a house in that neighborhood because it is populated by a large number of well-to-do Jewish families.

As I continue to listen to WOOK, I'm getting more and more excited, and I pledge to myself that I will get to second maybe even third base tonight. After all, she isn't Jewish, so what's it matter. As soon as I hear the words come out of my mouth, I'm appalled. Why should it matter that she's not Jewish? But isn't that the rule? You can take liberties with shiksas, but not with Jewish girls. Who made this rule? What's the point? If you mistreat Jewish girls and shiksas, won't they both cry and learn to hate men?

At 7:35, Shannon comes out of the house and walks to the car with her head down. As soon as she enters the car, she starts bawling. "Oh Izzy, I'm so miserable. My heart is broken. How could he do this to me?" She sits really close to me and nuzzles her head into the crook of my arm. She cries all the way to Valley Street. When I park the car, Shannon puts her cheek to mine and says, "Izzy, please hold me. Hold me tight." I am caught between lust and empathy. I feel myself becoming aroused by her closeness, by her soft blond hair and her breath on my neck. Yet having been dumped on several occasions by girls I thought I was in love with, I can imagine how she's feeling. She then looks at me with imploring eyes and moves in to kiss me. We start making out. "One Summer Night" by the Danleers is playing on the radio. The setting couldn't be more perfect, a balmy July night with the fragrance of honeysuckle in the air. I am so aroused that I completely forget my pledge. I just want to make her feel good. I kiss her neck and move my hand over her breast. She begins to moan a little and offers no resistance. I begin gently rubbing and tickling her back. I then put my hand under her skirt and she whispers, "Oh Izzy," and kisses me harder. I feel the soft, smooth skin of her inner thigh and know that I am close to coming. But as I move my hand further up her thigh, I feel something different, something very strange. I feel a covering that seems to possess little perforations. The covering feels like rubber or something. This material is so beyond my realm of experience that I haven't a clue as to what it might be. I suddenly bolt upright and exclaim, "What is that? What are you wearing?"

"Oh, you mean my girdle? My mom bought me this Playtex Living Girdle. She said I had gained too much weight and I needed to flatten my tummy."

"Well, it feels like a rubber chastity belt," I complain.

"Well, it does offer extra protection for my virtue," she says sarcastically. "Besides, would you be so fast with your little Jewish girlfriends?"

"I don't have any Jewish girlfriends."

"I know how you Jewish boys think. I'm a Shiksa. See I even know the lingo. I'm a Shiksa and you think it's alright to get as much as you can off me." I'm stung by her lumping me with other Jewish boys.

"Shannon, you don't realize how I feel about you."

"Izzy, you tell any girl who lets you kiss her that you love her. And if they let you feel them up, you'd be their devoted slave forever. I know you! Besides, we're just friends, remember."

The mood is completely broken. All hope of love and lust evaporate as I sit sullenly, trying to cope with my disappointment, frustration, and shame. My hangdog look pisses off Shannon. "Poor Izzy," she offers in that mock sympathetic tone that always infuriates me, "You look like the runt of the litter who knows he won't get fed. Do you even know what the meaning of love is?" she continues. The conversation becomes very complex and abstruse because of her obsession with Western philosophy. As Shannon attempts to explain the differences among the varieties of love-- Eros, Phileo and Agape, I zone out. No feeling is possible after a dose of Shannon's pedantry. "Enough, Shannon. Let's go home," I angrily say. She can see I am annoyed but she says nothing. As I'm getting ready to pull away, I see a light in my side mirror. It's a policeman shining a flashlight into the car behind me. I become entranced by the intense discussion that ensues between the burly policeman and the unseen driver about the nature of the activities that are taking place inside the car. At first, I can't make out what's being said, but as the two raise their voices, I hear the driver say, "But Officer, we were only necking." The policeman retorts, "Yeah? Well put your "neck" back in your pants and follow me to the police station." When I hear "police station", I pull the car out of its parking place in a hurry and speed away before a similar fate awaits us. When we know we're beyond the reach of the policeman, Shannon and I start laughing so hard that I almost swerve into a parked car.

As we are driving back to her house, Shannon gives me her sweet, compassionate smile. "Izzy, I am sorry if I hurt you. That's the last thing I want to do, because you are such a great friend." At the sound of the word "friend", my sense of shame rears its ugly head. Always a friend and never a boyfriend; this is my tragic fate. When she points out with a smile that I'm blushing, I feel even worse. She thinks I'm embarrassed by her compliment. In fact, I'm ashamed of my shame. I do not reply. All I can think about is how much my mind, my heart, and my balls hurt.

When we reach Shannon's house, she looks at me with an expression of sincere, solicitous concern, an expression that gives her commonly pretty features the appearance of elegant beauty.

"Izzy, will you be ok?" she finally asks.

"Yeah, Shannon, I'll be ok. I'm always ok," I reply, unable to keep the sarcasm out of my voice or the tears from welling up. At a loss for words Shannon gives me one last pained look and gets out of the car. When she reaches her front door, she turns and enthusiastically waves with a smile so bright it almost illuminates my internal night. But when the door closes behind her, I feel empty, lonely, and lost.

What she had said about her being a Shiksa cuts me deeply. I don't want to think that way. I hate it when I hear Jewish guys talk about Shiksas as if they are the lowest of the low. The conventional wisdom is that one can kiss, touch, and feel up Shiksas anywhere they will let you. And they will let you because they don't have the self-respect that Jewish girls possess. In fact, there are many Jewish girls who are labeled Shiksas because they "put out", letting guys get to second or even third base. In my crowd there is little distinction between the words Shiksa and slut. No Jewish guilt need apply.

Yet, it is at least partially true that I, like all of my male peers, come to believe that the female gender is divided into two categories: the pure and the "fast". It's assumed to be difficult to find a fast Jewish girl, but Shiksas are thought to be genetically programmed to "put out". In the presence of the "pure" female, one is supposed to experience transcendent feelings, worship her on one's self-constructed pedestal, but never touch. With the fast girl, the tramp, the slut, one respects nothing. A boy is supposed to degrade and then enjoy such girls sexually, or in the current parlance, "Get what you can off of her." My problem is that I accept only half of the double standard. I wax poetic about the pure, pity the tramp---and touch neither. Shannon is the rare exception. When I do touch her, I fall in love. She is probably correct when she says I would tell any girl who allowed me to kiss her that I loved her. The fact that she let me touch her breast did make me her slave. Whenever we "made out," I would wet my pants with an orgasm of monumental gratitude. From then on I could never say no to Shannon. Emotionally I seesaw between being quite withdrawn from girls and leaving myself completely unprotected. Of course, Shannon is not the only girl with whom I allowed my vulnerabilities to show. Such emotional display often scared girls into predatory acts. I would then be dropped or inexplicably used.

Many of the attitudes of my Jewish peers are so distasteful that I often want to flee my own Jewishness. Too many of my Jewish peers and their parents view gentiles with the same contempt that many gentiles possess for Jews. Next to "Schwartzeh" the most demeaning Yiddish term I hear is reserved for gentiles: a goyisher kop. Literally this is translated as a gentile's head, but it always conveys the idea that gentiles aren't very smart. I hate to see myself aligned with people who are so hostile to the differentness of others when I feel so different myself. Yet I crave acceptance from both Jews and gentiles. I want acceptance from gentiles because I hate the thought of being forced to limit my associations to just Jews. I crave acceptance from Jews because I fear the gentile's perennial hatred of Jews. Add to this dilemma the fact that I don't know what it means to be a Jew. Is a Jew someone who believes in and follows the commandments of the religion Judaism? What if I don't believe in God? How am I then a Jew? Am I a Jew because Jews are actually a separate race of people? What is race? Am I not white? I anxiously want to fit in and yet I keep my distance from every group. I want to be liked by everyone, but not to be constrained by the demands of any group.

I hate these categories that can turn my good mood into rage, humiliation, and despair. I see in my dark reveries, hanging over me like ghostly vapors, images of the arrogant and condescending gentile, the irresponsible, barely articulate Negro, the mean-spirited redneck; the arrogant WASP scion of the moneyed families that presumably rule the country, the filthy rich Jews who presumably rule the world. I lament these stereotypes that plant myths in our brains and lead to hateful segregation. The toxic fruit of such stereotypes, I think, poisons all hope of human kindness and understanding. I remember as a child the openhearted way I would greet another child. We would accept each other instantly as merely individuals with common interests and unique qualities. I never was concerned with the child's race, class, or even gender. Inevitably, I lost, as we all do, the simple "take you as you are" attitude toward other children. Eventually, this immediately granted acceptance is soon eliminated and replaced by cruel and ugly images of one another, images that separate us forever. It is a different person that I would encounter through the looking glass of these categories. Or so my 17-year-old mind has concluded.

On a scorching hot day in August, I take myself to Rock Creek Park to contemplate the confusion of my existence. I sit on a huge boulder in the middle of the creek, swatting away flies and mosquitoes. I imagine myself as two very different people in the same body. There is Izzy the way I think people perceive him and then there is the way Izzy truly feels inside. I was co-captain of the basketball team, Senior of the Year, president of my homeroom class, a popular B student, a scholarship winner and seen by others as an "all around nice guy." But inside I am burdened by lust, guilt and fear in relation to my sexual feelings, confused about my Jewish identity, bewildered by the clannishness of social groups and my marginal presence in all of them, hungering for more than a superficial relationship with a girl, and sitting in silent judgment of the people around me. And in a few short weeks, this confused, marginal boy with Negrophobia, will enter Howard University.

Chapter 5.

I've Got the Heebie-Jeebies

My first day at Howard begins in an inauspicious manner. I have to be on campus by 8 a.m. for orientation, and my alarm clock fails to go off. After the briefest of showers, I stumble in the dark in search of my closet. Never a stylish dresser, I at least want to be presentable. Without turning on the light, so as not to wake my brother with whom I share a bedroom, I grab what looks to be a relatively clean and dressy pair of black slacks and a white shirt. On my way out of our apartment I reach for what I hope is a sandwich that is to be my lunch. Avoiding the elevator, which always takes more time than a leisurely walk down the stairs, I virtually fly down the stairway the four floors to the lobby. True to its name the Suburban Hill apartments sits on a largish hill and so once outside I race down 30 more steps to get to street level.

I'm still smarting from the fact that we moved to the "burbs" right after my high school graduation. Since I can't afford a car, I'm forced to hitchhike. There I am at seven a.m. standing at the corner of New Hampshire Avenue and Ruatan Street in Langley Park, Maryland. I can barely open my eyes. I have traded the darkness of my apartment for the blinding ash-white morning sunlight. Seven a.m. and already the Avenue is heavy with cars and noise. As my eyes begin to adapt to the light, I can now see the ribbon of suburban commuters slipping over the camel-humped hills of New Hampshire Avenue leading to the city. The horns' blare and the tires' squeal leave me dazed and irritable.

As I wave my thumb toward every passing car, I notice how so many of the drivers won't even look my way. I begin to feel invisible. I lean forward into the road as if I'm ready to thrust my entire body in front of an on-coming car in order to stop it. A 1958 blue Ford Fairlane approaches. My thumb almost makes contact with the car as it passes by. The driver, in passing, holds up two fingers. "Two blocks? I BET you're only going two blocks. Goddamn liar." It's 7:15 already, and I conclude I have to employ a new strategy. In a frantic dead run I head for the next street which has a traffic light. There the cars have to stop which gives me a chance to knock on the windows and by means of exaggerated pantomime communicate my desperation. Reaching the light I reassure myself, "Now they'll have to stop. Now they'll have to deal with me." But the first driver I approach doesn't even look my way, even after I rap my knuckles on the car window and holler, "Going straight mister?" The driver sits motionless. "That's right, you heartless bastard! Pretend I'm not here!"

When the light turns red again, a brown and cream 1959 Plymouth Fury with those marvelous wing-shaped rear fenders pulls up to the light. Its sleek beauty leaves me speechless and unable to repeat my desperate pantomime. Instead, I merely point straight ahead. The driver nods and leans toward the door handle on the passenger's seat side to open the door. Thank God! As I ease myself into the car, the light turns green. The car speeds away with a great squealing of tires and the low, loud burbling of mufflers. I look curiously at the driver wondering what manner of creature is "chirping" his tires at this hour. What I see is a man about 30 with bituminous eyes and longish black hair that is combed straight back and coerced into ducktails. The blackness of his hair and eyes accentuate his gaunt, Anglo-Saxon features. The driver is vigorously chewing a piece of gum; and because of the noise of the cracking gum, I can barely hear him ask, in a distinctive southern drawl,

"Where ya goin' bud?"

"Are you going anywhere near Howard University?" I ask in a barely audible voice. He gives me a peculiar look as if to say, "Are you crazy or just pulling my leg?" Instead, he asks, "You go there?" making no effort to disguise the incredulity in his voice.

"As a matter of fact I do," I answer as if it's the most natural thing on the planet.

"I thought that's a nigger school. What's a white boy like you goin there for?"

"It's a very good school!"

"It's a nigger school!"

"It's still a good school!"

"It's a nigger school, how good cain it be?" I stare straight ahead, trying to master the murderous feeling that has overtaken me. We both sit in silence waiting for the traffic light to change.

We are moving again before I notice that the driver was smiling. I tense up in anticipation of some further racist observation. The smile turns into a chuckle.

"A white boy at a nigger school, don't that beat all! Hey boy, you the only white boy at that nigger school?"

"Don't call me boy!"

"Well, are ya the only white that goes there?"

"No," I rebut defensively, "There're plenty of white students there!"

"No shit! How many?"

"Well, that's hard to say. I..."

"What d'ya mean hard to say? Caint you tell black from white?"

"Actually, I don't know how many white students go to Howard."

"How come?"

"Well, this is my first day and I..."

"First day? Then you don't know shit from Shinola, do ya boy?" the driver bellows triumphantly. "You don't even know if you can stand to be with all those dumb, smelly niggers for more'n five minutes, do ya? How do ya expect to get an education going to school with niggers?"

Now I'm losing my composure. "You're crazy you know that! Negroes are no dumber and no dirtier than a lot of white people I know."

"Knee-grows? He guffaws. "You call niggers knee-grows, and you call me crazy?"

We ride in silence as we cross the District line at the intersection of New Hampshire and Eastern Avenues. The treeless, hump-backed hills are gone. The land begins to flatten out, and the Avenue narrows. As we ride on a few needles of sunlight filter through the clouds, flash against the windshield and disappear. I'm deep in reverie when I catch a distasteful whiff of alcohol on the driver's breath and I look over only to see the driver staring at me curiously. I return the curious stare. The driver's features seem to suddenly change shape from curiosity to panic as if he's stricken by a sudden perception of a painful truth. In a hushed voice, he asks, "Hey boy, you're not a nigger are ya? You're not a high yaller trying to pass on me?"

"No mister, I'm white."
"Only way it'd make any sense your going to Howard if you a nigger or a nigger-lover, and right now, I don't know which'd be worse to be drivin' around in my car."

"Hey look, you want me to get out here? Because if you do, I'd be happy to oblige."

"Now hold your horses, boy. Hold your horses. If you say you're white, I'll take your word for it."
"Thanks a lot!"
"Don't mention it."
The driver now has a nasty smirk plastered on his face. "How come you go to Howard any way, boy?"
"I said, don't call me boy!"
"Well, what's your name then?"
"Izzy."

"Oh shit, I got me a nigger-lovin' Jew boy in my car. Then you must be a Commie. Jewish Commies love niggers too, don't they? I hope you're not a Commie, Izzy?"

"No, I'm not a Communist. You know, it's actually people like you that led me to choose Howard."

"What d'ya mean, people like me? You don't know me!"

"All my life I've been hearing about how Negroes are inferior, dumb, dirty, lazy, shiftless, and so on. But the people I hear it from won't have anything to do with Negroes, except maybe to hire them to do their dirty work. All this hatred seems based on ignorance in my humble opinion," I say without a trace of humility. "I believe that if only whites and Negroes were exposed to each other, got to know each other as friends, all this hatred would disappear. I've gotten to know a lot of Negroes, and none of them seem lazy or dumb to me. Anyway, I want more exposure, and going to Howard seemed like a good way to do that." A wave of shame comes over me for revealing myself to this numbskull.

"It'll never work, boy. Race-mixing cain't come to no good. Niggers are different than whites. That's the way it is, and that's the way it'll always be. You're still wet behind the ears, but you'll see."

"How come you hate Negroes so much?
"

"There ya go with that "knee-grows" stuff again. I don't hate 'em, I just wouldn't want my sister to marry one. Would you?"
"I don't have a sister."
"But, if you did, would you want her to marry one?"
"That'd be her business."
"Jesus, boy, all I want to know is how you'd feel about it."
"I don't know how I'd feel about it."
"You wouldn't like it one bit, you don't have to tell me."

"Look mister, you don't know me well enough to say how I'd feel about it.

You know, you're straight out of a textbook, talking about keeping niggers in their place and crap like that! You probably never had any contact with Negroes. You probably don't know a thing a bout 'em."

"Boy, you don't know what you're talkin' about!"

"You ever listen to yourself? I mean, you're so blatant. You don't even say, Some of my best friends are black."

"Well, I'm friendly with some good niggers I know."

"Good Negroes! Boy, the stereotypes keep coming don't they?"

The driver's expression shifts now to contempt. "I know how you think. You are a nigger-lover, and I'm supposed to love you for it, right? I'm supposed to say, ain't this boy something, he don't have no prejoodice against nobody. Nobody except me that is. In your eyes, I'm just manure, ain't that right?"

"I didn't say that."

"No, but you're thinking it, ain't ya?"

In fact, I am thinking that, but I don't want to offend him anymore than I already have. I mean if he's a Southern bigot, he must be carrying heat, right?

"You talk about love so much. Tell me, boy, have you ever laid a nigger-woman?"

Despite his crude expression, I began to think of Desirie, Deserie, with the smooth brown skin and those lustrous ebony eyes, who I met in my high school chemistry class. I thought of how I ached to be with her and how the "nameless dread" had held me back from ever asking her for a date.

"Well, have ya?"
"No," I sheepishly replied.
"How come?"
"I haven't had the opportunity."
"Bull-shit. With all those fine-looking nigger-women runnin' around at that school, who you tryin' to kid?"
"I haven't seen them yet. I told you, this is my first day of college."
"Well, boy, you have a lot to look forward to. Don't keep your nose in all those books. Not with all that black pussy around. It's all pink on the inside."

His crudities suspend me between lust and disgust, and I'm rendered speechless. We cross Georgia Avenue at New Hampshire and eventually make our way onto Sherman Avenue. On top of a high hill, I saw where once stood Garfield Hospital, the hospital in which I was born. Garfield has since merged with two other hospitals to form the Washington Hospital Center.

Mercifully, I see the light at Euclid Street. "You can let me off at the light," I say with undisguised dejection in my voice. "Thanks for the ride," I half-heartedly offer. The driver says, "Don't mention it. Remember one thing, boy. Don't let those smart-ass niggers at that school mess up your mind. Remember, you're white!"

As I walk up Euclid Street, I can't get the driver out of my mind, his hatred and his arrogant presumption of white supremacy. "Why are people like that?" I ask myself over and over. As I play and replay this dispiriting conversation in my head, I keep searching for something clever or profound that I should have said. But nothing comes to mind. I'm ashamed that I even wondered whether any of his caricatures of Negroes is true. Just by wondering, my mood shifts from anger to alarm. Once again I've got the heebie jeebies when I realize that momentarily I will be surrounded by a large number of very dark human beings. Before that ride, I had been excited about the prospect of starting this new adventure. Now I'm a quivering, quaking, collection of nerves.

I'm so much in my thoughts that I fail to notice that I have walked right by Howard Place, the street that takes me up the hill to the entrance to the University campus. When I finally reach the entrance, I'm struck by the mammoth iron gate that opens to the Upper Quadrangle of the University, known colloquially as "The Yard". As I pass through the gate, I see two long lines of students slowly merging into one line to enter the Rankin Chapel in which the Opening Convocation is to be held. One line begins in the middle of the Yard, just adjacent to Frederick Douglass Memorial Hall and continues past the Religion building and Founders Library, which is just a few yards east of the Chapel. The other line comes from the opposite direction beginning down in the Lower Quadrangle (The Valley) where many of the science buildings stood. Students come up the steps and angle leftward to the Chapel.

I have never seen so many black people in my life, and this stokes up my level of heebie jeebies. I thought that I might be a little nervous at this initial immersion into Howard life, but I am unprepared for the way I actually feel once I see who my classmates will be. At that moment I feel so much the outsider, so much the minority, and I wonder if I have made a terrible mistake. As I look over the crowd of students, I notice that both lines are infrequently peppered with white persons. I feel a sense of relief that I'm not the only white student at Howard. This is a silly thought because I already knew several white students who went to Howard, including my own cousin Jason who is starting his third year in the School of Pharmacy.

"Why are you here?" I heard a voice say. At first, I think it's my own voice, giving vent to my fears. But then I hear, "Hey, white boy, why are you here?" I look behind me to see a tall, thin, light-skinned brown man glaring at me. My fear switches to defensive anger. "Why shouldn't I be here," I say huffily. "Cause you're white and this is a school for Negroes."

"Where's it written that only Negroes can go here?"
"Well, you won't let us in your universities, why should we let you in ours?"
"First of all, I haven't stopped anybody from going anywhere. And in the second place, haven't you ever heard 'two wrongs don't a right'?"

Suddenly, the tall, thin brown man begins to shake with laughter. "Hey, I'm just playing with you," he says. "You don't remember me, do ya?"

"Well, you look kind of familiar..."
"Think basketball; Interhigh playoffs? Flunky Coolidge vs super-talented McKinley-Tech? "

"Oh my God! You're the guy who kept beating on me every time I drove to the basket."

"Blocked your shots you mean!"

"You may have gotten a piece of the ball, but you also took a piece of my head with you."
"Hardly touched you at all white boy," he says with a smile."

"Yeah, well, I got half my points from the foul line because of the beating you gave me." I'm now laughing and feeling much more at ease.
"In case you don't remember my name, I'm Courtney Cartwright."
"Cartwright! Of course!"

"You guys sure gave us a scare. I think we took you white boys a little too lightly. We thought we had an easy road to the championship game."

"Hey, we weren't all white. Remember Henry Hill?"

"Oh yeah, he had been our third string center. You know he transferred to Coolidge so he could get some playing time. He was rotting on the pine at Tech."

"Yeah, well, he was making a mess of your center for three quarters."

"And then he faded like a deflating balloon. You see we knew something you didn't. Henry had a little problem with 'Stam Me Na'," he says with the biggest of grins while moving his head from side to side with each syllable.

" You know, I still have nightmares about my shot in overtime that kept rolling around the rim and finally rolled out."

"Yeah, I actually felt bad for you....for about two seconds." Cartwright cracks up with laughter.

It took us another 15 minutes to reach the entrance of the chapel. During this time, I learn that Courtney Cartwright was not only an excellent athlete but a stellar student as well who easily could have gotten into an Ivy League school. But he came from an upper middle class family in which a long list of his forbears had attended Howard. Of course he was going to go to Howard, whether he wanted to or not.

From the outside, the triangular, redbrick archway makes the Chapel seem deceptively small. Once we enter, however, the 90 by 50 foot structure feels cavernous. Yet the truth is somewhere in between. Three columns of 20 rows slope downward toward a raised stage. Thirty-three stained glass windows contribute to the illusion of the Chapel's immense size and gravity. Courtney and I find seats in the next to the last row. After a few minutes, the humming chatter of several hundred excited freshman dissipates as a dark-skinned man in clerical robes strolls toward the podium. He is Dr. Evans Crawford who is only the third Dean of the Rankin Chapel since its inception in 1895. He asks us to bow our heads as he leads the group in the opening prayer.

I feel very uneasy and very Jewish in this starkly Christian atmosphere. I sense a very familiar disturbance in my stomach that informs me once again that I'm "a stranger in a strange land." I, who fear being different more than just about anything, have voluntarily placed myself in this overwhelmingly alien situation. I only seem to be bowing my head. In fact, I'm doubled over by pains in my stomach. Here I am a white Jewish agnostic, who has little use for organized religion and who rarely shows his face inside a synagogue, much less a church, is sitting in a sea of black Christians.

After a few moments during which I am convinced that I will completely embarrass myself by vomiting in the pews, I look up to see another distinguished looking gentleman striding toward the podium. He is Dr. Mordecai Wyatt Johnson, the current President of Howard University. Dr. Johnson was the first African-American President of Howard and his tenure began way back in 1926. In fact, he is beginning his last year as President. I cannot believe my eyes. I'm looking at a white man. His skin color is the equivalent pale of my own. He's a hair less than six feet and has a scholar's eyes and a preacher's bearing. In a smooth Tennessee drawl, he begins:

"Members of the faculty, fellow students, we have assembled here today for the opening of another school year in what may be properly termed a minority University—a University maintained primarily as a matter of historical fact, for the disadvantaged tenth of our population whom we call Negroes.... Because the members of the founding group were wise, they did not say, 'We are founding a Negro University.' They said, 'We are founding a university that shall admit all persons, regardless of race, creed or color.'

And so it has been our fortunate history since the beginning of this institution, never to be wholly a Negro institution either in student body or faculty. On Howard University's Faculty, for example, are Negroes and whites, men and women, Protestants, Catholics, Jews, Freethinkers and Atheists; Americans, Europeans, Latin Americans, Asians and Africans. We even have a few Republicans."

This line brings the house down. If his bellowing voice doesn't wake you up, the sustained laughter will. While his speech is laced with such wit, he continues a bit too long for most of us. Upon seeing a number of the freshman falling asleep on him, he suddenly changes the decibel level of his talk from barely above a whisper to a bellowing crescendo, "The Lord told me to speak, but He did not tell me when to stop!"

After we register for classes, Courtney suggests we get a bite to eat at the Kampus Korner. Situated at the corner of Georgia Avenue and Euclid Street, directly across the street from the campus; the "Korner", as it was known to most, is a jumping, jiving social hub. As we enter the crowd eatery, the blended aroma of fried chicken, barbeque ribs, and burgers gladdens me. I'm salivating like a Pavlovian dog. The jukebox is blaring with the latest hit of Washington DC's premiere Rhythm & Blues group, the Clovers. "Love Potion No. 9" is one of a growing genre of comedic ballads made popular by such groups as the Coasters, the Cadillacs, and the Clovers. I could use a little love potion no. 9 the way my love life is going; but that's a story for later.

Courtney begins introducing me to some of his friends. All are very pleasant and very tall. David Trane, Vincent Rice, and James Robinson are all over 6'2", and all are pre-med liberal arts majors. Even Courtney's "main squeeze", Claudine Taylor, is about 5'10" and stunningly attractive. They're all intrigued to meet a white boy who is going to Howard. In the middle of our conversation, Ray Charles's "What I'd Say" boomed out of the jukebox, and Courtney and his friends begin dancing. They all are beckoning me to join them. I stand motionless, paralyzed by the "nameless dread". Claudina comes up to me and grabs my hand. She starts dancing in front of me and urges me to join her. The music finally trumps my fear, and I join the group in the "pony", the "slop", and the "snap". In high school, I had won several dance contests with my moves, but I'm flat-out amazed by Vincent and Claudine's more polished version of these dances. But they too are impressed. "Look at that white boy dance," Claudine exclaims. "I've never seen a white boy move like you." As Claudine moves back into my orbit, we begin to move together as if our bodies are having a conversation. Each of our dance moves communicates to the other what should come next. While dancing with this lovely black woman, a feeling of pure joy overtakes me. Not only am I taking a step toward conquering my Negrophobia, but I finally have a dance partner who instinctively understands my moves and who makes me look better with her own. That has never happened with any of my white partners.

When the music stops, Vincent opines, "You must be part nigger." I'm shocked by his use of the N-word, but nobody else seems to be. In fact, everyone is laughing at Vincent's anthropological speculation. "You might be on to something there Vince," says David. "Hey Izzy, where did you learn to dance like that?" Courtney asked.

"By watching the Milt Grant Show,"
"You say what?" Courtney asks in an incredulous tone.

"Yeah, the Milt Grant Show on Channel 5. It's on 6 days a week and get this, they reserve one day a week for black teenagers to be on the show. I would study how black teenagers dance. It was so much smoother and more rhythmic than the white kids. I just love watching black kids dance, and I want to dance something like that."

"I watch it," James pipes in defiantly.

"You DO?" the rest of the group asks in unison.

Yeah, particularly when they let us on. They call it Black Tuesday."

"Ain't that some shit, Vincent complains. "One day a week? And I bet we're not allowed on any day there are white kids dancing."

"Hell no," James acidly exclaims. "The station owners are terrified that we might despoil the girls and "nigrafy" the boys."

"Nigrafy?" Vincent inquires, cackling. "You made that word up."

"What if I did? It's a good description of what's happening to Izzy here. The Milt Grant Show has turned him in to part jungle bunny."

We all have a good laugh at that. At the same time I feel like my worst fear is coming true. I'm becoming nigrafied!

"Jungle bunny, my ass," proclaims an unfriendly voice coming towards us. "He's a pretender, a wannabe. Hey White, what're you doing here anyway? Why did you come to Howard?"

The voice belongs to Jason Sharpe. He is muscular, mouthy, and generally combative. I had first met him when he was a point guard for Cardozo High School. He would talk trash to me the entire game. Our rivalry spanned two basketball seasons. It began when we both played junior varsity and continued when we moved up to our respective varsity squads.

"Well if it isn't Mr. Jason Sharpe. Listen Sharpe, we're not on the court now so you don't have to keep talking trash to me." I mean this as a joke. He takes it as a challenge. His smooth, soft chocolate brown features belie his combative expression.

"I'm not talking trash. I'm just tellin' it like it is. You haven't answered my question. What're you doing here?"
"I chose Howard because it's a good school and I can afford it."

"Sure you're not just slummin' with the jiggaboos, White?" Sharpe retorts with a malicious smile on his face.

Courtney can no longer contain his impatience. "Sharpe, what's your problem?"

"I ain't got no problem. It's Mr. White boy here who has a problem. He don't realize he's in the wrong part of town."

"It's a free country," I lamely offer.

"You're right, White. I forgot.... for white people it is a free country."

"Now here comes his patented speech about the revolution," Vincent announces. Sharpe just looks at Vincent and decides to shift his focus from animosity to ridicule.

"And what do you call this shit?" Sharpe does a mocking imitation of my dancing, exaggerating my best moves into a hilarious parody. None of us can avoid cackling at his grotesque impersonation. But I'm shaking inside with rage and humiliation.

"Let me show you how it's done, son," as he launches into a silky smooth and-- I have to admit-- superior version of the pony, the slop, and the snap.

"Well, I'm gonna pony on out of here because I gots me an ASSignation. I'll dig you sad cats later." He cracks himself up with that line. And out he goes dancing and laughing.

"Don't pay him no mind, Izzy," Courtney says after Sharpe is out the door. "He always has a bug up his ass about something."

"No problem, Courtney. His words don't bother me, but his dancing puts me to shame."

"I love the way you dance," Claudine says, coming to my rescue. Mercifully, no one comments on my blushing.

"Well, I have to get home," I say finally. But it was great meeting you all."

"Be cool, White," says Vincent. "I hope we can dance again soon," says Claudine cheerfully.

As I'm walking toward the door, Courtney yells out, "Hey Izzy, I'm glad you chose Howard."

"Thanks!" And for the first time today I think so am I.

I'm feeling high as a helium balloon as I walk up Georgia Avenue to find a good position from which to grab a ride home. These are warm people that I have just met, except for Sharpe. But I already knew his game. I feel surprisingly at home after just one day at Howard. Maybe this won't be nearly as hard as I imagined.

When I reach the traffic light, I immediately approach a green Chevy Impala waiting there. Much to my amazement, the driver beckons me in. He is a largish Negro man with broad features. He is mocha-hued and possesses a definite twinkle in his eye.

"Where are you going?' he asks.

"I need to go all the way to Langley Park. Are you heading up New Hampshire Avenue by any chance?"

"As it happens, I am. I live near the District line at Eastern Avenue if that will help."

"Great," I reply, excited that I have obtained a ride on my first try. "From there, it'll be easy for me to get a ride the rest of the way. Or I can take a bus if I have to."

The driver cheerfully offers, "I'm happy to oblige." He gives me a huge grin. When he smiles, he reminds me of the pictures that I've seen of Fats Waller with the same expressive eyes.

After looking at me for a moment, he asks, "What are you doing in this part of town?"

"I go to Howard University," I respond with a surprising amount of pride.

"Really," he says in genuine amazement.

"Yes, this is my first day."

He gives me a curious stare. "What made you choose Howard?"

Oh God, Am I going to have the same conversation in reverse?

I explain that I have two main reasons for choosing Howard. One is that the price is right. The second reason is that I know I have taken on some racist ideas and feelings, and I thought that if I really got to know some Negroes, I could eliminate these feelings. I believe that education can cure racism, especially mine.

The driver looks at me like I'm clearly certifiable. "Never in my entire life have I heard such a speech from a white man," he says with great astonishment. "You must be a very unusual individual to choose Howard and for those reasons." He ponders for a moment and then adds, "Wait a minute! I got it! You're Jewish, aren't you?"

"How did you know," I ask as cheerfully surprised as I could. What I am really thinking was "Oh God, here it comes now, the 'Jews are bleeding heart liberals' speech."

Instead, the driver explains, "Look, I know Jews are tight with money. I also know that many Jews are quite sympathetic to the plight of the Negro, and I am very grateful for that. I know your people feel a common bond with us, you know, because of slavery and all. Jews are a different breed and that's a good thing. Not Anglo Saxons, though. They are some of the meanest people on earth. I don't know why that is, but they sure hate them some Negroes, ooo wee." The driver says laughing. But the more he rails against Anglo Saxons, the more upset he seems to get. He pulls a handkerchief from his pocket and begins mopping his brow. I don't know whether to feel complimented or insulted. I cannot recognize myself in these stereotypes, positive and negative. I don't have any money to be tight with.

That's why I'm going to Howard. And I am sympathetic to the Negro's plight, as he put it, not because I feel a common bond because our ancestors shared slavery, but rather because of simple justice and respect.

"By the way, my name is Miles Taylor. What's yours?"
"Izzy, Izzy White. "
Miles' face breaks out into a big grin, but he remains silent. That smile says to me,
"Do I know a Jew when I see one, or what?"
"My people all hail from Maryland's Eastern Shore. They lived near Tuckahoe where Frederick Douglas was born. You've heard of him, haven't you?"

"Well, I was in Frederick Douglas Hall today, is that the same person?"
"Oh yes. He was a great man, a great orator. You should read his autobiography some day. Anyway, many of my ancestors were slaves, and I heard so many stories growing up about the cruelty of their Anglo Saxon slave owners. It's as if I've inherited my dislike for the race. Every time I think about the fact that we are almost a hundred years away from the end of slavery and Anglo Saxons still treat me like shit, I get so angry I don't know what to do with myself. I don't think anybody who isn't black can dig how much rage there is in the Black man." Anglo Saxons better watch out. The Black man will not remain docile forever." Miles begins mopping his brow again. I'm taken aback by the intensity of his feelings. We both remain silent for a while. I just stare out the window noticing for the first time how circuitous a road New Hampshire Avenue is from Georgia Avenue to the District Line.

"So you don't dislike all white people?" I finally ask him.

"Naw, lots of white folks are nice, particularly you Jews. The source of the Negro's problem and his greatest enemy is the Anglo Saxon. And it's not like a lot of Anglo Saxons aren't poor and haven't experienced humiliation, discrimination, and hard times. But instead of those hard times making them sympathetic, it makes them all the meaner. In fact, some of the most vicious racists are poor redneck farmers and Georgia 'Crackers.'"

"What's a Cracker?"
"Well, a Cracker is a poor, black-hating white man."
"But where does the term come from?"

"Well, there are two theories about that, Izzy. One theory holds that the slaves themselves invented the term to describe a whip-cracking slaveholder. The other theory says it arose when slaves were analogously comparing white soda crackers to ginger cookies."

"But are all Crackers mean? Are all rednecks racist?"
"Just about son, just about."
I immediately thought of the driver who gave me a ride in this morning.

We're approaching Eastern Avenue when Miles says, "Well, I turn left here. It has been a pleasure meeting you and talking with you, young Izzy, and I hope our paths will cross again real soon."

"Thanks, Miles. Me too!"

I quickly get a ride from a middle-aged man in a middle-aged car. Fortunately, he is not in the mood for conversation. Alone with my thoughts, I begin to review my first day at Howard, the first fruits of my unusual choice of colleges. I'm struck by how every person I met talked in stereotypes about other people. Whites, Blacks, Jews, Anglo-Saxons are all summed up in simple global phrases. I know that I share some of these stereotypes, but at the same time feel that they violate my own experience of the wide variety of personalities that I have already encountered in my young life. Isn't this part of the problem? Wouldn't education remedy these inaccurate portrayals of each other? I am deep into the perplexity of these thoughts when the driver announced that we had reached my destination. "Isn't that Suburban Hill there on the left?" He asks. I thank him and get out of the car.

I race across New Hampshire Avenue and receive for my effort the loud blare of the horn of an oncoming car whose angry driver is upset that he has to slow down to keep from hitting me. I bound up the many steps to get to the back entrance of the building and once again avoiding the intolerably slow elevators, I run up the steps to the third floor. I enter my apartment and see my father sitting at the dining room table having a cup of coffee. "Well, how did it go today with the "Shwartzehs"? He asks. I just glare at him. Without answering, I go to my room and close the door.

Chapter 6.

That's Your Mistake

It takes a full nine weeks for me to get used to the heavy schedule I am required to take. I'm taking 19 credit hours that includes Chemistry Lecture and then additional time devoted to laboratory work; Humanities, English, Natural Science, and Analytical Geometry. Since these were Honors level courses, the amount of homework that accumulates in a week's time blows me away. In high school, I never put in the amount of time necessary to complete my homework assignments. And thus I found a new reason for the heebie jeebies, the fear of academic failure.

The Chemistry Building is only 23 years old, but it seems much older. The halls are dark and the laboratories dreary. Rusting Bunsen Burners lie among the other dilapidated equipment on tables that appear to be products of the Civil War. A rotten eggs smell pervades the entire laboratory, and I wonder whether gas masks are regularly handed out during chemistry experiments. This is not my idea of a cutting edge chemistry laboratory.

Chemistry had been the subject of my only intellectual romance in high school, and I had received one of my few "A's" in my high school chemistry class. By a process of elimination it became my major. That rare "A" grade catapulted my imagination to the belief that I was destined to become a successful chemist. This belief becomes a full-blown fantasy during my freshman year at Howard when I convince myself that my ultimate purpose in life is to earn a Ph.D. in chemistry. This will allow me to eventually earn a $100,000 a year salary. By pocketing such a yearly sum, I would live a luxurious lifestyle that would eliminate financial worry while rocketing me forever out of the orbit of my lower middle class origins.

My hope and enthusiasm are initially expanded by the elegant, droll, and ultimately intimidating presence of our professor. Dr. Moddie Taylor is a rising star in the world of chemistry. He was a 1943 Ph.D. from the prestigious University of Chicago. In 1945, he worked at the U. of Chicago for two years on the top-secret Manhattan Project. From him I know that I will get a good education in chemistry. But his status is a two-edged sword. I am in constant fear of embarrassing myself, which I manage to do virtually every other class. Here is a prototypical example: Dr. Taylor asks the following question, "Who here can describe Aristotle's view on the theory of the atom?" I raise my hand frantically with a feeling of excited certitude. "Yes, Mr. White," Dr. Taylor says, expectantly. "Aristotle believed there are four kinds of elements, Earth, Air, Water, and Fire," I answer triumphantly. Dr. Taylor peers at me with a gentle, avuncular smile of forbearance and says, "I guess Aristotle said a lot of things, didn't he, Mr. White." "Anyone else?" he asks, turning his gaze in a completely different direction.

The same dark omen awaits me in the laboratory. For a time, I am at home with the putrid smells, the dirty reagent bottles, the clattering of test tubes, the smoking acids carving trails across the laboratory tables. It isn't long, however, before the foul smelling and mood killing epiphanies I encounter in those dark dank chemistry laboratories threaten my fantasy of a successful career in chemistry and an opulent life. Initially, I think it's coolly avant-garde to be playing in the smelly, smoky laboratories, creating oozing, odorific concoctions. And I am thoroughly enjoying my tablemate who seems not only to share, but also to revel in my macabre sense of humor. As we transfer our concoctions from one test tube to another, we both give out with an overly loud maniacal laugh. This earns us a look of disapproval from the lab instructor. When I proclaim with faux hysteria "It's alive! It's alive!" the lab instructor is quickly in my face with a rather unpleasant verbal reprimand. My tablemate muffles his laughter with a mouth-covering hand. After the lab instructor returns to his seat, I hear a laughing voice behind me say,

"Hey, Dr. Frankenstein, got any sulfuric acid left? I'm all out."

"Sure Courtney, here you go. God, this stuff smells."

"Some chem. major you are. You can't even take the smells. You know the odor stays with you, Izzy, all day long."

"Are you talking about the chemicals or your b.o.?" I crack up at my own joke, but Courtney responds with a sour smile. I'm surprised by the easy camaraderie that has developed between me and Courtney Cartwright. Even though we had played on rival basketball teams in high school and had met again our first day in line for the Opening Convocation, it's only in Howard's laboratory that we actually become friends. By now we have been tablemates for nine nose-withering weeks.

"Courtney, what the hell are you laughing at?" I ask.

"Your hands, man, your hands," Courtney answers with a high-pitched chuckle?

"They're almost as brown as mine now. You better watch out, Izzy, my color's beginning to rub off on you." I look at my acid-stained hands and with effort manage a smile. But some nameless dread seizes me. Will the stains ever come off, I wonder. Courtney interrupts my reverie. "Come on, Izzy, let's take a break. This experiment's a snap. We'll have it done in no time." Courtney reaches into his briefcase and pulls out a box of doughnuts. As he lifts the doughnuts out of the box, the powdered sugar falls off, dusting his hands and wrists. I watch in fascination as Courtney's hands lose their mocha color to the fine layer of white powder. Courtney leans his lanky frame against the lab table as if he is sidling up to a bar for a drink. With a deft motion of his wrist, he pushes the entire doughnut into his mouth. Courtney suddenly gets a look of dismay on his face and attempts a muffled apology as he belatedly offers me a doughnut. The heebie jeebies return as I take the doughnut from Courtney's hand. I stare at Courtney's hand and then at the doughnut. I am paralyzed, unable to bring the doughnut to my lips. Courtney is puzzled and getting frustrated with my reluctance to eagerly consume his gift. "Go ahead, eat it man!" Courtney exclaims a little too forcefully for my taste. "It won't kill you. The acid's dry by now. It won't come off." I'm not worrying about the acid. I finally work up enough nerve to swallow a bit of the doughnut. I scrunch up my eyes and wait for "the great change" to overtake me. I am near panic as I wait. Will the change be permanent? Will I forever after be viewed with contempt as a Negro with all his imagined faults and foibles? Did I just eat myself into second-class citizenship? When some moments pass and nothing happens, I am consumed again by the familiar tumult of shame. By the time class ends, I'm sick to my stomach and wondering how I will be able to stand my upcoming humanities class.

I'm already late for my humanities class, but the need to evacuate is so great that I make a detour to the largest bathroom in the Chemistry building. I enter the ancient men's room. I must confess I am appalled by what I see. The concrete floor is cracked and stained with what appears to be old blood. What light there is comes from a single fixture that hangs from the center of the ceiling. A dozen bathroom stalls are lined up against the back wall, but none of them has doors. Privacy and dignity are dispensed with apparently along with the toilet paper. Given my imminent need, I frantically race from stall to stall until I find a lonely roll in the last stall closest to the bathroom's entrance. Because I've waited so long, I'm in considerable pain. I attempt to ease my pain by massaging my member and thinking of Shannon. My fantasy is so compelling that I don't initially notice the figure standing at the entrance of the bathroom. He is a tall tan-skinned man who is eyeing me curiously. With his muscular arms crossed, he leans against the wall that supports a line of sinks and a mirror above that spreads across the entire wall to the adjoining window. I hear his voice but at first I can't make out what he's saying. After he moves a few feet closer, I can see him clearly and unfortunately, he can see me clearly.

"That's quite a long cock you got there," he says matter-of-factly, as if he is viewing a work of pictorial excellence.

"I don't think so," I reply.

"No, no really," he reiterates, "That's quite a cock. "Why don't you let me massage it for you?"

"I don't think so," I say again, this time with greater force.

"Seriously," he says with greater insistence. "Why don't you let me massage it for you?"

"No thanks," I answer, trying to remain polite but firm. After a third invitation, I stand up and with all the manly assertiveness I can muster, I say, "I think you better leave." He has a good six inches in height and 40 pounds in weight over me, but I don't care. It's a matter of principle. If I say I don't want my member massaged, I want my wishes to be respected.

"OK, but you don't know what you're missing," he finally opines and disappears from my life forever.

I'm a bit shaken by this strange encounter. Again I feel ashamed because he obviously saw what I was doing and kindly wanted to take over the task. I also consider this as an inauspicious beginning to my career at Howard. Here it's the first semester of my freshman year, and I am invited to engage in a homosexual tryst of the briefest and most anonymous kind. My father's words come back to haunt me. "Howard's filled with queers," he lectured, hoping that he had delivered the coup de grace to my collegiate plans. What I originally took to be a statement of desperation on his part now appears prescient. How did he know? What experience did he have? With Howard? With homosexuals? Why would it be a problem even if what he said is true? Yes, I was momentarily discomforted when the tan-skinned man wanted me for his sexual purposes, but I put a stop to it. There was no violence, no conversion to homosexuality. No harm, no foul. Besides it was only one encounter. I can't conclude that Howard is filled with queers. Granted it's only my first semester at Howard, but this could be my first and last episode.

I can't stop the questions. Why was tan man interested in my member? Was it because I was the only person in the bathroom? Or did he think I was a queer? Do I look like a homosexual? I don't lisp when I talk. I don't walk funny? I don't use flamboyant gestures when I talk. Ok, I do use my hands when I talk and I was a first tenor in my junior high school choir, not a bass or a baritone. But that doesn't automatically make me a feygela.

I wonder what it's like being a homosexual, having such unusual desires. I just don't understand where they put it...and why. Is it about love or sex? Do homos really love one another? Do they actually fall in love? On the other hand, why does it frighten people so? Ok, it is a bit unusual, but why the hatred and the anger? They're still human. They're humans who do things differently. Big fricking deal! It's all a big mystery to me. Maybe I should try it? I wonder what I am missing. But if I am to try it, could I do it with a black man? Would that not be having sex with the wrong race? The wrong gender? I carry these troubling thoughts with me up the stairs to my humanities class. The only image that would give me respite is the memory of making-out with Shannon.

Without interrupting himself, my humanities professor gives me a quick glance of disapproval and turns his attention back to the class. I tiptoe my way to a vacant seat in the front row. Professor Frank Snowden is the first Negro that I ever heard with a Boston accent. What I have taken as the generic Negro accent is actually a southern drawl tinged with Black-based inflections. But here he is a Harvard trained classical scholar who had attended Boston Latin High School before that. He is a dynamic and articulate professor. And every time he opens his mouth, I am so enraptured with his accent that I almost miss the many pearls of wisdom that pours forth from this elegant and educated man. We are currently reading "De Rerum Natura" or On the Nature of Things by the first century BCE Roman poet, Lucretius. Although his poetry is dense and hard to fathom, Lucretius is brought to life by the passion and clarity of Dr. Snowden's explanations. Lucretius was a devotee of Epicurus and his philosophy of seeking long-lasting intellectual pleasure (rather than ephemeral sensual pleasure) and avoiding pain. It is a philosophy that perfectly captures my aspirations. My mental state is a fairly constant barrage of heebie-jeebies, and I fervently wish for the calm that intellectual pleasures supposedly would bring.

But there is another reason that this class fills me with such joy. I'm so impressed with myself because I am reading an obscure Roman Poet whom I have never heard of. Here at Howard where my father is convinced I will receive an inferior education. And this is the University's Honors Program in which Dr. Snowden who doubles as the Dean of the College of Liberal Arts has placed me. It is vindication of the choice I made and a refutation of my father's fear-ridden anti-Negro diatribe.

The students in this class are an academically talented bunch. Their comments during the class discussions drive home the point that I am no smarter or better prepared academically than this group of Negro students. A surprising number of these students come from countries in the Caribbean, particularly Jamaica and Trinidad. There is one student, however, who stands out among all the rest: Winston Basil McKenzie, a gangly Jamaican whose demeanor is a shock to my system. He is the first intellectually arrogant Negro that I have ever met. His arrogance, however, seems almost wholly justified. He is brilliant and articulate. And he's not shy about letting you know how brilliant and articulate he thinks himself to be. He is fond of telling everyone he knows, "I am committed to 'the Good, the True and the Beautiful'." My day is incomplete if I do not hear McKenzie tell me about the Good, the True, and the Beautiful. The more I listen to him, however, the more I get caught up in the Good, True, and Beautiful fever. Through his inspiration, I find myself for the first time in my life thinking critically about morality, searching diligently for the truth, and opening my eyes to the pleasures of the visual arts. Of the three, he is most committed to the truth, particularly the truth about the impact of white racism on American Negroes. He disdains the myth of white supremacy and pities its brutalizing and warping impact on poor and bourgeois Blacks.

Our relationship gets off to a rocky start because he keeps asking me if I have read this book or that book, none of which I've ever heard of.

"Izzy," he says to me one day, "You've must have read Black Bourgeoisie by E. Franklin Frazier."

"Uh, no Winston, I haven't," I say in a heebie-jeebies' voice. I don't know the book or its author.

"But mon, Dr. Frazier is on our faculty," McKenzie replies with great incredulity. His lilting Jamaican accent seems to become more pronounced in his disdainfully shocked reply. "He is the Chairman of Howard's Sociology Department and one of the most respected black scholars in the world," he adds with a self-satisfied look.

"No, I didn't know that either," I respond, wanting desperately for this conversation to end.

"I guess your high school education wasn't so superior, was it Izzy?" Winston's tone reeks with condescension. "I guess not," I mumble spinelessly.

"Don't you think it's odd that a white boy like you is named White?" Winston adds finding new ways to humiliate me.

"Not until now," I answer. "Why do you have such an interest in my reading habits anyway?" McKenzie places a foot on my chair and leans his 6' 2" frame towards me. He has close-cropped hair, deep brown eyes, a striking mustache and a wisp of a goatee. He's wearing brown, sharply creased pants and a cream-colored turtleneck shirt. "Well, Izzy, where I come from in Jamaica there are not too many white people. Everybody looks like me and this is true throughout the Caribbean. Yet we hear all these stories about the superiority of the white race, particularly in comparison to the descendents of former slaves in America. The movies we see and the characters in the books we read from the U.S.A. all seem to have this underlying feature. The white man is superior. This is so beyond the ken of my experience that I feel a necessity to check it out with every white student I meet. And here you are in the Honors Program at Howard University and yet I am wondering about your fund of knowledge, particularly about the Good, the True, and the Beautiful."

"Well, I'm sorry to be such a disappointment," I retort.

"You're not," he replies with a wide grin. "In fact, you are proof that the ideology of white superiority is a myth." "I never claimed to be superior, Winston." My tone of voice communicates an equal measure of apology and injury.

"For that I give you full credit for candor," Winston says unkindly. His haughty demeanor and hovering presence seems to suck all the air out of the room. I am feeling a bit claustrophobic since I see no easy way to move beyond him to leave the now-concluded humanities class. Eventually, Winston senses that I need to move and he removes his foot from my chair. "The t'ing is, Izzy," he continues, "You need to know that a change is gon come, a huge change in the way people treat one another. This change is gon be worldwide. Maybe you can help us bring about this change."

"What kind of change?" I asked, intrigued by the unclear scope of this undefined change.

Although I have been a student at Howard for nine weeks, I have yet to eat in the school cafeteria. Today, I want to change that fact, and I make my way over to the eatery in an advanced state of hunger. As I approach the largish building, the aromas emanating from within are not encouraging. I go in and immediately encounter a large room filled with a surfeit of aging tables and chairs and a very busy cafeteria line. Despite whatever I might think about the aromas, the cafeteria is mobbed. This inspires hope that the food will be better than my first sense impressions. I enter the cafeteria line that is now so large that it winds back around the line closest to the food and heads for the entrance to the building. Fifteen minutes later, I finally face some food. What I see, however, almost makes me bolt. There are barbeque beef sandwiches that look days old. The meat's grayish tint leads me to question the nature of the animal from which it is carved. Gray seems to be colour du jour for today's lunch. Even the specialty of the day, lamb chops, along with the accompanying mashed potatoes, approached the color of gunmetal. I settle for the wrinkled hot dog and purchase a bag of Wise potato chips and a watered down fountain draft of Coca Cola. I search for a free table and find one with only one other occupant. "Mind if I join you?" I ask the studious-looking fellow with his nose in a textbook. "Not at all," he answers without looking up. His body language makes it clear that our physical proximity is acceptable, but that I can expect no conversation. He's obviously cramming for a pending exam, but I can't understand how he can concentrate in the din produced by a hundred conversations swirling around us. I was therefore left to my own devices and my wrinkled hot dog.

As I eat, I watch the people moving back and forth from the cafeteria line to their respective tables; people moving from table to table or people leaving the cafeteria. I'm amazed at the range of skin color in the people passing by me. There are very black people, people with more of a chocolate brown complexion; also mocha-colored individuals, and there are a fair number of people who are very light-skinned, so light in fact, that I wonder if they're white, Negro, or what? At first, I keep these ruminations to myself. I am having an intense internal dialogue with myself on the deep philosophical question of what the term race really means or refers to? What does it mean to be white? What determines whiteness? How come these seemingly white people identify as Negroes? I soon tire of this internal dialogue and force myself on my tablemate.

"Excuse me, can you answer a question for me," I asked.

"Yes, what is it?" he responds with some impatience.

"You see these people walking by us? Many of them look white. Are they white students or light-skinned Negroes?"

"It all depends," my interlocutor answers.

"On what?" He picks at his beard, which I have noticed for the first time, and looks at me with an expression of weary condescension, an expression that seems to say to me, "Why are you pestering me with these questions, and what are you doing at Howard University anyway?" Instead, he says, "It depends on how they choose to identify themselves."

"They have a choice?" I ask in utter disbelief.

"Well, to a certain extent. Have you ever heard of the 'one drop rule'?

"Sort of, but I'm not really clear what it means." His weary, condescending expression becomes even more weary and condescending. He sighs heavily and expounds, "You white people have decided that if a person has one drop of Negro blood, then he's a Negro no matter how white he looks. But some Negroes are so light and so lacking in what are called Negroid features that they can easily 'pass' as white. Now most, if not all of the people you see here, identify themselves as Negro, but there may be a few who think of themselves as white, but their ancestry will reveal that much more than one drop of Negro blood is present." I remember my conversation with Mrs. Prescott and how members of her family lived as white and how she had indeed "chosen" to identify as Negro. This is confusing. In a society that seems to be so rigidly defined by race and color some people actually have a choice to identify as white or black.

Now convinced that he is not going to get any more studying done, my interlocutor introduces himself. "By the way, my name is Michael White." I can't help myself. I burst out laughing. "What's so damn funny?" exclaims the other Mr. White as his brown face takes on a crimson glow of embarrassment.

"I'm sorry. I'm laughing because my name is White too, Isadore White. But everyone calls me Izzy. I guess you're the black White and I'm the white White." Michael hesitates turning crimson again. But a moment later, he starts to laugh at the absurdity of this coincidence.

"Where are you from, Izzy?'
"D.C. "How about you?"

"I'm originally from New Jersey, but my parents died when I was 6 years old and I lived with my grandparents in Durham, North Carolina."

"How come you didn't go to Duke?" I ask in all sincerity. It's Michael's turn to burst out laughing. "You know, I don't believe you. Here you are, a white boy going to Howard University and you don't seem to know much about what's going on in this country."

"What do you mean?" Michael makes little effort to hide the scorn in his voice.

"Don't you know how segregated the South is? I can tell you it is pretty bad in North Carolina. The K.K.K. is still large there, man, and if you violate the segregationist code, you're liable to get your ass killed: Like that GI who came home from the war, sat in front of the bus in Durham and the bus driver shot him cause he moved too slowly to the back of the bus. It took the all white jury all of 20 minutes to free his ass. It goes without saying that Duke don't allow no 'nigras' within its sacred portals," he says in a voice laced with resentment.

"I thought that was changing there like it is here," I protest. "I guess what I've experienced growing up in D.C. is a kind of polite line in the sand. Social mixing just isn't done. Whites and Negroes live in different places, go to different places for recreation, shopping, dining, etc. I never thought that there would be violence if the line was crossed."

"Izzy, where have you been?" Michael cries out in exasperation. "How can you be so naïve and yet decide to come to Howard? I knew white people were crazy, but boy, you are something new under the sun. Didn't you follow what happened in Little Rock a couple of years ago?" Michael asked, hoping against hope that the school integration crisis at Central High School would ring a bell.

"Well, yeah," I say with embarrassment, "but it was too painful to watch."

"Too painful?" Michael sputters. "Izzy, you haven't a clue. Look, I believe you've got a good heart or you wouldn't be a student here, but you've GOT to get an education."

"That's why I am here," I answer, "I came to get an education."

"I mean you need to find out what is going on between the races, man. Black people been takin' shit from white people for far too long and a change is gonna come in the very near future. And that change is gonna rock white people off their self-constructed pedestal." Michael is pointing his finger directly at me as he ends his diatribe. He's the second person today who warned me of a great change coming in race relations as I recall Winston McKenzie's own Jamaican flavored jeremiad. But neither one is specific. What change? How dangerous is this gonna be?

"Listen, Izzy, I don't hate white people. I know there are fair-minded, good-hearted Caucasians. But you don't understand how difficult it is to face someone who looks like you and not feel hatred."

"But I haven't done anything to you!" I complain.
"That's not the point, Izzy. Your color is the color of the oppressor."

"I don't get it Michael. I'm not even a white Anglo Saxon, I'm Jewish and as far as I know there were no Jewish slave owners."

"There's where you're wrong, my man. There were in fact several Jewish slave owners in the South. And Jew or not, they had all of the prerogatives of any other white southern slave owner. You check the history and you'll see I'm right about this."

I try to cover my shock and disbelief at what Michael is saying. "I have to get to my English class," I say as neutrally as I can. "It was great meeting you, Michael, and I hope we meet again soon. I think you have much you can teach me."

"I look forward to it, Izzy. I look forward to it very much," he answers with a big grin.

As I walk toward Douglas Hall I feel as if I have just swallowed a hunk of hard bread. My stomach is unsettled; I have pains in my chest. My thoughts are racing-- sure signs of the heebie-jeebies, but this time laden with melancholy. Jewish slave owners? Negroes who view whites in the same stereotypic fashion as whites view Negroes? These views are as difficult to swallow as the aforementioned bread. In the past, I was afraid that black teenagers wanted to kick my ass. Now I'm hearing that there is a long history of reasons why they might want to. Michael's words keep reverberating in my mind. "You are the color of the oppressor!" True enough! But I personally didn't do anything to Negroes. Am I still guilty? If so, of what? Are all whites to be thought of as guilty? How is this different than thinking of all black people as criminally inclined just because one black person commits a crime? The logic escapes me. Yet this is the logic that I had heard all my life from people who share my color.

The Upper Quadrangle gleams in the sunlight. The day is one of the jewels that Washington, D.C. occasionally gets in early November. The Indian summer sun is bright and gently warming. I stop by the "Dial," the Sundial which stands in the epicenter of the Upper Quad. A stone backless bench is nearby and I sit there for a few minutes hoping that the warming sun will bring me some tranquility. Within moments a student about my age asks if he could sit for a moment. I cordially invite him to do so. He is a little taller than I and just as slim. He's quite dark and his hair is combed high off his forehead in a kind of Pompadour. Since my quest for solitary tranquility is eliminated by his presence, I turn on my affability button and cheerfully introduce myself. "My name is Izzy White. What's yours?"

"I'm Rick Frazier, but my friends call me Bee Bop cause I like Jazz so much."

"What kind of Jazz?"

"I dig Miles Davis right now. That man blows a cool trumpet. How about you? Ya dig Jazz?"

"Don't know much about it," I answer.

Bee Bop begins to wax enthusiastic. "Man, you've got to hear his new platter; called 'Kind of Blue'. This is the best jazz album yet. Davis's talent is bodacious and he's got some of the best Jazz musicians who ever lived joining him –Cannonball Adderley and 'The Train on sax; Bill Evans on piano, Paul Chambers on bass, and Jimmy Cobb on drums."

"I never heard of any of these guys. Who or what is 'The Train?" I asked. Bee Bop is blown away. "You don't know who the Train is? You never heard of John Coltrane, the most creative saxophone player ever?"

"Sorry. I'm much more into Rock 'n Roll, Rhythm & Blues, and Doo Wop."

Bee Bop's voice suddenly takes on an ingratiating tone. "Oh yeah, that stuff is pretty cool, but it lacks the intellectual heft of jazz. I sure hope someday you'll listen to some jazz. If you do, you'll see the connections between Rhythm & Blues and Jazz."

"By the way, Bee Bop, where're you from?"

"My people are from Gastonia, North Carolina, outside of Charlotte. But we moved up to D.C. when I was a baby. We ended up in the Barry Farm projects in Southeast, you know, near St. Elizabeth's Hospital. It was a real hellhole, all kinds of violence and shit like that. I'm lucky to be here. So many of my friends are either dead or in prison. Early on, though, I could see the dead-end street my friends were on, and I promised myself that I was not gonna end up like them. I caught a lot of shit because I studied. My friends accused me of acting white because I got good grades, particularly at Anacostia High School. I lost some friends but kept my life. But there were some good times." He adds wistfully. " How 'bout you, Izzy, where're you from?"

"I was born in D.C. and grew up in the northwest part of the city. We lived a mile south of Walter Reed Hospital and not far from Silver Spring, Maryland."

"Never heard of those places," Bee Bop says somewhat dejectedly.

"I went to Coolidge High School," I add. Right after graduation we moved to Langley Park.

"Oh, Coolidge," Bee Bop said excitedly, "I know Coolidge. We used to beat the stuffing out of Coolidge in football."

"You guys had a good basketball team too. If we hadn't lost to McKinley Tech in the playoffs, we might have played Anacostia."

"Did you play?" Bee Bop asked.

"Yeah, I did." But before I start bragging on myself, I get up and say, "Listen, Man, I have to get to my English class. It's been great talking with you Bee Bop and I hope to see you again."

"Same here." Bee Bop looks at me with a peculiar expression on his face and says,

"You know something, Izzy, this is the first time I've ever had a conversation with a white boy as an equal." Bee Bop Frazier turns and walks away without looking back. My jaw drops and remains that way as I watch him head toward the "Valley". This simple conversation, man-to-man on an equal footing between a Black man and a white man has been forbidden for much of the country's history. A heavy sadness overtakes me, then molten rage at the unending hypocrisy of the American Creed: All Men are Created Equal, my ass! The more accurate reading is If You're White, You're Alright!

My mind is reeling with a kaleidoscope of images of the people I've met today. The arrogance of Winston MacKenzie contrasted sharply with the humble, but enthusiastic Bee Bop. Because of my skin color, the former gives me a heaping dose of condescension while the latter shows me an equal dose of deference. My partial namesake, Michael White, warns me of a perilous future for race relations, while my chemistry tablemate, Courtney Cartwright jokes about my acid-driven color change. And I freak out that his generous offer of a doughnut might turn his joke into reality. How different these fellow students are and how- like me- obsessed they are with their own idiosyncratic perspective on race and color.

Several weeks later, these thoughts continue to buzz inside my head like bees around a hive as I enter my English class in Douglass Hall. The class is presided over by the very distinguished Dr. James Lavelle. He is about my height, tan colored and balding. He has marble black eyes that always possess an expression of dramatic expectation. He is almost pretty with a thin straight nose and a pencil thin mustache. He is quirky, funny, and sophisticated, and he is an intellectual snob. He clearly believes his mission is to turn us all into intellectual snobs. "The New York Times is the only newspaper worth reading," he always says. "All of you should be reading the

Saturday Review and at least two books of fiction a week," he adds. "You're college students now and you need to kick it up a notch with your reading. Now, I realize that many of you are still stuck on comic books, tabloids, and those literary jewels—God help me--Jet and Ebony. But ladies and gentlemen, you need to raise your vision. With your noses stuck in such magazines, you are unable to see the light. Come out of that self-imposed cave filled with the baubles of the Black Bourgeoisie. They are fool's gold that appears to shine with the alleged improvements of the Negro Race. There is so much of true value out in the world beyond the ghettoes of your minds. It is all there for you to learn and to treasure." With his oratory completed, he looks around the room, and mentally takes attendance.

I sit in my usual seat and fumble through my notes. We have been covering the speech-giving section of the course for the last two weeks, and today is my turn to give a speech before the class. "Ah, there you are Mr. White," Dr. Lavelle says with a little laugh and a look I cannot fathom. "Mr. White," he continues. "I believe it is your turn to give a speech. What is the title?" he asks. "The Brotherhood of Man," I reply. Dr. Lavelle rolls his eyes. I can't fathom the eye rolling either. By last night, I finally arrive at a comfortable place with my speech and its many oratorical flourishes that I either purloined from the likes of Thomas Jefferson or that are paraphrases of several heartwarming American platitudes. It sings of brotherhood, waxes poetic over equality, and prophesies that equal justice under the law is just around the corner. Now in light of my encounters today with Courtney, Winston, Michael, and BeeBop, I feel very differently about my speech. It seems naïve and childishly idealistic. But I have to give it as is.

I stand there looking at a class of black students; because in this class, I am the only white person enrolled. I normally come down with the heebie-jeebies whenever I have to give a speech before a group of people. But now I, who possess the "color of the oppressor", am going to talk about how we are all created equal to a group composed entirely of students who are the color of the oppressed. My heebie-jeebies advances to panicky paranoia. I'm terrified that I will unintentionally offend Dr. Lavelle or my classmates without having a clue as to what is considered offensive. My terror changes the whole tone of my speech. The words are as I had written them, but my sonorous encomium to brotherly love comes out as one muffled, maudlin Mea Culpa. My words are fired by hope and confidence in a changing world. My tone seems to beg forgiveness from every Negro in America. When it is over, I look imploringly at Dr. Lavelle, hoping that in his hearing there are at least a few redeeming morsels in my speech. "Mr. White," he finally says after looking at me for an uncomfortable length of time. "Your speech would have been infinitely more interesting had you taken the opposite point of view."

My head reels with confusion. I can't believe what he said- the opposite point of view? What is he saying? Did he want me to stand up in front of an entire class of Negroes and defend white supremacy? Did he want me to deny that these terrible things had happened to Black people? Maybe he's being subtle, speaking on some rarefied level of intellectual discourse that soars over my head. All I know is that I'm missing something.

I carry my confusion with me to The Student Union in Miner Hall. I am about to sit down when I notice a lively card game that is taking place nearby. There are four players each with a stash of bills on the table. Several other students are standing around watching the game. I ask a fellow standing next to me, "What are they playing?"

"It's dealer's choice," he says. "By the way, my name is Rayford Dixon."

"And I'm Izzy White. You seem like a student of the game here."

"Not really. I'm just watching my good friend Archibald Green. He's a card shark without peer. In fact, I don't think he ever goes to class, because he seems to be in here playing cards all the time. I watch the game for about a half hour and Archie Green wins every hand. The other players have had enough and the game ends for lack of "marks". Ray introduces me to Archie and the two of them invite me for coffee. Ray is tall and thin, while Archie is about my height, but with a parabola-shaped belly. It's clear that their primary interest is in finding out why a white boy is attending Howard. Their curiosity requires me to repeat the Q&A session that I have now engaged in many times during my short tenure at Howard. Such repetition compels me to mess with their minds a little bit. "How do you know I'm white?" I ask. Their eyes are wide with incredulity. "Well, you look white to me," says Archie Green. "So does a third of the Howard student body," I retort. "Amen to that," Ray says laughing. After they complete their Q&A, I start one of my own. I want to know if they think that a change is coming in race relations and if so what kind of change. Archie responds first. " Nah, man, it's gonna be the same shit forever. The white man has too many guns, bodies, and too much money for us poor niggers to fight for our rights. White people are so sick in the head about race and skin color I don't see no chance of things changing for the better."

"So you don't think students at Howard should get involved in destroying segregation?"

"A waste of time, man, a fucking waste of time." Archie says this with a vigorous shake of the head. "The only thing liable to get destroyed is a group of sorry, addle pated niggers." Hoping for a different more hopeful answer, I ask Ray if he agrees with Archie. "Shit, yeah, man. Us Black folks have never had the power to change our miserable fate. It's not so much integration and respect we need. It's power. If we had the power to shape our own fate, we would command respect. But it's difficult to create power when you are one tenth of a population that hates your guts. We need to work with white allies and they are few and far between. The only allies Blacks have usually had are Jews and Socialists. So I figure that you are one or the other....or maybe both. Which are you, White?"

"Well, I'm Jewish, but I'm just learning how bad things are between whites and Negroes. I don't know if I'm an ally yet, but I certainly hate the ugly things I'm learning that people of my color have done to people of yours." At this point, Archie jumps in. "Then let me school you, White. The only task we are allowed to perform is to figure out how a Negro survives in a racist culture. One thing I've learned is not to try and succeed in a white man's world. Even if you are lucky enough to make some money or achieve some fame like Jackie Robinson, you're still a nigger to each and every white man whether he's trailer trash or the owner of General Electric. The well-to-do or famous Black man will still be harassed by the police, won't be allowed to live in certain neighborhoods, eat at most restaurants, be denied room at most inns. It's bullshit man and it really makes me sick with rage if I let it. So the Black man has to find any way he can to survive. If he wants to go back to Africa, that's a way to survive. That's not my way, but it's an option. If he's light enough and he wants to pass as white, that's a way to survive. It's not my way, but it is a way. If a Negro wants to become a well-to-do member of the Black Bourgeoisie, I don't judge him. I know he's doing what I'm trying to do—survive! If he has a chance to form an all- Black community that is run by Blacks and for Blacks like they did in Eatonville, Florida, that's a way to survive, but it's not my way. My way, White, is to become the most skilled card-playing Negro in the country and make a good living plying my trade. Now I plan to get a degree from Howard...eventually. Just in case things do change and the professional work I seek to do is finally accepted; and I'm paid a living wage; and I'm allowed to live where I want. But if that day never comes, I will survive by my card-playing wits and my ability to read the minds and emotions of my opponents."

"What about you, Ray? How do you plan to survive?

"I wouldn't mind becoming a member of the Black Bourgeoisie. If I can't have power, then I want money. And I want my picture in Jet and Ebony." This produced a group cackle. "And Izzy, what are you doing here? I scratch my head in the hope of stimulating some intelligent thought in my otherwise blank mind. But all I can come up with at the moment is, "I'm here to learn. The problem is the more I learn the more there is to learn. It all seems hilarious and depressing at the same time."

Chapter 7.

Desirie

By early December of my freshman year, the golden days of Indian Summer have given way to the chilly drafts and dreary light of late fall. The change in the weather contributes to my growing disenchantment with having to hitchhike to school. In fact, I am sick to death of my daily hitchhiking hassle. Monday, Wednesdays, and Fridays, I have an 8 am Natural Science class; and because of the unpredictability of my means of transport, I am out on New Hampshire Avenue by 7:10 am with my thumb in the air. It's the same thing every day-- the drivers' incredulous looks, the same racist banter, and the same sexual obsession. The driver could be male, female, old, young, rich, or poor. It doesn't matter. The last question is always, depressingly, maddeningly the same, and always asked in a conspiratorial whisper: "Hey, have you ever been to bed with a black woman? What's it like?" But the worst part of the ride is what comes after. I'm on the verge of being late for almost every class. I make a mad dash up Euclid Street, across Georgia Avenue, up Howard place, past the Rankin Chapel and down the stairs to the Valley. The last phase is a sprint on the diagonal to the Biology Building and up to the second floor. Virtually every day, my white professor, Dr. Anson Stillwell, is watching me out of the second floor window. And every day, he greets me with sarcasm. "Ah, Mr. White, I am so happy to see that you have your track shoes on today." Or, to the class, "We must all emulate Mr. White's commendable effort to improve his physical stamina." Dr. Stillwell is a man in his early 50s. I refer to him –not to his face, of course—as "Dr. Sneerwell" because his face is irreversibly set in a condescending sneer. His blond hair is beginning to grey and is parted in the middle, as if we still lived in the first decade of the 20th century. He wears wire-thin glasses and possesses small pointy eyes. He is slightly taller than I, but his body resembles a loaf of barely kneaded dough. This collection of features leads me to view him as an anachronistic, arrogant alien.

For the duration of my two-semester course in Natural Science I'm constantly late, and Dr. Stillwell just as constantly metes out the punishment of sarcasm. But this morality play possesses a unique ending. In the late spring our last class is a field trip to the Agricultural Center in Beltsville, Maryland. Upon our return, I know the bus will come within blocks of my apartment in Langley Park. Instead of returning all the way to Howard only to hitchhike my way back home, I have previously arranged with the bus driver to let me off when we are in walking distance to my home. When we approach the intersection of University Boulevard and Piney Branch Road, I signal the driver to let me off. As the bus is coming to a stop, Dr. Stillwell asks "Oh, Mr. White, do you live near here?" I answer, "Yes I do." Pointing to the left, I continue, "I just shoot down Piney Branch Road all the way to New Hampshire Avenue, and I live right there at Suburban Hills Apartments." Dr. Stillwell gives me a funny look. "You know, Mr. White, I live in the other direction on Piney Branch, just a few blocks up. You could have come to class with me in the morning," he offers. The weight and pain of my having to bear his humiliating sarcasm day after day, class after class, almost overwhelms me. At that moment my rage destroys the power of speech, and I run out of the bus to keep from punching Dr. Stillwell in his snooty nose.

In contrast to the Chemistry building that sits next to it, the Ernest Just Hall Biology Building is much newer and looks it. Constructed in 1956, the building is dedicated to Ernest Everett Just, a prominent marine biologist. It is bright, spacious, and comfortable. I take my accustomed seat on the end of the third row. I immediately begin to search the room for her. When I do not see her right away, I feel a sense of desperation. I keep scanning the room, but she is nowhere to be found. My mood switches from eager excitement to hopeless desolation. Until, that is, I hear a voice from behind me say, "Hi Izzy." I turn around and there she is, Desirie Jackson, in the seat directly behind me displaying her sparkling smile.

"Hi Desirie," I utter in a barely audible voice. "What brings you here?" I stupidly ask. In mock anger, she scolds, "Now, Izzy White, you darn well know why I'm here. The same reason you are. We both have to take this course. What kind of question is that?" Her smile now is turned up several degrees of brightness and that only increases my mortification. I keep my eyes on her perhaps a little too long and she gives me a quizzical glance.   I quickly look away and turn myself around to face the professor. Instead of taking notes, I am writing her name in my notebook over and over. It's difficult to pay attention to "Dr. Sneerwell" because my mind is captivated by images of Desiree. Today, she wears her hair in a French twist, which makes me think that she is way more sophisticated than I. Her creamy chocolate complexion, ebony eyes, and thin nose give rise to lust, longing, and finally to the heebie-jeebies. I am smitten and terrified of feeling smitten.

Besides the fact that Desirie's presence is sending my physiology into orbit, there is another reason why it's difficult to listen to Dr. Sneerwell. He is going on and on about the Krebs Cycle, the complicated set of cyclical chemical reactions by which food is converted into energy. His monochromatic delivery, however, is converting my energy into a state of leaden sleepiness. I try to wake myself up by stealing a quick glance at Desirie. My head is snapping back and forth between quick glances at Desirie and speedy attempts at presenting the illusion of paying rapt attention to what Dr. Sneerwell was saying. The manikin-like movements of my head make Desirie giggle. I don't know whether to feel pleased or embarrassed. I go with the former. I'm so taken with the musicality of her laugh that I turn my robotic head movements into a little chair dance. My head moves to a syncopated beat while my shoulders shiver. This brings more soul warming laughter from Desirie. And just as I'm really feeling the groove, I hear… "Mr. White!" It is Dr. Sneerwell in his most pompous voice. "I would have thought that given your diligent and speedy efforts to make it to class on time that you would be motivated to pay attention to the course lectures. Instead, I find you performing a parody of Fred Astaire in a chair.

Now would you be so kind as to pay attention to—and absorb--my pearls of wisdom?"

Well, fuck him, I think as I make myself as small as possible in my seat. Why is he picking on me, I wonder? Is it because we are both white and it's easier for him to chastise me than anybody else in the class? Is he afraid to say something harsh to any of the black students? All I know is that I seem to be on the receiving end of all of his bricks. And I don't like it.

The time remaining in Dr. Stillwell's class moves with all the alacrity of an unhurried snail, which I conclude is apt punishment for my classroom misdemeanors. When class finally ends, it just so happens that Desirie and I leave the classroom at exactly the same time. Despite my fear, I take the opportunity to ask her where her next class is. She says she's heading for her English class in Douglass Hall. Since I'm heading there too for Analytical Geometry, I ask if I can walk along with her. "Sure, Izzy," she replies with surprising exuberance. We walk together toward the steps leading up to the Yard. She is wearing a beautiful maroon colored coat, which has large black buttons and a broad collar that is pulled down. As we approach the steps, the wind begins to kick up. She pulls up her collar, which now completely covers her tiny clam-shaped ears. I want desperately to say something clever or witty or at least insightful. But all I can muster is, "So how do you think Howard compares with Coolidge? I mean we're in college now. Does it seem very different from high school?" She looks puzzled. Then she smiles. "Izzy White! That is the worst pick up line I have ever heard." I'm shocked by her bluntness. But rather than admitting that my stupid question was a bizarrely poor effort at flirtation, I deny it.

"No no," I protested. "I really want to know what you think."
"You're not very good at this are you?" she responds.

"No, as a matter of fact, I stink at it," I finally confess. She looks at me and I feel penetrated to the core. "Have you ever come on to a black woman before?" She asks softly.

"No, but I think of myself as an equal opportunity blunderer. I'm likely to strike out with girls of all races, religions, and nationalities." Desirie laughs heartily. As I watch her laughing, I feel a great craving—lust, if you will—for her company. I love being in her presence, listening to her laugh, anxiously awaiting the next surprising thing she will say to me.

When she finally stops laughing, she says with a serious look, "Well, you're the first white boy to come on to me."

"I find that hard to believe," I opine. At this she becomes wide-eyed. "Izzy," she exclaims, "DC is still a segregated city. Even though I transferred from Roosevelt to Coolidge in my junior year, there wasn't a lot of social mixing between the races during my two years there."

"Things will get better."

"Bullshit," she says louder than she wants. She immediately claps her hand across her mouth and squeals with laughter. I have the same wide-eyed expression, and I too laugh at her unexpected critique. We enter Douglass Hall and I walk her to her English class. "This is my prison cell." she says, "Where's yours?"

"In the room just above you," I answer. As we say our goodbyes, I am seized with a sense of urgency and hurriedly ask her, "Desirie, can we meet after class for lunch or coffee?" She looks at me as if she were trying to discern my motives or perhaps her own. "OK, Izzy," she says hesitantly, "If you like."

Desirie is not available for lunch so we plan to meet for coffee after our classes. I show up at the Student Union ten minutes early for our 3:30 meeting. I'm so nervous that my stomach is giving a live concert before a sparse crowd in the Union. This kind of nervousness is painfully familiar. I feel this way whenever I'm going on a date with a girl that I like. The fact that she is black adds a new dimension to my worrying. What will people think? I anxiously scan the union to see if I can pick up any clues from the people sitting at the various tables. Only six tables are currently occupied. At three of these tables I see black couples who are into one another and oblivious to everyone else. At another table are two black men engaged in animated conversation punctuated by loud laughter. They are "playing the dozens".

First Man: "Hey, look-a-here."

Second Man: "What's that boy?"

First Man: "You've got some nerve callin' people ugly; why you so ugly the hospital you was born at oughta be closed for repairs." (cackle, guffaw, chortle).

Second Man: "That's alright; after yo mama gave birth to you, she had to be quarantined." (cackle, guffaw, chortle).

I didn't know what "playing the dozens" was until Miles told me on one of my frequent rides with him from Howard to the District line. He informed me, much to my utter astonishment and horror, that the term the dozens referred originally to the slave trade in New Orleans where deformed slaves were sold in lots of a cheap dozen. To be sold in such a manner was considered to be the lowest form of degradation. Playing the dozens though refers to a competition in trash talking where the object is to humiliate your opponent until he can no longer respond with a clever retort.

At still another table, there are several individuals clothed in traditional African garb joyously conversing in their native Swahili. The musicality of their language captivates me. I am so lost in the percussive sweetness of this African colloquy, that I do not hear Desirie trying to explain her late arrival. "Izzy, are you listening to me? I am so upset." Her distress yanks my attention away from the Swahili concert as if it were a hooked cane. She holds her face in her hands while continuing to stand over me. "What happened, Desirie?" I ask as I motion for her to sit down. "Professor Davis gave me a B- on my midterm exam," she says as she dissolves into tears. I don't know quite how to respond. I want to be empathic, but I'm expecting a more consequential calamity like losing her purse or that she was mugged on her way from class. "Gee I'm sorry, Desirie," I reply unconvincingly. She gives me an angry frown, but quickly shifts her expression to a sheepish smile. "I am sorry, Izzy. I don't mean to act like a hysterical female, but I really expected an 'A'." She sits down, removes her coat and again begins to cry. "My father's going to kill me," she says shaking her head.

"Just because you got a B-?" I ask in disbelief.

"You don't understand, Izzy. My father demands nothing but 'As'."

"What does your father do?" I ask annoyed by such perfectionism.

"He's a lawyer, but he works in the Department of Justice," she answers with a mixture of pride and fear in her voice. Desirie seems to be distracted. She keeps looking around the student union. I wondered if she is doing what I had been— seeing who might be seeing us together.

"Are you looking for someone?" I ask, still annoyed, but now at her.

Still scanning the room she replies, "No, no one in particular." A moment later our attention is abruptly drawn to the beautiful doo-wop sounds emanating from the male students who had just been playing the dozens. They have been joined by a third student, and the three of them begin to sing a very good version of "For Your Precious Love", the first--and in my mind-- best song ever recorded by Jerry Butler and the Impressions. Their harmony is so tight and thrilling that I can't believe they're not in an echo chamber. Desirie looks over at me. Her face is now wide with astonished amusement. "Why Izzy, you're blushing." Her voice now filled with the harmony of teasing and laughter, she asks me, "Who you thinking of, Izzy? Who you been getting next to, Izzy?" Even though I turn a brighter shade of crimson with every mocking sound she makes, I can't help being charmed by the phrase "Getting next to". It speaks to me simultaneously of longed for closeness and wild sex. I desired both with Desirie. After a long pause, I said, "I don't have a girlfriend, Desirie."

"Well, you look like you were thinking of someone," she continues to tease.

"I just love this song, that's all," I say, trying to divert her from her mocking tactics. Her eyes sparkle when she teases me, and I fall deeper into my love fantasy.

"Liar!" She counters triumphantly. She mocks, jeers and teases me into a confession.

"Okay, I was remembering someone I thought I was in love with," I replied, even though it was she I was thinking of.

"Finally, Izzy White tells the truth," she says as if she were giving a closing argument to a jury.

"Tell me more. What was she like?" Desirie seems to warm up to the prospect of learning about the girl who broke my heart. I tell her about Sophia, the endless nights I pined for her, and the devastating way in which she had humiliated me last New Years Eve. When I tell her how Sophia and Sonny Henson began making out in front of me, Desirie's eyes grow big. She cups her mouth with her hand and squeals out her unique form of shocked laughter. She can't believe this bizarrely ludicrous ploy of the girl of my dreams. "Oh Izzy, I am so sorry to laugh, but never in my born days have I heard of such a cold, cold play. You were the victim of some rare, creative bitchery, I've got to tell you. And you loved this girl?"

"I thought I did," I feel my face flush once more. "Okay, enough about me. It's your turn. Tell me about your love life. Have you ever had your heart broken?" She hesitates for a moment, gives me a searching look to see if there are any traces of ridicule in my expression and then says, "Yes. Just once."

"Go on," I prompt.

"Have you ever heard of Oak Bluffs?"

"No. Where and what is it?"

"It's one of the little towns on Martha's Vineyard."

"That doesn't help much because I know next to nothing about Martha's Vineyard." First she gives me a history/geography lesson. Oak Bluffs was a resort town on the island of Martha's Vineyard off the coast of Cape Cod. Originally known as Cottage City when it was incorporated in 1880, its name changed to Oak Bluffs in 1907. Although most of the people who lived in this seven square mile area were white; by the 1930s, a small area of the town had become a popular summertime resort for very well-heeled Black people. (I had no idea such people existed). The white part of town had been a Methodist retreat. Ironically, but not surprisingly, the inns and hotels were segregated until the 1960s, including the Methodist-owned 100 year old Wesley hotel.

The Black elite play on a narrow strip of the beach in Oak Bluffs that they named the Ink Well. As much as the whites disdained the Blacks, the older and richer residents in the Black community developed their own form of within group snobbery towards more recent arrivals or less well-off Blacks who were coming to the island in increasing numbers to vacation.

"Last summer," Desirie continues, "my father was invited to spend two weeks at his brother's place in Oak Bluffs. My uncle is a very successful lawyer in New York who then made a fortune off his real estate investments. Even he isn't completely accepted by the oldest Black residents of Oak Bluffs, but he charmed his way into being one of the more popular new arrivals. He used to host these grand parties and invite virtually every black family in Oak Bluffs. I spent most of my time on the beach. I loved the Ink Well and met so many interesting people there. And the young Black men were so fine! Anyway, my first day there I was lying on the beach when this light-skinned man with a thin moustache came up to me. He knelt down on one knee and said, 'Hello my gorgeous sister that's some fine tan you have there.' I looked up at him, and I noticed he had the sweetest smile on his face. And it did not escape my attention that he was built like a brick ... well you know what I mean. I was a good bit darker in hue than he was and I felt a little sensitive about it in this neighborhood. 'Are you making fun of my color?' I asked him. "No ma'am,' he says, 'I luuv chocolate. In fact, chocolate is my favorite flavor.' All the while he's grinning like somebody placed a juicy steak in front of him. It was obvious that this man did not lack for self-esteem, but he was too fine to be sent on his way. Still grinning, he says, 'Allow me to introduce myself. My name is Carter Woodson Wyatt. My father idolized Carter Woodson and that's how I ended up with my name.' Well, Izzy, I know I should have known who Carter Woodson was, but I hadn't a clue. His smile transformed into shock when I told him I didn't know who Carter Woodson was. 'You don't know who the father of Black history is? He was a great historian who started the Journal of Negro History. He was only the second one of us to get a Ph.D. from Harvard. And in 1926, he founded Negro History Week, which takes place every year during the second week of February.' I'm sure he thought I was an ignoramus, but he asked me out anyway. And that began a wonderful two weeks of romance and adventure. I had never met anyone like him and I confess I fell for him hard."

"What happened?" I begin to feel inside the first gull squawk of jealousy.

"We spent many days at The Inkwell. At night, we would go dancing or walk for miles on the beach. And on one moonlit night as we walked hand in hand on the beach, he told me he wanted to make love to me. Much to my surprise, I heard myself say yes. He took me home and there I lost my virginity. By the end of the night, I was so in love with that man, my mind was in a fog for days."

Desirie had told me the very thing I did not want to hear-- that I hoped I wouldn't hear. Throughout her monologue I try my best to be matter-of-fact about what she's telling me. But I can feel the jealousy squawk becoming a lion's roar. "And then what happened?" She begins to tear up. She takes a moment to pull a wad of tissue from her purse to dab her eyes. When she is able to continue, she tells me how Carter wanted her to meet his parents; how the four of them had dinner at the Wyatt's palatial beach house. She begins to cry when she describes his mother's shocked expression when she first laid eyes on Desirie.

"She didn't even have to say a word," Desirie says plaintively. "I could see it in her eyes. I was too dark for her son." More tears pour out of those breath-taking eyes. Her expression changes instantaneously to a flash of anger. "She looked at me like I was a geechee nigger," Desirie cries out.

"Whoa, what is that?" I am taken aback by her use of such a derogatory term.

Desirie looks at me puzzled at first, a look that suggested that of course I should know what that means. Then a look of recognition comes over her and her face turns crimson. "I'm sorry Izzy, that's the first time I have ever used that phrase with a white boy. For a moment, I forgot who I was talking to." I feel like a door has been slammed in my face. I am enjoying the warm sense of closeness that I have been feeling with Desirie, and then I was suddenly cast into the category of the Other.

"You know, Desirie, you make me feel like I'm from another planet."

"In a way, you are, Izzy. I mean, I look at you and I see the white slaver, the overseer, the oppressor of my people. Now I might be willing to try to get past that because I can see that you seem to be a sweet boy, but it is hard work. And I believe you must have the same problem on the opposite end. Tell me that you don't." The challenge in her voice throws me a little, and I shift uncomfortably in my chair.

"I see a beautiful girl," I finally offer.

"Sweet words, Izzy, but is that all you see?"

I look down at my trembling hands because the truth is it's not all I see. I see Aunt Jemima, Sapphire from the Amos and Andy Show, and Ethel Waters, Lena Horne and Dorothy Dandridge. I also see Beulah, the maid of radio and TV fame, but I also see the very real black maid we had when I was five years old and whom my mother blamed for my TB scare that turned out to be a false positive. I see all of the caricatures of black women perpetrated by radio, TV, and the movies. To tell her that, however, not only feels rude, but also like a capitulation to everything that I hate--in society and in me. I desperately want to get past that.

"Well, Izzy?" Desirie asks, waiting not so patiently for my answer.

"You're right, Desirie. I have work to do too."

"Okay, then. Look Izzy, I like you and I sense that you like me. If we are going to do this—to spend time together, we need to do it with our eyes open and we need to be totally honest with each other. Lord knows I don't need to add any more trouble to my life. I can already hear the disapproving glares and smirks of people on my side of the fence when they learn I'm taking up with some cracker boy. And I don't want to hear that you won't get the same treatment from folks on your side the fence."

"Different words, same message," I respond in depressed tones as I contemplate the reactions of my family and friends.

"Well I hope you have some cojones, Izzy," she warns.

"What does that mean?" I ask. "I'm unfamiliar with that Spanish term."

"It means you better be a man about this."

I smile and look at her with apprehension and with an indescribable feeling of admiration.

She gets up to leave and I follow her lead. "By the way, what is a geechee nig...you know...what you said?" Desirie smiles at my efforts to avoid the slur. Her eyes suddenly get big and soulful and in her best impersonation, she exclaims, "Oh dat a nigger fun de Sout who don' speak de langwedge so good." As I look at her with astonishment, she's bent over double with laughter.

Chapter 8.
Devil or Angel

As I make my way toward Georgia Avenue to begin once again my annoying quest for a ride home, I'm in a state of complete befuddlement about Desirie. Her easy ridicule of a certain sub group of Black people disturbs me. Her constant ability to surprise charms me. Despite my ignorance of--and alienation from-- the experience of Negroes in America, I find myself increasingly drawn to this beautiful Black woman. But who is this woman from another world?

Yet I am most befuddled by the color prejudice among Negroes. It makes no sense to me that a group of people that has been hated, demeaned, insulted, and denied their basic rights as Americans because of the color of their skin also engages in this form of color-based human diminishment. The only reference point I have for understanding this is Jewish self-hatred. I am painfully aware of my own fear that I might inadvertently display tendencies that Jew haters around the world have proselytized and continue to proselytize as self-evident truths. I fear being too loud, pushy, or aggressive. When in the company of gentiles, I constantly monitor my behavior for any signs of being overly concerned about money.

But this within group color prejudice feels different to me. I become even more perplexed when Desirie tells me, as we make our way together toward Founders Library, of her painful quest to join AKA. She was rejected when she failed the "paper bag test". Once again she is too dark to be accepted. She is now pledging the "Deltas" and seems happy about it, but I can see that the shame of rejection still pains her like an unlanced boil. Where does such prejudice come from? What is it about? I need answers. When a familiar green Chevy Impala pulls up and I recognize the driver's Fats Waller grin, I hope to get some of my questions answered by Miles Taylor.

"Greetings, Master White, " Miles greets me with no intended irony.

"Hi Miles," I return the greeting in an emotionally flat voice.

"You seem preoccupied today, Izzy. What's happenin'?"

'I'm so perplexed. I met a girl..." And before I can continue, Miles jumps in. "Oh, I bet she's fine. There are so many fine looking women at Howard, I can hardly keep my mind on the road whenever I drive by the campus. " Miles finally sees that I have my mouth open and correctly observes that I'm in mid-sentence. "Sorry I interrupted you, Izzy, What demon's eating at your soul?"

"This girl, this beautiful brown girl told me a story that really blew my mind. I just don't understand it." I told Miles the whole story that Desirie had shared with me about her time in Oak Bluffs and how Carter Woodson Wyatt's parents rejected her because she was too dark. "How can Negroes discriminate against other Negroes because of the color of their skin after all the prejudice and hatred that all Negroes experienced and still experience at the hands of white people? This makes no sense to me." Miles looks at me earnestly and pulls on his imaginary beard with one hand while driving with the other. "To understand this, Izzy, we have to go back to slavery times. You remember I told you that the meanest people on earth are Anglo Saxons?" Without waiting for me to answer, he continues. "Well, one of the meanest things that Anglo Saxon plantation owners did was to rape their female slaves. I mean an attractive African woman was at the mercy of her owner and mercy was the one thing a slave owner never showed. The slave owner would rape whoever he wanted whenever he wanted. And the result was a growing population of mulatto children. The lighter skinned children of the slave owners were definitely favored by their white fathers. They would get more and better food, easier jobs, and often were educated and allowed to travel. The darker slaves worked the fields. And, by the way, the dark slaves were the ones that were beaten, burned, and hanged, the ones permanently condemned to being low man on the totem pole in the great United States of America. It was even illegal for these folks to get an education. The light-skinned slaves began to look down on their darker brothers and sisters. Sometimes plantation owners would deliberately sow discord between lighter and darker slaves as a way of preventing unity and therefore the possibility of a slave rebellion. This was a real 'pigmentocracy,' for Negroes, a caste system based on color. In Charleston, South Carolina, a group of free Negroes started the Brown Fellowship Society in 1790. This group allowed only brown men of good character to join and they had to pay an admission fee of $50. Darker skinned Negroes actually formed their own business organization called the Society of Free Dark Men.

After the Civil War, light-skinned mulattoes further disassociated themselves from darker skinned Negroes by forming elite clubs like the Bon Ton Society right here in DC and the Blue Vein Society in Nashville. If you wanted to join the Blue Veins, you had to be fair enough so the blue veins on their skin were visible. Fraternities and churches would use the paper bag test. If your skin was darker than the bag, you couldn't join." At this point, I interrupted Miles and told him how Desirie explained to me the paper bag test and how she failed it trying to join AKA. Miles nods his head and continues. "And it's not just about skin color. Hair texture is critical too. So-called good hair is straight and finely textured. Bad hair kinks up and is easily tangled up in a comb. Sometimes sororities would use the "comb test". A fine-toothed comb was hung at the door. If your hair got caught in the comb, you were not allowed in the sorority. This kind of in-group prejudice, which is now called Colorism, is a cancer on the body of the black community. It is our dirty little secret that has caused so much pain to our darker-hued brothers and sisters. And the pain is both physical and emotional. Many of our sisters have suffered great pains at the hands of their own mothers who have tortured them with hot combs in an effort to straighten their kinky hair or with skin creams to lighten their skin tone. Our darker brothers have been shamed by many light-skinned Negro parents, who tell their daughters not to bring home any dark meat.

"This is all too depressing," I intone.

"Look at me. In case you haven't noticed, I am intensely brown. Guess where I fall in the pigmentocracy. Don't you think I've been victimized by this bullshit. Even today, my lighter skin brothers and sisters look down on me because of my skin tone just like those mulatto bastards—and I do mean bastards literally—two hundred years ago looked down on their darker brethren who were slaving their lives away in the cotton fields of their father's plantation." I can see tears welling up in Miles eyes. I don't know what to say. All I can manage in a pathetically weak voice is "I'm sorry." My apology does not have its intended effect. It seems to anger Miles.

"You're sorry? I'd say you're lucky. Most white people consider you Jews white and you get all of the advantages of being white. Now I know there're many white people, particularly in the South, who don't think Jews are fully white and as far as white people go, Jews are probably low man on the totem pole. I mean I heard some Jews and some non-Jews talk about the Jewish race as if it were something separate from the Negro race and the white race. But whether being a Jew means you're a member of a different race or a different religion, you are still white to me, and that means you are more favored in this world than I am. Do you realize that you are white, Izzy, and what that means?" Miles seems to ask me this with sadness, curiosity, and a whole lot of resentment. I'm stung by his referring to me as "You Jews" as if I have become another enemy. I don't know how to respond. When I see that we are approaching my usual drop-off point, I can only manage to say, "I'm gonna have to think about that question, Miles, but here's Eastern Avenue where I get off. I hope I see you tomorrow." Miles looks at me pensively for a long moment and finally says, "Me too, Izzy," I'm not sure I believe either one of us.

Miles' question grabs me by the short hairs. I'm so troubled and preoccupied by it that I walk a mile down New Hampshire Avenue before I stop at a traffic light to thumb a ride home. I have really never thought about my whiteness and what it means to be white. Of course I know that there are non-white people in the world, but my horizons are so limited that I have had contact with very few people who are not white. Until integration came to Coolidge High School, the most exotic people I had encountered were the large number of Greek kids that I had met in the nearby neighborhoods and on the close by playgrounds. Native Americans, Asians, even Hispanics barely register a blip on the screen of my life experience. I obtained most of my ideas about members of these groups from TV and the movies. This was also true of my experience with Negroes. But now I'm adding some real life experience with Negroes to the myths and stereotypes I had absorbed from the media. And I am slowly becoming aware that I have implicitly thought of whiteness as natural and everybody else as the Other. This awareness was achieved through electric shocks to my assumptions. In one of my classes a rather dark young woman responded to a professor's question by vociferously complaining about the "white standard of beauty" and how Negroes' allegiance to it makes it next to impossible to appreciate the beautiful features of black people. I was so perplexed. White standard of beauty? Is there more than one standard of beauty? I fall into a reverie about the women I consider beautiful. Images of Elizabeth Taylor, Jean Simmons, and Marilyn Monroe flood my mind. Doesn't everyone agree? It has never occurred to me that I possess a white standard of beauty. When I discovered Lena Horne, I thought she too was beautiful. But she is light-skinned and possesses thin lips and a delicately thin nose. My reverie continues with images of the many fine-looking, light-skinned women I saw at the Howard student union and all of them approached the white ideal of feminine beauty. But then I think of Desirie, Dark Desirie, who is clearly darker than all of the light-skinned girls at the Union. Dark she may be, but she possesses a slender nose and luscious, kissable lips.

When I reach my apartment, I'm happy to find I'm alone. My parents and my brother are all working and I have my bedroom—a bedroom I share with my brother—all to myself. I pull out my stack of 45s and put on "Desirie", a beautiful doo-wop ballad recorded by the Charts in 1957. The lead singer Joe Grier's falsetto intro sends me into an altered state of consciousness. After spending about a half hour in this altered Doo-Wopadized state of mind, I decide to call Desirie. I need to talk to her. She lives in Crandall Hall, which is a freshman women's dorm in the Harriet Tubman Quadrangle (better known as the "quad"). The quad is located on Fourth Street between Howard Place and College Street and actually houses five dormitories: Baldwin, Crandall, Frazier, Truth, and Wheatley, which are connected by a series of tunnels. Over 500 women live in these dorms. When Desirie finally comes to the phone, I'm so nervous that I utter a barely audible hello. I can hear female voices in the background presumably waiting in line to use the phone.

"Who is this?" Desirie asks with perceptible annoyance in her voice.

"It's Izzy, Desirie, how are you?" I say in a more confident voice.

"What is it Izzy? What do you want?" She sounds even more annoyed. I hear in the background a voice saying "Izzy? Isn't he that white cat I saw on campus." (Laughter). "Is he Izzy or is he isn't?" Another voice says. (More laughter). The girls in line begin to clap and chant, "Is he Izzy or is he isn't."

Desirie, evidently embarrassed and angry says, "Izzy, this is not a good time. I will talk with you in class." And she hangs up. This is such a departure from the tone of voice I have been hearing from Desirie that I shatter inside like crystal. The pain is so intense I need to medicate it. My drug of choice is Doo-Wop music. I rummage through all of my 45s and finally find the one I am looking for, "Devil or Angel" by the Clovers. I long so for an altered state of consciousness. After about three plays of this song, the hurt begins to ease. But it is soon followed by anger, a soul-searing inner cry of injustice. Why treat me this way? I've done nothing to deserve such a curt dismissive reaction to my phone call. In my reverie of rage, Desirie's sweet smile transmogrifies into a malicious cackle that seems to say, "Take that white boy." Then I see her with Carter, see them making love and I'm there watching. I get so angry I storm out of the bedroom and I hear her say—just as I heard Sophia say to me last New Year's Eve—"Aw Izzy, don't go. We're supposed to see the New Year in together. I want to be with my boyfriend and my best friend." I scream in protest. Desirie then turns into Sophia, only Sophia is now a Negro. And I am standing over her like an Old Testament prophet berating her for her immoral behavior. "God punishes fornicators," I hear my prophet self bellow. Now I start to laugh because I want nothing more than to fornicate with Desirie. It is now me with Desirie in bed and I don't know what to do. Desirie looks at my "equipment" and says, "Is that all there is, Izzy? I mean Carter's is so much bigger..." Imagining her saying this to me feels like she has pushed me into an icy river of penis-paralyzing, soul-shriveling shame. And I get angry all over again.

The weekend arrives and brings an icy December day. I have made plans to go with the Three Miscreants to Ledo's for pizza. Ledo's is situated on University Boulevard in Adelphi, Maryland, not far from the campus of the University of Maryland. Ledo's has the best pizza in town as far as we all are concerned. Unlike most pizza palaces, Ledo's serves their pizza in squares and rectangles rather than circular pies. The pizza is always served steaming hot, and the flavor of the cheese and the tomato sauce is exquisitely unique. James is our chauffeur and as usual, he treats University Boulevard like a racetrack. Why he never gets a ticket for speeding is beyond my comprehension.

As we enter the restaurant, our senses are assaulted by the din of the crowd and soothed by the wonderful pizza aromas that permeate the entire restaurant. After a short wait, we are seated and virtually no time has elapsed before an attractive but taciturn waitress comes over to take our order. She takes our order after uttering only a single word-- "Yeah?" Given the large number of patrons that are always present at Ledo's, I'm amazed at how quickly our pizza is served. We have the habit of diving into our food and then beginning a conversation rather than the other way around. This requires the utmost in attentiveness if we're going to understand each other amidst the crowd noise and our own stuffed mouths through which we attempt to speak. We resemble four Demosthenes speaking with pizza rather than pebbles in our mouths. Peter begins the muffled colloquy. "So Izzy (Which sounded more like, "Tho wiffy"), "How's Howard? Have you become black yet?" Peter says, with an open-mouth grin that revealed fragments of unmasticated pizza. "Come on, Peter," I complain, "I've only been there a few months so I'm not even high yella yet." Bobby chimes in, "What's it like to be in such a minority? I mean you were a big fish in high school and now you're a little white fish in college. " Everyone laughs.

"Yeah, and a little white fish is good with a bagel and some lox and cream cheese." When I feel attacked, I often get silly. James gives me his "You're weird," stare. Bobby L ignores my attempt at humor and continues his interrogation. "Have you met any black women yet?" He asks with a salacious smile on his face. I hesitate, I blush, I stutter and before I can more fully answer, Bobby starts laughing his high-pitched, hyena laugh and triumphantly bellows, "You have, you have, you have!" All three of my friends now stare at me with great attentiveness waiting for my confession. After too long a pause for their comfort, Peter coaxes, "Come on, Izzy, spill. Give us the details man. Like, what's her name?" With great dignity, I announce, "Her name is Desirie Jackson." The Three Miscreants look at one another and say in sequence, "Desirie?" "Desirie?" Desirie?" Peter waving his hands like a bandleader directs, "Hit it boys!" The three of them commence to caterwaul the worst version of "Desirie" my ears have ever been subjected to.

The three of them collapse in a heap of giggles. I can't help but laugh at their ghastly rendition of this beautiful song.

"What's she like?" Peter asks with genuine curiosity.

"She's beautiful," I rhapsodize, "And she's really smart. I never know what she's gonna say or do next." Then Peter asks me the inevitable question, "What does she look like? I mean, er how dark is she?"

"Oh for Christ's sake, Peter, what does it matter?" I disgustedly reply.

"It matters, "he answers, defensively. "Look, Izzy, I know you have your head up your ass about race, but it really does matter. What do you think people are gonna say when they see you walking down the street with a Black girl? And Black people will be just as surprised and maybe as appalled as white people." Peter continues his hectoring. "I think you're out of your mind doing this. But then I thought that about your going to Howard." James put his hands behind his head and leans back in his chair, gives me an earnest look and lapses into "Roll Over Beethoven". We look at James who has a big grin on his face and laugh at his rhythm and blues parable. Excited by James' cryptic support, I suggest with a smile in my voice, "Now James here has the right idea, Peter. You have some screwed up ideas about race. Why can't whites and blacks be together and, if it happens, love one another?" Peter in an exasperated voice answers, "Izzy, that may be the way the world should be, but it's not the way it is. You have to deal with the world as it is."

"But it's stupid!

"Yes, but it is real."

I can feel myself getting angry and more animated. "So then we need to change the real world!" Bobby jumps in. "Calm down, Izzy. You are not that powerful. You can't save the world." My God, I thought I was listening to my father. His variation on this depressing theme is "You can't carry the world on your shoulders. Nobody gives a shit about you, anyway, except your family. So why should you care what happens to a bunch of Schwartzehs?" As I replay this chronic argument with my father in my mind, I find myself saying to him, "How about because I've fallen in love with one."

As I watched my three white friends stuffing their mouths with pizza, I'm suddenly struck by how different a world I live in with my white friends than I do with my acquaintances at Howard University. I look around Ledo's and see no black faces. At Howard, there are a few white faces, but these are literally few and far between. My borrowed rides from home to school and back seem like interplanetary excursions between the worlds of black and white, worlds that are separated by a distance measured in psychological light years. I wonder how or whether this expanse can ever be bridged? Even my frequent rides with Miles Taylor serve less as a bridge and more like a running commentary on the reasons why the bridge hasn't been built. Ironically people from both worlds ask me the same questions. Why are you going to Howard? What are black/white people really like? Are you sleeping with any black women? Why are you messing with long-established taboos? The rides between the two worlds are not the long, lonely excursions that I imagined trips in outer space to be. The agonizing loneliness comes after I land. At Howard, the question is how do I adjust? How do I fit in? But when I return to my pale suburban world, the question is how do I continue to fit in. I have been at Howard only a few months and already I feel myself changing and beginning to leave the orbits of each of my uncomprehending friends.

It is now January 1960, a new decade. I am filled with hope that the putrefying hand of old ideas will loosen its grip on the human mind. I spend the bulk of the Christmas break goofing off, going to dance parties, and wasting time with Peter, Bobby and James. On occasion, I ponder what I have thus far learned about the state of race relations and do not like what I have learned. The gulf between blacks and whites seems even greater than that between Jews and gentiles. And the reasons for these divisions strike me as idiotic. It seems that whites never got over being slave-owners and therefore are unable to accept any black person as an equal. Many blacks carry the stigma of slavery through many generations and find it difficult to think of themselves as equal to whites. I know that is not the whole story and I know it's beginning to change. What I don't know is how to change myself and rid myself of the remnants of white supremacy. My hope is that with more education and more exposure, I will begin to feel cleansed. I no longer want to be a prisoner of my own putrid ideas.

I don't see Desirie again until our natural science class resumes. She is cordial but cool and seems to want to keep her distance from me. This only enhances my hurt and anger. Instead of driving me away, however, I begin to pester her. I ask her to have coffee with me, and she refuses. She won't take my phone calls. Every rejection brings a new and more desperate entreaty. The more she rejects me, the more in love with her I feel. Desirie is now every girl who has ever rejected me. In my agony, I fall again into reverie and remember the exquisitely humiliating experience of my first date. When I was in the 11th grade, I sat behind the cutest redhead I had ever seen. Sally Oster was always smiling, always had a twinkle in her eye. She smiled at everyone so there was nothing special in being smiled at by Sally Oster. But when she smiled at me, I became convinced I was her special love. It took me six months to work up enough nerve to ask her out. When she said yes, I thought I had found heaven on earth. Although I had just turned 16, I had no car and had to double date with James. He was dating Shirley Kaplan who was enamored of James' unique forms of communication— stares and rock n' roll lyrics. We went to the MacArthur Theater to see The Green Man with Alastair Sim, a hilarious British comedy that advertised itself as a mystery. I was surprised that all four of us liked the movie, because only Sally and I possessed intellectual pretentions. After the movie, Sally and I bored the other couple with our hymns of praise to the profundity of British comedies. To rouse himself from his boredom, James drove faster than usual. In no time at all, we had made our way from downtown DC to suburban Maryland to feed ourselves at our favorite fast-food drive-in, Tops Sirloiner. There everyone ordered the eponymous hamburger with the magic sauce and a milkshake. Afterwards, we dropped Sally home first, and I walked her to the door. Gentleman that I was, I nervously asked her if I could kiss her goodnight. She replied, "I better not. I might burp from my milkshake." I was so astonished by her answer that I stood there wordlessly staring at her with a moronic grin on my face. She slowly closed the door and I fled down her steps in tears. In their laconic fashion, James and Shirley tried to console me. This time, however, James was unable to come up with any appropriately consoling lyrics from Chuck Berry or Elvis Presley.

When it becomes clear that Desirie will not take my calls, I finally show up in person at Crandall Hall. As I enter the dorm, there is a group of about five Negro women standing in the lobby. My entrance draws their attention and in unison they look at me, as if to say, "Umph, umph umph and what brings your white self around here?" "Is Desirie Jackson available?" I ask. One of the women answers, seemingly for the group, " Available for who?" She queries with a sardonic smile on her face and moving her head from side to side. "Izzy White?" I answer. They hear the question in my voice. "I don't know," jokes the spokeswoman. "Is he white? You sure look white to me. If you don't know, who does?" All five of my tormentors begin cackling with their hands over their mouths and their bodies bending toward one another in a circle. Finally, one of the women finds an ember of kindness in her soul, smiles sweetly at me and says, "Let me get her for you, Izzy." I wait for 10 to 15 minutes before Desirie appears in her maroon coat.

"What do you want, Izzy?" She clearly wants to get away from me as fast as she can.

"Can we talk, Desirie?" I ask in a hurry-up voice.

"We have nothing to talk about," she answers.

"What is going on with you? We had talked about seeing one another."

"I don't think that's a good idea, Izzy." She hurries out of the dorm and I struggled to keep up. "Why not?"

"It just isn't, Izzy. Now leave me alone." I can hear that she is crying.

I stand there mute, uncomprehending, and flooded with questions. What have I done? Is it me? My color? What? I remember what I had said to her when we first met—that I was an equal opportunity blunderer, and that I turn off women of all races, religions, and nationalities. What I originally meant as a joke now feels like a devastating truth. Once again I have tasted the bitter fruit of my heart's desire. I watch her walk away across the Valley and up the stairs toward Founders Library. For only the second time since I arrived, I entertain the unacceptable idea that enrolling in Howard University has been a terrible mistake.

Chapter 9.
NAG (Nag nag, naggety nag)

I spend the winter in despair. My heart is as frozen as the mounds of plowed snow that remain for weeks after a sudden January blizzard. My morning routine is to weep upon awakening, have breakfast and weep again. I cry behind closed doors because I don't want my parents to see that another girl has broken my heart. I look in my mirror and see an even paler white skin than usual. I'm beginning to hate my white skin because I believe it's the sole reason that Desirie wants nothing to do with me

It's difficult being in the same class with Desirie As before, she sits behind me. I do not look at her or speak to her; and despite our close proximity for much of our time in class during the winter/spring semester, I try everything I know to wall off my feelings. I even imagine that she is not there. Occasionally, I sneak a peek at her as she leaves the class. This is a mistake because each time I do, my heart and tear ducts spring a link. By the end of February my feelings are entirely frozen over and not just for her. Little in life is capable of arousing any feelings in me. I inadvertently see her one more time before the end of the school year. I'm looking out the window of my Douglass Hall classroom during English class. Spring has just been reborn. The trees are sprouting their resplendent green leaves. The warming noonday sun is high in a clear blue sky. Noontime on Friday means that all the fraternities and sororities are gathered at their special spots, singing their special songs, moving to the beat of their own unique choreography. Right out front of my window, not two yards away, are the Deltas. Across the yard are the dark and brainy women of Zeta Phi Beta. Down a ways from the Deltas, but on the same side of the Yard, are the Kappas and close by their sister sorority, Alpha Kappa Alpha or AKA. Omega Psi Phi, the "Ques", have circled the sundial in the middle of the yard. Each fraternity and sorority has adapted its songs of praise and fealty to the current rock n' roll hits of the day. I am thankful that such a joyous cacophony just outside my window manages to create a brief release from my despair. The Deltas, whom I can most clearly hear, are singing the virtues of being a member of Delta Sigma Theta to the tune of "Step By Step", a new hit by Johnny Maestro and the Crests. As I watch the Delta sorors swinging and swaying, I see the smile that stands out among all the smiles, the face that shines above all faces. I can see in her face and in her smile the joy Desirie feels because she is now a full-fledged Delta. My heart starts to pound and I want to cry out her name.

With my efforts to numb myself of all feeling for Desirie obliterated, I give vent to such howling over the course of the next few weeks that I feel like a hound dog baying at the moon. What finally terminates my ululations is a conversation I have one day with Winston McKenzie. "Hey White!" McKenzie calls after me in his irresistible Jamaican accent. He is looking particularly sharp this day in his dark-colored turtleneck sweater and tan slacks. "A word with you, if you please, " he pompously proposes. The wisps of his goatee quiver with every word. "In fact, do you have time for coffee? There is something of great urgency I wish to discuss with you. "

"I guess so." As we walk toward the Union, he begins his inquiry. "White, are you aware of what college students are doing in the South?" Since I can't read what he's driving at, I treat his question with a great deal of caution. "I'm not sure what you mean."

"The 'sit-ins'! Don't you know about the sit-ins?" Now I'm completely befuddled. Why is he asking me about the sit-ins? "I vaguely remember hearing something back in February. Some Negro students sat down at a segregated lunch counter and were harassed and beaten."

"Yeah, Mon, that was February 1st. Four Black men from North Carolina A&T sat down at the lunch counter at Woolworths in Greensboro, North Carolina. Instead of getting their food, they got a whole lot of shit, mon. A whole lot of shit! A bunch of angry white people poured ketchup on their heads and hot coffee. Some of these mean bastards started beating the four men. They were not arrested as they expected, so they stayed until the store closed. Do you know what has happened since then?"

"No, what happened?" Now I am genuinely interested.

"Two days later there were 60 students from NC A&T and from Bennett College for Women. Then the Klan came in with their Neanderthal followers and gave these students a very hard time. But these brave Africans were undeterred. In the next few days, sit-ins spread to Hampton, Virginia, Rock Hill, South Carolina, and Nashville, Tennessee. Now there are sit-ins in virtually every southern state. The South is on fire Mon! On fire!" I am surprised by how animated McKenzie has become. He has always struck me as cool and cerebral; and when he answers questions in class or offers a comment, he sounds more professorial than our current professor, a gentle German Quaker who has taken over teaching duties from Dr. Snowden for the second semester of Humanities. Here McKenzie is flailing his arms, raising his voice, and his cultured Jamaican accent devolving into the Jamaican patois of his youth. We climb the wooden steps of Miner Hall and McKenzie soon finds us his usual table in a quiet corner of the student union. A couple of McKenzie's friends are sitting there waiting for us. "Gentlemen, this is Izzy White. Izzy, these intelligent brothers are Bob Kinnard and Phil Workman." We exchange greetings. Phil Workman catches my wide-eyed look of shock as we shake hands and says, "Yes, Izzy, I'm white too. You're not the only one." I knew there were other white students at Howard. In fact, I had seen a couple, but they are few and very far between. Before I could play "racial geography" with Phil, McKenzie interrupts, "Izzy, have you ever heard of NAG?"

"Isn't that what you're doing to me now?" I cracked. I look over at Bob and Phil and see that they are both trying to suppress a grin. McKenzie is not amused. "No mon, NAG, the

Non-Violent Action Group.   We are a group of politically savvy Howard students and some non-students who believe that we no longer can wait for our elders to get off their bourgeois asses and correct the pervasive injustice experienced by Black people. We want to organize the student body to engage in social action. We are mostly Black students, but you can see by Phil's presence here that not everyone interested in helping to bring about justice is Black. In the short time that I have known you, Izzy, I can tell that your heart is in the right place even if you are politically naïve."

"I appreciate the compliment, but what is NAG planning to do?" McKenzie strokes his wispy goatee thoughtfully and then suddenly thrusts his head toward my face. "We are planning a number of non-violent demonstrations of segregated facilities in D.C. and surrounding areas. I'm talkin' sit-ins, stand-ins, lie-ins and any other kind of "ins" we can think of to embarrass the proprietors of said stores and facilities." When McKenzie finished his thought, his head recedes back toward the top of his turtleneck sweater. This alternating thrusting and receding of McKenzie's head resembles nothing more than a turtle thrusting his head forward in search of food. When he repeats his thrust, I begin to feel like a particularly tasty morsel. "We want you to become a part of NAG and help us organize these demonstrations." McKenzie's head remains outstretched and inches away from my face. "Why me?" I ask. His pompous tone once again evident, McKenzie answers, "As I mentioned before, I know your heart is in the right place. Besides, you are a Jew, are you not?"

"Yes, but how did you know? And what does that have to do with anything?" I add as the snake of defensive fear begins to coil and recoil inside my chest.

"Oh my intuition about people is beyond compare. Your people are renowned for your commitment to social justice; and in the earlier iterations of our struggle, Jews have been our greatest allies."

"Really?" I say, unable to keep the skepticism out of my voice. My reference point is my family and my Jewish peers who collectively seem to me to be as big a fan of white supremacy as any southern bigot.

"Ain't this a shame!" Bob Kinnard finally weighs in. "Izzy, you truly are in need of an education, but not just about my people but about your own as well." Bob had come to Howard from Gainesville, Georgia, known as the chicken capital of the USA, and was well scarred by a life spent in the shaming "prison without walls" that is segregation. The separate drinking fountains, the consignment to only the balcony seats in the local theater, the necessity of lowering one's eyes so that a Black person never makes eye contact whenever he comes upon white people; the thousand and one indignities that he and his people suffered. As valedictorian of Carver High School, he had given a stirring speech about the responsibility of his generation to finally make the American Creed apply to Black people. Although his original plan was to come to Howard and eventually become a physician, he took his own valedictory words seriously; and since the first day he arrived at Howard has searched for ways to get involved in the struggle for civil rights. He had lately been inspired by Martin Luther King's latest book, Stride for Freedom, an account of the Montgomery Alabama bus boycott.

"Don't you know," Bob continues, "that some of the founders of the NAACP were Jewish and that liberal Jews have supported our cause since the turn of the century?" I turn crimson and sheepishly answer, "No, I did not."

"Come on, Izzy, be a good Jew." Now I thought this was a low blow. Bob is appealing to a side of me that is blissfully dormant, a side that has the power to pick at the scab of my shame. A good Jew? I'm not sure what that means having spent my youth suppressing any evidence, any manifestation of Jewness. Even here I'm unclear. All I know is that I fear whatever goes on in the fetid imaginations of anti-Semites when they conjure up their caricature of a Jew. It's only when I can relish my sense of being an outsider that I feel pride in being Jewish.

With my eyes cast downward, I mumble, "I think I'll pass."

"You say what?" Bob asked, "I didn't hear you."

"I THINK I'LL PASS!" I yell, surprised by the resentment in my voice. McKenzie composes his face into his characteristic sneer. Bob, however, has a big grin on his face and says sharply, "I thought you were passing. But that's all right, Izzy, I'm not gonna give up on you. Cause if you're White, you're alright." Bob, Phil and McKenzie collapse in a harmonic chorus of guffaws at Bob's play on words.

A week later, I'm sitting on the bench by the sundial, the same bench where I first met Be Bop. It is a gloriously warm day in late April. All the trees in the Yard are graced with pale green buds, a sight that always fills me with optimism. Early spring is suffused with an aroma that I always find intoxicating. I fall into a deep reverie about my life thus far at Howard University, so deep in fact that I neither hear nor feel Phil Workman sitting down next to me. My startle reflex kicks into high gear when I turn my head and see a white face very close to mine. It is shockingly out of context to be jarred from my reverie by the close proximity of a white man.

"Izzy, I need to talk to you." Phil seems agitated. I prepare myself for some intimate personal revelation that he is about to share. "What is it?" I ask in a solicitous voice. Phil lights a cigarette and looks around the Yard to see if anyone might be eavesdropping on our conversation.

"Listen, Izzy, NAG needs you. Needs us, I should say. There aren't that many white students at Howard and NAG should have a strong presence from the few white students who are here."

"Why?" I ask. I am truly perplexed because it's beginning to be clear to me that it is the obsession with race that is behind so much of the hatred and mistreatment of Negroes. Why do we need to over-emphasize racial differences?

"I thought NAG's concern is simple human justice."

"It is about simple justice. But justice has never been simple in this country. Listen Izzy, despite what you were told in your high school history classes, the United States is not a paragon of democratic freedoms. And every freedom that we do have, we have to fight for every day. The cruel treatment of Negroes is probably the most obvious and blatant example of the denial of freedom and justice. But labor unions have fought for decades for their rights and their existence. The workingman has been denied his rights in this country for almost as long as Negroes. And Black laborers suffer the most. To me it seems so obvious that there should be a natural alliance between Negroes and whites of the working class. But even as big business sticks it to the white working man, we still have segregated unions. Company bosses maintain control by dividing black and white laborers from one another. The Negro without a vote or a union card has little to say about his wages; and whatever job he's offered, it is 'take it or leave it'. At the same time, the bosses can threaten poor whites who want to better their economic position by throwing them out of their jobs and offering them to Negroes, who, desperate for money, will work for less. I joined NAG to do my part to break down the walls of segregation, but my larger hope is that the push for Negro rights will merge with progressive voices in the labor movement. We need a liberal labor party committed to the fight of the Negro for equality, of the workingman for improved living conditions, and of the farmer for the fair share of his produce. Izzy, I just finished a pamphlet on the history of the movement for civil rights and I want you to have a copy. Please read it, Izzy, and give serious thought to joining NAG." I look at the pamphlet and rapidly thumb through it. I make a mental note to read it. But I'm pondering Phil's motives. He seems to be on the same page as

McKenzie about Negro civil rights, but there is a new wrinkle in his thinking. Labor unions? The workingman? McKenzie never mentioned either. Since my father had been a butcher for much of his working life and changed careers only when he hurt his back, I resonate with this new emphasis on the workingman. But it troubles me that only Phil has mentioned this concern. And why is he coming on to me like a hard-sell car salesman? Why is it so important for me to sign on the dotted line, as it were, right this moment and commit to joining NAG? I must have had a deep frown on my face because Phil anxiously asks me, "What's the matter, Izzy?" His earnest stare emanates from a face that was much too close to mine. I instinctively arch my body back away from him. I notice for the first time how much he looks like the young (and slim) Orson Welles. He has the same intense but femininely pretty eyes.

"Nothing," I answer. "All this attention and interest in my political opinions is new to me. I feel like I'm rushing a fraternity."

"You are," Phil replies. "NAG is a fraternity engaged in social and political change." I'm both troubled and gratified by the trace of a seductive smile that I see on his face. What does Phil really want from me? Yet it is indeed a rush to feel so wanted. I'm less clear, however, about why they want me and what they want me for.

With my nose filled with the intoxicating smells of early spring and my head filled with the new ideas I have absorbed from Phil Workman's impassioned plea, I make my leisurely way to my usual hitchhiking spot on Georgia Avenue. Before long, a familiar green Impala comes by and a grinning Miles Taylor gestures for me to get in. As we drive off, Miles continues to grin at the radio. He seems to be in such a good mood. I have never seen him this up. He's in a head-shaking, shoulder-boogieing groove as the pulsing radio played Little Anthony and the Imperials' Shimmy Shimmy Ko Ko Bop. "Ooo wee, I DO like that song," Miles offers. When it's over, he turns down the radio and asks, "And how is my favorite pale male?" "I'm okay, but I have a question for you." Still grinning at me, Miles replies "Ah Negro-ology, lesson 3. Lay it on me, my fine young scholar."

"Before I do, I want to know why you're so happy today?"

"That's an easy question to which there is a simple answer. My girlfriend, Yvonne, and I 'got next to one another,' if ya dig." As he says this, Miles performs a dead-on impression of the eyelash batting and wide grinning Fats Waller.

"Is she your main squeeze?" I ask.

Miles seems put off by my question as if I have violated some unspoken understanding that we have. His expression of offense quickly shifts back to his imitation of Fats Waller. "One never knows, do one?" He turns right on New Hampshire Avenue and heads toward the Eastern Avenue District line. In the small yards that we quickly pass by, we both take in the promising new growths of spring. We can see shoots of crocuses, daffodils, and forsythia. After a long pause, Miles turns his head towards me and asks, "What was your question?"

"Have you ever heard of NAG?" I ask. Looking perplexed Miles' face takes on a bug-eyed expression and he answers with a question, "Nag? You mean like being a pain in the ass and asking me questions all the time?" With that, Miles bursts out laughing. "I'm only playing witcha, Izzy. Yeah, I know about NAG, the Nonviolent Action Group. They're a group of radical young bucks on your campus who believe they can change the world. I applaud their idealism, but fear their political naiveté."

"Do you know anyone in NAG personally?" I ask.

"Not really, but I have a nephew who was contacted by some NAGGERS and who has flirted with joining. He told me about the only meeting he attended. Maybe 15 to 20 people showed up. There were several women and a few whites. As far as my nephew could make out, NAG wants to employ a two-pronged approach to the struggle for Negro rights in America. They want to organize the Howard student body to get them actively involved in the national struggle, but to do that they know that they have to begin by focusing on student rights on campus. Howard University is run by a frightened bunch of bureaucrats. Fear makes the administration authoritarian in their approach to students. So they become the perfect foil for NAG to attack in order to entice students into the larger struggle. The struggle for campus rights is clearly a means to an end, which is to shake the foundations of segregation and white supremacy. These cats do not dream small dreams." My experience with Howard administrators thus far revealed no signs of fear so I was genuinely perplexed by Miles' statement. "Why are they so afraid?" Miles looks at me like I was a less than adequate student in the realities of life, which of course I am.

"Well, its kind of long and complicated story, but I'll try and give you the Reader's Digest version. The first thing you need to know is that Washington, DC has no representation in Congress, that is the city has no senators or congressmen to represent the views of Washington residents. And DC has no real control over the running of the city. Furthermore, what's true for the city is true for Howard University. Since it opened in 1867, Howard has mostly depended on the good will of Congress for its financial well-being. But starting in 1928, Howard administrators got money to run the place from an annual appropriation set by Congress. The problem is the House Committee for District Affairs is controlled by racist southern Congressmen who do not want black people to thrive. And they're the ones that decide how much money the Department of Health, Education and Welfare gets. Howard's annual appropriation comes out of the budget of the education wing of HEW. The Howard administrators always have to walk a fine line between supporting Negro advancement and not offending the white racists in Congress who control Howard's purse strings. So Howard prospers when their bureaucrats err on the side of caution. Ya dig?" Finally getting the drift, I spontaneously add to Miles' monologue.

"So when NAG harangues the bureaucracy for student rights or even worse organizes the students to challenge the racial status quo, the Administration starts shaking in their boots and becomes dictatorial."

"You got it now, Izzy. You know, you ain't as dumb as you look," Miles says, grinning from ear to ear.

"Do you think they can really make a difference, Miles? "

"Well, I have my doubts, but those cats who sat in at Woolworths in North Carolina have sure made a lot of noise and seemed to have started something big." I look at the big grinning brown man sitting beside me who hails from a world so different than mine, and I marvel at how comfortable I feel with him. How easy it is to talk with him. Inside our private universe of his green Impala, we're just two human beings enjoying each other's company. Color, race, and all of the other social distinctions that human beings have created to separate us from one another, and to deny us the possibility of emotional connection and intimate friendship, are nowhere to be found inside our moving green world. I feel safe, cared for, and respected, and I instinctively reciprocate the same gifts. Miles is becoming a beloved mentor.

As the light turns yellow at New Hampshire Avenue and North Capital Street, Miles hits the gas in order to make the light. As he crosses North Capital, a 1956 blue and white Ford Fairlane comes speeding up North Capital and clips Miles' Impala. His grin transmogrifies into the look of a wounded angry animal. He lets out a loud stream of obscenities and then begins the hard work of calming himself down with a series of slow, deep breaths. Miles gets out of his car with the intension of exchanging insurance information. The driver of the Ford Fairlane gets out of his car, but has malice written all over his face. He is white and almost the same size as Miles. "Where did you learn to drive ya big dumb nigger?" Miles's eyes bug out, his face becomes crimson with rage. "You honkey asshole, I'm gonna teach you some respect." The two men grab each other and start to wrestle. Their combat is abruptly interrupted by the wail of a nearby police siren. The police car screeches to a stop and two officers jump out in a flash. They separate the two combatants and ask what happened. The white man answers in a voice laced with offended pride, "This black ape caused the accident." Miles, who knows from years of confrontations with white policemen that it is necessary to calm down and present his case in a polite, mild-mannered way, gathers his composure and calmly says to the officers, "This gentleman is lying." The Ford driver looks at the police officers and asks with incredulity in his voice, "Who're you gonna believe, this jungle bunny here or me, a white man?" The police officers look at each other. One nods to the other to go to their car so that they can discuss the matter privately. After a few whispered interchanges, the two policemen return to the combatants. The older looking policeman says, "We are giving you both a ticket for reckless driving." Miles is enraged but uses every fiber of his being not to say a word to the policemen. The Ford driver screams in protest. The policemen seem to be upset by the scowl on Miles's face, but since Miles remains quiet, they do nothing more than hand him the ticket. Despite the Ford driver's invective toward the policemen, they hand him his ticket and quietly caution him to calm down. Miles coldly looks at the three white men and says nothing. He looks at the ticket, then back at the white men; and after a long moment turns and gets back into his car. He can't even look at me, and I can see his eyes welling up with tears of humiliation. Miles is silent the rest of the drive. As we approach the District Line at Eastern Avenue, Miles slows his car to a halt. He continues to look straight ahead, still seething with rage, his face set in a rigid scowl. Without looking at me, Miles says in a low, stony monotone, "You best get out of the car now, Izzy. I can't bear looking at your white face right now." This hurts me deeply. "Yes, I'm white but I'm not Anglo Saxon," I protest. "I thought you said Anglo Saxons were the problem?"

"Izzy," Miles says sharply, "Right now, I can't tell the difference. Now get your damn self out of the car!" The curtain of race and color has once again come down between Miles and me.

And what about that feeling I had of safety, comfort and ease? Gone like a cool breeze.

Chapter 10.
Just Two Kinds of People in the World

I catapult myself from Miles' car and walk in a fog of fury to the corner of New Hampshire and Eastern Avenues. I listlessly stick out my thumb in search of a ride, but it's difficult for me to concentrate. The painful irony is almost unbearable. Someone I thought was a friend is rejecting me because of the color of my skin. I go numb. I'm confused. My experience at Howard thus far has convinced me that there really are two kinds of people— the tolerant and the bigoted. My logic has convinced me that people who are bigotry's victims would understand its pain and would avoid it like a plague. Yet here is this black man who I thought was my friend rejecting me; not for any crime I have committed against him but because of guilt by association. The great stain of racial animus that has been transmitted—much like a genetic mutation—from generation to generation to the brains of light and dark people in the U.S. for over 300 years has separated Miles from me. This is the last ride I ever took with Miles.

I stay in my room the rest of the day and evening foregoing dinner and the balm of human friendship. Instead I mope and ruminate. In one short academic year at Howard I have made and lost what I thought were two great friends, Desirie and Miles. I reached across the racial barrier and thought I had found a great love and an inspiring mentor. Both have rejected me because I'm white. What a mistake I've made by choosing to go to Howard. What idealistic folly. What makes me think I can change the world? My father's words come crashing down on my head once more. "You can't change the world. Nobody gives a shit about you except your family!" I hate to admit it to myself, but I'm beginning to think that he might be right.

When my freshman year comes to an end in early June, I think I will soon be free of all the pain inflicted on me by my association with Howard —the rejection by would-be lovers and friends, the racist horseshit I had to endure on a daily basis from my vehicular benefactors who transported me to the urban black world of Howard and back to the white world of suburbia; the sarcastic putdowns from my white biology professor as he watched me sprint to his class, invariably late because of the temporal vicissitudes of hitchhiking. But that is not to be. One more blow comes to me when I receive a letter from the University. The letter informs me that my cumulative grade-point-average for my freshman year is 2.97. Because I have failed to reach the minimum GPA necessary of 3.0, my academic scholarship has been cancelled. Cancelled!! What are they talking about? I have to read the letter three times before its gist penetrates my brain. Because I was .03 points under the required GPA, I no longer have the money to support my college education. Is there no wiggle room? I can't believe it. I keep putting the letter down on our dining room table and picking it up again to reread it. I'm overtaken by a massive wave of panic, the likes of which I hadn't experienced since I was five years old. At that time, for some reason, the truth of my mortality came crashing down on my head. I was going to die someday. The world would go on for thousands of years—without me. Unacceptable! Electric shocks of fear ran up and down my spine, I had severe stomach pains and I became light-headed. I ran to the toilet and sat, dazed and dizzy in hopes that I could evacuate this terrifying idea. As it did then, the fear runs its dizzy-making course, not because I was mortal, although I felt like dying, but because I had foolishly squandered the means for my affording an education. My friends try to console me, but it is like talking to a zombie. For most of the month of June, I walk around glassy-eyed, jobless, broke and broken.

I know I need a job, but have no idea how or where to look except for a position with one of the many D.C. playgrounds. I had enjoyed my two previous stints as a staff member at Rudolph and Takoma Playgrounds. So when I learn that a summer position unexpectedly is open as Assistant Director of the Shepherd Park Playground, I submit my one and only job application. When I worked at the Takoma Playground the summer before, I had a boss who was more philosopher than manager. Every day he treated me to one of his endless pearls of wisdom. One day we were sitting together and waiting for the mad crush of kids that would arrive around 10 am. With a grave look on his face, he said, "Izzy, I want to share with you a remarkable life lesson. There is no greater joy under heaven than taking a good crap." With such a philosopher to guide me, why do I need to go to college?

My life begins to turn around on Thursday, June 30th. The mail comes early that day and I receive a letter from the DC Recreation Department informing me that I have been hired to work at Shepherd Park. Then Peter calls. He has had enough of my moping and orders me to go with James, Bobby, and him to Glen Echo. After the myriad of suggestions that the three of them keep making to try and raise my spirits, Glen Echo catches my fancy. Memories of many fun times there have broken through the dam of my sadness and flooded my mind. I remember the roller coaster, The Whip, the Dodge M Cars, the Crystal Pool, and the Fun house with the mechanical wooden fat lady whose nonstop infectious laughter whips and stirs my enthusiasm. James has agreed to drive if we all chip in money for gas. En route, Bobby proposes that we all go to Atlantic City in August. He promises that even James and I would score with the chicks on the Boardwalk. As my mood lifts, the colors of the world return. I take these felicitous events to be an omen that my life is about to change again—this time for the better.

As we approach the entrance to Glen Echo's parking lot, we see a streetcar on MacArthur Boulevard stop and let people off. It seems exceedingly odd for this urban means of transport to appear in this more sylvan setting. As we pull into the graveled entrance, we notice a picket line on the grass. I immediately recognize Winston McKenzie, Bob Kinnard, and Phil Workman, all from NAG. Then I remember the plan to picket Glen Echo that the three of them had talked to me about. I completely forgot that the place is segregated. Phil is the first to recognize me. "Hey, there's Izzy. Hey Izzy," he yells, "What are you doing going into that place? Don't you know it's segregated?" His face is framed in disapproval. James slows the car, but does not stop. Before I can respond, we are rolling down the graveled hill into the main section of the parking lot. "I have to join them," I told the group. "Join what?" Peter asks annoyed. "The picket line, " I answer, "I have to join that picket line. "

"Aw for Christ's sake," Peter whines. "Look, we came here to have fun not to fight for Negro rights."

"Come on, Peter, you know it ain't right."

"What's so wrong with it. Colored people have their places to go and white people have our places," Peter opines as if it were common sense.

"You know, gentiles said the same thing about Jews, and they used the same logic to justify restricted covenants to keep us out of their fancy neighborhoods like Spring Valley and exclude us from the Chesapeake Bay Beaches like Beverly Beach and many top-rated universities like Harvard." Peter just grumbles. "Well, I don't want to get in no fucking picket line; not with a bunch of coons." I frown at Peter and though I hate leaving him, I say, "Well, I'm going. James? Bobby? Are you with me?" Bobby looks at Peter then back at me, and smiles. "Cool. Let's do it!" James ponders the choice for a moment, then turns to Peter and says, "Don't be cruel to a heart that's true." Peter shakes his head and says, "I'm going in with or without you guys. James turns to me and sings, "It was a brown-eyed handsome man that won the game, a brown-eyed handsome man." With that, the three of us begin walking back up the hill to the entrance to the park. I look over my shoulder to see Peter standing there with a look of pained horror and disbelief plastered on his face. He is mouthing some obscenity that none of us can hear.

When we get to the top of the hill, Phil Workman comes out of the picket line to welcome us. I introduce Phil to James and Bobby. They both are surprised to see that Phil is white.

"Welcome to a NAG picket line, boys," Phil almost sings with enthusiasm. "I assume that you will join us in our righteous cause?" The three of us look at the band of about 15 picketers marching in an elliptical pattern with signs held aloft bearing a variety of declarative captions: "STOP! Glen Echo is segregated" "Freedom and Justice For All" "Discrimination is Not For Our Generation". "Jim Crow Must Go". Much to our surprise, we discover that there are a number of whites in the line besides Phil. While we try to make peace with our fear and awkwardness, Phil keeps talking. "You know we're gonna be successful. We already scored a victory in Arlington earlier this month. We picketed segregated lunch counters; and after 10 days, the owners agreed to let Negroes eat at the counter. Lunch counters in Alexandria and Fairfax have taken their cue from Arlington. What d'ya say boys?" We look at one another and solemnly nod. We're each handed a sign. Mine says, "Glen Echo Should Echo Democracy". I love the play on words. As we enter the line, Phil gives us a cautionary spiel, "By the way, you should know something from the get-go. We all could get arrested. We're trespassing on private property." Cold fear shoots through me. I have to struggle to hold on to my sign. I finally get a handle on the task and am soon marching proudly and displaying my sign as if I'm showing heaven my sign of honor. Out of the corner of my eye, I see Peter watching us. None of us noticed that he trailed behind us all the way up the hill. He seems lonely and curious. Phil has noticed him too and once again leaves the line to invite a newcomer. Peter walks toward the line with Phil as an escort. Peter's expression and the leaden way he now walks toward us suggest a man en route to his own execution. He looks very uncomfortable, but it's also clear that he does not want to be left out. Bobby and James laugh at him. I'm proud of him. Soon the four would-be revelers are engaged in the serious business of protesting a social evil. I realize that I'm proud of me.

As we continue our oblong march, I notice the wide diversity of people in the picket line. The majority are Negro college students from Howard. But there is a white woman with her baby in a stroller, a Catholic priest, a Protestant cleric, and a rabbi (no joke). At least three other picketers are Jewish men and women from the very well-to-do Bannockburn section of Bethesda. I feel a twinge of shame about my prior thoughts concerning the prejudices that Jews hold toward Negroes. These people prove that McKenzie, Kinnard, and Workman had been correct. Many Jews are supportive of integration and back their beliefs with action.

We have been marching for about 15 minutes when a blue souped-up 1955 Mercury slows down to gawk at us. The faces that we can see in the car collectively form a tableau of menace. In unison, the car's occupants throw beer cans at us, and scream out, "Die, Nigger-lovers." We are an agile group and no beer can makes contact with human flesh. We are most worried about the baby in the stroller and many of us make solicitous noises to the mother. Peter is angry, embarrassed and conflicted. He doesn't know whether to be upset with the vehicular racists or the people in the picket line. I feel a pure and purifying anger. They're-the bigots- and we are the good guys. We are righteous, and they are ignoramuses indulging their irrational hatred. I can't remember when I have felt so virtuous. This is the only incident during our time in the line, but I take it to be my baptism of fire. I now pronounce myself an active member of the Civil Rights Struggle.

All the way home, I pontificate to the Three Miscreants about the importance of our participation in today's picket line. Peter continues to fume. Initially, he's enraged at the punks in the Mercury. But on the drive home, he castigates all of us for abandoning him. The trip to Glen Echo provides Peter with more evidence for his deep-seated conviction that we really don't care about him. I accuse Peter of feeling sorry for himself and of missing the true importance of our participation in the picket line. He accuses me of being a know-it-all and complains that my going to Howard has changed me for the worse. We argue all the way home while Bobby and James look at us in turn as if they are watching a tennis match. They have huge grins on their faces, and they nod to one another their wordless message, "There they go again.

By August I begin to heal and make my peace with the loss of my academic scholarship. My hope hangs precariously on the lifeline thrown to me by the Head of the Psychology Department. Dr. Meenes told me that if I bring my grades up during my third semester so that my cumulative grade-point-average reaches the critical 3.0 mark, my scholarship would be reinstated for the rest of my undergraduate career. This is enough to free my mind, at least until school starts in a month. And it allows me to feel a little bit of joy about our upcoming vacation in Atlantic City. The Three Miscreants and I leave on a cloud stricken August Monday, our mood as gray as the weather. Peter is the first to complain. "I've been waiting for this day to come for weeks and the fucking weatherman says rain in Atlantic City for the next three days. How am I gonna get my tan?"

"Yeah, this weather eats it," grouses Bobby. " All I've been thinking about for weeks is the beach stuffed with all those gorgeous half-naked babes." James, who as usual is the designated driver, just tunes out the bellyachers. He looks straight ahead and he seems to be singing to himself in a barely audible voice. He is mumbling "Maybelline".

Although I share their disappointment with the weather report, I'm still high from the news I received from Dr. Meenes. I attempt, as best I can, to cheer up my horny friends. "Come on, guys. We're gonna have a great time come rain or shine. We have one whole week doing whatever we want, whenever we want."

But Peter is inconsolable. "Yeah, we won't be able to do shit if it rains the whole week." By the time we reach the Pennsylvania line, the weather turns even darker and so did our mood. Rain begins to pour down and all of the car's occupants except James let out with a collective groan. James is still singing under his breath.

"For Christ's sake, James, shut up! I can't take the muttering." Peter sounds like he is at a breaking point with James' mumbled melodies. "What are you saying anyway?" said Peter with undisguised hostility in his voice. "All I hear is mutter, mutter, mutter." "He's singing," I answer for him. "You know, Chuck Berry. James has gone through all 20 hits that Chuck Berry has made since 1955."

"Man, can't you give it a rest," Peter complains more quietly. Without looking back at Peter, James gives him the finger and continues with his singing while bopping up and down in his seat. Then James suddenly bellows the title of latest musical muttering, "ALMOST GROWN". Bobby cracks up at this. "If you're gonna sing, James, sing so we can hear you," Bobby says playfully. "Oh no, you don't want that," James replies with a laugh. "Look the reason I'm singing is that my damn radio is on the fritz, and I sure as hell don't want to spend the entire drive listening to your whining. So I'm singing in self defense."

On the Delaware Memorial Bridge, the rain is so heavy that looking out over the water is like trying to peer through a translucent glass window. "Great vacation," Peter gripes. "I can't even see the water." As usual, when I get so sick of Peter's complaining, I begin to make stuff up to placate him. "Come on, Peter, the sun will be out tomorrow. I promise." "Oh listen to Mr. Sweetness and Light over there." I can hear the gears of his mind grinding out a play on words. "Hey Sweetness and Light, if you're so light, how come you're going to Howard?" This cracks him up. When he sees that I all I can give him is a nervous laugh, Peter suddenly turns serious. "OK, Izzy, you've been there a year now; what's it like?"

"Do you really want to know?"

"Yeah, I do," Peter replies, "I can't imagine being a minority in a school filled with jigaboos." Peter catches my look of disgust. "I'm sorry, Izzy, " Peter insincerely apologizes, "I mean a minority in a primarily Black school."

Bobby joins in, "Yeah Izzy, do tell. What are the black babes like?" I can always count on Bobby and Peter to be predictable. Peter is obsessed with color, Bobby with women. I never could understand Peter's hostility toward black people. Negroes hadn't done him any harm as far as I knew. If Bobby has any reservations about Negroes, it has to do with an inchoate belief that the mixing of the races is somehow inappropriate. But this vague sense of the appropriate is obliterated whenever he thinks about women (which is every seven seconds). Then color seems to have no bearing. If a girl is fine, he wants her. Before I can answer Bobby's question, Peter intervenes. "But aren't you afraid that you might become like them?"

"Maybe I already have," I tease. Peter gives me a look of shocked disgust. "You know, Peter, none of us have any idea what life's been like for Negroes, particularly in DC." Before I can go into my history lesson, however, Peter interrupts me. "But wait, you haven't answered Bobby's question. What are the black babes like?" As I think about their question, I warm to the task. "Guys, you best believe there are some fine-looking girls on campus, and man they come in all shades from ebony to cream. Several girls I've seen look so white I don't understand why they even think of themselves as Negro. In fact, I don't understand why people make such a fuss about skin color. One thing I'm learning is that beauty comes in all colors." Peter is unrelenting. "Yeah, but have you been to bed with any of them or made out with them? I mean is it any different?" I'm getting annoyed with my friends' questions. "Why would it be any different? You act as if black girls come from a different planet. It's absurd to think that it would be any different. We're all human aren't we?" But I realized I have the same questions. Would it be any different if I touch and kiss a Negro girl the way I touched and kissed Shannon? I don't know. I have no basis for comparison.

Inevitably, my contemplations make me think of Desirie and unfortunately reawaken my dormant feelings for her. What would it be like to make love to Desirie? I want to find out.

The rain has stopped by the time we turn onto Atlantic Avenue. All four of us simultaneously cheer as the sun peeps through the scattering gray clouds over the ocean. Oh, but we can see the ocean and it's such a cleansing sight. All of the irritations of the rain-spotted drive, the catastrophic predictions about how our vacation is going to turn out, and our fears of wasting precious dollars that we had wallowed in for most of the trip evaporate with the sight of the ocean's great expanse, the smells of the sea, the sound of the waves breaking toward the shore, and the coital cries of the seagulls.

It's four in the afternoon when we arrive at our motel. It is located—as advertised --about two blocks off Atlantic Avenue, but it's much shabbier than we had expected. The watery blue stucco sides of the motel look as if it has been punished for years by recurrent hurricanes and thus are peeling badly. We have reserved two adjoining rooms and draw straws to see who will be rooming together. Then we draw again for the pick of the room, not that there is much difference between them. Both rooms have a heavy, stale smell of cigarette smoke and a hint of urine. They're otherwise identical except for the arrangement of the furniture. As luck would have it, I draw Peter, but we do get the room closest to the ice machine. A fair trade-off, I think to myself. Before we even unpack, the four of us get into our bathing suits and make a mad rush to the beach. We're surprised to find how sparsely populated the beach is. Many people are beginning to leave, frustrated by the relative lack of sun. Despite the gray clouds and the peek-a-boo sunlight, the heat is oppressive. We jump into the water, kicking our legs up high and flailing our arms. We are ten years old again and play all the silly water games of an earlier age. We splash water on one another and jump on one another's head trying to force it under the water. Then we challenge each other to walk straight into the now powerful waves to see who can remain standing. None of us can. The waves smash into us sending us tumbling backwards towards the shore. After about a half-hour of such play, we conclude that we have had enough of an initiation, pronounce our vacation begun, and pledge to spend most of the next day on the beach.

I have to rouse everyone up from his nap at 7:30 because I'm starving. By 8 pm, we're on the Boardwalk hungry for food and female companionship. Food comes first. The oppressive heat from before has dissipated, replaced by a gentle, cooling breeze. The Boardwalk is already crowded with people of all ages. One can hear the sounds of the carousel no matter where you are on the 6-mile long Boardwalk. People are frequently dodging the numerous Rolling Chairs, the wicker, canopied chair-on-wheels that serves as a relaxing means of transport pushed by wisecracking attendants along the entire length of the Boardwalk. We pass by the Steel Pier, which is the central locus of entertainment on the Boardwalk. One ticket allows you entrance to every concert, film and attraction on the Pier, including the impressive Ferris wheel. All the major entertainers played the Steel Pier during its heyday from the 1920s to the 1950s. All along the Boardwalk, there are an uncountable number of food stands, souvenir shops, ice cream parlors, and penny arcades. The smell of French fries, hamburgers and tantalizing egg rolls is unrelenting and is with us no matter where we walk. The dizzying combination of enticing smells, compelling sights, and joyful sounds leave me disoriented. I am pulled in so many directions at once that I don't know what to do first. "Let's eat," I hear one of us say, and my attention finally focuses on my most pressing need.

When it comes to food, this night the four of us are on the same page. At one stand, we purchase a hamburger and the best French fries any of us has ever tasted. Next door, we buy a foot-long egg roll that puts to shame any that we have had in a Chinese restaurant. The feast is completed with the cold sweet slide of frozen custard down our grease-heated gullets. We are so full we have to sit. We locate one of the numerous benches on the Boardwalk where people can sit and stare at the ocean.

"Now this is the life," Peter contends with a belch. James sings us another song title, Don't You Just Know It. Bobby is holding his stomach and groans, "I'm so happy I could hurl." I feel so relaxed and free of worry that I have the rare experience of being speechless. We move on after awhile when we can finally focus attention on our next hunger. We ogle every girl we see. James and I are mostly silent while Peter and Bobby make rude comments to all the girls we see in short shorts. "Hey shake it, but don't break it," Peter cries out to a group of three wiggle-walking women not far ahead us. Bobby asks a cute girl pulling up along side of us, "Would you like to see the submarine races with me?" "No thanks," she says sweetly. "I already get enough sleep." "Oooooh," we all croon in unison.

We haven't moseyed very far down the Boardwalk before we see three fine-looking young ladies. All three are curvy, dark-haired sirens in white short shorts and halter-tops. We stop them and engage them in conversation. As soon as they open their mouths, we know they're all from "New Jurzee". "Where ya boys from?" asked the prettiest of the three. Peter and Bobby respond together with dopey grins on their faces, "Washington, DC." "Oh, the Southland," a second girl says. "I hear it's very dark in DC these days," she continues. The three girls start snickering and giving each other looks. I blush but Bobby doesn't catch their drift. "No, DC has about the same amount of sunshine as New Jersey," he rebuts. This drives the girls mad with laughter. As the conversation continues in this vein, a guy walks by, obviously from New Jersey and ogles the girl Bobby is interested in. The stranger says to the girl, "Gee, I'd like to get in your pants." The girl responds, "What's the matter, d'chu shit 'n yours?" Her friends laugh heartily. We, however, laugh nervously because we are shocked. I lean over and whisper in Bobby's ear. "A woman of unusual refinement." Bobby chortles and whispers back, "Yeah, but what a rack." The stranger gives her the finger and swaggers off down the Boardwalk.

The three girls have wordlessly made their selections. The prettiest girl is clearly interested in Peter. The second girl is smiling large at Bobby. Despite his cluelessness, she thinks he's cute. James has been "conversing" with the third girl by giving her his sexy stare. She keeps blushing and smiling at him. I feel like I have just lost a game of musical chairs and decide to return to our motel room. The Three Miscreants make a pretense of feeling bad about my leaving and insincerely "beg" me to stay. But I almost can hear the sighs of relief as I turn and walk away. An old tape begins to play in my head. Why can't I attract girls the way they can? Am I that ugly? I stop for a moment and look out at the ocean. The moon has laid a shiny carpet of light on the ocean. The gentle breeze on my face feels like a caress. It's difficult to whip up a good pity party on such a night in such a place.

It's a few minutes shy of noon before the four of us get ourselves together and go to the beach. Unlike the day before, the bright blazing sun is almost blinding, and the beach is packed with people. My three friends have made a date to meet the three nubile girls from New Jersey with whom they presumably have spent an undisclosed night of romance. The plan is to meet them near the Lifeguard stand. Despite the specificity of the location, it takes us twenty minutes to find them. We all smile. Mine is a sheepish odd-man out smile. My friends give their newfound loves a leering look, which the girls happily and seductively return. Out of fear that they will abandon all social restraint and begin to copulate before this huge crowd, I wander away in search of a seductress of my own. This seems like a hopeless cause in this anonymous multitude of bikini-clad females. A feeling of loneliness suddenly overtakes me. I think of Desirie and how she would stand out on this white beach with all of its white occupants. I imagine the two of us flying a few dozen feet above the beach, holding hands and laughing together over the effort of so many white people trying to darken their color, yet the same people would be appalled if they had to share the beach with Negroes. I feel myself drifting away from this world. I have completed one year at Howard, and it is changing me.

The intermittent breeze fans the beach with the unmistakable smell of suntan lotion. As I continue my sandy sojourn, I think I hear a familiar voice calling my name. I give it little credence at first and wonder whether I'm hallucinating from inhaling the fumes of all that suntan lotion. The voice becomes clearer as I unwittingly approach its source. "Izzy! Over here." It's Shannon Creamer sitting up on her beach towel with her hands behind her re-hooking the clasp to the top of her hot pink and black polka dot bikini. I have actually felt more of her naked skin than I have ever seen and I'm dazzled by the degree of her feminine pulchritude. She's one choice-looking girl and I feel hornier than all get-out. "Shannon?" I exclaim with a huge grin on my face and a false note of question in my voice. I know damn well it's her, but I want to appear "cool". I never do cool well and Shannon laughs at my pitiable attempt. "Izzy, this is Meghan my roommate from the University of Maryland." I have been so enraptured at seeing Shannon that I see for the first time that she's sharing the blanket with another human being. I see an attractive sultry-looking brunette, a well-tanned body in a sky blue bikini. "Hi Meghan," I say with a smile frozen on my face. "Izzy goes to Howard, Meghan. Can you believe that he goes to school with all those colored people?" Meghan just smiles and shakes her head. Ironically, the loudspeakers on the beach blare out the new hit comedy song,

"Itsy Bitsy Teenie Weenie Yellow Polka Dot Bikini".

"Who'd you come with?" Shannon asks.

"You know, the usual suspects, Peter, Bobby, and James," I answer.

"Izzy, you sure hang out with a strange bunch." Shannon never cared for any of the Three Miscreants. "Where are they now?"

"I suspect that they are making out on various nearby beach blankets with some local yokels they picked up last night." Shannon tilts her head and looks at me with an expression of make believe commiseration. "So they left you all by your lonesome?"

"No, I chose to remove myself from a very uncomfortable scene," I answer in a voice that suggests this is the best decision that I've made in years.

"Well then, Izzy, you can take me to dinner and a movie tonight. Meghan here went and got herself a date and is leaving me all by my lonesome."

"Sure," I say as nonchalantly as I can, when in fact I am having trouble keeping my feet rooted in the sand. With a stunning smile that disorients me, Shannon exclaims,
"Great! There's a new Hitchcock flick at the Atlantic Theatre. It's called Psycho." As
she sounds out the name of the movie, she manipulates her voice into a fearful warbling sound. With a smile still frozen on my face and in an emotionless tone, I manage, "It sounds scary."

At 6:30, I meet Shannon at the entrance to the Million Dollar Pier. After she calls my name, I turn around to see a paragon of loveliness, garbed in a sundress of blue and yellow pastel stripes and sandals topped with a floppy flower. We both are in a cheerful mood probably for the same reason—that neither one of us has to be alone tonight. I had promised to take her to the place I had found whose egg rolls were the "most". As we walk up the boardwalk toward the stand, Shannon talks the whole time about everything that she and Meghan have done so far on their vacation. I'm not too interested in her conversation but am happy to be in the company of such an attractive girl who wants to be with me. I reach for her hand. Shannon is momentarily taken aback by this gesture. She brightens at this unexpected invitation and seizes my hand with surprising vigor. She holds my hand tightly as she continues on with her monologue. At the food stands, we order and eventually scarf down two egg rolls apiece, two large cones of French fries, and almost as an after thought, a hamburger. We discover that we not only had overeaten but we are running late to make the 7:45 show. I think the two of us are going to barf as we walk/run to the movie theater. We make it in time for the endless previews and give each other a barfy look that acknowledges that after all, there was no need to run. When the credits for the movie begin to roll and the scary music blares, Shannon grabs my hand and fearfully squeezes it. She has caught two of my knuckles in just the right juxtaposition so that they seem to be begging my mouth to scream at the top of my lungs. With great effort, I'm able to manfully suppress my scream and inadvertently turn it into a wimper. "What's the matter?" Shannon asks with concern in her voice. "Nothing," I reply. "Nothing at all." The knuckle mash was nothing compared to what comes afterward. During the shower scene, I receive even greater punishment. As Janet Leigh steps into the shower and minutes later when Tony Perkins, as Norman Bates dressed up like his mother, starts to slash and stab his beautiful victim to death, Shannon starts screaming while simultaneously digging her long painted fingernails into my left forearm and releasing a significant amount of my blood. I see my blood running down my arm and spilling off my fingertips and I let out with a scream. This scream I cannot suppress. The audience, however, hears me loud and clear and starts laughing because my baritone scream has mingled harmonically with the soprano screams of just about every female in the theater. I count myself fortunate that I emerge from the movie theater alive—bloodied but unbowed.

Shannon invites me back to her motel room. She says she wants to minister to my wounds. When we arrive at the motel, she makes a cursory examination of my cuts, makes sure the bleeding has stopped, and then washes my arm. After she has completed her ministrations, we settle ourselves on the pull out sofa. She faces me with her legs tucked underneath her knees and gently touches my hand. Her whole demeanor has suddenly changed. "Izzy," she purrs softly. "I have something to tell you."

"What is it?" I ask. Her tone begins to make me nervous. "You know we have been friends for a long time." My anxiety spikes as I think, "Oh God, another rejection."

"But when I saw you on the beach yesterday," she continues, "I don't know. Something came over me. It just hit me that this is a guy who's always cared about me, been there for me, told me the truth. And yet I've been chasing one jerk after another with only one thing on their puny minds. All they want is to get in my pants and use me. But you, Izzy, with all your brightness and sweetness, you're the real deal. Let me show you what I mean." She leans in to kiss me, but I'm a step behind because I can't believe what is happening. We bump noses and both of us laugh nervously. Finally, we reach serious liplock, and her tongue is making unfamiliar intrusions into my mouth's interior. She is kissing me in ways that I have never experienced before, either with her in our make-out sessions on Valley Street or with any other girl for that matter. "Oh Izzy," she sighs, "I think I'm falling for you." She grabs my hand and begins moving it down to the hem of her dress. She guides my hand under her dress. "Please touch me," she demands with fierce urgency. She feels me tighten up as I begin to remember our previous encounter in this neighborhood. As if she's reading my mind, she says again, "Touch me, Izzy. I'm not wearing my Playtex Living Girdle." I almost burst out laughing. No girl has ever uttered such a phrase to me. In the heat of the moment, I am struck by its absurdity. As I become more aroused, I keep seeing the television ad in which a very fetching blonde dances around in her Playtex Girdle while the unseen announcer waxes poetic over its slimming and liberating powers. My cock alternates between tumescence and deflation—mimicking the action of a slide trombone. Shannon's moans free me from my absurd dilemma. She is wet with pleasure, which helps to increase mine; until, that is, my mind's eye is suddenly filled with the smiling image of Desirie. Shannon sees, feels, and hears the change that has come over me and asks, "What happened Izzy? What's the matter?" After much hemming and hawing, I tell Shannon my long tale of woe; how I met Desirie and the way our relationship has played out. Shannon tries her best to listen to my tearful tale of unrequited love, but the effort it takes to shift gears from pre-orgasmic bliss to selfless sympathetic friend sends her mounting frustration through the roof. When it finally dawns on her that my failure to "finish the job" is due to my feelings for another woman, she becomes apoplectic. She burst into tears. "How could you, Izzy? How could you leave me high and dry because you were thinking of another woman." Then the final realization turns her into a screaming banshee. "Oh my God, Izzy, Desiree is colored isn't she? You were trying to make love to me while thinking about a colored woman? And a colored woman who has dumped you? You're pathetic Izzy, and I hate you for the way you've humiliated me!" No apology, explanation, or appeal will mollify her. "Just get out, Izzy," she wails mournfully.

"But Shannon..."

"GET OUT!" She screams, as she runs into her bathroom and slams the door.

Chapter 11.
Is You Is or Is You Ain't

Shannon is right. I am pathetic. I had the opportunity of my lifetime, something that I've wanted to do with Shannon for years and I blew it. Why? Because I'm thinking of a girl who doesn't want me. A Black girl yet who comes from another world, a world I know nothing about. It's pathetic. But what is Shannon's anger about? Is it because I was thinking about another woman or because I was thinking about a Black woman? Oddly, the thought that she was offended because Desirie is Black eases my pain a bit. Shannon has become one of them— the prejudiced, the bigoted—and therefore unworthy of my tears.

Still in pain, I walk down to the ocean and watch the waves breaking to the shore with a rebuke that pulls the water back and with it the earth's sand and shells into the thrust of the next wave. As I watch enthralled by the water's energy and strength, the waves' rhythmic cresting and crashing, a wave of hope crests within me that I can be lifted out of the dark mood in which my encounter with Shannon has left me. The smell of the salt, the heat of the sun, and the blasting sounds of the ocean lift me out of my funk and into a feeling of wellbeing. I see two dolphins moving in an arching pattern rising above and then dipping into the water's depths. The dolphins disappear, and in their place appear four pelicans swooping down into the waves and then flying upward in a movement so graceful and elegant that the loudest sound I hear is my own gasp. I return to the ocean as much as possible for the rest of our vacation so that I can take in nature's drug in the needed daily dose.

After we return home, I go back to work at the Shepherd Park Playground. During inclement weather, I'm confined to the school lunchroom with typically a dozen kids creating exquisite crafts, gossiping, or dancing to the latest rock n' roll hits. I really get into the dancing and am thrilled to teach them how to do the Pony, the Slop, and the Snap. On nice days we walk out onto the blacktop where there is a basketball court and picnic tables that are constantly occupied by kids playing board games. Down the hill are the two baseball fields where my 12-and-under and 14-and-under baseball teams play. Late in August my 12-and under team plays for the championship against Takoma playground. With the score tied 1 to 1 in the final inning, Takoma has men on first and third. The Takoma batter hits the ball right back to the pitcher. Elton, our star pitcher and homerun hitter, has a mental lapse and throws the ball to first base. The man on third easily trots across home plate with the winning run and the championship. I lose i-t and blast Elton for his "idiotic error". Elton lets loose with a flood of tears, but I can't let go of my rage.

My work at Shepherd greatly distracts me from the pain I feel about Desirie, about Shannon, the lost scholarship, and the realization that I do not feel at home in either my white world or my Black world. I'm about to start my sophomore year at Howard in a week and I feel no enthusiasm at all about my continuing education. As I contemplate my return to Howard, I'm clear about one thing. NO MORE HITCHHIKING! With a loan from my father, I am able to scrape together $150 to buy a 1954 Plymouth. I' m dizzied by the sense of freedom that this purchase produces. I'm free not only from the racist chatter that I had experienced on every ride to Howard, but also good old Betsy—the name I have given my new set of wheels—extends the range of my travel s and my education. Betsy takes me to parts of D C. that I have never seen or even knew existed. It has only been three years since Black people made up a majority of the residents of Washington D C., but as I travel in the Northeast, Southeast, and Southwest quadrants of the city, I see firsthand how segregated a city Washington is. I encounter very few white people in these three quadrants. I see fewer and fewer exclusively white neighborhoods in the city, and these are concentrated west of Rock Creek Park, the sylvan glade that runs from the southern part of the western half of the city to the northwestern District line and out into the suburbs. There are geographical, as well as psychological, reasons for my feeling stuck between two worlds as I travel every weekday from home to Howard and back.

I begin my sophomore year with my mind filled with contradictions. I'm not sure I even want to return. But return I do, still a Chemistry major when it is very clear that I have fallen out of love with the laboratory. Whenever I'm cooped up in the lab holding smelly test tubes, I look longingly out the window and crave human companionship. The dark world of Howard still feels strange, but I'm growing increasingly distant from my white friends. Many of my high school friends left town for college and most of these left my life forever. Several attend colleges in the Washington area such as American, George Washington, or Maryland University and consequently are living very different lives. The lines of connection formed in high school have either atrophied or died out entirely. The courses that I'm scheduled to take also cause me no reason to be excited about my education. I'm taking American Government, which had bored me to tatters in high school. I'm also required to take an English literature course that I dread. My scheduled chemistry course is Qualitative Analysis, which promises a meaningless search for metallic ions uncovered by a series of tricky chemical manipulations. My required math course is Differential Calculus, the front end of a two-course sequence that produces a week's worth of anticipatory nightmares. I'm also required to take a language and for some inexplicable reason, I choose German. Finally, my anti-military biases crash headlong into my necessary immersion into ROTC. None of these courses is of any interest and yet I have to do well in order to retrieve my lost scholarship.

I have lost track of what my friends in NAG were up to since we picketed Glen Echo together at the end of June I see them from time to time during the beginning of the new semester, and each time they would inform me of the great things NAG is doing and entreat me to join the group. Each time their entreaties leave me sympathetic, guilt- ridden, and fearful, and I would politely refuse. I learn from my politically active friends that with the establishment of the Student Nonviolent Coordinating Committee (SNCC) in April, NAG has become one of the new organization's chief affiliates. I learn that after I left the picket line on June 30, Gwendolyn Greene, a fellow Howardite that I had once briefly met, along with four other Black protesters was arrested for climbing onto one of the hand-carved wooden horses of Glen Echo's famed merry-go-round. Just hearing about her courage fills me with shame.

A chief topic of conversation on campus is the upcoming presidential election between John F. Kennedy and Richard Nixon. Although I'm still too young to vote, I'm an ardent supporter of Kennedy. I hang on his every word and search the papers for any clue to his political positions and policy prescriptions. I'm not alone because it seems like most college students want Kennedy to win. I don't think I have met anyone at Howard who supports Nixon. Yet the members of NAG, as well as many other Howard students, are suspicious of Kennedy and have serious doubts about his commitment to Negro rights because of his frequent attempts to placate the Southern segregationists in Congress. In October, Dr. Martin Luther King had been arrested for participating in a sit-in at Rich 's Department Store i n Atlanta, Georgia. The sit-in charges were dropped, but King received a four-month prison sentence for violating probation that he was placed on back in May when he received a traffic ticket. King was never informed that he was on probation. The judge refused to let King free on bail. Instead, King was secretly moved in the middle of the night to Reidsville State Penitentiary, infamous for its chain gangs and mysterious killings of Negro prisoners. . King's family and staff tried to contact both the Kennedy and Nixon campaigns. Nixon did not even respond. But Kennedy called Coretta King to offer his good wishes.

NAG's desegregation successes and its growing prominence are still not enough to turn me into a student activist. My heart is clearly with the developing student movement for equality, but I can't overcome my fear. I need a distraction from the assaults of recent events. My love life is a bust; my courses are a drag; and my fear of joining NAG appalls me. I need something that will prevent these worries from achieving a coup d'etat over my mind. It comes to me one day in Phys Ed. while I'm mindlessly shooting a basketball. "Basketball! That's it! I'll try out for the varsity basketball team," I exclaim to no one in particular. It's a long shot to make the team, but it would be fun to try and maybe I won 't worry so much about the rest of my life. Maybe I can surprise myself. After all, my success in high school came as a complete surprise to everyone- particularly me. In fact, the only reason I had tried out for my high school team was because no one believed I could make the team. "You're too short," they said. "You don't stand a chance," they said. When, in my senior year, I had become the team 's leading scorer, my friends now assured me I was too short to play college basketball. What better reason...right? The first day of try-outs, however, merely gives me another thing to worry about. The cracker-box gymnasium—a refurbished Quonset hut—is fragrant with perspiration. The water rises from the sprinting bodies in miniature geysers. The reeking oppressive odor is all around me, leaking out of every pore of the undersized gym. Is it worse than in high school? The odor inspires me to wonder. I can't remember. A bolus of racial myth and fear presses inside my stomach as the ten brown men sprint by me. They do smell different! Ridiculous! No, it's not! The debate rages within me while I watch my competitors, in a furious scrimmage. The panic comes on, and the world changes. Everything in the dilapidated gym inspires fear. The thump of the basketball reverberating against ugly walls creates strange auditory patterns as if someone is being beaten with a rubber hose. The staccato pounding of basketball shoes in continuous motion suggests to my overwrought ears a stampede of, well, bison. The players' frenzied chatter is an eerie echo of doomed tortured voices. What am I doing here, anyway? These guys are big, strong, fast, and BLACK!

I watch the returning starters from last year's team and consider how I had watched them before, but only as a spectator. Now I have to play against them in order to one-day play with them. There is George Black, the size of a college guard, who wants to be the team's leading rebounder. He is only 5' 11" tall, but he easily out-jumps and out-rebounds men several inches taller. At the age of nine, on a Northeast Washington DC playground, he vowed to all who would listen that he was going to grow to be over 6 feet tall. When his growth stopped just short of his goal, he was inconsolable and unforgiving, although he did not know who to blame. So he blamed everyone, his parents, his peers, and especially anyone who was over 6 feet tall. To compensate for his cruel fate, he spent most of his spare time strengthening his legs and practicing his jumping. His leaping exercises were a familiar sight at the Turkey Thicket playground. From sunup to sundown, he would stand in the same spot underneath one of the basketball goals jumping and jumping like a solitary Yemenite dancer. The wound has never healed, and his hatred continues unabated for all men over 6 feet. In every game, under each basket, George Black can be seen jostling for position and yelling at the top of his lungs, "Come on six-footers! What's the matter six-footers, you can't out-jump ole 5' 11" George Black?"

Hard as he tries and high as he jumps, George Black cannot out-rebound Lincoln Haskins. Linc, after all, is 6' 9" and weighs 260 lbs. In the pivot, or under the basket, Linc looks like one of the giant boulders of Stonehenge. Opposing players fall off him like luckless, ill-fated mountain climbers. Linc is the only member of the team who thinks seriously about playing professional basketball, who thinks he even has a chance to make the pros. Whenever he begins one of his patented, fluid moves to the basket, the nearest players can hear him muttering under his breath, "I'm pro caliber!

By far the fastest member of the team and its second leading scorer after Linc is Whee Willie Watson. Whee Willie got his name from the Howard University fans. Whenever he flashes by his opponent, the crowd bellows, "Wheeeee Willie!" He's a joy to watch, his body a beautiful moving sculpture. With his thin mustache he resembles a brown Ronald Coleman. At 6 feet, Whee Willie is small enough and quick enough to dart around bigger opponents. His great strength, however, also gives him an advantage over men his own size and smaller. He seems capable of every move and skill I have ever acquired. His shooting accuracy from 20-plus feet is equal to mine. What can I do against that?

Watching Whee Willie glide into his favorite move—a fake to the left and then a swift move to the right—I suddenly see how it is done. For the first time, I notice Whee Willie's sudden shift of the hip to the left and a subtle drop of his shoulder in the same direction. Then, with unseen speed, he shifts his entire body to the right. It looks very similar to a move that I use consistently to gain an initial edge on my opponent. But I use my shoulders more. Whee Willie's hip fake is even quicker, and it is something one can do off a full-speed dribble. "I can do that," I think, now eager to enter the game. "White! Take Johnson's place and cover Whee!" I leap from the bench as if I have been ejected from a burning cockpit, and I search for the Ronald Coleman smile. For the first few minutes, I do little more on offense than pass the ball off to my teammates. I'm too nervous to move freely. Soon the rhythm will come—I hope— and my jittery awareness that I'm now actually trying out for a college basketball team will fall away. While I ease myself into the game, Whee does little to reassure me of my chances for making the team. First he applies the move I have just mastered and fakes me out of my shoes for an easy lay-up. Then he lofts a feathery jump shot over my head for an easy two-pointer. On his third attempt, I time my jump perfectly and partially block his shot. But I foul him badly in the process. "Hold on, white boy, this ain 't no playground ball," Whee Willie fumes. "You can't do that shit here".

The next time I have the ball Whee's covering me so closely that I can feel breath on my forehead. His sunshiny grin never leaves his face. "Come on, white boy, show me your stuff." It 's a gentle taunt, just enough of a challenge for me to relax and get into my rhythm. After giving an unconvincing fake left I dribble to the right, behind a teammate who blocks Whee Willie from me. I know my jump shot is good as soon as it leaves my hand. It's a beautiful soft parabola from 24 feet. The "regulars" start laughing and hooting, and getting on Whee Willie.

"Hey Whee, you gonna let that little white boy show you how to play?" Whee just laughs, but a look of caution appears on his face. I let some time pass before I challenge Whee Willie again. Instead, I try to concentrate on setting up plays and good shots for the other players. I know if I have any chance at all for making the team, it is as a playmaker, not as a heavy scorer. But Whee Willie's gentle taunting continues and it's infectious. I start talking back. "Listen here, Whee Willie," I say, "I'm gonna beat you at your own game. I'm gonna blow right by you on your left side."

"Listen out there all you niggas," Whee calls to his teammates laughing. "Listen to what the man say." I use Whee Willie's own move on him—a hip fake to the left and a quick move to my right. I manage to get a step on him. He's surprised by my quickness, but his own speed allows him to recover before I can reach the basket. Frustrated, I pass the ball off to a teammate. "You move mighty quick for a white boy," he says, still smiling. I can't remember the last time anyone recovered from my usually quick-enough-first-step the way Whee Willie has just done. The next time I have the ball I fake to my right and go left. Just as before, Whee Willie recovers before I can advance any closer to the basket. But I pull up short after my first step by Whee and loft a soft jump shot from 15 feet. A lovely swishing sound can be heard as the ball touches nothing but the strings of the basket. Whee Willie's teammates begin hooting once more.

"Hey white boy, you all right," Whee says.

"You're not bad yourself...for a Black boy." I can't believe I have just said what I said. It spills out of me like a leaky faucet. Everyone in the gymnasium stares at me wide-eyed with perplexity. The place is eerily quiet for what seems like a millennium. Whee gives out with a raucous laugh, and the rest of the players soon join him. Then he puts his arm around my shoulder and yells over to the coach. "Hey coach, if this white boy don't make the team, can we keep him as a mascot? We'll call him the Albino Bison."

"It's alright with me as long as I don't have to sit at the back of the bench," I retort. Even the coach joins in the players' laughter.

The coach blows his whistle and calls the scrimmagers over to the bench. "That'll be it for today, men. Same time tomorrow! First cut will be next Monday and the final cut will be the Monday after that. We eventually plan to carry no more than 13 players. Unfortunately, that means we'll have to get along without the services of 12 of you hotshots. On Monday, however, we will trim down to 17. Then we'll take another look at those of you who make the first cut for a week and make the final cuts the following Monday. That's all, gentlemen!"

We file out of the gym, heads down, shoulders sagging, tongues hanging out, a poignant tableau of exhaustion. I notice the coach watching us with a worried look on his face. Only Whee retains his bounce. "Hey White," he calls, "How about a beer after a shower? Rise up in the world, my man, and join the stars of the team at the Kenyon."

"Sounds great!"

When I enter the shower room I immediately go into traumatic shock. There I face 20 brown men in their astonishing birthday suits. I cannot believe what I see. There's Gavin Dillard with what appears to be a huge, black rubber hose between his legs. Henry Brown, who has been stimulating himself possesses a large brown member now curved like a sickle. Thank God for Harry Gaines who seems to possess a more normal sized organ. Little rainbows are hazily visible through the billows of steam that rise from the showers. I can barely see several of the players—on the pretext of washing—pulling on their organ so that it would show as long as possible without being erect. This masculine competition requires consummate skill in self-manipulation. I turn my body to the wall and wash myself.

Four of us walk the three blocks up Georgia Avenue to the Kenyon Grill. It is dark, smoky and small. We sit at the bar and order beers. We split into two conversations, Linc Haskins and George Black and Whee Willie and me. While Linc and George are engaged in their usual mutual putdowns about who's the better rebounder, Whee leans over toward me, his face almost touching mine. He seems to prefer this physical almost Bedouin closeness when he talks. "You've got a nice little game," he begins. "Fact, I don't recall ever seein' white boys move the way you do. Where did you learn your game, anyway, in New York?"

"No, like you, on the DC playgrounds. Probably spent more time playing with Negroes than with whites. In fact, I originally copied my shot from a fellow from Roosevelt High that I used to play with."

"Is that where you went to high school?"

"No, I went to Coolidge, but I played pick-up games with guys from all over the city. You went to Spingarn, right?"

"That's right."

"Yeah, I remember seeing you play in high school in the interhigh finals against Dunbar."

"Oh yeah. Whee Willie put on a show that day, didn't he?"

"You were mighty sharp, Whee Willie."

"So was you today, my little white flash. You made a mess of me out there. What you doin' at Howard anyway? Most white folk I know of want to get away from niggers as fast as they can." I laugh at the way he phrases it, but there's nothing in my experience that tells me he's wrong. I spare him my idealistic rap and tell him that the price was right. "Tuition is only $200 a year."

"What about an athletic scholarship?" I look at him perplexed. "You know Howard doesn't give athletic scholarships." His face takes on a pained look suggesting that I'm missing the obvious.

"I don't mean Howard, man. I mean a scholarship to one of those big white schools." Now I look at him like he's missing the obvious. "I'm not that good, Whee. At my height, I'd have to be someone extra talented for say a state university to give me a scholarship."

"Oh shit, man, I've seen sorrier players than you on fine athletic scholarships!"

"Well, nobody's been knocking down my door to make me an offer."

"What you need my man is a public relations agent to make you a star."

"Are you applying for the job?"

"Sure enough, white stuff. The Whee Willie Watson Public Relations Corporation is gonna make you a star!"

"It'll take more than public relations, I'm afraid."
"Don't you worry about that. Don't you know behind every great white man is a nigger doing his dirty work?" The remark itself stuns me, but I'm even less prepared for the malevolent smile on Whee Willie's face. It suggests to me that there is a well of bitterness in him that I don't particularly want to get to know. So I ignore the smile. "Listen Whee, all I want to do is make this team. All I want is to be a Howard Bison."

"That's my loyal white boy." I'm growing more anxious. I can't follow Whee's sudden shift from gushing support to implacable sarcasm—a sunshiny smile alternating with darkening clouds of hostility. Whee lights a cigarette and proceeds to puff small billows of smoke. He never inhales in training, but seems more comfortable with a cigarette in his mouth. Whee stares at me for what seems like forever and then assuming the voice of a conspirator, he asks, "Have you ever been with a Black woman?"

"No I haven't."

"There's nothing finer than a Black vagina," he says with a low conspiratorial cackle. He chug-a-lugs his beer and, without waiting for me to ask, Whee adds, "White women love me! They just love my lovely brown ass."

"How nice for you," I retort with some sarcasm of my own.

"Here's what I'm gonna do for you," Whee says, totally ignoring my sarcasm. "If you fix me up with one of your white girlfriends, I will find you the finest piece of Black ass in DC." I start laughing because Whee is asking a 19-year-old virgin to procure a white woman for him. Up to this point in my life I have been unable to find any girl white or Black to be my girlfriend much less a sexual partner.

"Why are you laughing?" Whee asks in a hurt and angry tone. "Ain't I good enough for your snooty white girlfriends?"

"It's not that, Whee." I'm eager to drop this topic of conversation. I sure as hell don't want to tell him the truth.

"What is it then?" He won't change the subject.

"It's not that easy," I lamely argue.

"You won't be breaking no law. This is DC, not Mississippi!"

"I know that, Whee," still trying to beg off. Now he's really pissed. "You know, you come to Howard and you give everybody the impression that you're not a racist. But you're just like every other white man I've ever known. You can't stand the thought of me or any other nigger getting next to a white woman. You people are crazy. You think civilization is gonna come to an end if a Black man and a white woman get together."

"It's not that, Whee. I could care less who you're with. That's not the problem!"

"What's the problem then?" I'm utterly stuck. I'm completely out of evasions. "God damn it, Whee, I'm a virgin! I can't find a girl for me, much less you!" His laughter begins with a low hum and builds to a cackling crescendo. "A virgin?" The rolling laughter continues. "Look, don't say anything to anybody, will you? I've got enough on my plate here." I try to keep a begging tone out of my request. Whee's laughter catches Linc and George's attention. Linc yells over, "What's happenin' there?" Whee, still laughing, says, "Aw nothing man, Izzy just told me a wild joke. It's a gas man, a gas." Whee turns his attention back to me and says, "No problem, Izzy, I just have to school you in the fine art of pressing women."

"I've signed up for enough courses, thank you very much," I protest. "Oh no, it's my solemn duty now to help you find a woman you can bust a nut with."

"Yeah, what's your fee?" I say with a smirk.

"Already told you. You find me a fine white girl and I'll fix you up with a very willing Black girl.

"Well, I hope hell freezes over!"

On Monday, I learn that I have made the first cut. The eight guys who are let go are all would-be forwards or centers. As the rumor mill has contended, no guards would be cut. The rumors help staunch my fear, which has been bleeding out of me since the coach first mentioned the word "cut". My joy, however, is muted by the realization that the final cuts will primarily focus on the guards. The week of practice features a virtual war among the guards who are on the bubble. You might think there are no rules in the game of basketball the way the guards claw, paw, bump, and hammer one another. Since I am the smallest of the guards, I take a real pounding. But every time I get hit, I pledge to myself that I will out-quick, out-score, and outwit my competition.

At the end of the week I am battered and confused about my chances. The weekend is a welcome relief from the physical punishment, but the mental punishment I put myself through is even worse. By Sunday night I'm an utter mess. All I can think about is the list I'm going to see the next day. "Will I make the cut?" is the question I ask myself a thousand times over the weekend. I can't eat or sleep. I just don't know what to do with myself. When I began the tryouts, I told myself that I would give this my best shot, but it was no big thing if I didn't make the team. But my initial nonchalance melted in the heat of battle, and the thought of being cut is now unbearable. At this moment I want nothing more out of my college education than to play varsity basketball for Howard University.

Mom is busy making a pot roast that I usually salivate over. It was the one dish that she cooks with some skill. Tonight the smells increase the queasy feeling that settled in my stomach at daybreak. I keep playing over and over in my mind every play, every shot, every defensive gaffe and gem that I can remember. I try to compare these with my competition. I wince at every memory of another guard's triumph and secretly draw hope from my competition's mess-ups.

There are six other guards who along with me are contending for two guard spots. One of them is my old nemesis Jason Sharpe from Cardozo High. He's still talking trash to me, but I have become inured of its effects. However, there's one jibe that does get to me. He is so convinced of my inferior talent that he frequently and vociferously offers his considered opinion that if I do make the team, it's because the coach wants a token white player. That comment, I must admit, really burns my ass.

What Howard needs most is a respectable point guard to quarterback the offense. My dilemma is that, although I'm a fair point guard, I much prefer playing shooting guard. But everyone knows that's Whee Willie's spot. So it's point guard or oblivion. At dinner I'm in a zone. My parents attempt to engage me in conversation and on their fourth attempt, I respond with monosyllables.

Dad: "Do you think you'll make the team?"

Me: "Maybe."

Mom: "How do you like your dinner, dear?"

Me: "Fine."

When I finally hit the bed at around 1 a.m., I just lay there trying to find a way to minimize the pain and shame of being cut. In a reverie I imagine several scenes of my explaining to friends and relatives the reason why I was cut. (a) Everyone is right. I am too short to play college basketball; (b) Coach is prejudiced against whites; (c) I never told anyone I was injured; (d) Coach seized on one bad play I made; (e) I pissed Whee off and he told the coach he won't play with me on the team; (f) Since I knew the coach would never choose a short Jewish boy, I didn't try my best; (g) It was an administrative error. Coach really meant to cut someone else; (h) Coach took umbrage when I told him I thought Jerry West was better than Oscar Robertson.

Not a convincing rationalization in the bunch so my ruminations continue into the wee hours in the morning. I finally fall asleep for about two hours; and when I wake up, I realize I'm in danger of being late for my 8 am class. I scarf down my breakfast that I don't taste at all, jump into my 1954 Plymouth, and race onto New Hampshire Avenue in a high state of terror. Because of my preoccupation with the "list", it's a wonder I make it to school in one piece. The problem is the list won't be posted until 4 pm when we all show up for practice. The long day stretches before me like an endless sojourn in the desert.

I'm not much in the mood for plumbing the depths of Beowulf, our current reading assignment in my 8 am English class. It is nearly impossible to focus on such jaw-breaking names as Hrothgar, Hrothulf, Hildebuhr and Wiglaf. I recently heard of an English professor who named her son Hrothgar in honor of Beowulf's king. My thought is that such an act in the 20th Century constitutes a serious form of child abuse. But there is one passage that catches my ear given my current state of mind.

> Each of us must one day reach the end
> Of worldly life, let him who can
> Glory before he dies: that lives on
> After him, when he lifeless lies.

I hate to admit to myself, but I want the glory of making the team and not just because of my love for the game. I really do want to be the first white varsity basketball player at Howard. And I want to be picked on merit, not as a token white. Echoes of Jason's jibe continue to wound me.

Analytic Geometry is no better. I could care less about turning graphs into algebraic formulas and vice versa. I call this course Descartes Ravings in honor of the antiquated French philosopher who created this misbegotten math. Worse yet, I'm saddled with a professor who promised to fail 80% of the class, and judging by the several posted grade sheets under his name, he usually keeps his promise. In one course he failed everyone in the class and then apparently changed his mind (or was forced to). The tell tale smudge of an eraser makes clear that he had converted one "F" to a "D". I don't remember a thing that went on in class today.

By lunchtime I'm experiencing some hunger pangs that are shouting down my queasiness. I take myself to Ben's Chili Bowl down at 12th and U. I'm in no mood for conversation, and I need to stretch my legs. Ben's Chili Bowl had opened last summer. A husband and wife team, Ben and Virginia Ali, had renovated a building that had been the Minnehaha, Washington's first silent movie house. It was later taken over by Harry Beckley, one of Washington's first Black police detectives who turned it into a pool hall. Mind you, the Alis took this risk at a time when the national business failure rate was 60%. Anyway, they make the best Chili Half-Smoke in the city, and the restaurant is fast becoming a major icon in the city. My lust for the half-smoke completely eliminates my queasiness and is also an effective antidote to my anxious cogitating about who did or did not make the team.

On my way back from lunch, I stop at Waxie Maxie's Quality Music store near 7th and U. I listen to For Your Precious Love by Jerry Butler and the Impressions and moon about Desirie. After listening to this beautiful song twice, I leave the record store in such a state of calm and good feeling that I am now ready to face the prospect of being cut from the team. As four o' clock approaches, my fear returns. I dash across the Yard, past Greene Field to the Quonset hut that houses Howard's inadequate gym. When I see that the list has been posted, my dash-induced rapid breathing turns into hyperventilating. Now that I rushed so fast to get to the list I'm afraid to look at it. I freeze some ten feet away immobilized by fear. I don't want to know. I do want to know. I try talking to myself: Come on, Izzy, you need to know....

At that moment, the old silly refrain roars inside my head, Is you is or is you ain't? Is you is or is you ain't? I remember how my father said this in his effort to mock Negroes' use of grammar. Then I remembered how Joe Turner sang it in his hit, Lipstick, Powder, and Paint, with all the sass and fun he could muster. I start singing it aloud with a syncopated beat. Soon I'm dancing to my own music and singing over and over,

Is you is or is you ain't,
Is you is or is you ain't'
Is you is or is you ain't

A member of the Howard B-ball team?

Some of my fellow hopefuls have gathered and watch in amazement as I sing and dance my fear away. "Hey White! What's happenin' man?" one of them yells. I finally recognize that it is Jason Sharpe. "Does that poor excuse for dancing mean you made the cut?" he asks.

"I don't know? I haven't looked at the list yet."

"You are one crazy cracker," Jason says with a superior laugh.

"If I'm so crazy, why don't you look first?"

"That's alright, you were here first." I laugh at his false bravado. The absurdity of our behavior finally registers and I inch toward the list. The names are arranged alphabetically. I see George Black's name and Linc Haskins', of course. Down the list I see Jason Sharpe's name, but with mock sadness I look and point at him and slowly shake my head. He blanches for a second and then recognizes the impish smile that I'm trying to hide. "You dumb motherfucker!" he protests. I keep going slowly down the list...William Watson and there it is. Dead last on the list, Isadore White.

"Yes! Yes! Yes!" I bellow and break into my dancing again.

"I guess the white boy made the cut," says Jason somewhat dejectedly.

I laugh and announce, "I'll spare you the trouble, Sharpe. You made the cut too. You made it too."

Chapter 12.
What Am I To Do?

"It was the phone call! That's why Kennedy won,"
gleefully answers a very intellectual looking student in black
horn rims. I'm in my Government class the day after the
presidential election and Dr. Dorsey has just asked no one in
particular why John Kennedy has just beaten Richard Nixon. The
student ad-libs, "Black people matter. Black people now have
power." "Explain yourself, Mr. Jones!" Dr. Dorsey bellows as he
paces back and forth in front of the class while making circular
motions with his hand on his glaringly protruding stomach.
Stanford Jones then launches into an appalling story of the
routine injustice that takes place in the segregated South. His
monologue is a dance—every part of him moves in a rhythmic
sway.

"Well, don'tcha know, Dr. Martin Luther King was
arrested back in February in Atlanta for driving with just an
Alabama license. Don'tcha know, he just moved from
Montgomery to Atlan—" "MR. JONES, " Dr. Dorsey loudly
interrupts, "Would you PLEASE stop beginning every sentence
with 'Don'tcha know.' You sound like a corn pone Negro." "Sorry
Dr. Dorsey, " Jones says sheepishly. "Anyway, Dr. King was just a
few days past the 90-day deadline for getting a Georgia license.
But this white cop was upset because Dr. King was driving with a
white woman. Dr. King had to pay a $25 fine that the judge
imposed on him, but he wasn't told that he was on probation. So
back in early October, Dr. King participated in a sit-in at Rich's
Department Store in Atlanta and was arrested. Now here's how
white people do. The judge drops the charges for trespassing but
sentences him to four months in jail for violating the traffic-
ticket probation. And, get this, he refuses to let King out on bail
while the ruling is being appealed. Dr. King is shuffled off in the
middle of the night to Reidsville State Penitentiary where a lot of
niggers end up strangely dead." To quell the groundswell of
laughter, Dr. Dorsey intervenes with a stern "Mr. Jones, you are
pushing the limit."

"Sorry again, Dr. Dorsey. Anyway, fearing the worst, Dr. King's family and supporters tried to contact anyone they thought could help. They called both the Kennedy and Nixon campaigns. Nixon didn't do diddly." "Mr. Jones," the rotund professor again interrupts, "Would you please render that sentence into proper English."

"Yes sir. Nixon did nothing. But Senator Kennedy made a personal call to Coretta

King to offer his sympathy and promised to see what he could do. His brother Robert called the judge and asked why Dr. King did not receive bail on a misdemeanor charge. The judge relented, granted bail and Dr. King was released after being jailed for eight days. Now a lot of Black people weren't too keen on Kennedy's Catholicism, but after that phone call which led to Kennedy being endorsed by King's father, Black people rallied around Kennedy. Kennedy got 68% of the Black vote."

"Well done, Mr. Jones," Dr. Dorsey opines. Despite your ham-handedness with the English language, you gave a plausible rationale for your contention."

As it happens, we have been discussing the voting patterns of Negroes throughout American history and the revolutionary nature of Franklin Delano Roosevelt's successful weaning of Negroes from their traditional preference for Republicans to an increasing affiliation with the Democratic Party. This trend continued into the election of 1960, which was quite an achievement since the Democrats were heavily influenced—if not dominated by—Southern racists committed to an ideology of white supremacy. Dr. Dorsey peers at us through wise and tired eyes and makes his usual demand with his usual feeling of dread. "Now please turn in your homework. " Dr. Dorsey's gaze transmogrifies into a stare of malevolent suspicion as he witnesses a lot of faux fumbling by the students in their bags and brief cases. "How many of you do not have your homework ready to hand in?" More than half the class slowly and tentatively raises their hands as if they are volunteering for a potentially lethal assignment. This is the final straw. After two months of admirable restraint, Dr. Dorsey loses it. His voice rises to a shriek. "YOU KNOW THE WHITE MAN BELIEVES YOU ARE INFERIOR. DO YOU KNOW WHY HE BELIEVES THIS?" Several students automatically shake their heads. Dr. Dorsey continues at the same ear-shattering level. "HE BELIEVES THIS BECAUSE YOU ARE INFERIOR. YOU ARE LAZY, UNCOMMITTED, INFERIOR STUDENTS, AND THE NEGRO RACE WILL NOT ADVANCE A JOT OR A TITTLE BEYOND ITS CURRENT SORRY STATE UNTIL YOU-- THE SUPPOSED CROP OF BLACK INTELLECTUAL TALENT-- GET SERIOUS!!!" As I look around the room at my humbled Black fellow classmates, I become so self-conscious about my white skin that I imagine myself to be an alabaster extraterrestrial. As Dr. Dorsey bellows I shrink into my chair trying to become as invisible as possible. The bell mercifully rings at this moment. As I gather my books together I think I see a few of my fellow classmates frowning at me as they leave the classroom, but it could be just my paranoia.

We're only three weeks away from our opening game and our practices have picked up in intensity. At times it's like war out there—particularly between me and Jason Sharpe. We're both competing for the second point guard position. It's a stretch for both of us because we're both shooting guards. The two of us work furiously on our skills in distributing the ball— mostly to Whee Willie or Linc--, improving our court vision, and mastering the art of penetrating the defense and dishing the ball to a player who comes open when the defense collapses on the penetrator. The competition is marked and to some degree marred by the constant trash talking we heap on one another.

"Come on, White boy, show me what you got," taunts Jason when he's covering me. He sticks so close to me, I think he's Velcro. "Mr. Chocolate, here, is gonna show you how to play this game," Jason continues. Just as I begin my patented fake to the right, he swiftly flashes an unseen hand in my direction and niftily jars the ball loose from my grasp. As he races down the court for an unchallenged layup, I hear him yell, "JUST LIKE IN HIGH SCHOOL." He's reminding me of the time that he stole the ball from me in the exact same way when Coolidge and Cardozo played one another two years before. I return the favor by pump-faking Jason up in the air who then lands on top of me with some extracurricular punches thrown in. Despite the abuse, I go up as he comes down and I make the shot. "A little white bread for Mr. Chocolate to spread himself on," I taunt. He growls and then mumbles. I think I hear him say, "Fuck you, Honky," but it could have been just my paranoia.

Unfortunately, we take our trash talking into the locker room when practice ends. Jason continues with his oft-repeated refrain, "The only reason you made the team is because Coach wants a token whitey."

"Well, this token is sure scoring on you pretty easily."

"Yeah, you got lucky, but you can't guard me either."

"Maybe I could guard you if you stopped knocking me outta the way to set up your shot. In a real game you would have fouled out in the first quarter."

"You white boys are such cry babies."

"You're the one that's crying about my skin color. How come you put everything I do on my race? I'm my own player. I got my own game. I don't play white ball. I play Izzy ball."

Jason is momentarily speechless, but only for a moment. "Well it looks like white ball to me. And you're white ain't you?" At the very next practice, Jason pump-fakes me into the air just as I had done to him the day before. I land on top of his head fists first. He's not amused. He gets right in my face and yells, "I'm gonna kick your mother-fucking white ass."

"I'm terrified," I retort, my voice dripping with sarcasm. In fact I am terrified. I take a moment to have a private conversation with myself that goes as follows: "What are you saying? Are you nuts ? This guy 'll pulverize my Caucasian behind." In fact, Jason was about to punch me out when Whee Willie sees what's happening and jumps into the fracas. "Will you two candy asses cut it out. We've got a game in a week and the two of you need to focus on learning this offense. Now get your heads out of your asses and into the game. Jason glares at me but says nothing more. I turn away and surreptitiously wipe away the cold sweat that has formed on my forehead. "Thank you, Whee Willie, thank you," I mumble to myself. And then, much to my surprise, but probably because I hear it everyday on the Howard campus, I hear myself saying, Thank you Jesus!

Farmland and more farmland! That's all I see as the bus rambles toward the campus of Lincoln University in Southern Pennsylvania. I have gotten it into my head that a northern Black University that bears the name of our 16th President is located—like Howard University--in an urban area. As the bus pulls into the entrance of the university, it goes under a beautiful arch—two flag stone pillars holding up a gently curved grid in blue with orange lettering spelling out Lincoln University. The Alumni Arch, as it is called, is a memorial dedicated to the Lincoln men who served in World War I. A tree-lined drive takes us into the heart of the campus that opens to a mixture of modern red brick buildings and the older Gothic buildings situated on gently rolling hills.

We unload at the gymnasium and make our way to the locker room. I'm shocked to see that their locker room is even older and gloomier than Howard's. The grey lockers and faded blue and orange paint give the impression of a sports program past its prime as if the all too frequent losses have seeped into the walls. The Lincoln Lions have hardly roared for years, at least not in football or basketball. But then neither have the Howard Bisons bellowed. Overconfident we're not. Since there's only two hours to game time, the Coach is dubious about our eating anything and assumes we will play better anyway if we're hungry. We dress in our away uniforms—white numbers on a field of deep blue. I proudly don my jersey with the number 11 on it. My number in high school was 12, which ironically was my per-game scoring average. I would be more than proud if my scoring average at Howard ever equals the number on my jersey. We're in for a second shock when we enter the basketball court. The dilapidated locker room does not prepare us for the beautiful and spacious basketball arena in which we are about to play our first game of the season. It's an attractive regulation size court with bleacher seats on either side that rise to the ceiling. A large number of people are fanning into these seats, and the Lincoln Cheerleaders are already engaged in their shaking and stomping cheers. The atmosphere is becoming electric and I'm surprised by how nervous I feel. I look over to the Lincoln lay up line. They are in their home whites with dark blue and orange numbers. I spot two 6'9" "trees" in the line easily dunking the ball, one after the other. I find that a bit intimidating because our center, Linc Haskins, is the only player we have who even approaches 6'9". I see their sharp-shooting guard, Clyde Bell. He too is easily dunking the ball even though he's just 6 ' tall. I imagine that I'm the only player on the court who can't dunk the basketball. Welcome to college basketball. Whee Willie notices the "look-of-the-condemned" expression on my face and says to me, "Aw White, they ain't nothing; just a bunch of niggers who think they can play." Most Black players I've seen who think they can play, can play, so I find Whee Willie's words less than reassuring.

We know we're in trouble as soon as we begin to shoot around in our pre-game drills. To our Quonset Hut-trained eyes, the gargantuan appearance of a regulation-size court is disorienting. The baskets seem to have lids on them and appear to be miles away from our usual shooting spots. No one's shot is going in. Our horrendous shooting during the warm-up carries over into the game itself. Lincoln takes a quick lead and never relinquishes it. Their two stars, Clyde Bell and Elton Henderson, do the bulk of the scoring. At halftime, Lincoln is leading 30 – 23.

We make a run at them during the third quarter because of the sterling play of Whee Willie and Linc, but Lincoln begins to pull away during the fourth quarter. When the game is out of reach, Coach puts me in. I am petrified. The first time I touch the ball I immediately throw it to a Lincoln player. Moments later, I steal the ball and I race down the court as if I 'm running for my life. I overrun the basket and miss the layup. After missing my first three shots, I finally make a 15- foot jump shot and later make one of two foul shots after one of their trees hammers me on my way to the basket. We lost 65 to 54. I sit by myself at the end of the bench for a few minutes caught between sadness and exhilaration. We lost, but I am now a college basketball player.

The team goes south without me for the next three games. I'm terrified of taking off a whole week of classes, not with my trying to reclaim my academic scholarship. The coach is none too happy with me, but he tells me he understands. But I'm miserable that whole week because I badly want to play. The team goes one and two for the three games. They beat St Paul in Lawrenceville, Virginia, lose to Johnson C Smith in Charlotte, North Carolina, and lose again to Virginia State in Petersburg. When the team has its first practice after their return, I'm so excited to be playing with them again. I greet every teammate as if he's my long lost brother. The next game is against Hampton Institute near Norfolk, Virginia. Since the game is on a Saturday and we return Sunday, I'm able to make the second trip south.

We head for Hampton's campus compliments of "Mr. Greyhound". We stop at the Richmond Greyhound bus station for lunch; and for the first time in my young life, I'm faced with a moral dilemma that requires an immediate decision. Upon entering the bus station, I notice that it houses two separate dining rooms. "This is odd," I think. Why would a company that supports an economy-based means of transportation have two dining rooms? Then I see the signs. To the left is a fairly modern looking` dining room with a sign above its entrance that reads "Whites". To the right is a more dilapidated looking dining room whose sign reads "Colored". I have grown up with "white" and "colored" classified job ads, but, living in a completely white world, I never had to make a segregation-forced choice. I had only experienced segregation as the absence of Negroes-- in swimming pools, restaurants, and movie theaters.

The twelve of us appear to be paralyzed as we stand together equidistant from either dining room. "What are we going to do?" asks Henry Gaines in a fear-distorted warble. For a couple of moments, we just stand there looking at one another. Linc finally announces, "I'm starving, and I need some good food. Come with me." He leads a progression of eight large Negro men and a not-so-large white boy into the whites only dining room. Three of our teammates think it more prudent to eat in the colored dining room. I sandwich my small, fear-racked body between 6'9" Linc and 6'6" Ellis Anderson hoping to make as grandly inconspicuous an entrance as possible. There are about six patrons having lunch. All six look stricken. Their horrified expressions make me think that they're looking at a pack of hungry vampires intent upon sucking the blood out of their "Southern way of life". The look of horror gives way to the infamous hate stare--eyes narrow and cutting, mouths locked in a grim and rigid expression of disgust. But there is no violence and no one says a word. After a few minutes of their wordless unwelcome, all six people go back to their food and pay us no further attention. And much to our surprise, less than a year after the first sit-in, we are served without incident. We revel in the nurturing food of spontaneous social action.

Hampton's campus is an exquisitely beautiful peninsula surrounded on three sides by the Chesapeake Bay. The school opened a year after Howard as the Hampton Normal and Agricultural Institute for former slaves. It was renamed Hampton Institute in 1930.

Holland Hall looked even bigger to me than Lincoln's gym. Most seats are taken and that's no surprise to anyone. The rivalry between Hampton and Howard dates back to the 1920s. We even have the same colors, blue and white. They are in their home "whites". Their jerseys have blue numbers on a white field. We have the reverse. But I'm focused on the size of the court. We now have played four games on courts larger than our practice court, and we are just beginning to adjust our shooting to the more spacious dimensions of our opponents' courts. We spend extra time during the warm-up period on our jump shot drills. Whee Willie has found his sweet spot on the left wing and is dropping in rainbow jump shots in bunches. However, there's practice and then there's the game. During the first half, Whee Willie would go to his spot, but the ball would not drop; and Linc is being bottled up inside by two big men. The points are hard to come by. Home court advantage is real this night. For every shot that Whee Willie misses, Hampton's star guard, Walker Winslow makes his. At the end of the half, Hampton is up by seven, 33-26. Early in the second half, much earlier than I'm prepared for, the coach puts me in. As I make my way onto the court, I quickly scan the crowd of dark faces and the realization finally washes over me that I am the only Caucasian in the building. As I continue to look at the crowd, Whee Willie somehow intuits that I am petrified by my minority status. He walks over to me and says, "Come on, White, pretend you're in Mississippi." I crack up and in the process lose my heebie jeebies. I feel a surge of confidence and energy suffusing my body. Unfortunately, the energy is accompanied by delusions of grandeur. It's up to me to save the team, I think. The first time I touch the ball, I make a 15-foot jump shot from the corner. As I trot down the court, I see members of the crowd looking at each other and I hear them asking, "Is that a white boy?" Two minutes later, I fake a jump shot from the same corner and drive by my defender for an easy layup. In seven minutes, I score 11 points. The team greets me at the next Time Out with surprised glee and enthusiastic high fives. Even Jason Sharpe. The coach is more ambivalent about my scoring and says to me in a voice loud enough that the entire team and some nearby fans can hear, "Now maybe, my little white star will do his job and pass the ball?" "Yes Coach," I reply, still reveling in my performance and the cheers it brought me.

In the fourth quarter, we catch up with Hampton and we are trading baskets until the final minute. Hampton's second string forward is fouled with 30 seconds left, and Hampton is up by two points. He makes one of his two free throws. Whee Willie scores our final jump shot from 25 feet and we lose by one point, 58-57. That shot is from so far out, it should be counted as three points; then Whee Willie's Rainbow Beauty would have tied the game.

Several of my teammates are originally from Virginia and are very much craving "Southern Black Food". So they talk the coach into having the entire team go for dinner at Mama Hannah's, the best restaurant of its kind in Hampton, Virginia. It is a cold December evening when the 14 of us (12 players, the coach and the team manager) enter Mama Hannah's. Although the decorations are nondescript, the place has a warm and cozy feel. There is even a small room in the back in which all of us are barely able to squeeze into. As we pass the other diners, they all seem to be staring at me. Their gaze is not hostile, more curious, as if they are collectively thinking, What's this peckerwood doing in this part of town? There is no serving off the menu for us. Dinner was pre-planned. I am starving, but also nervous about what I am about to eat. The aromas seeping in from the nearby kitchen are promising. Out comes a traditional southern Black Meal: fried chicken, macaroni and cheese, hominy grits, collard greens, fried okra, and corn bread. Although I have recovered from last year's debacle in chemistry class when I panicked as Courtney Cartwright handed me a doughnut, I still am a little anxious about eating traditional black food. I no longer fear becoming "nigrafied", but I have my doubts whether I will like the food. And as I said, I'm starving. Wrong again! I loved everything. The food is a revelation and I keep asking for more. Mama Hannah comes out of the kitchen. She wants to see who is eating so much. She looks at me stuffing my face. She howls with laughter, "Oh my, that little white boy sure can eat!" Everybody in the small room laughs as I continue to eat. The one dish I cannot get passed my lips is chit'lins. Nothing about it attracts me. Whee Willie leans over and whispers in my ear. "I know white people make fun of all this nigger food, but the irony is that a lot of this food originally comes from Indians-Cherokees and Choctaws mostly. And chit'lin's are originally from Europe. Go ahead and give it a try." He could neither convince me that he is telling me the truth or to eat them.

"Aw Whee Willie, you're always making up stories."

"No, Izzy, I'm not jiving you. Look it up." Later, I do look it up, and I learn Whee Willie is telling the truth.

We return to our assigned dorm rooms on the Hampton campus. A half a dozen of us are stuffed in an upper level room that looks and feels like an attic. The radiator heat is going full blast; and when we try to turn the heat down, nothing works. So we open the windows and a cold blast of air hits us in the face. We try to position ourselves in a way that balances the cold blast with the high heat. Needless to say, it is difficult to get any sleep. Since we cannot sleep, we have only one option: engage in the traditional college bull session. And as all college bull sessions must, the topic soon turns to sex. Yet our discussion combines race and sex. It quickly becomes apparent that I, a 19-year-old virgin, am designated the spokesman for the sexual habits of white people.

"Hey Izzy," asks Henry Gaines, "Is it true that white men like to eat pussy?" Now what do I say? "So I've heard," I reply authoritatively.

"Why man? It's disgusting." Hmmm, he might have a point.

"I think because they find it pleasurable. Or at least the women do?"

"Yeah, but the pussy is so near the ass it must smell terrible." With hand on chin, I pretend to ponder his answer. Finally, I say, "Men do many strange things for love."

"Or for a piece of ass, " Henry, says, cackling wildly. "OK, tell me this. Why are white women frigid?" They are? I ask Henry for elaboration. "You know, cold. They don't get into sex. They don't move, and they don't come. I mean I've only been with a couple of white women, but that's how they do."

"Well, Henry 'a couple' is a small sample size. We need more data."

"What we need is more ass, but that's why I'm asking you. You're the expert." I'm so happy that Whee Willie's not in the room, because he's the only one who knows that I'm a virgin.

"You've got to realize, Henry, that there are lots of differences among white women. Some are hot and some are cold. You need more experiences with different types of white women." I'm really on a roll now. Henry leans in closer to me and in a conspiratorial whisper asks, "Can you help me get some?" This sends him into prolonged, high-pitch laughter. "OK, Henry, let me ask you a question. "Are Negro girls easy?" "Naw," he says, it's just that Howard boys talk more. To tell you the truth, Howard girls are tough. Very few 'give it up.'" I can't help myself. I retort, "They don't give it up in general or they don't give it up to you?" Several guys nearby laugh at my comeback. One of them says, "Look at Izzy playing the dozens on Henry. Laughter fills the attic and Henry is not happy. "Kiss my ass, White," Henry replies emphatically, and moves away from me.

I love being the sexpert, cause I'm learning a ton.

Fourteen sleepless members of the Howard University basketball team stumble zombie-like onto the bus that will take us home. We fall into our seats hoping not to fully awake so that we can finally acquire some elusive shut-eye. The cacophony produced by the snoring passengers resembles a lumber mill and eventually wakes a few of us up. Since sleep is impossible, those who are awake start complaining about another missing vital necessity. "I'm hungry!" comes a cry from the back of the bus. "Me too!," complains another. Still another says, "Can't we stop and get some food?" Coach, who was the last to awaken says, "Can't you guys wait until we get home?" A chorus of grumbles erupts. "Come on, Coach, we're starving." "Listen, men, I don't think that's a good idea." "Come on, Coach, we had no problem at the Richmond Greyhound station," Linc Haskins implores. "Yeah, but we're not near any major city. Petersburg is the nearest and that's a hour away." Linc has become the self-appointed spokesman for the team. "We can't wait that long, Coach." "Alright, it's your funeral." I wonder if the coach is speaking literally. Ten minutes later we see a diner and the ravenous group convinces the Coach that the bus should stop here. Thirteen black men and I pile out of the bus and head for the entrance to the diner. We are met by two of the owners. These two burly men in their 50s, I would say, bar the entrance. "Ahm sorry, but we don't serve nigras here. You best be on your way," says one of the burly men. I look inside and the same expression is plastered on the face of each and every patron. I don't have a word for it, but it is a combination of intense fear and hatred. We don't want to make a scene so we turn around and dejectedly make our way back to the bus. Coach turns to me and says,

"White, go order us some sandwiches." "Me, Coach?"

"Yes, you, White. You're the only white man here." I head back toward the diner and, once again, the two burly bouncers greet me. "Ah said, we don't serve nigras here."

"But, I'm white."

"Ya caint be if you're with that group. You is either a high yaller or a nigger-lover and we don't serve neither." It's all I can do to keep my cool. "Look, all I want to do is order some sandwiches for my team. You don't want to lose the money, do you?" The two men confer with one another. "Alright, go around to the back and we'll make you your damn sandwiches."

"Pardon me, I think I said ham sandwiches, not damn sandwiches." I look at the menu and decide to keep it simple. I order 14 ham sandwiches and 14 cokes. The menu says that ham sandwiches are 50 cents and a coke is a nickel. So I figure the bill should come to $7.70. The coach had given me a ten-dollar bill, which should have been enough. When the sandwiches and cokes come, I am handed a bill for $15.40. When I point out the disparity between the menu prices and my bill, I am told, "Take it or leave it." When I tell the Coach I need more money, he says he doesn't have any more money for those honky thieves. "I'm sorry, White."

"Don't be sorry, Coach, They are a bunch of honky thieves." I have to go around to everyone on the bus in order to scrounge enough money to pay the rest of the bill. Two years ago when my cousin integrated Howard's football team, he had to do the same thing. When the team went south, Jayson had to get food for the entire team. These Southern racist crackers are the pits!

Because of my scoring spree at Hampton, I'm promoted to first string, and I start my first college game a week later against West Virginia State. I mostly do my job in distributing the ball to our scorers, but as a scorer I come up with a big blank—zero. We were crushed 67-48. Our next game occurs ten days later during a Christmas tournament at Montclair State University in New Jersey. In the first game of the tournament we battle Albany State. As the game begins and I dribble the ball down the court, I'm suddenly overtaken by a feeling of disorientation. Here I am the starting point guard of a Black basketball team playing against an all-white team. The feeling passes, and we play hard against what I truly believe is an inferior team. Our shots, however, do not fall during critical moments, and we spend the entire game a few points behind chasing Albany State. The final outcome is 64-59. After the game, the five starters sit around long after our other players hit the showers perplexed by the loss and trying to analyze how it could happen. We all sit in the same position with our heads in our hands and elbows on our knees. I'm enraged at myself for missing so many shots, and in my rage I spontaneously cry out, "How could we lose to those CRACKERS?" My four fellow starters look at me with incredulous laughter. Whee nudges Linc and says in between his guffaws, "Look who's calling who a cracker." All four of them just laugh and laugh. Whee finally says to me, "You know what White. I'm gonna start callin' you Izzy Black."

On my 19th birthday, we begin playing our home games at the Capitol Arena, a 2,000-seat arena that mainly hosts wrestling and boxing matches and the occasional country music and jazz performance. We're scheduled to play Lincoln University for the second time. We had lost to them in our first game of the season back in December, and we're hungry for revenge and hungry to end our 6-game losing streak. As a birthday gift to me my parents decide to come see me play for the first and only time. I think they're truly surprised by the royal treatment they're given. They have a special welcoming committee who meet them at the entrance and accompany them to some of the best seats in the house. As we go through our lay-up drills, I can see them being ushered to their seats. My father is wearing a suit and my mother is in an evening gown. You might have thought they're going to a nightclub instead of a basketball game. They're able to see me clearly and wave to me. Although I can see them, I'm too embarrassed to wave back. Yet I'm so happy they have come that I find myself leaping as high as I can during the layup drill. A number of Howard students in the crowd begin to chant my name to a syncopated beat. "Dunk it White! Come on and dunk it! Dunk it White! Come on and dunk it" I'm so moved by this that I try as hard as I can to at least touch the rim and each time I fail by a few inches. I'm the only member of the team who cannot dunk the basketball, which—at that moment-- makes me feel odder than the fact that I'm the only white player on the floor.

The Arena is surprisingly well lit given that it is usually shrouded in darkness during wrestling and boxing matches. The lighting, I am convinced, improved our shooting accuracy by at least 10 to 15%. It's the first time that as a team we are in good condition. We have finally shaken off the limitations of our practicing in the undersized Quonset hut at the University. During our painful and humiliating losing streak, we consistently can't find the shooting range during the early part of the game and run out of energy during the last quarter of the game. I find the size of a regulation gym distorting after the Quonset hut, and I shoot many an "air ball" because my shooting position on a regulation court is further away from the basket than the corresponding spot in the hut.

By this point in the season, we're feeling in top form and finally have learned how to play together. We jump on the Lincoln team very early and never trail. Linc is having a field day. It seems he is getting every rebound and making every shot. He ends up with 40 points and 15 rebounds. Whee Willie is unconscious with his outside shot. He sinks eight rainbow jump shots from over 20 feet. Even though I'm the point guard, I use set screens to hit my jump shot from long distance. Then when my defender tries to over guard me, I blow by him for the easy layup or dish-off to Linc. We are playing our best basketball of the season thus far. In one memorable play, I steal the ball from my opponent and race down the court. Out of the corner of my eye, I see Whee Willie trailing me on my left. As my defender commits to covering me on the developing 2-on-1, I fake going up for a layup and throw a behind the back pass to Whee Willie for an easy layup. The crowd roars its approval and the chanters begin again. "Alright White! White's alright! Alright White, White's alright!"

The other memorable moment of that game is also my most embarrassing. Early in the game I make the mistake of attempting to steal an offensive rebound. As I go up against the two 6' 9" forwards for Lincoln to get the rebound of Whee Willie's errant shot, one of the forwards grabs the ball out of the air and swings his elbow, which catches me right in the mouth. The impact of the blow dislodges my partial plate that houses my two front teeth, and the plate goes flying onto the court. While the other nine players are racing down to the other end of the court, I'm on my hands and knees searching for my plate. The referee, thinking that I am hurt, blows his whistle to stop the action. A spontaneous search party forms and several players from both teams are on their hands and knees looking for my missing dentures. Some of them are not even sure what they are looking for. A great storm of applause erupts in the Capitol Arena when the missing partial is found. We win the game by the lopsided score of 101-59.

As the three of us walk out of the Capitol Arena, I feel like I am being mugged by the cold. The blast of frigid January air that attacks my face and ears fiercely contrasts with the heated confines of the Arena. Linc and Whee Willie are jumping up and down beating their hands against their upper arms. "Man it's cold as a witch's pussy out here," says Whee. I look at him dubiously and question, "I thought the phrase was 'cold as a witch's tit'?" Whee looks at me as if I am a child needing instruction and opines in a mock professorial tone, "You see, Izzy, white men say 'witch's tit,' but black men say 'witch's pussy'."

"Really?" I ask. Whee replies, "It's obvious that you have a lot to learn". Then he looks at Linc, and they both roll their eyes and commence to cackle. They are doubled-over with laughter. After a moment of searing embarrassment, which brings back a flood of memories of my perennial gullibility, I start laughing too. Still laughing, we pile into Linc's 1958 Ford Fairlane.

"You got some brew in this tank?" Whee asks in a desperate tone.

"As it happens, I do," Linc replies with a triumphant grin. As we crack open our beers, I feel a warmth with these two black men that I never thought possible. The warmth of our bodies creates a fog on the car windows that lies like a protective blanket sealing in our friendship. For the first time since high school I experience a great desire to be part of a group. I want more than anything to be "one of them". Linc is just saying how

Whee Willie is his "main nigger". I laugh again at their easy use of this horrid word. The usual controls I place on my speech melt in the warmth of this camaraderie, and without thinking about what I'm saying, I announce, "Well, you guys are my main niggers." Their faces each take on the same shocked and wounded expression. Linc tries to cover up his pain by laughing nervously. But his expression turns grave, and he says to me with barely contained rage, "Izzy, if you ever call us niggers again, we're gonna kick your white ass from here to kingdom come."

"But why?" I protest, " I would never use the word as a slur. Every time I hear you guys call each other nigger, I feel so left out. I just want to be one of the guys, that's all."

Whee Willie's index finger jabs the air in order to emphasize each syllable, "You ain't one of us. You never can be one of us. You're white, Izzy, and that makes all the difference."

"But why?" I ask again, "Skin color is so superficial. Why should it separate us?"

"It's not skin color, Izzy," says Linc, "It's history! Don't matter the context, the word nigger out of a white man's mouth brings nothing but pain and memories of pain."
"And Izzy, " adds Whee Willie, "I'm telling you this for your own good. In every black man you meet there is a scar as old as slavery and you best not poke at it. You can't see it, but by God it's there!"

The light and easygoing mood has disappeared. The three of us sit stone-faced staring at the road ahead as Linc drives us back to the Howard campus. Whee Willie's words prick me, and I feel the beginning of my own scar. I fall into a reverie, imagining what it must have been like to be a slave, to be stolen from one's homeland, forced into middle passage; the agonizing voyage across the Atlantic, chained together and packed like sardines in the suffocating darkness. And if I had survived such a terrifying transport, which I seriously doubt, the nightmare life will have only just begun. A life robbed of freedom, dignity, and one's own name. My faint powers of imagery, which in no way can make real the searing demoralization of such a transformation of one's life, nonetheless brings me such pain and despair that I do not understand how anyone could bear it. I have no real reference point in my own experience to approach such horror. Or so I believe until my mind seems to automatically turn to images of a different kind of human depravity. The terrors of the middle passage turn into the horrors of the holocaust, the systematic slaughter of millions of my tribe. Here I feel for the first time the emotional linking of the degradation of two oppressed peoples who experienced human cruelty in its purest form. As I see in my mind's eye naked dead bodies stacked like cord wood, or naked and barely live ones walking unknowingly into the gas chambers, I begin to feel the same rage, the same scarring disfiguring of my soul that slavery has appeared to inflict on my two teammates. Even as I feel a new closeness to them, they are feeling an increased alienation from me. The remorse I begin to feel is excruciating.

"I'm really sorry, guys," I finally am able to utter. "I wouldn't hurt you guys for the world. You're my main....guys." Despite their anger at me, they laugh at my pitiable effort to revise my offending phrase. Linc drives me to my car, which is parked on Georgia Avenue across from the Kenyon Grill. As I'm getting out of the car, I notice that Whee Willie has a sly smile on his face. "Now don't forget, Izzy," he begins. "If a nigger calls another nigger a nigger, that's cool. But if you or any white man says nigger, that's jivin'."

In February, Morgan State traveled down Route 40 from Baltimore to the Capitol Arena for our second meeting of the season. I was not available—again for academic reasons-- for our 10-point loss to the Bears back in January. Because of that previous absence, the coach put me back on the second team, and I dejectedly ride the bench through much of the first half. Late in the second quarter the coach puts me in and I immediately hit three straight jump shots from about 23 feet. By the third shot the crowd noise has risen to a roar. As I trot back down the court, I give the crowd a quick glance to allow myself to briefly bask in the warmth of their cheers. But I cannot believe the beaming brown face that fixes my attention. It's Desiree jumping up and down, her face suffused with a bright, gleaming grin. That smile takes me completely out of my game. Even as I try to concentrate on the game, my brain is crowded with thoughts of Desiree. I miss my next three shots. My ordinarily quick moves are slowed by thoughts of her, by the pain of missing her, by the yearning I feel for her. Fortunately, Whee Willie and Linc are literally scoring at will and lead us to a 98-91 victory. I manage only two foul shots for the rest of the game.

There is a special sweetness attached to beating an opponent who has already beaten you. It rivals acing an exam after nearly failing its predecessor or rekindling a lost love. All three joys happen to me on this stingingly cold day in February. So I join the raucous celebration in the locker room with the silliest hoots and the loudest hollers. Whee Willie throws water on my head in an attempt to calm me down, but to no avail. Linc and Henry Gaines are both doing the "pony", which is quite a sight because both are naked and well hung. The sweat-soured locker room is soon filled with snapping towels and flying jockstraps. And everyone's game is meticulously dissected for evidence of the grossest deviations from excellence. "Hey White," I heard Jason Sharpe yell from across the locker room. "What happened to your shot? After a couple of lucky rainbow "Js", you went colder than a white woman's pussy." Linc sauntered over to me with a big grin on his face, put his arm around me, and leeringly told the team, "I know why Izzy's game fell to pieces. He kept checking the crowd like he was looking for someone special. And sure enough, there was someone special because I saw Izzy make eye contact with a fine-looking brown mama. Fine as cherry wine she is. And when Izzy made a shot, ooo wee, she was jumping up and down like she was just voted Homecoming Queen." Now Jason joins the leering party and with a malicious grin rhetorically asks, "Who knew that Izzy is trolling for trim on the dark side of the river?" I blush a bright crimson and the heat of it makes me doubly mortified. I'm rendered speechless by this obscene reference to my romantic reawakening.

"Come on, White, spill!" Jason goads. "Who is she?"

"The girl in the crowd? Her name is Desirie and I happen to like her a lot." As soon as this bit of intelligence leaves my mouth, I know I have made a terrible error. At the sound of her name, at least six members of the team mockingly form into a singing group and begin to sing the Doo-Wop hit, Desirie. The sight of six naked brown men huddled together bending their arms and snapping their fingers in perfect synchrony tears from me uncontrollable laughter.

"Almost as good as The Charts, " I say. I really mean it. They're so good I'm in shock and I wonder whether any or all of these guys spent their teenage years on urban street corners mastering the harmonies of Doo Wop in hopes of receiving a recording contract.

The musical entertainment abruptly ends any further inquiry about Desirie. My teammates fall into their usual cliques and whispered plans hiss throughout the locker room. Whee comes over and quietly invites me to join him, Linc and Henry to a party they're going to in Northeast Washington. Whee tries to entice me with promises that there will be an endless supply of beautiful, easy black women who are dying to wrap their legs around me. Whee sees the thin furrow of fear that settles across my forehead; and before I can answer, he says,

"Not your scene, eh Izzy?" With a sheepish smile, I answer, "Not yet, at least."

I sit alone in the locker room, fully dressed and with my winter coat on, lost in thought about why I've just refused Whee Willie's invitation. I can neither stop nor sort through the growing pile of self-accusations that weigh upon my brain. Did I refuse because I am a racist and think it beneath me to associate with Black women? Did I flee from this opportunity because I 'm afraid of Black People? Black women? All women? Or just afraid I'll make a fool of myself? Any thought of success or having a good time lies deeply buried beneath the rubble of my self-doubt. I next begin to brood about my performance during the game, its sterling beginning later ruined by her presence. Why did she show up? Why did her presence affect me so? I take these thoughts and myself out into the icy February evening. My ruminating is interrupted by the soothing sound of a familiar voice. "Hi Izzy," Desirie says with an enthusiastic grin on her face. I can't speak. I just stare at her. She's wearing the same maroon coat she wore when we first met last year. And, as before, she wears her collar turned up, which gives her a regal appearance.

"Hi Desirie," I finally respond. "I was surprised to see you. I haven't seen you at any of the other home games." With a coy smile, she replies, "Well, Izzy, I've been thinking a lot about you lately and I decided I had to see you play. And you were wonderful, Izzy, just wonderful—at least at first. What happened? You made a bunch of shots and then you went cold."

"Uh...speaking of cold, I'm getting cold standing here. I'll walk you to your car. Where did you park?" "I'm just a block away on 14th Street," she said as she reaches for my hand. I am surprised by this gesture and reluctantly take hold of her tiny freezing hand. I immediately feel a jolt of warmth, a dissolving of longing, followed by resentment. What is this about? She has avoided me for so long, presumably because I'm white. I know I haven't changed color. What does she want? I go with the feeling of warmth and contentment and fail to ask her.

"So, Izzy, what happened?" She asks with a smile bright as the full moon. I'm so flummoxed I don't know what to say. I sure as hell wasn't going to confess that I went cold because I saw her in the stands and that destroyed my concentration.

"Izzy?" She asks again.

"Well, you can't make every shot," I alibi.

"Yeah, but you were on fire. Then you went so cold so quickly. It was like somebody poured ice water over your head." I feel pinned to the wall with her questions.

"What's it matter to you?" I ask with bitterness leaking into my tone.

She's taken aback by my response and responds with a loud protest, "I was in the stands rooting for you, Izzy, for you. It matters. You matter." I feel her hand loosening in mine. I 'm so appalled by my snottiness that I immediately conclude that she wants nothing more to do with me. I let her hand go, thinking that is what she wants. But she looks even more hurt. "Well, I gotta go, Izzy," she says sounding profoundly disappointed. "If the spirit moves you, why don't you call me sometime," she utters without looking at me and hurriedly climbs into her car.

I watch her drive off into the freezing night. When she finally disappears from sight, I yell into the night, "WHAT THE HELL JUST HAPPENED?"

Chapter 13.
A Thousand Miles Away

My befuddlement lasts for days. Desiree is a mystery to me and that makes her all the more alluring. I finally weary of my thoughts about her, about us, about the maddening stupidity of racial separation. It's time, I conclude, that I go stick my head in the gathering snow piles outside my apartment window. As I get up to go, the phone rings. Bobby is calling to remind me of our conversation from a month ago about going to Fort Lauderdale for Spring Break. He's just finished the book "Where the Boys Are" which tells of thousands of college students engaging in their annual spring break flight to Lauderdale for suds, sun, and sin of the sexual kind. He's convinced that his recent drought in sexual conquests will come to a glorious end in Florida. "Come on, Izzy, we'll end our sexual drought," Bobby continues his hectoring. Drought? We're talking here about a lifelong ice age.

"Well, I don't know about sex, but I sure could use the sun and the warmth."

"Fucking A, Izzy, it'll be great and I'll drive. Maybe we can get a couple of other people to go to help with the gas."

"Like who?" I ask doubtfully.

"You must know some guys at Howard."

"Actually, I don't. But what I can do is put a note up on the bulletin board in the Student Union and maybe we'll get some nibbles."

"You best believe we will," Bobby crowed with enthusiasm.

My doubts are quickly extinguished when after two days I find several people had responded to my note. Two, in particular, fit all of our requirements. They want to leave and return the same dates, agree to Bobby's no smoking in the car policy, and will pony up money for gas up front. One of our pending travel-mates is a fellow Coolidgite, Len Rothstein. Neither Bobby nor I know Len very well, but our brief encounters in the past have found him to be a very funny and unassuming guy. We didn't even know he is attending Howard. The second fellow is another Izzy, Isadore Brown, who was from Scandia, Florida, right next to Hollywood, a little south of Fort Lauderdale. This Izzy has kinky hair. Except for that, he looks like an ordinary Anglo Saxon with his thin nose, blue eyes, and buttermilk complexion. I know he has an interesting story to tell.

On the last day of February, Bobby and I drive down to the Howard campus where we previously planned to pick up Len and Izzy Brown. From inside a heated car, the day outside looks like the middle of summer. The sun is bright and only a few puffy clouds populate the azure blue sky. In fact it's 18 degrees outside and the slight breeze that blows seems destined to remove an ear from its owner. After a 15-minute wait, we see Len and Izzy, with small suitcases in tow, approaching from different directions in the Yard. Izzy is heading toward us from Cook Hall at the northern end of the campus and Len is approaching from the Student Union on the Yard's southeastern side. They pile into Bobby's 1959 Chevy Bel Air and Izzy and the three of us make our introductions. As we drive off, Len starts in with his complaints about his dorm mates in Cook Hall. "I'm so glad to be going to Florida. I need to get away from Negroes for a while. The Negroes in my dorm are all noisy slobs...." Bobby and I are looking aghast at Len, and Izzy is looking down at the floor. "What?" Len asks, clueless about his faux pas. "Uh, Len, I demur, "Izzy Brown here is a Negro." "No!" Len blunders on, "That's not possible, he's as white as I am. " Finally, Izzy Brown speaks up. "Sorry to disappoint you, Len, but it's true, I'M A NEGRO." Izzy Brown's face is contorted into a horrifying scowl, his impression of Michael Landon in "I Was a Teenage Werewolf," in full lycanthropic transformation.

"Izzy, I am so sorry," Len apologizes abjectly with his hands together in prayer mode.

"That's OK, Len, you can't help yourself." Len completely misses Izzy's pejorative edge and blunders on some more. "Well, Izzy, if you don't mind my asking, how come you're a Negro when you're as white as I am?"

"Well, Len," Izzy replies, imitating Len's pompous tone of voice. "I do mind, because you are the 10 thousandth Ofay to ask me that question. But I'll tell you anyway."

None of us knows what Ofay means. But it doesn't sound good, and each of us makes a private decision not to inquire.

" I am the 10th and last child of a white father and a black mother who live in the black section of Scandia, Florida. Negroes there, like virtually everywhere in the south, live across the railroad tracks. It's like a little town and my father was chosen as the unofficial mayor of this town. We call it Hopetown, while our friends across the tracks call it Niggerville. I have five brothers and four sisters. Each one of my siblings is three years older than the kid below. So my oldest brother is 47. And this may surprise you, every one has completed college, so it's on me to complete the cycle." The more Len hears, the more nervous he becomes. He keeps adjusting and readjusting his glasses. "But your father was really white?" Izzy cut his eyes at Len and says, "I know that question has meaning for you Len, but your binary racial code just can't handle the reality." Len adjusts and readjusts his glasses several more times. "My father was originally from Sweden, but his mother was an American with Seminole blood in 'er. She had married a German named Braun, which they anglicized to Brown when they immigrated to America. My father eventually married a beautiful Negro woman who was living here in DC. And her grandmother was white but was also one fourth Cherokee. After a couple of unhappy years here, she talked him into moving to her hometown in Scandia. He was congenial to the idea because Scandia was originally settled by Danes, Swedes, and Norwegians; All Scandinavians-hence the name Scandia. However, when they got to Scandia, he discovered he had to live across the tracks from his fellow Scandinavians, and because he lived and associated with Negroes, they considered him a light skinned Negro, unworthy of their association, although they never said it that nicely." Len's astonishment grows more intense. "But didn't your mother warn him?" Izzy gives him a smirk and answers, "Let's just say she committed a sin of omission. But my father was the most adaptable man I ever met. He just made the best of whatever circumstances that he found himself in. He soon became a favorite in the community and was thought of as Hopeville's unofficial mayor."

We discover that after a reluctant start Izzy Brown is just getting warmed up. He goes into great and colorful detail about his parents' history in Hopeville, the competitive strife among his siblings, the history of race relations in Southern Florida, how important tomatoes were to Broward County in the early 20th century, and his soporific coup de graces, an extended description of every last detail of his youngest sister's graduation ceremony from Spellman College. His monotonic monologue gets us to the North Carolina border at which point he has put himself and Len to sleep. I too am nodding off, but I fight it in order to keep Bobby company. His eyes never leave the road. He's determined to make it to Florida in one day without going to sleep either behind the wheel or in a motel room. For the next hour or so, we carry on a conversation without his once looking at me. With his eyes fixed to the road, he begins to share intimate details of his relationship with his girlfriend, Judy. They have been entangled in an on-again, off-again relationship for the past two years. Judy is a smart, emotionally needy girl whose constantly fighting parents agree on only one thing—they both hate Bobby. During our senior year in high school, Judy had been forbidden to see Bobby even though it was their clear intention to go together to our senior prom. To facilitate their being together on this propitious night, I collude with them in an act of what Bobby referred to as "stunning friendship". Bobby had hired a limousine and Judy had told her parents that I was her date for the senior prom. I put on Bobby's tux and traveled in the limo to pick up Judy at her house. The limo then drove back to my house and I removed the tux, which Bobby then put back on. They drove off together to a prom that I did not attend. But that is a long and painful story for another time. I hadn't lost sight of the fact that I was once again a decoy, a stand-in for another boy, as I was with Sophie and Sonny Henson a couple of disappointing New Years Eves ago. But this time it was of my own choosing. As we remind each other of that ludicrous tale, we laugh. But the story turns out to be a prelude to a long and sad tale that Bobby relates. With his eyes fixed on the road he tells of their painful, ecstatic sexual relationship. Because I'm a stranger to the act, I'm envious of the fact of their sexual relationship, amazed by the joy of it, charmed by the love that was in it, appalled by the pain of it, and saddened by its absence in my own life.

By the time we enter South Carolina, Izzy Brown and Len have awakened and desperately need to pee. In fact we all do. Before exiting the car, Izzy B puts on a battered old fedora. "What's that for?" I ask. "You see those two buildings over there?" Izzy B points to a brick building on the left that looks like it has seen its best years about two decades ago. Then he points 20 yards to the right to a broken-down shack with nails popping out of the hastily assembled flat boards with vines growing over the roof. "The brick building is the bathroom for white people. The outhouse on the right is for Black people. From here all the way south to Scandia, that's what you'll see for bathroom accommodations for niggers. I ain't no "nigger" and I ain't going in that one. It's disgusting and degrading. So this hat covers my nappy hair and I'm heading for the white bathroom. My advice is for you guys to hope for the best and prepare for the worst." The three of us wail a collective "Oh Shit!" We watch Izzy for a moment as he heads for the white bathroom. Then I say to Len and Bobby in a conspiratorial whisper, "We're not too conspicuous, are we, standing here together gawking at Izzy?" We walk quickly in three different directions and engage in our idiosyncratic ways of being inconspicuous. Bobby sticks his hands in his pockets, hunches his shoulders, and arranges his face in a rather off-putting scowl. Len pretends to read a map while continually adjusting and readjusting his glasses. And I begin to whistle as if I were walking past a graveyard. Izzy Brown seems to be taking a very long time to pee. The longer we wait, the more difficult it is to maintain our nonchalant poses. Beads of sweat begin to appear on each of our brows. A gas station attendant finally appears and asks Bobby, who is closest to him, "You want to fill er up?" The attendant is no taller than Bobby with a snout for a nose, a mean mouth and thin lips. He is straight out of central casting for the part of a paranoid redneck. Bobby says yes and asks the attendant if he would also wipe the windows. Bobby's scowl seems to move itself to the attendant's face, except the attendant's scowl is real. He apparently does not like the sound of Bobby's accent and begins to eye each of us suspiciously. His glare annihilates our nonchalant poses, and our faces simultaneously acquire a guilty look. "You boys from up north?" The gas station attendant asks icily. "Yy-yes," we respond in unison. "Whereabouts y'all from?" His beady, bituminous eyes seek an answer from each of our faces in turn. The air seems to become extremely heavy.

"We're all from Washington, DC, " I finally answer. The attendant mumbles something to himself. I can't be sure, but it sounds something like "Fucking Yankees". Before we can inquire, the sound of footsteps draws everyone's attention to Izzy B making his way back to the car. The attendant stares at Izzy as if he knew. He makes a final inspection of each of our faces and says, "Where y'all headed. "Fort Lauderdale," Bobby answers. "Scandia!" Izzy B suddenly says. He sounds defiant and his tone stirs the attendant's suspicions. He moves toward Izzy, and Bobby; Len, and I look at each other, and we each see the same fear that the others felt. The attendant addresses Izzy. "You from there?" "Yeah," Izzy says, his own suspicions now stirred. The attendant's expression suddenly softens and with a smile he says, "I got a cousin there named Delbert Throckmorton. Ya happen to know 'im?" We could see Izzy relaxing his defensive stance. "As a matter a fact, I do. He runs the pharmacy in town." "That's right," the attendant is now excited. "Well, how about that. I haven't seen Delbert in at least 10 years. Say hello to him for me, will ya. Mah name is Macarthur Blade. Just tell 'm Mac the Blade asks how's it hangin'." Izzy B works hard to suppress a guffaw and responds with feigned enthusiasm, "I sure will, Mac." We wait until we get back on the highway before the four of us explode into uncontrollable peals of laughter. It's as much a release of tension and fear as it is an appreciation of the absurdity of the moment. For us, it's a true bonding moment.

Much of the rest of the drive involves the three of us sleeping off and on while our indefatigable driver, Bobby, remains wide awake the entire time. Whenever I look over at him, he seems lost in deep thought. Is he replaying in his mind his doomed relationship with Judy? Or is his trying to discern the reasons why it's so difficult for him to let girls know the real Bobby Levine? I can't tell. But I do know he is a skilled thespian with every girl he ever tried to get close to. I think it both ironic and an honor that he confides in me more than in any other human being on the planet. Yet, what he most desires and fears is to have an intimate relationship with a girl, a lover and confidant rolled up in one voluptuous and nurturing female. Bobby's reverie triggers my own as a team of images of Desirie and me together step dance in my mind.

No one—not even-Bobby-- thinks we will reach Lauderdale in one day. With this certainty deeply planted in our minds, we made our motel reservations in Fort Lauderdale for the next day. When we reach the outskirts of our destined city at 9 pm, we know we will have to continue on in search of lodgings for the night. We drop Izzy B off in Scandia and make plans for where we would meet in a week to have him join us on the return trip. Afterwards, the three of us ponder where to go from there. Len pops up with the following suggestion: "Let's go to Miami. I've never seen Miami." With no objection forthcoming from Bobby or me, off to Miami we go. To our astonishment, we quickly get a room in a lovely little hotel on Collins Avenue that has its own private 20' x 20' square of beach. Exhausted from the trip, we flop into bed early. We want to rise early in order to spend some time on the beach the next morning before we make our way back to Lauderdale. We have plenty of time since we can't take possession of our room until 3 pm. By 10 a.m., we're lying prone on our private beach with the sound of seagulls lulling us to sleep.

Bobby and I know enough to come out of the intense Florida sun, but when we try to rouse Len, he resists. He promises that he would return to the room shortly. Back in the room, Bobby and I become lost in conversation and an hour goes by before we realize Len hasn't returned from the beach. Fearing the worst, we run down to the beach. There we see Len, his back is lobster red from a deep sunburn, and his face is contorted in agony. In his attempts to rise from his blanket, he resembles nothing so much as a beached whale. Bobby grabs one of Len's arms and I grab the other and we try to yank him from the blanket. He howls like a cat in heat. "Owwwwww," he cries. It sounds like the penitent lamentation of the damned. His piercing cry of contrition continues all the way back to our room. When we finally let go of his arms, he bellyflops onto his bed with a shriek that eventually turns into a muffled moan. His pillow now covers his face. The moan then metamorphs into a snore as sleep overcomes his pain. Sleep, the balm of burned backs.

When we begin our drive to Fort Lauderdale, Len stretches out in the back seat and alternates between snoring and moaning for the entire trip. An hour later, we're at our hotel. We store Len on a couch in the lobby where he immediately proceeds to curl up in the fetal position while Bobby and I register. When we enter our room, we help a staggering Len to a bed where he resumes his concert of snores and moans. We leave Len to his dreams and go to explore the grounds of the hotel. We soon happen upon a courtyard where at least 20 college students have already begun their vacation. Several couples are already seeking Nirvana through intertwined lips and tongue. One gentleman is meticulously stacking beer cans on top of one another. The rest, who already seem well plied with alcohol, are listening to a one-man hootenanny. A rather rotund smooth-voiced fellow is enthusiastically singing "Dr Freud", a hilarious satire on Freud's line of work. At this point in my college career, I know little about Freud, but I have convinced myself that I'll appear sophisticated if I express great joy over the cleverness and sentiments expressed in the song. I proceed to do so. "Oh excellent," I chirp in a British accent. "How devilishly clever," I continue. Bobby follows my lead with "Quite so. Quite so." Observing our anglophile antics are three butterball beings sitting to our right. At first, I think they're triplets. They all have blond flat top haircuts and beer bellies of identical proportions. Their identical tee shirts display Fordham University in huge white letters against a solid maroon background. The butter being in the middle says in an overly loud, aggressive voice, "You guys are from Harvard, aren't cha. I can tell from your accents. Continuing my imitation of an Oxonian accent, I correct, "Not Harvard.... Howard!" The three Fordham butter beings look at each other and begin to smile. The smile soon turns into a chortle and then into a cackle. The three cackling butter beings keep this up for a couple of minutes. Bobby and I respond with a pretended yawn as if we're totally bored by such adolescent foolishness. Finally, the middle butter being says through his laughter, "Howard; ain't that the nigger school in DC."

"Many Negroes go there," I pompously concede. This response elevates their cackling to the level of guffaws. "What the fuck are you guys doing at Howard?" queries the butter being on the right. The face of the middle Fordham flattop assumes the expression of someone who has just had an epiphany. "I got it! You're liberals. I heard that Howard's filled with liberals. And liberals like big government. And that means you're really socialists. And socialists really are no different than communists. That's it. You guys're communists and that's why you go to Howard." After contemplating the meaning of this razor sharp parsing of the political landscape for a few minutes, Bobby and I look at each other in total incomprehension. Bobby asks, "What are you guys talking about? We're not even political."

"So why are you going to that school?" Without hesitating, I reply, "Because the price is right. What's it cost you to go to Fordham?" The butter being on the right answers, "I don't know, maybe about $1,000 a year." "Well it costs a little over $200 a year," I say triumphantly. Middle Butter Being responds just as triumphantly, "Well, we don't have to go to school with niggers and we got academic scholarships." Bobby and I give each other wide-eyed bemused looks because we have no way of understanding this oxymoronic statement. "See ya around," Bobby and I respond in unison to our peers from Fordham. The atmosphere seems to us to be heavy and claustrophobic, and we beat a hasty retreat from the hotel courtyard. We walk the two blocks to Highway A1A that we have to cross to get to the beach. An endless caravan of cars is making its way slowly in both directions. The drivers are carrying on a running conversation with the onlookers standing on both sides of the highway gawking at the train of autos. In a red Ford convertible a very short young man is standing up in the back surveying the scene for appropriate-sized females. Spotting a diminutive but shapely female in short shorts walking in the opposite direction of his car, he yells, "Hey baby, where ya been all of my life." Accepting the compliment, she smiles sweetly, but walks on in silence. People on both sides of the highway applaud the short man's bravado, sharp eye, and philosophy of "faint heart never fair maiden won." The caravan moves so slowly that some intrepid occupants leap out of their cars and ply virtually any female in their line of sight with various pick-up lines. Once they're rejected, they climb back into their cars that have traveled only a few yards. They repeat the process two minutes later and 20 yards further down the road. At one intersection a policeman stands on top of a flat-roofed motel directing traffic through a bullhorn. He manages to convey the laws of the land with a great deal of goofy humor. The entire spectacle is suddenly interrupted by the crack of thunder. Lightning stabs the sky. These are auras of an ensuing cloudburst. As the furious sheets of rain pour down on all our heads, what a moment ago has been a charmed audience of a leisurely display of auto-transported narcissism now turns into a frantic exodus of people from the beach and the scattering of the shelter-seeking sidewalk audience. With no audience to admire their wonderfulness, the caravan of cars close their windows, zip up their convertible tops and zip off. Bobby and I run as fast as we can to get under a building's awning or overhang. Upon our return to our hotel room, we find Len still snoring and moaning. We sense that Len will likely remain in his painful sleep until morning. Bobby and I collapse onto our beds thinking that all three of us will be fine going to bed without our suppers.

The next day we're on the beach early and so are 30,000 other college students. By 10 a.m. the air is redolent with the fragrance of suntan lotion. The sun is already dazzling and intense. The blare of thousands of transistor radios drowns out all other sounds, and the erotic lure of brightly colored bikinis dapples the entire beach. I can't take it all in. The smells, sights, and sounds overwhelm my ability to make sense of it all. In such situations, I zone out and begin a simple reverie of the hungry search for love. "Izzy? Izzy?" The faint voice calling my name finally reaches audibility, and I can make out that Bobby is trying to get my attention. "What?" I ask as I slowly come out of my altered state of consciousness. "Back in your dream world, Izzy?"

"Well, it seems more pleasant there." Bobby is shocked. "Are you crazy? With all these gorgeous half-naked women to look at and pursue."

"But that's just it. I don't see the point of the pursuit." Bobby looks at me like I'm an inpatient out on a weekend pass from the local loony bin. "The point is, Izzy, that you get laid," Bobby opines. Len, having roused himself at the sound of "half-naked women" adds for emphasis, "Laid, Izzy, Laid." The enthusiasm in his voice communicates that there is no greater quest and no great achievement.

"And then what?" I ask in all seriousness.

"And then you put another notch on your gun," Bobby answers.

"And then you can brag to your buddies what a great cocksman you are," he adds with increased annoyance. "And then you don't have to suffer horniness for at least the next 24 hours," Len chimes in. The three of us laugh at the invocation of this well-known state of adolescent malaise. "You know, guys, I was reading the other day that many psychologists believe that all human motivation can be traced to drive reduction." "Drive reduction! What's that?" Bobby interrupts.

"The idea is that humans are born with a number of drives that have to be satisfied. And our behavior is motivated by the search for whatever activity will reduce the tensions in our body caused by these instinctual drives. For example, the hunger drive is satisfied by food consumption, the sex drive, by sex." "I get it," Len says excitedly. "Fucking reduces the horniness drive." "You best believe it," Bobby says, grinning from ear to ear. Our prolonged cackling is interrupted by the sound of a siren. "It sounds like an air raid warning," Bobby guesses. With a look of horror on his face, Len cries out, "The Russians are coming to bomb us!" There are no school desks to climb under. In the wide- open setting of a crowded beach, we are all seized by the heebie-jeebies. We look around the beach to see how other students are reacting to the siren. Just as we expect, hundred of students are running off the beach as fast as they can. "Oh my God," I shout, "We're gonna die. Len picks up my hysteria and wails, "I'm too young to die." Bobby yells, "Stop crying and keep running." We follow the crowd into one of the bars on the boardwalk. But instead of diving under furniture, everyone is yelling out an order to the bartender for his or her favorite alcoholic beverage. "What the hell?" Len grouses. "We're about to die and everybody's gonna get drunk?" "Well, there are worse responses to our pending demise," I suggest. "The hell with demise, we're dying Izzy," Len says with panic written all over his face. He starts yelling at the crowd. "Why aren't you people doing something more constructive than drinking. We're about to be bombed. Didn't you hear the air raid siren?" This provokes peals of laughter from everyone within earshot. A voice already well lubricated with alcohol proclaims, "We're all gonna get bombed, but not by the Russians." More peals of laughter. A golden Adonis with bleached blonde hair says, "That was no air raid siren. That was the signal that the bars are now open." Len looked at his watch and asks incredulously, "At 11 am?" Adonis replied, "Welcome to Spring Break in Fort Lauderdale." As we begin to calm down, we finally hear rock n' roll music filtering through the din. After about 20 minutes, many of the bar's occupants are at least two sheets to the wind. A chorus of slurring baritone voices begins to sing "Bring on the tee-shirts! Bring on the tee-shirts!" The drunken heralds' serenade is successful. As if on cue, several muscle-bound beachcombers hoist four more-than-willing college women on top of four separate tables. They're attired in cut-off shorts and white tee shirts. Another group of males are pouring carafes of water down the girls' chests. The resulting translucence makes it perfectly clear that they were braless and well endowed. With each liquid baptism, the crowd cheers. The girls start modeling and posing. One bends over putting her hands on her knees and thrusting her tuchas out behind her. Unfortunately, I'm in the line of fire and her cheeks meet mine at nose height sending me reeling into the crowd. Bobby and Len can't stop laughing. "Enjoy it, Izzy," Bobby cracks, "That may be the only ass you get on this trip." The likely accuracy of Bobby's prognostication turns me crimson, and I just glower at him. The crowd is instructed to vote with a vocal cheer for the winning wet tee shirt-clad woman. The winner, as determined by a deafening cacophony of growls, whistles, and lust-filled yells, is a tall blonde whose chesty charms is a work of art. She begins to imitate a prototypical winner of a Miss America Pageant by cupping her hands over her mouth in disbelief, shedding copious tears, and hugging each of her three competitors.

After about an hour of imbibing and ogling, the three of us leave arm and arm, mainly to hold each other upright. We stumble out of the bar into the bright sunlight in search of girls. Successful we aren't. So, to fill the growing sense of emptiness, we eat and drink too much. For the next several days, our lives gyrate in a repetitive cycle of beach, bars, and bathrooms.

On the day before we have to go back to our ordinary life, the three of us make different decisions. Bobby and Len want to conclude our trip with a day of extraordinary experiences. I want to be alone. After breakfast, the two of them take off with the enthusiasm and openness to new experience that I imagine characterized the great hunters and explorers of the past. I make my solitary way to the beach. I am alone, pensive, and disengaged from the legion of bare-skinned bodies that surround me. I want no new experiences, but rather just to observe my environment and reflect on my private thoughts. Before me is a peach of a day. The sun shines brightly and its warmth comforts me. The cries of the sea gulls flying overhead bring me an odd sense of peace, a rare appreciation that it is not only tolerable, but also enjoyable to be alone. I notice without feeling or lust the dozens of beautiful young women within sight in bright bikinis that barely cover their breasts and loins as they preen and stretch on their blankets. Many of them have their butts in the air as they lie on their stomachs clutching their untied halters so that no bra strap line will interrupt an otherwise seamless tan. Through the misting glare of sunlight, I'm able to make out from the crowd of beach-walkers another young woman sashaying and sauntering on the wet sands abutting the ocean, stopping every few yards to let the rivulets of incoming water roll over her feet. She is darkly tanned and is about the size and shape of Desiree. I sit bolt upright and try to get a sharper view of her. I know full well that Blacks are not allowed on these beaches. Yet I can't help myself. My heart starts beating furiously and my attention is now acutely fixed on this shadow in the sunlight. I know it isn't her, but the mere possibility that it might be brings up all the pain of longing for Desirie that I have tried to keep at bay during this entire vacation. I am suddenly furious that every woman on this segregated beach is trying their best to shed their white exterior. And Desiree's innate darkness is not allowed here. I rage against the stupid cruelty of Society. Who makes these stupid laws anyway, and why should they be allowed to interfere with my happiness? My happiness. That's a laugh. In my life, happiness has been as elusive as wisdom. I have found precious little of either so far. Is it my fault that I am not happy or is the very idea of happiness twisted and warped by the society in which we live, by prejudice, ignorance, and fear? And then another voice enters the fray. How talented am I. I have fallen and fallen hard for a woman who is taboo, who Society rejects without even knowing her, and my feelings for her make it impossible for me to get interested in any girl that Society might deem appropriate. In reveries and nightmares, I find myself seeking her, pursuing her, and asking myself why I'm so afraid to rebel against these miserable mores. I am 19 years old and already I feel world-weary.

My rant and reverie is interrupted by the appearance of Bobby and Len. Each is standing above me with a girl on his arm. Trailing slightly behind is a shy but attractive girl in a bikini, whose color matches her green eyes. All three girls are cute and curvy, but it is clear that Bobby has pre-assigned the three. It is also clear that he has chosen for himself the most attractive of the three. "Izzy, I want you to meet my new friend, Veyda Minnit." Veyda is blond and blue-eyed. Her entire demeanor exudes sexual desire. Her fire-red bikini adds to this impression. Len follows suit. "And this is Mara Nating." At the sound of her name, Mara clings more tightly to Len's arm and gives me a proprietary smile. "Izzy," Bobby continues, his voice assuming a greater degree of formality, "I particularly want you to meet Miss Claire Azmud." Claire blushes crimson, which adds an interesting contrast to her black hair, green eyes and deep tan. I get up to shake hands with each prize catch of Bobby's feminine treasure hunt. I'm staring at three sets of gorgeous, smiling teeth. My gaze lingers on Claire's face. There is something familiar about it, but I can't place where I might have seen her before. From behind me, I hear Bobby say, "Listen, Izzy, do you mind keeping Claire company? The four of us want to hit the bars and Claire doesn't want to go." I turn toward Bobby and roll my eyes in dismay. I look back at Claire and see that she's staring uncomfortably at the sand. Politeness trumps dismay, and I reply "Of course." Claire and I watch the giggling quartet running toward the bars inadvertently kicking up sand that lands on the sun-tanning occupants of the many blankets they pass. We can hear some choice cuss words from the near-by victims of the quartet's human-made sand storm. This invective produces only more giggles from the insouciant four as they attempt to pick up their pace. More speed, of course, leads to more flying sand and more cussing.

After they're out of sight, Claire and I look at each other confusedly, not knowing exactly what to say. I gesture with my hand inviting her to sit with me on my blanket. Still perplexed by where I might have seen her before, I stare at her with a puzzled expression. She catches me staring at her. For a moment her face registers her embarrassment and then quickly hides behind the camouflage of her brilliant smile. "Why are you looking at me that way, Izzy?" She shyly asks. I can feel myself blushing and the shame beast crawling up my back. "I guess, I guess I find you very attractive," I lamely answer. She smiles in gratitude, but remains silent.

"Claire, where are you from?"
"I'm from a small Florida town called Ocala. Ever heard of it?" For the first time I notice the slight southern twang of a native Floridian. "No, where's it near?"

"Just south of Gainesville. That's where the University of Florida is."

"Is that where you go to school?"

"That's right. I'm a Gator. I just love that school." As I listen to her soft, sultry voice, I feel an attraction to this dark creature. It's a familiar feeling that I thought I could only feel for

Desirie. In fact, I finally realize that she reminds me of Desirie with her black hair, green eyes, and deeply tanned skin. Maybe I've met someone that I could love that Society won't bust my balls about. The possibility thrills me.

Did I feel something for Claire because she reminded me of Desirie?

Was she a stand-in, a Desirie with impunity? A white Desirie?

Our conversation, which becomes increasingly intimate, continues for the next hour—our thoughts rubbing like lovers. We are so into one another that we do not notice that a small crowd of scowling teenagers has gathered around my blanket. The spokesman for the mini-mob is a portly, beady-eyed Aryan, not quite a candidate for Hitler's master race. He barely opens his down-turned mouth when he barks, "Hey you! Nigger-lover! What's she doing on our beach?"

"Listen, my friend," I say with all the sarcasm I could muster, "She is not a Negro. She just has a great tan."

"Don't bullshit me. I know a nigger when I see one," he howls, his eyes now bulging.

"And she can't be here. It's the law," he adds with judicial authority.

"And, by the way, no nigger-lover can be a friend of mine."

"In that case, why don't you mind your own business and peddle your twaddle somewhere else." The portly Aryan and two of his like-minded goons move closer to us. With a malevolent smile, he offers this gem of an idea, "How 'bout I kick your ass instead and physically carry you two off the beach."

"Oh, big man," I hiss, "You need the help of your two scholars there. Portly turns red at this defamatory challenge. He turns to his buddies, still grinning maliciously, and says, "I got this, fellas." He lunges toward me, but tripped on the sand and lands with a great thud on my blanket. He manages to grab hold of only my leg. Claire lets out with an ear-piercing scream. I'm able to dance my way out of his grasp and assume a defensive crouch. He too assumes a crouch, but his globular, drooping belly makes him look like a Sumo wrestler. Portly's crowd of goons cheers him on. This sound, in combination with Claire's screaming, quickly brings the police. Claire manages to convince the two Fort Lauderdale policemen that she is a well-tanned Caucasian. They order Portly and his entourage not to bother us and to go on their way. We decide, however, to leave the beach and repair to the nearest bar for a drink. We don't know what to say to one another. We make our silent way to the Parrot Lounge where we order a couple of brews. As I replay our confrontation with Portly and the gang in my mind's eye, I suddenly realize that I have just lived the same ironic experience that Mrs. Prescott had shared with me a couple of years back. I now had the experience of defending a Caucasian friend accused of being a Negro even though I lack the other ironic piece of the story. I'm not Black.

We are both at a loss for words; we just look at each other. After an uncomfortably long period of silence, Claire smiles at me. "You were very brave, you know."

"Very foolhardy more likely. I'm lucky the police came before that fat tub of racist lard squashed me like a grape." Claire laughs heartily at this image. "Why'd you do it then?"

"I can't take it anymore. Segregation is so stupid. It's psychotic. It makes no sense." Claire looks at me in earnest and says, "I don't agree. I think beaches should be segregated. We have our beaches and they have their beaches. Birds of a feather, and all that jazz. But white people should know that I'm white. In fact, I'm insulted that those goons thought I'm a common nigger."

"WHAT!!" I can't believe my ears. "What are you saying? Thousands of women and dozens of vain men are lying on the beach right now trying to become as dark as they can. And now you're saying that dark people and white people should be segregated?"

"Come on Izzy, you know there's a difference between being a tanned white person and a nigger."

"Would you mind not using that word?"

"What's wrong with it, Izzy. It's a good word. It means that Black people are inferior to whites. That is literally God's truth. It's the way God made us."

I can feel the poison of her words murdering every newborn shoot of positive and romantic feeling that I have so quickly developed for this lovely ignoramus. The painful truth washes over me: She's no Desiree. I feel even more lonely, lost, and alone than I had felt at the beginning of this trip. I make a pretext of looking at my watch and say,

"I have to go."

"Oh Izzy, don't be that way. I really like you."

"Claire, I really have to go." I quickly make my way out into the bright, cleansing sunlight and begin walking back to my hotel. I'm dumfounded and angry and I want nothing more than to bring this date, relationship, and spring vacation to an end. I am ready to go home.

Chapter 14.
See Saw

The "war of no words" between Desirie and me comes to an abrupt end one sun-blessed day in March when she pulls me aside after class and asks if she could speak to me. "Of course," I say trying to manufacture as much nonchalance in my voice as I can. Yet I'm keenly aware of an icy sensation of fear beginning to slither its way through my body. I can see that she's gathering up her nerve to tell me something.

"Izzy," she finally begins, "I know that I haven't treated you very well in the past, but I've been doing a lot of thinking. Despite the fact that you're white...."

"Oh, that warms the cockles of my heart," I interrupt.

"Let me finish, Izzy. It may never have occurred to you, but it's not so easy on my end to go against this stupid color taboo. But I like you. You are a kind person even if you are a little dense when it comes to women...."

"You're killing me with compliments today."

"Izzy, please listen. I want you to ask me out on a date. I know that presents some difficulties for you, but it does for me as well. I sense that you like me too, but something is getting in the way. I suspect it has something to do with the color of my skin. I hope we both can be brave and just be two college students beginning to date. You know, it may not work out, but I'll be damned if I want this ugly social prejudice to deny us the opportunity to find out. What do you think?"

I admire her guts and her ability to speak her mind. She eagerly waits for my answer, her face painted with an uncharacteristic shy smile. "You may be braver than I am," I answer. "Let me think about it." Her expression grows stormy. "You do that, Izzy White," she fires, "You think about it." With that, she spins on her heel and rapidly walks away. As I watch her walking across the "Yard", I descend to a new level of desolation.

Fool! Idiot! Dimwit! Why do I do this? Why do I keep pushing away the very person that I desire above all others?

I sit alone on my favorite spot-- the stone bench next to the Sun Dial. I lift my closed eyes to the sun and feel its warmth hoping it will cool the burning shame that has engulfed me. I open my eyes and see dozens of black strangers walking by me. I watch them parade by, laughing and jiving, and I wonder who they are and what their lives are like. I now have been a Howard student for a year and a half; and despite the fact that I have been on the basketball team and my name consequently has traveled around the campus, I know so few people. I feel more than alone. I feel alienated. It's as if I have taken myself to a planet in another galaxy where there is indeed life, but it is life unfamiliar, a mysterious culture that I have difficulty taking in, a culture that I presume has no use for my white skin. Yet in the midst of this primal loneliness, I have met someone who seems so familiar, and I want so urgently to be close to her, to bathe in her warmth, to meet her skin on skin and to eventually feel growing between us the web-like entanglement of human love. And perhaps through her; I will be taken in by this strange culture, and I will allow myself to become part of it. The prospect of such binding growth also terrifies me. It feels dangerous, unnatural, a one way ticket to self-destruction.

The first day of spring is not auspicious. I awaken to a cold and rainy start to a new season one I hope will promise better days. The chilled silence between Desirie and me does nothing for my mood, which varies a pimple's height from gloom to doom during the six weeks since I last saw her. For better and worse I cannot stop thinking about her. Despite the dreary day just the thought of a new season, a season of rebirth, brightens my mood and cements my courage. I will ask Desirie out on a date.

The ringing phone is dwarfed by the sound of my pounding heart. Desirie's melodious hello renders me momentarily speechless. "Hi, Desirie, it's....it's Izzy." First silence, then an enthusiastic almost seductive "Hello, Izzy. I'm glad you finally called." I'm happy that she had been waiting for my call, but I can't entirely ignore the rebuke in her voice. "Well, Desirie, here's the thing. I want to ask you out but I don't know where to take you that is...uh safe."

"I do!" She quickly interjects. "We can go to the Bohemian Caverns, near 11th and U. They have wonderful jazz shows there and it's an integrated crowd."

I'm dubious, but I say OK. "Are you free this Saturday?" I ask. "I will be," she replies without explaining her use of the future tense. "When's a good time to get there?" She answers around 8:30 pm because that's when the main show begins.

"Great, how about I pick you up at the dorm around 8." There is a pause on the line. Desirie seems to be thinking something over.

"Izzy, why don't you come by around 6:30 and we'll have dinner first."

"Alright," I agree, but I clearly feel that she's dragging me beyond my comfort zone. It isn't that I'm worried about the extra money that I'll l have to spend for dinner, but I know nothing about the quality of the restaurants near campus. Nor am I sanguine about their reception of an interracial couple. Then I remember Chinatown. Maybe one oppressed minority group will be more accepting of another. In an earlier instance of minority removal disguised as urban renewal, Chinese immigrants were kicked out of their original location on Pennsylvania Avenue Northwest where they had lived since the 1880s. When the Federal Government in the 1930's decided to build the Federal Triangle, a complex of government buildings, they moved to the current location of Chinatown between 5th and 8th streets and E and H streets Northwest. One of my favorite restaurants there is the China Doll. Of all the Chinese restaurants in Chinatown, the China Doll seems to me to be more authentically decorated in Chinese scroll paintings, porcelain statues and intricately carved dragon pieces. My favorite knick-knack is a porcelain laughing Buddha (that always makes me laugh) situated next to the cash register. It also is bathed in romantic, even seductive, lighting. An amber glow permeates the entire restaurant. The food is outstanding, if not, in fact, particularly Chinese.

I arrive 15 minutes early at Crandall Hall and therefore sit in the lobby for almost a half hour. When Desirie makes her appearance, it is well worth the wait. I hold my breath when I see her in a halter-topped satin dress of pale lavender that perfectly frames her brown beauty. She is wearing a paisley print shawl over her bare shoulders with colors that meander from a deep plum to a grey that matches her grey suede shoes. Diamond-shaped silver earnings dangle from her clam-shaped ears. I feel under dressed in my blue blazer, tan slacks, white shirt, and skinny striped tie. I secretly pinch myself to make sure I'm not dreaming. I just stare at this beautiful young, brown woman who deigns...No that's the wrong word...desires to go out with me. "Hi, Izzy,' she croons with a smile that sparkles like a cut diamond.

"Hi, Desirie," I return, squeaking like a new teenager whose voice is beginning to change. When I finally gain my composure, I add, "Desirie, you're beautiful. You're a vision."

"Thanks, Izzy." I see crimson suffusing her coffee-colored cheeks. After an uncomfortable pause while I stare and she blushes, she says, "Shall we go?"

It's odd that in almost two years as a student at Howard, I still don't know the area east of campus very well. I need directions from Desirie to get me back to Georgia Avenue. She instructs me to head south on Fourth and make a right at Bryant Street, which ends at the familiar landmark of Georgia Avenue. Once I make a left on Georgia, I know where I am, and it's a straight shot to Chinatown. The heat of the unusually warm day has dissipated, and the night air possesses a refreshing coolness. I leave the driver's side window of my 1954 Plymouth partially open to let in some air. "Let me know if it's too cold in here." Desirie is smiling at me. "I'm fine, Izzy. The air is wonderful."

As I drive down Georgia Avenue, which shortly becomes 7th Street, my head keeps turning as if it's a mechanical toy to look at Desirie. Then I have to forcibly yank it back to focus on the road. Once my adoring gaze lasts a bit too long and Desirie screams, "IZZY, WATCH OUT!" I'm heading right into the path of a 1958 Chevy coming in the opposite direction. I barely manage to avoid smashing into a car filled with Black teenagers who give voice to a resentful chorus of "Dumb motherfucker". Much worse is Desirie's look of fearful disapproval that I have to endure. "Sorry," I utter in a pitiful voice. Much to my surprise, I find a parking spot on the street not far from the restaurant. Once we enter the soft glow of the China Doll, I relax. That lasts until we're seated. I look around at the half Asian, half Caucasian crowd and wonder what they're collectively thinking. Desirie and I are the only interracial couple in the restaurant. She picks up on my swivel-headed fidgeting and says with a frown, "Izzy are you ashamed of being out with me?"

"No, not at all," I answer in a voice that registers close to zero on the truthfulness meter. Her rebuking question brings me back to the joy of the moment. I'm out with the girl I love or think I do. Her loveliness dazzles, the aromas that float around the restaurant have me salivating, and the combination puts me in such good spirits that I can finally give her my complete attention. With greater conviction, I tell Desirie that far from being ashamed, I'm thrilled to be out with her. She smiles and coyly buries her head in the menu, "What are you having Izzy?"

"I always get the same thing here, "Shrimp Chow Mein and Egg Drop Soup. This combo's so good, it's hard for me to be adventurous."

She gives me a sly smile and said, "I think it's hard for you to be adventurous about anything, Izzy."

"How can you say that?" I protest. "I'm out with you, ain't I?" With a pained expression, she asks, "What does that mean?" By this time our voices are raised, and I notice that patrons at nearby tables are looking at us curiously. I'm angry with myself for blurting this out and abjectly apologize.

"What are you sorry for, Izzy, for telling the truth? For thinking that you are some kind of racial pioneer by deigning to go out with a poor little nigger like me?"

"Come on, Desirie, that's not what I meant."

"Well, what did you mean?" Glints of amber light are reflected in her angry green eyes. I'm helpless and undone by her anger, and I'm clueless as to how to turn her temperature down from fiery fury to loving warmth.

"Can we just order? What are you having?"

"No, Izzy, I want to hear from you first. What is this date about for you? I thought you liked me, but I'm beginning to wonder whether you're just trying to prove to yourself what a great white liberal you are." She might as well have branded me "white liberal" with a branding iron. I howl with pain and rage. "If that's what I wanted, I could've picked any black girl, but I picked you. I've had the hots for you since the day we met, and I think you know it, have known it. Besides, you're the one that rejected me because of my skin color or don't you remember that?" Her face went crimson but this time not because she's flattered by my compliment but because I have held a mirror up and she sees that she's guilty of the very crime she's accusing me of. Chastened and drained of her rage, she softly states her apology. "You're right, Izzy. This is what I want to avoid--having this stupid social taboo make it impossible for us to get to know one another."

The soup course comes and the seductive aromas calm us. The combination of my egg drop soup and her won ton sets us both to smiling, first at the soup and then at each other. The flavor of my soup is so subtle and satisfying that it sends my mind back to a nine year-old memory when my uncle took me to Philadelphia. He wanted to show me "where Democracy was born". But I was more interested in the food. One night we walked a few blocks from our hotel and found two Chinese restaurants that were next-door neighbors. Ravenous, I bounded up the steps of the restaurant on the right. "Izzy, come back here," exclaimed my uncle, clearly perturbed. "What?" I asked. "I'm starving!"

"Just wait a minute," he ordered. "Just be patient." The way my hunger was gnawing at my innards, I knew that patience was quite beyond my 10-year old control. My uncle watched and waited. I paced back and forth, occasionally giving him a silent imploring look. After a few minutes, people emerged simultaneously from both restaurants; except the patrons on the left were all white and those on the right were all black. "We'll go here," my uncle said authoritatively, pointing to the left. I saw no logic to his decision and I asked why here. He said, "This will be fine. Come along now." My hunger blotted out all awareness and contemplation of the real reason for his directional tilt. The restaurant he chose, however, was truly elegant. I had never seen such elaborate decorations in any Chinese restaurant in Washington, and I immediately concluded that Chinese people who live in Philadelphia must be rolling in the moolah. "I know this place's reputation, Izzy; let me order for you. I know this is hard for you, but regardless of how awful the name of the food sounds try not to judge it by its name. Just taste it." This was very difficult for me. When I find something I like, I order that dish over and over again because I know I won't be disappointed. Trying something new always felt very risky to me. Out comes the first dish—Jellied Egg Drop Soup. "Jellied?" I cried. "What does that mean, Uncle Sol?" I imagined great globs of grape jelly hiding under the otherwise familiar looking soup.

"Just taste it, Izzy," my uncle barked impatiently. I gingerly collected some soup on my spoon, scrunched up my nose and reluctantly place the spoon in my mouth. It was magic. I had never tasted anything so marvelous. The taste was so new, unexpected delightfully velvety on the tongue. The first swallow created an itch that was impossible to satisfactorily scratch. I kept going back to the beautiful soup terrene that was decorated by a succession of dragons linked tail to mouth all around the bowl's circumference. More helpings followed until I drained the terrene entirely. My uncle gave me a disapproving look. "I hope you have room for the other dishes," he said with his mouth turned down in disdain.

Here I am now having my usual egg drop soup and shrimp chow mein for the same reason I ordered this combo 10 years ago. I look up from my soup to see Desirie smiling at me. "Izzy, what are you thinking?" Her voice is as velvety as the texture of my soup. " Oh, nothing much. Just how much I love this food. How about you? What's percolating inside that capacious mind of yours?" Did I just say capacious? How pretentious.

"I was just imagining my parents' reaction if I brought you home."

"Why, are your folks prejudiced against whites?"

"Distrustful is probably a better word. My father can't imagine any white man wanting to be with me except for sex. Mom's not as bad, but she worries about me having sex ...with anybody. She's not in a hurry to become a grandma." This conversation is generating pictures in my head of our being naked together. Although I'm in a sharing mood, I decide not to share that picture with her.

"I know you told me that your father is a lawyer at Justice. Does your mom work?"

"Yes, she teaches history at Terrill Jr. High School."

"I know Terrill. I was there once when I played basketball for Paul Jr. High School. Terrill was one of first Black schools I was ever in. I was flabbergasted. We were held in the locker room until an announcement came over the PA system that it was time for the teachers to escort their particular classes to the game. Then and only then were we allowed to enter the gym. And the gym was beautiful, much newer and bigger than the gym at Paul. The game was also a novel experience. Several of the fans were firing paper clips at us. We all got hit. During the game we spent as much time dodging the paperclips as we did trying to escape our defenders. We also experienced the fast break for the first time in our lives. Those young boys ran us off the court. We left with a loss, but with our lives intact and happy for it."

Desirie is beaming at me again. Embarrassed, I quickly change the subject back to her. "Do you have any brothers or sisters?"

"Yes, Izzy, I have a brother and a sister."

"Are you the oldest?"

"No, I'm the youngest. My brother is four years older and my sister is two years older." This last piece she says with a hard edge. And then added, "You know, Izzy, I'm beginning to feel interrogated."

"I'm sorry, Desirie. It's just that I want to know all about you." Not taking the hint, I keep up the interrogation. "What do they do?' She shoots me a look that expresses both annoyance and resignation. "They're both ordained ministers and both graduated from Howard's divinity school. "

"Oh, a case of sibling Biblery, eh?" Desierie guffaws at this silly pun. She clasps her hand to her mouth to prevent the extrusion of some yummy but seriously masticated egg foo young. "Izzy, you slay me. Your joke happens to be true. My brother Thomas graduated from Howard's divinity school last year, and Lydia is now a junior there. Poor Lydia has to put up with her professors constantly singing Thomas' praises. 'Oh I hope Miss Jackson that you will do as well in my class as your brother Thomas. He was one of my best students ever.' And Thomas has always resented the fact that whatever he tried, Lydia had to imitate him. Would you believe that both of them were track stars in high school and excelled in the same events? And to hear them argue over who knows more about the Bible, Lord have mercy. At every family holiday, they quote scripture at each other as if they were firing bullets."

"Are, are you religious, Desirie?" I ask tentatively, afraid of her answer.

"Not like they are," she answers. "I do believe in God, don't you, Izzy?"

"Well, I'm not sure. Even if there is a God, it's hard for me to believe that he is a merciful God or even a very good engineer." I see her eyes widen with shock and I become nervous. "What are you talking about, Izzy? What are you saying?" She makes no attempt to hide the dismay in her voice. "You've heard of the Holocaust?"

"Of course I have, Izzy?"

"Well, how could a merciful, all-seeing, all-knowing God allow six million of His allegedly chosen people to be systematically murdered?"

"Oh come on, Izzy, that was not God's fault, that was man's."

"And who made man, supposedly in His image? Like I said, not a very good engineer. Whether He lacks mercy or skill, He does not deserve the reverential praise that believers lavish upon Him. I choose not to believe in such a deity. It is the only rational conclusion I can draw." We lapse into a commonplace discussion of faith versus reason that produces more heat than light. And the more heated we grow, the colder our food becomes, and the more it loses its delectable flavors. To bring the temperature down, we're silent throughout the final stages of the meal.

Our silence continues as we leave the restaurant.

The spring evening air has drastically cooled, as if the season changed while we were having dinner. As we make our way to my car, our breaths forming parallel puffs of smoke, I wrap my arm around Desirie to ward off the dying winter chill. She does not reject this proprietary kindness. Once in the car, I'm gratified to find that the car miraculously starts right up. I head north on 7th Street in search of Florida Avenue. The inefficient car heater compels Desirie to move closer to me and the great thaw is on. I don't know if it's the continuing silence or the feeling of her body touching mine that gives me the heebie-jeebies, but I try to calm myself with a mousy-voiced plea to be restored into her good graces. "I'm sorry if I upset you," I said with a tear in my voice. "I'm not upset with you, Izzy, I just don't understand you." This is said with such forgiving softness that my heebie-jeebies completely melt away. I want to make another attempt to explain my views, but I'm afraid I will lose the developing closeness between us. Instead, I beat a hasty withdrawal from the topic of God, a topic that torments me on a regular basis. I want to believe in a loving, merciful God, but the concept makes no intellectual sense to me; not with the overwhelming evidence of human depravity, unanswered prayers, and unrewarded virtue that I have collected through experience, reading, or from watching the always painful NBC evening news. I think if I share my views, Desirie will be even more perplexed.

Instead I give all my attention to driving and the search for Florida Avenue. I'm so concerned that I might miss the turn that the heebie-jeebies return. "Am I close? Do you know how soon we will get to Florida Avenue?" I ask, my voice and pitch rising with each question. "It's two blocks up, Izzy. Stop worrying! I'll tell you when to make the left turn," Desirie replies with a hint of exasperation in her voice. I'm a stranger driving in a strange land and fearful that Desirie is beginning to see me as strange. "It's coming up now, Izzy. Make a left at the light." I had recently learned that Florida Avenue was originally called Boundary Avenue because it represented the northern boundary of the original city of Washington. I feel like I'm crossing some boundary and entering an unknown, unexplored part of the city, an area in which I do not belong. We cross 9th street and Florida Avenue has become U Street. Two blocks later we arrive at the Bohemian Caverns. "You know, Izzy," Desirie says enthusiastically, "this jazz club opened in the 1920s in the basement of a drug store and was originally called Club Caverns. They later changed the name to the Crystal Caverns and only two or three years ago did it become the Bohemian Caverns." She can barely contain her excitement as she continues. "All the great black jazz artists played here, including Duke Ellington, Cab Calloway, Louis Armstrong, and Miles Davis." "That's amazing," I say, as I try to convert my heebie-jeebies into genuine excitement. We enter the darkened cave-like structure and find the room filled with little round tables, each with a small lamp that barely illuminates the table. The walls have been artistically rendered into faux stalactites and stalagmites. The ambience exudes cool on so many levels. A low buzz of conversation fills the room while the live entertainment is on break. As I survey the room, I see that most of the couples are Negro. The sight of several interracial couples helps me relax, and I notice one or two white couples. We both order whiskey sours; and while we wait for our drinks, Desirie begins touting the talents of the featured act, The Modern Jazz Quartet. I have never heard of them, but she is "deeply in love with MJQ".

"Izzy, MJQ has introduced a whole new cool and mellow sound to Jazz. The group started about a decade ago by Milt Jackson who plays the vibraphone." Her enthusiasm is infectious and I find myself getting wound up before I have even heard a note. We're sipping our drinks when the MC begins his introduction.

"LADIES AND GENTLEMAN (he's screaming) THE BOHEMIAN CAVERNS IS PROUD TO PRESENT THE MODERN JAZZ QUARTET WITH MILT JACKSON ON THE VIBRAPHONE, JOHN LEWIS ON PIANO, PERCY HEATH ON BASS AND CONNIE KAY ON DRUMS." For such a small place, the applause is thunderous. I imagine that everyone but me is deeply knowledgeable about the merits of MJQ.

MJQ begins its set with the eponymous "Bag's Groove" written by Milt "Bags" Jackson. I'm hooked from the first colloquy between Jackson's vibraphone and Lewis's piano. This mellow new sound, aided by the alcohol I'm by now too rapidly imbibing, slides effortlessly into my brain. I'm well into my second whiskey sour when I think I notice the faux stalagmites undulating. Everyone in the Caverns seems to be undulating as well, all in the same direction, as if they're gesticulating toward the quartet. And Desirie is moving her head in such a sensual, rhythmic sway that I'm once again filled with desire for her. Every once in awhile, she turns toward me and bathes me with a joyous smile. The quartet moves through a number of their previous hits such as "Django", "Nights in Tunisia", "Pyramid", and "Round Midnight". After the first set, I'm still slightly woozy from the alcohol. Desirie's head seems to be swaying to the sound of silence. So I try to mimic what I see. "Izzy? Izzy, the music has stopped and your still boppin'." I begin to drum a syncopated beat on the table to accompany my awful singing:

The music's stoppin'
But I'm still boppin'.
The music's stoppin'
But I'm still boppin'.

Desirie starts laughing. "Oh Izzy, you're drunk."

"No, I'm not," I protest. "I'm just doing what you're doing... boppin'."

"But I'm not doing anything. It's all in your pickled brain. I've never seen a drunk white boy before," she muses. "Well am I any different from a drunken Negro?'

"The black men I know who have been drunk are either mean or boisterous. You're just silly." As I lapse into a paraphrased version of the Clover's hit, "Ting-A-Ling",
Desirie's eyes spread wide with horror. "Izzy, stop!" I see and hear her say this but her entreaty does not register. I get up and do the snap and continue singing the chorus to "Ting-A-Ling". Desirie starts tugging at my jacket trying to pull me back down into my seat. "Izzy, you're embarrassing me." The audience is laughing at me, but clapping loudly to spur me on. I comply with Desirie's forceful tugging and clumsily fall back into my seat. "What was that about, Izzy?" By now, Desirie is angry. I look into her eyes with a doleful, imploring gaze, and utter with mock solemnity and in the Blackest accent I could muster: "But, honey, I'm just a po' white boy." Desirie is furious. "Now you're just being an asshole."

"Desirie, I'm serious. I know I'm a little tipsy but I'm trying to tell you that I have strong feelings for you."

"Yeah, right. By making a fool of yourself? By embarrassing me? By imitating a Black singer? You've got to be jiving me." With a downcast look, Desirie stares into her drink, and gently and slowly shakes her head. She looks like she has lost her best friend, and I feel like my hopes that she will reciprocate my intense feelings for her are obliterated by my inadvertent minstrel show.

We're silent throughout the MJQ's second set and leave quickly when it is over. As I head back to her dorm, Desirie breaks the silence. "Izzy, I don't think this is going to work out. Maybe we should end this now before we both really get hurt."

"Why are you saying this? I got a little drunk and acted silly. Is that such a crime?"

"Look, Izzy, I'm not upset just because you made a spectacle of yourself. It's the way you did it, imitating a black accent, dancing like your idea of a black man dancing. It wasn't just silly; it was offensive. I know you didn't mean to be insulting, but you're trying too hard to be what you think I want you to be. You're trying too hard to be Black and that's not what I want."

"Well, what do you want? Before you rejected me because I'm white."

"I rejected you because I was frightened," she fiercely rebuts. Then more softly, she adds, "I just want you to be yourself, Izzy, that's all." When we arrive at the dorm, she quickly collects her things together, hurriedly gives me a peck on my cheek and curtly says, "Goodbye Izzy." And she's gone.

I just sit in my car, bluer than I have ever been. I turn on WOOK in the middle of "Music for Lovers Only". The announcer is about to play The Closer You Are by The Channels and he is listing the requesters: "This goes out for Bob and Carol, Gerald and Livonia; for the Bossman and Anita, Clarence and Sweetlips; for Claudina and Louis, Snooky & Dreamgirl; for Ramon & Jackie, and...........

Chapter 15.
A Change is Gonna Come

I sit in the car for the longest time feeling underwater, drowning in grief. My tears won't stop. I can't lose her. I have to get her back. I can't bear to be without her. I look up at the shaded floor window of Crandall Hall and see the dark silhouette of three women apparently engaged in a gabfest. I imagine them to be Desirie and her two closest friends talking about me and my ridiculous antics at the Bohemian Caverns. I imagine that I can read the lips of the dark silhouette I took to be Desirie. She's waving her hands in disgust and telling her friends, "What was I thinking trying to date a white boy, especially a white boy as crazy as Izzy White. Moments later, I see the three silhouettes bobbing up and down in apparent laughter. I'd swear on a stack of Bibles that Desirie is recounting every embarrassing thing I said and did throughout the course of our relationship. I sit here in my car with my head in my hands sobbing and feeling the chilled blanket of shame straight-jacketing my entire body.

That imaginary scene of Desiree and her laughing friends freezes me. I believe in my image completely and conclude that she wants no part of me. As much as I want to contact her, I'm too ashamed, too vulnerable to try. I see her every week in our sociology class, but I make no effort to speak to her. If I catch a glimpse of her coming or going from class, I turn my head away. Oddly, I think about Desiree only when I'm on campus. She completely slips my mind when I'm home or with my white friends, only to again haunt my thoughts when I return to campus.

It's a warm day in April when I am wandering on campus, lonely as a cloud, and lost in thought about Desirie. I feel a hand grab the scruff of my neck. I jerk myself free fearful that I'm being attacked. I whirl around to see who my "attacker" is and I am shocked to find that the hand that has grabbed me-- and the person to whom it belongs--is white. It's Phil Workman who's staring intensely at me with a predatory grin covering his face. "Hey, Izzy," he says in an overly cheerful voice, "How's it hanging?" I show him my hangdog expression and reply, "It's hanging like a dead weight. How're you hanging?"

He stares at me out of large black saucer eyes. "Izzy, I want you to do something for me that I think will redound to your great credit." Redound? Never heard that word before, but it sure is lovely.

"What do you want, Phil?" His eyes get even bigger, approaching the size of frisbees.

"I want you to go with me to a NAG meeting. The next meeting is Sunday, April 2nd at the Newman House."

"Well, I don't know."

"Come on, Izzy, you'll meet some wonderful, committed people who want to bring some long overdue justice to this world. Look, I'll even pick you up. Where do you live?"

"Langley Park."

"Oh shit!"

"Phil, you don't have to pick me up. I'll drive down and meet you there."

"THEN YOU'LL COME?"

"YES, I'LL COME," I said, mocking his enthusiasm.

I leave my apartment around 11:30 on Sunday morning. I want to get on campus early because I'm not quite sure where the Newman House is located. I arrive around 12:30, and it takes me another 30 minutes to find the place. No one has informed me that it's located several blocks off-campus. I walk into the house and am immediately confronted by a giant crucifix, which set off alarm bells. What the hell am I doing here?

I find the meeting room in which about 25 people have congregated. Among the group are about a half a dozen white students, many of whom I've noticed around campus. They're all listening with rapt attention to a bespectacled Negro gentleman talking about the various demonstrations that NAG has engaged in DC, Maryland and Virginia protesting against segregated restaurants and other business establishments. I scan the room hardly listening. I see another crucifix on the wall and am disturbed again by an inner alarm. I finally espy Phil who turns around to survey the room. Spotting me, he nods with an ear-to-ear grin. Then I see her….Desirie…. sitting two rows in front of me and off to my left. From that point on, I see nothing else nor can I take in any of the people. I only faintly hear the political strategizing, the self-praising of NAG's efforts to organize the campus and their call for volunteers to participate in the pending Freedom Rides. Desiree must have come to the meeting from church because she is done up in her Sunday finery, white dress and a white wide-brim hat. I thought she had not noticed me, but she made a special effort to track me down after the meeting. "Izzy. Oh Izzy, I'm so glad you came. Isn't it exciting?"

"What?"

"The Freedom Rides. This is our chance to get on the front lines of the struggle; to change the world."

"I'm not sure what you mean, Desirie."

"Didn't you hear all the talk about what CORE is doing?"

"Well, I had trouble hearing the speaker," I alibied. OK I lied. "Why don't you fill me in? In fact, do you have time to get some coffee at the Student Union?"

She looks at me probingly for a moment and then says, "Sure."

As we walk over to the Union, she tells me about CORE's plan to challenge segregation in interstate travel on buses. Segregation, in fact, had been ruled illegal by the Supreme Court last December in a case called Boynton v. Virginia. Bruce Boynton was a Howard University law student who was arrested in 1958 for attempting to desegregate the Richmond Trailways terminal. The Court ruled that state laws requiring segregation in lunch counters, restrooms, and waiting rooms are unconstitutional. The purpose of the Freedom Rides is to make sure this monumental change in the law is being enforced. The fact is that despite the Court's ruling, Negroes are still being arrested and harassed if they try to desegregate bus terminals or sit in the no-longer valid "whites only" section of a bus. James Farmer, CORE's Director, and his associates came up with a plan for a "Freedom Ride" from Washington, DC to New Orleans. When we finally sit down at an available table, Desirie continues.

"Anyway, CORE is trying to recruit a dozen or so volunteers, bring them to Washington for three days of intensive training in nonviolent tactics, and then leave on May 4th. The Freedom Riders, as they will be called, will be split between Greyhound and Trailways buses. They'll travel through Virginia, the Carolinas, Georgia, Alabama, and Mississippi and be in New Orleans on May 17th, which just happens to be the 7th anniversary of the Brown v. Board of Education decision. Isn't it exciting? And Izzy, I've volunteered."

"You've what?" I get the heebie-jeebies just thinking about what a mob of Alabama rednecks might do to her. "Desirie, this Freedom Ride sounds extremely dangerous!"
"It is, but I'm prepared to put my life on the line for our freedom."

I just look at her, speechless with fear and apprehension. However, I'm not prepared for what comes next. "And Izzy, I want you to volunteer too."

"You what?" Are you out of your cotton-picking mind?" I guess picking cotton is not quite the metaphor I was striving for. "Seriously?" She says with a pained expression.

"I'm sorry. You know what I mean. I' m just so afraid you'll get your head bashed in by a bunch of crazy Crackers." Now she laughs. "Izzy, your metaphors are something else. Look, I know it's dangerous, but the Freedom Ride is a wonderful opportunity for us to be together, sharing in a struggle we both care about. I know you hate segregation and injustice. You wouldn't be at Howard if you didn't."

We sit in silence for what seems a millennium, just looking at each other. Her imploring expression dissolves into the warm smile that always sends my physiology into perturbations. "Well, Izzy," she finally asks, "Will you come with me? Will you volunteer?"

"I don't know, Desirie. I have to think about it."

"Yes, Izzy, do think about it. And think about acting on your convictions. Or are you all talk?"

"Listen, Desirie, the truth is that I have thought about it and I can't go."

"Why not?" Her eyes are now wide with frustration.

"Well, first of all I'm on scholarship and I can't afford to take two weeks off from classes and homework. You know what happened to me last year when I lost my scholarship. I can't afford to lose it again." Now she's angry. "Oh Izzy, you're smart enough to make the work up. "

"Well, I guess so," I respond sheepishly.

"Then you'll volunteer?" I look at her eager face lighting up with hope, and know that I cannot disappoint her. I tell myself that it's all for a good cause.

"OK, Desirie, I'll volunteer, but they probably won't take me," I say, trying to prepare her for the strong possibility that I won't be going with her.

"Oh, Izzy, that's wonderful. I'm so proud of you." She just grins at me for a long moment, and I see that tears are welling up in her eyes. "Well, Izzy, I've got to run." She leans in and kisses me on the cheek and hurries off. Without looking back, she waves the back of her hand and cheerfully says "See you at the training sessions." I watch her bounce away until she's no longer in sight. And when she's gone, my body sags from the weight of what I have just promised her. I am scared out of my mind. Once again the internal debate begins. This is not my fight. I mean who ever helped the Jews? Maybe the idea of Freedom Rides is too radical an approach to change. Maybe I'll lose my scholarship again. But I know the real reason for my doubts. I don't believe I will make it back alive, and I do not relish the idea of dying so soon. I can hear the southern white bigots screaming, "Let's get the nigger-lover. He'll wish he'd never brought his Commie ass into Dixie."

The consequences of my decision hit me full in the face when I have to sit down and write a required essay explaining how and why I have become committed to nonviolence and civil disobedience. I'm not sure I'm fully committed to either. An even more formidable obstacle is obtaining my parents' permission to volunteer. CORE required parental approval for all volunteers under the age of 21. Somehow I cobble together an essay that even Gandhi would have been proud of. Then I convince my mother to let me go and leave her the unenviable task of informing and convincing my father. With essay, permission slip and suitcase in hand, I show up at the Fellowship House down on L Street between 9th and 10th late Sunday afternoon, April 30th to begin three days of intensive training in nonviolence. I meet the other dozen or so volunteers at dinner who range in age from 19 to 61. There's an elderly white couple from Michigan that catches my interest. I really look forward to getting to know them and learn how they come to volunteer for the Freedom Ride. I sit next to Desirie at dinner and think to myself that this is an odd venue for us to have dinner together. I enjoy it nonetheless.

In the morning, James Farmer, the National Director of CORE, starts the training session by telling us in his booming baritone of the importance of CORE, of the Freedom Ride, and of the imperative to remain nonviolent regardless of the provocation. He outlines the itinerary of the Ride and the possible positive and negative outcomes. After he speaks, CORE's general counsel orients us about constitutional law, federal and state laws pertaining to discrimination in interstate transportation and informs us of what we should do if we get arrested. Other speakers make us aware of the racial mores in the South and the lengths to which the local citizenry will go to force compliance with these social rules. One speaker tells us what's really going to happen to us and that we could be badly beaten or even killed. Later during that first day, we read the classic texts of nonviolence, including Thoreau's groundbreaking essay on civil disobedience written in 1849, and Gandhi's rules of civil disobedience.

The first day goes well. I'm becoming more attracted to the philosophy of nonviolence despite my initial grave doubts. My doubts are less about the validity of the philosophy then my ability to be nonviolent under provocation. At dinner that evening, I'm filled with joy and love for all of humanity as I sit next to Desirie for a second straight night. I can't imagine ever being happier for I have simultaneously found a love and a cause. After dinner, Desirie and I sit around with a number of the volunteers talking about the upcoming Freedom Ride. The discussion soon turns into a philosophical debate about power, violence, and nonviolence. It takes me awhile to open my mouth, but when I do I spill my guts about my admiration for Gandhi's Rules of Civil Disobedience, and my fears that I won't remain nonviolent if a bunch of angry ignoramuses start knocking me upside my head.

"But Izzy, that's what this training is for. We all have that fear and that difficulty," said a white volunteer from Arizona.

"I know, I know," I exclaim, frustration and fear pouring from my voice. "But can I do it? Can I remain nonviolent while being beaten to a pulp?"

During the second day of training, the intensive role-playing sessions begin. These sessions are designed to serve as rehearsals of the shit that is to come our way. Before my turn comes, I watch people being called awful names, slapped, kicked. Coke and other unpleasant substances are poured on their heads. The more I witness, the more uptight I get. When it's my turn, I feel no Gandhian sense of calm, but rather I sit on the imaginary bus station stool hunched over like a cornered beast. During the exercise, I surprisingly can handle being called a "nigger-lover", but when they pull me out of my chair, start kicking me and calling me a Commie Jew, I spring to my feet and grab one of my tormentors around the waist and tackle him to the floor. I immediately let my victim go and apologize profusely. "Not quite what we have in mind, Izzy," suggests the trainer in charge. "I know! I'm sorry! Let me try again." On the second pass, I grab the coke bottle and pour some on my fellow volunteer. On my third and final attempt, I end up screaming at the volunteer, "You goddam Peckerwood..." This provokes peals of laughter from the entire group. I'm at a loss. I have no clue why I can't control my anger. The trainer in charge calls me in and tells me that I'm not cut out for this work and that I best find another way to contribute to the Civil Rights Movement. I am devastated. All my self-doubts are realized. Desirie is not happy. She's ashamed of my performance, angry and disappointed that I won't be with her on the Freedom Ride. "How could you fail?" she cries. "You're white! "It should be easier for you." Now I'm angry. "How do you figure? I think they hate white people more for joining the Negro cause."

"Oh so now it's just a Negro cause, is it? Not about simple justice and respect."

"Come on, Desirie, you know what I mean. You act like I failed this on purpose."

"Well, did you?" I can't bear her accusatory stare. "Don't be like that, Desirie, I couldn't control my anger; I don't know why."

It's a lonely, shame-weighted ride home. The pain of failing is almost unbearable. Despite my initial reluctance to volunteer for the Freedom Ride, after the first day of training I was eager to go. I had already begun to think of myself as a civil rights activist serving a righteous cause. And now, through my own miserable lack of control, I have denied myself the opportunity to share with my righteous brothers and sisters an historic effort to change the world for the better. It hurt even more to see the anger and disappointment in Desirie's eyes. I have no idea where I stand with her. One minute she's smiling at me, and in the next she looks as if she's fraternizing with the enemy.

When I arrive home, my mother is standing in the kitchen with her hands on her hips frowning at me. Her eyes are ablaze with annoyance "I wish we could afford another phone just for you, Izzy," my mother complains. "The phone's been ringing off the hook and the calls are all for you. Peter called, then Bobby called, and I just hung up from James." "Sorry, Ma," I reply as I quickly dart into my bedroom. A couple of phone calls later, the four of us plan to meet at 6 P.M. for some Liedo's pizza. James volunteers to drive and offers to pick me up on the way to Liedo's. My apartment is only a mile or two away from the restaurant.

There is truly something different about Liedo's pizza. The cheese is more flavorful than any we have ever tasted. The tomato sauce has an unusual tang that's almost addictive. As we enter the restaurant, the smells are intoxicating. Like four Pavlovian dogs, we sit at our table with saliva-filled mouths, anticipating the never disappointing rectangular dish of pepperoni-topped pizza. I always eat more than my capacity and the subsequent stomachache I suffer is well worth our gluttonous sojourn to pizza heaven.

It's not an ideal time for them to start the interrogation given the pain in the belly I feel, but Peter can't resist. "So you're not going?"

"Like I said, I failed the nonviolent test. I didn't mind being called a nigger-lover, but I couldn't stand it when they called me a Commie Jew." My voice sounds like an old crone. It's the only sound I can make while clutching my gas-bloated belly. Peter has his characteristic smirk, the one his face assumes whenever a sarcastic jibe is about to leave his mouth, "I would've punched somebody out at nigger-lover." He laughs his nasal laugh and I just stare at him. "You know you're out of your fucking mind to even consider it. "

"Why?" I ask indignantly.

"Because you would've gotten your ass stomped, that's why, and it's not even your fight." Peter has reinforcements. Bobby chimes in that while he shares the sentiment that people should be treated fairly, he thinks me hopelessly naïve in imagining that I can change the world. I glower at him and ask sadly, "Et Tu Bobby?" Then with resentment, "Yes, I know your philosophy. The individual is nothing. We had that discussion before when you justified petty larceny on the basis of the insignificance of the individual. The crime is miniscule and the criminal is even less." Although I intend my statements to be critical, Bobby relishes my recounting of our previous discussion. "Yes! That's right!" he says in a self-congratulatory tone, "And the same is true here except that people like you who think Negroes should get their rights are rare birds in this society." James is silently taking all of this in between bites of his pizza. The three of us look at him to see if he'll say anything. He stares back at us and responds with a barely intelligible "Wha?" Bits of pizza cheese and pepperoni came flying out of his full mouth as he speaks, and rivulets of red tomato sauce slide out of his mouth and dribble down his cheek. He looks like someone has just punched him in the mouth and he's bleeding and blowing teeth. The three of us break out into loud guffaws as James continues his garbled reply. "We can always count on James for a pithy statement that will settle any argument," says Bobby as he falls into his characteristic high-pitched laughter. "Screw you all!" James says in a clear voice and with a smiling mouth now completely vacated of food.

Out of the corner of my eye, I catch Peter staring at me. His expression is one of utter puzzlement, a look he gets when people are saying or doing things beyond the borders of his experience. "What?" I ask in an annoyed and accusatory voice. "I don't get you."

"That's obvious from the look on your face. You're looking at me like I'm a Martian or something. What's your problem?" His expression does not change.

"Why are you doing this?"

"Doing what?" My annoyance is growing.

"Going to Howard, becoming a political radical. I mean you always had this obsession with blacks, listening to black music, dancing like a nigger. I mean I don't get you. You're becoming…. I don't know what….Niggerized." James, Bobby and I look at each other in incredulous amazement. "Niggerized?" we say in unison. "Is that even a word?" Bobby asks.

"Well, if it isn't, it ought'a be," Peter answers haughtily. "I don't know you anymore. You're becoming strange to me." This he says with detectable apprehension in his voice.

"Do you guys feel the same way?" I ask looking first at Bobby and then at James. They both hem and haw. Bobby then says "Well you are changing. I mean you never talked about politics before, and now you're ready to risk your life for a political cause. What's that about, Izzy?"

"It's called education!" I retort in a self-congratulatory tone. "I mean it's true. Going to Howard is changing me in a lot of ways, but I'm still me, the same old lovable Izzy White." This brings gales of laughter from the three of them.

"Well, had you gone on those Freedom Rides, I do believe your education would have come to an abrupt and painful end," Bobby half-facetiously adds.

"Yeah, but segregation is ignorant, stupid, and evil and has to change. I feel awful that I won't be going on the Freedom Ride."

"You're nuts," Peter opines.

"Amen," agrees Bobby. James says nothing. He just nods his head; and the expression on his face tells me that he's sorry, but he has to agree with the others.

"Well, somebody has to do something," I say, feeling defeated. Peter picks up on my expression and tries to cheer me up. "Look Izzy, don't feel bad, the Nigs are obviously doing something so you don't have to." I am furious. "Peter, you just don't get it. This struggle is not just for Negro rights. If one group is oppressed, nobody's free."

We're so full of pizza that the four of us stagger out of the restaurant. We all laugh at the bodily results of our pig-out. But on the way home, we are silent. I look at the Three Miscreants who have been my best friends for the last half dozen years and feel a growing sense of distance and alienation. It hits me that I had the identical feeling on campus-- distant, alienated, and disoriented. I am drifting away from my "white" world and yet do not belong to my new black world. I am lost and suspended between these two worlds and yet unable to avoid participating in both. I exist on the margins. I truly have become a marginal man.

For the entire month of May, I'm glued to the newspaper and the TV, trying to learn as much as I can about what is happening to the Freedom Riders. And every night in a state of terror I dream of Desirie, hoping she'll survive the Freedom Ride. Coverage is fairly sparse until Sunday, May 14th. I cannot believe my eyes when I see on the evening news a Greyhound bus in flames outside of Anniston, Alabama. The Ku Klux Klan has firebombed the bus. I'm not positive, but I think Desirie is on that Greyhound bus. I try to get word of her fate from a couple of her friends on campus, but no one knows what has happened to her or on which bus she might be. I can't decide whether to hope she's on the Trailways bus now bound for Birmingham, because the violence against the Riders could be a lot worse. A few days later I read that the CORE Freedom Ride is over. Since they can't find any drivers who would drive them on the next leg to Montgomery, several freedom riders fly to New Orleans. Was she on that plane? God I hope so.

On Friday, I read a short piece in the Washington Post about 10 riders who are now in a Birmingham jail. But the article maintains that the freedom riders that have been arrested are from Nashville. Nashville? Who are these students? They aren't the ones who left from Washington, D.C., the ones with whom I had begun my aborted training. Now I'm thoroughly confused and out of my mind with worry for Desirie's safety. As the month drags on, and I still haven't heard from Desirie, I am sick with apprehension. I mean physically ill, nausea, stomach pains, headaches. I'm a mess. Terrible things apparently happened in Birmingham and Montgomery, Alabama and then Jackson, Mississippi, but the details are sketchy and I have no idea whether Desirie was attacked or not. I'm not even sure she's still alive. I keep trying to reach her, but to no avail. I finally decide to go to her dorm. As I enter Crandall Hall, I see a tall, attractive light-skinned woman coming toward me. It's Desirie's friend,

Francis Carter. "Fran, have you seen Desirie?" She gives me a grave look; and after searching me with her eyes says, "Look, Izzy, Desirie was badly beaten in Alabama and was traumatized by the whole experience." I become sick to my stomach. "Is...is she ok?" I ask, making no attempt to hide the foreboding in my voice.

"Physically, she's ok, but mentally, she's not doing well at all. Izzy, she's been back for two weeks, mostly hiding out in her dorm room."

"Oh my God!"

"After she was released from the hospital, she flew home and spent several days with her parents. They bombarded her with questions that she wasn't ready to answer. One morning she packed, left a note for her parents, and fled to her dorm room where she's been in hiding ever since."

"Did she get my messages?"

"Yes, Izzy, she got them, but she couldn't talk to you. She could barely talk to me." Fran looks at me like she's trying to decide something. "OK, Izzy, I'll tell Desirie that you're here, but I'm not sure she'll see you. Wait here." After a 20- minute wait, Desirie comes into the lobby in tight jeans, turquoise shirt, and a wine-colored scarf over her head. It looks as if she'd made an effort to be presentable, but her demeanor suggests that she just wants to hide under the covers. She looks profoundly sad, and exhibits none of her typical cheeriness. There are deep purple bruises on both sides of her face, and the scarf is poofed up in the back of her head. It's covering a massive bandage that protects an apparent deep wound. "Hi Izzy," Desirie says, in a voice barely above a whisper. Her mood seems 10 feet below sea level. I attempt to hug her, but she makes no effort to return the hug. It was like hugging a Raggedy Ann doll. "Is there a place we can go and talk?" I ask after I release her from my embrace. "I'm not sure I feel like talking, Izzy." But she dutifully follows me to an open area in the lobby where there is an empty table and two chairs. We both sit down, but Desirie can't look at me. She stares at her clasped hands resting on the table.

"Desirie, tell me what happened. I've been worried sick about you."

"Oh Izzy, please don't make me. It was horrible." Her hands rise to cover her face as she burst into tears. I need to know so badly that I disregard her request. "Desirie, please talk to me." She looks at me and then quickly looks away. "I don't know where to begin," she says, shaking her head. "Begin with a happy scene if you can." This seems to calm her down. "Oh Izzy, we were all so full of hope. We had a wonderful dinner at the Yenching Palace the night before we left. We were nervous but eager to get on with our righteous mission. People kept making jokes about the Ride and about the dinner. Someone called it the Last Supper. By the end of dinner, I think we all felt like a brand new family. After dinner, James Farmer let us know that we still had time to drop out of the Freedom Ride. No questions asked. He even said we could tell him privately or not show up at the bus terminal. I didn't sleep at all. I was so scared, but I felt a deep stirring within that said to me I had to go; I had to be part of this change. My people need us to restore their dignity. Second class citizenship is no longer tolerable. The law is now on our side, and every American needs to respect the law. The next morning we met at the Greyhound and Trailways Bus stations. Six of us were assigned to the Greyhound bus and the other seven would get on the Trailways bus. I was assigned to the Greyhound bus. We were given our last instructions and seating assignments. At least one Negro Freedom Rider on each bus would sit in the section reserved for whites, and at least one interracial pair would sit next to one another. The other riders spread out into different parts of the bus. And one rider on each bus would act as if he was just a regular passenger respecting segregation, so that at least one person wouldn't get arrested. When we finally took off, no one seemed to get upset about where people were sitting. Our first stop was in Fredericksburg,

Virginia. I got really scared when I saw the Jim Crow signs on the restroom doors and the separate lunch counters. One of the white riders used the colored bathroom and one of the Negroes bought a drink at the white lunch counter. I held my breath, but no one said or did anything. There were no problems, Izzy. I mean no problems at all. And this was true in most of the towns we went through in Virginia: Richmond, Petersburg, Farmville, and Lynchburg. It was only in Danville, the last town we passed through in Virginia, that we met with some problems. But even there we prevailed. We were all amazed. There were no problems in Virginia. Can you believe it, Izzy?" Without waiting for my answer, she continues.

"Our amazement grew when we were received cordially in most of the towns we stopped at in North Carolina. I kept bouncing back and forth between relaxing when we were treated like regular people and becoming very frightened when I thought about our traveling into the Deep South. We finally hit some real trouble in Rock Hill, our first stop in South Carolina. That did not surprise me a bit. Rock Hill has been a prime target of CORE and SNCC for the past 15 months, and the site of many sit-ins and three months ago of the "jail-in". A bunch of tough-looking Crackers... " Desirie smiles sheepishly, "I'm sorry, Izzy." I just laughed. "Now we're even." "Anyway, the rough-looking white boys in ducktails and leather jackets blocked the entrance to the WHITE waiting room at the Greyhound station and then attacked John Lewis and two other white Freedom Riders. But a white police officer stopped the beatings before they got too bad. Then two of us got arrested for trespassing in a small town called Winsboro. After that incident, we rested for two days in Sumter, South Carolina, before making our way to Augusta, Georgia. We had another surprising shock when we were treated courteously in Augusta. The next day we had similar good experiences in Athens and Atlanta, and I was beginning to believe that not only were we going to succeed to desegregating the buses and bus stations, we were gonna have an easier time than any of us had imagined. Our spirits rose even higher when Martin Luther King joined us for dinner. Oh Izzy, he kept praising us for our courage and our commitment and he was genuinely enthusiastic about the stories that we told about what happened so far during the Freedom Ride. At one point, some of us encouraged him to join us on the rest of the Ride to New Orleans. We were all shocked when he refused. And then more bad news; James Farmer got word that night that his father died in DC and he would be temporarily leaving the Freedom Ride. The thought of wading into Alabama Klan hatred without our leader put the fear of God back in my soul, and whatever optimism I had felt about our mission had completely vanished." The memory of the loss of James Farmer brings more tears. After dabbing her eyes she continues, "Anyway, during the ride from Atlanta to Birmingham, there was very little talking among the Freedom Riders. I think we all knew that we were riding into deep trouble. Our fears were confirmed when another Greyhound bus going in the opposite direction motioned to our bus to pull over. That's when we learned that there was an angry mob waiting for us at the Anniston bus station. As we pulled into the station, we could see that it was closed and eerily silent. As soon as the bus stopped, an angry crowd of men rushed the bus screaming, "Kill the niggers! Kill the nigger-lovers." One young man who couldn't have been more than 16 years old lay down in front of the bus to stop us from leaving. I saw men with pipes, chains, and clubs. They kept screaming and banging on the bus and then I heard the sound of breaking glass. One of the bus windows had been smashed." Desirie starts crying and shaking her head as if she's trying to rid herself of the ghastly images. "The bus finally took off and we thought we were gonna be safe. You could almost hear a collective sigh of relief. I momentarily felt sorry for some of the white passengers on our bus who weren't Freedom Riders." "What do you mean, Desirie?" I ask, "What other passengers?"

"Izzy, these buses weren't chartered. They were regularly scheduled Greyhound and Trailway buses; so there were other people on it besides Freedom Riders." I look at her in horror and ask, "You mean these people didn't know what they were getting into?" "That's right, Izzy, many of them didn't know."

I look at her for a moment trying to grasp the situation. "Then what happened, Desirie?"

"As I said, we all thought we were gonna be safe. But just outside of town, a car got in front of the bus and was weaving back and forth and slowing down, clearly trying to get us to stop. We finally had to stop. There must have been 30 cars and trucks following us out of town. When the bus stopped, the mob came running to the bus screaming. One man smashed another window with a crowbar while several other men were rocking the bus, trying to turn it over on its side. This went on for about 15 minutes. And then...and then..." Desirie now starts to sob, and I move closer to her and hold her. "Someone threw a burning object into the bus. There was a fire and horrible black smoke and all I could hear was the sound of enraged voices screaming, 'Burn them niggers! Burn 'em to hell.' Some of us were finally able to crawl through an open window. One of the fuel tanks blew up and the mob started running away thinking the bus was gonna explode. The front door of the bus was finally pried open, and the rest of the passengers staggered outside to escape the smoke and flames. Hank Thomas, from Howard, was the first one to manage to crawl out of the burning bus. A member of the white mob said to him, 'Boy, are you OK?' And before he could answer, the white man proceeded to smash him in the head with a baseball bat. That's when I got hit on the back of my head with a lead pipe. I was out for a few minutes. When I awoke, my face felt very sore and I didn't know why. It was much later before I noticed I had been punched several times in the face. I looked around, and I saw several Riders crawling on the grass, coughing and bleeding. As the mob moved toward the Riders to attack them, I noticed that some of them were dressed up in their Sunday clothes. They obviously had just come from church. Only the sound of a pistol fired by a highway patrolman stopped the mob from killing us all. I heard him say, 'OK, you've had your fun, now let's move back.' The self-appointed executioners then walked away disappointed. Oh Izzy, I can still feel the smoke in my chest. I can still see those white faces ugly with rage. It was horrible, horrible." Desirie collapses in my arms sobbing louder than I have ever heard anyone sob. I just hold her and stroke her face gently. I have never felt such tenderness for anyone. I keep stroking her, and then I kiss her cheek. I find her lips and kiss them softly. Her lips are like every set of lips I have known and yet like no other. These are Desirie's lips—sweet, sensual, and soft. She kisses me back with real passion; and as my feelings rise, I know I want her in every way. I'm in love with Desirie and with life. For the first time, I feel like it is my great good fortune to have chosen to attend Howard. Desirie kisses me again and just as suddenly pulls away. "I'm sorry, Izzy, I just can't do this." I thought she had stopped because she is afraid she will lose control and go further then she had intended. "That's OK Desirie, I probably shouldn't have moved so fast with you. It's just that I desire you so much it's difficult to stop once I start kissing you." Desirie looks at me with an incomprehensible scowl on her face. "You don't understand, Izzy. I can't do this because you're white. I look at you and I see those angry white faces wanting to burn me alive...I, I just can't." Desirie gets up and quickly disappears.

I watch her walk away until I can no longer see her. I can't comprehend what has just happened. What can I do? I can't help the way I look. Maybe if I put a paper bag over my head, she'll love me. How ridiculous is that. I finally meet a girl that I love, and who seems to love me as long as she doesn't have to look at me. I slowly get up and stagger to my car stunned, crushed, angry, and hopelessly in love.

Chapter 16.
Integration or Separation

On a warm, lazy day in the middle of August 1961, nothing much is happening at the Playground. Most of the kids who usually show up are away with their well-to-do parents at their well-to-do beach houses. The few who show up stay inside the school to work on their craft projects. One of the older teenagers agrees to supervise the small cadre of sun-avoiding younger teens and tweens. I take the opportunity to find a grassy spot off to the side of the tarmac, place a blanket on the grass, lay my troubled self down, and allow my mind free reign to wander aimlessly through the meandering pathways of one of my frequent reveries. The smell of the newly mown grass gladdens my heart. It always does. My mind floats right to a shaming memory—I'm walking with my cousin, Jason Davidoff, to the basketball courts on the grounds of Paul Jr. High School. He's 12 and I'm ten. We pass an open field that has just been mowed. The smell enchants me and I joyously exclaim, "It smells like Walter Johnson League grass." I am referring to the 12 and under baseball league in which we both are playing. One of the few joys of my being stuck out in right field every game is the smell of the grass. Jason thinks this comment is hilarious, and he mocks me with a singsong parody of my joyous metaphor the rest of the way to the basketball court. Jason and I are more like brothers than cousins. During our childhood, his behavior toward me alternated between Chief Protector and Chief Tormentor. He too went to Howard University, preceding me by two years. In fact, he just graduated from the Pharmacy program in June. I rarely saw him because most of my liberal arts classes were on the upper quadrangle while his pharmacy courses were held entirely in the "Valley". Jason had integrated the football team two years before I had done the same for the basketball team. Because he was the only white player on the football team, he had to order food for the entire team in the segregated restaurants of south. Two years later, I did the same for the basketball team. My reverie effortlessly shifts into the story of his one big play. Jason was a middle linebacker and reserve fullback who never got a chance to run the ball. He often begged the coach to let him carry the ball just once. The coach always refused, until, that is, the last game of his last season. "OK, Jason, here's your chance." Jason entered the game filled with nervous anticipation. The center snapped the ball and the offensive line opened a gigantic whole for Jason to run through. He ran as fast as he could straight for the goal line that was fifty yards away. But Jason was not speedy. Any other running back on the team would have easily scored a touchdown, but Jason gained about 20 yards before the two cornerbacks converged on him and brought his career as a running back to an end. As Jason jogged back to the sideline, the coach said with a smirk on his face, "Hey, Jason, I know you said you wanted to carry the piano, but I didn't think you'd stop and play it." Jason turned crimson at the sound of his teammates' laughter. I laugh at the memory.

The reverie now shifts back to basketball, and I can clearly see myself playing against Hampton University, scoring 11 points in seven minutes; my best game ever. I think I can be a star, but as the season wears on, I discover I have to work my ass off every day just to be competent. Most players I face are bigger, stronger, and faster, and I have to give 120% every game in order not to embarrass myself. I know I have to make a decision about whether to keep playing. I also know that I'm not NBA material. I replay Jason's last play in my mind's eye and it makes me think that my career in basketball is coming to an end. But I love the game. I love that I am playing at the college level, and to be perfectly honest, I love that I am the only white player who ever played varsity basketball at Howard University. Maybe one more year!

The sun feels hotter as my reverie moves on. I feel needles of grass pricking me through the blanket as if to remind me of yet another worry. I have to choose a new major. Chemistry perished inside a dank and smelly laboratory. I had routinely boiled away my test solutions and with it my dreams of becoming a successful chemist. My experiment with sociology ended in laughable humiliation. After taking two sociology courses and getting "As" in both, I presented myself to Dr. Marjorie Wilson, the Acting Chair of the Sociology Department, proud as a peacock, preening to be praised and informed of the great opportunities awaiting me as a full fledged sociologist. Her response is terse and crushing. "Mr. White," she says. "If I were you, I would get out of sociology. Unless you want to teach or don't mind becoming a cog in the wheel of a large research organization, there are no opportunities for you." I'm flabbergasted, deflated, and demoralized. My reverie now turns its fearful eye onto psychology. I'm listening to Sigmund Freud as he unravels the secrets of the human mind. I tremble at the thought of associating myself with this genius. How can I become a psychologist when next to Freud I'm clearly intellectually inadequate? I tell Freud I want to try and become a psychologist and ask him if he thinks that is possible? He laughs and in Yiddish says "What am I, a mind-reader?" The image of Freud darkens until all I can see are his teeth. The teeth grow whiter and the dark background assumes the contours of Desirie's face. Now she is laughing, but her laughter is not the laughter of ridicule. "Of course it's possible!" I imagine her saying. Her laughter is a gentle reproach to my tendency to doubt my abilities and myself. I'm so grateful for the support I hear in her laugh that I see myself hugging her. Soon we are in her bedroom, kissing and removing each other's clothes. We begin—Loving! ...Merging! ...Coming! At the moment of climax, I hear a loud thunderclap. "Just like in the movies," I muse. But as the rain comes flooding down on top of me, I realize that the thunderclap is real. The cloud burst has brought my reverie to an end. I grab my blanket and sprint for the schoolroom door.

Toward the end of September, I'm walking along the upper quadrangle of the campus in a rare state of wellbeing. I'm now a junior in college, a fact that gives rise in me both incredulity and self-congratulations. It's a golden autumn day and the leaves are just beginning to change color. The gentle warmth of the sun on my face seems to dissolve all of my worries. Nature has bestowed a gift upon us all. Every student that I can see appears to be walking with a light and lively step. One student in particular catches my attention. He's walking right toward me with a wide grin on his face. He approaches me with such confidence that I believe he must originally be from one of the islands in the Caribbean. "You are Izzy White, are you not?" he asks, continuing to grin at me as if I am a long lost friend. He is literally tall, dark, and handsome. He has very expressive eyes, an infectious smile, and an odd combination in his speech of a Bajan lilt and a New York accent that is irresistible.

"Yes, that's me. And you're Brandon Blackwell."

"Ah, so you have heard of me."

"Yes I have. I know you're originally from Barbados, went to Bronx High School. You love soccer and have already become a prominent voice in NAG."

"And you have done your homework, I see," he says with a welcoming grin.

"What I don't know is what you want with me."

"Winston McKenzie tells me you would be a good person to know."

"That surprises me because I thought McKenzie had nothing but contempt for me."

"Not true, Izzy," Brandon rebuts loosening the collar of his starched white shirt.

"And you can't believe that about Winston because I know he tried to recruit you for NAG last year. How 'bout we step into the Union so we can talk?" Brandon's movements belie his garb. He moves with an easy smoothness, the direct opposite of the tight rigidity of his sharply creased Navy blue pants and starched shirt. After getting some coffee, we sit at a corner table. Before he can get a word in, I start. "Why would McKenzie recommend me to you?" My guard is up as my paranoia begins to bloom. "All he did was put down my education and slam white supremacy. The irony is that I agreed with him on both counts." Warming up to our conversation, Brandon becomes more enthusiastic and informal. "He knew that, Jack. He knew that. He was so impressed with that, Jack, so impressed. He was also impressed by the fact that you are this white cat in liberal arts. They are few and far between, Jack. Most whites that come to Howard are in the professional programs—pharmacy, the med and dental schools. Then you have all these white girls from the suburbs that come to Howard to be dental hygienists. Not to work on black people's teeth, of course. They graduate and run back to their lily-white suburbs to work. But you; you're in the liberal arts program and you seem to be interested in social justice."

"So?"

"So, NAG needs people like you."

"I assume you too have done your homework. So what do you know about me?"

"I know you're a good-hearted Jew and Jews have been some of our best allies in the struggle for civil rights. Your father is a butcher, which means he is a solid member of the working class and therefore must lean toward the Democratic Party. I also know that you are excelling in the Honors Program here at Howard and that you played on the Howard varsity basketball team. And I know that you participated in a picket line at Glen Echo and you tried to become a Freedom Rider. Quite a feat for a little white, Jewish cat."

"You're scary. How did you learn all that?"

"Like you said, I do my homework." Brandon pauses, gives me a searching look, and then continues. "I don't know if you're aware that NAG has become the student affiliate group at

Howard for SNCC, the Student Nonviolent Coordinating Committee."

"I've heard of SNCC, but don't know too much about the group. I know just a little bit more about CORE because CORE was behind the Freedom Rides."

'That's right, but CORE, SNCC, NAG; we all have the same goal. We want to remove the humiliation of segregation and destroy white supremacy."

"That, I can dig!"

"So you do share NAG's goals."

"Well, yes, the little I know of them."

"Come join us then!

"What specifically is NAG trying to do? I mean, I know that NAG's primary task is to try to organize and influence the Howard student body so that as many students as possible will join the struggle for human rights. I also know that the bait is to help students to organize for improvements in student rights and living conditions on campus."

"That's right, Izzy. Student life issues are important, but our ultimate goal is to wake students up from their somnolent apathy, their materialistic obsessions, and take responsibility to help our people secure the rights that belong to them as Americans. For example, we've recruited a lot of students to participate in the Route 40 project. Are you familiar with that?

"Something to do with segregated restaurants on Route 40?"

"That's right, from Wilmington, Delaware to DC. Now this is some crazy shit. Restaurants, gas stations and other facilities all along Route 40 only serve white people. As you know, a large number of African countries have thrown off their colonial chains and have become independent. And they have become bona fide members of the UN, Jack. That means there are many African diplomats routinely traveling from the UN in New York to their embassies in DC. Route 40 is the primary means of travel. So none of these restaurants, gas stations and whatever is serving these diplomats, and it's become a national embarrassment to the Kennedy administration. Would you believe that Kennedy published an announcement of a new policy that would punish any place that refused service to dark skinned diplomats? Not Negroes in general, mind you, just dark-skinned diplomats. We're not gonna stand for that, no we're not! Members of NAG joined CORE in demonstrations and sit-ins all along Route 40. We even had students dress up in African garb and they were served. That policy was eventually cancelled, Jack, you bet it was."

"OK, but here's what I don't get. Why are you telling me your whole strategy since I'm one of the students you want to influence?" A smile plays briefly around Brandon's mouth and then fades.

"You're a commuter student, aren't you Izzy?

"That's right."

"So you're not so concerned about student life on campus.

"That's mostly right."

"But you do care about civil rights and social justice.

"Very much so."

"Also, you're on the basketball team, yes?"

"Yes."

"Well, dig it, Jack. That makes you a BMOC."

"At 5'7", not so very big." Brandon chuckles and nods.

"And BMOCs are listened to, ya dig?

"Even to white ones?"

"Especially to white ones." Do you ever read the Hilltop?"

"Yeah. For a school newspaper, I've been pretty impressed."

"Several of the Hilltop staff are members of NAG. That way NAG's messages and ideas can reach the entire campus. But the only student organization that has any money is the Liberal Arts Student Council. So several NAG members got themselves elected to the student council, including yours truly. Now we have a budget to help us spread progressive ideas." Brandon's intense stare unnerves me a bit, but I am also impressed by his passion. "So what's NAG working on now?"

"Have you heard of Project Awareness?"

"Yeah, I think I read about it in the Hilltop."

"Yes you did, Jack, yes you did!" Brandon's refrain emphasized that NAG's plan is already working. "Project Awareness is an attempt to raise students' consciousness on social issues by staging debates between well-known advocates on opposing sides of controversial questions. We've been careful to frame the proposal in terms of important academic values like freedom of inquiry, and open debate, and non-partisanship. You know the administration really doesn't trust us. They view us as a potentially dangerous radical group. So when we gave them this apparently even-handed proposal, those cats were dumbfounded. They were mighty anxious folk. They stalled and delayed their decision for months. Eventually, they sent the proposal to President Nabrit who doesn't trust us either. But he finally approved the idea in principal. Here's the kicker though. He's gonna review each and every debate before making any decision.

"When's the first debate?" I'm not sure where Brandon is going with this.

"October 30th."

"And who are the debaters?" Brandon has an impish smile on his face.
"Bayard Rustin, who by the way is a mentor to NAG and Minister Malcolm X of the Nation of Islam."

"Oh My God!" I respond in a quivering voice. Brandon laughs and says, "That's the same reaction we initially got from the Howard administrators. They were worried that the Dixiecrats in Congress would come down hard on the University's budget to punish Howard administrators for displaying such insolence in supporting so-called 'subversive' programs. Now NAG actually has some sympathy for them here, but we aren't going to let their problems become our problems. We're not going to stop putting on controversial debates."

"What are they debating?" I fight to keep the tremor out of my voice.

"We're calling the debate 'Separation or Integration?' The question is whether Black people are better off trying to form alliances with progressive whites or creating a black-oriented power-base. At least I think that will be the gist of the debate."

"And what is it that you want me to do?"

"OK, we need to fill Crampton Auditorium for this debate to prove to the Howard bureaucrats that Project Awareness is popular with the students. Since you're a Little Big Man on Campus," Brandon interrupts himself here with his own laughter. "I'm sorry man," he says, still chuckling. "Since you're a BMOC, we want you to encourage anyone you meet to come to this debate, but particularly the white students. The more white students we can convince to come, the more legitimacy the debates sponsored by Project Awareness will have with the bureaucrats. We think that Mr. White Basketball Player will have a large reach to help our cause."

"I have my doubts, but I'm willing to give it a shot." I say this more out of a response to Brandon's charisma than out of any real desire to participate in NAG's political machinations. One thing I'm sure of, I want to be at that debate. I am somewhat familiar with Malcolm X's Black Nationalism, but I want to hear for myself his anti-white diatribe.

Brandon and I say our goodbyes and agree to touch base with each other in a week or so. I find my favorite seat by the sundial, and in my mind's eye replay my meeting and conversation with Brandon Blackwell. Although his reputation has preceded him, Brandon's presence, passion, and power astonish me. I'm already in awe of him and I know we are in agreement about the goal of social justice. And I loved the idea of Project Awareness, and of bringing together speakers with diametrically opposed opinions on the important issues of the day to debate. This can only enrich the education of every student at Howard University. But I'm also troubled by Brandon's presentation. It seems as if he and NAG are less interested in the idealistic goals of Project Awareness than they are in the political and tactical significance for recruiting as many Howard students as possible to become activists. Yet being in his presence is intoxicating. I know I want his approval even as I question his manipulative approach to people.

For the next three weeks, I am the good soldier and I distribute announcements of the debate to as many students I can and encourage them to come. I especially seek out the white students. I'm amazed and appalled to learn that several professors encouraged their students not to attend the debate because of their fear and animosity towards Malcolm X. Nonetheless, I'm able to secure a few commitments from both black and white students.

The night before the debate, I get no sleep at all. I can't shut off the worry spigot. What if the debate turns ugly; What if my presence, or that of the white students I convinced to attend, is resented by the mostly black audience? What if anti-white feelings run high? What if there's a riot? Will I survive this debate? The only reassuring thought I have to challenge this avalanche of apprehension is my assumption that most people are going to support Bayard Rustin's position on integration. Even the radical members of NAG are going to support their mentor, Rustin, I think, over Malcolm X's expected hateful anti-white rhetoric.

I only have two classes on Monday, and my academic day is over by 3 pm. There's no sense in going home since the debate is scheduled to begin in four hours. I hear through the NAG grapevine that some members who also work for the Hilltop will be interviewing Malcolm for the newspaper and then will have dinner with him. I'm not invited. It's just as well because I have no desire to break bread with a white-hating (and, for all I knew, a Jew-hating) minister of the Nation of Islam. After hanging out in the library for a couple of hours, I make an early dinner stop at the Kampus Korner and make do with a fair-to- middling burger. By the time I finish my dinner and walk over to Crampton Auditorium, the place is beginning to fill up. It looks as if the new, 1500-seat auditorium is going to be completely filled and then some. Only a few white faces dot the large Negro crowd. I feel a sense of failure that I was unable to succeed in selling white students on the debate. But more worrisome is the return of all my anxious thoughts about the outcome of this debate. I go in and take a seat near the back in case I have to make a speedy exit. The auditorium is filled, and many people are still trying to get in before Professor E Franklin Frazier introduces the program and its speakers. I turn around and see the crush of people still trying to enter the auditorium. This only enhances my fears of an ensuing riot. I can see that the auditorium is packed, and there is a large crowd gathering outside the front door.

The lights dim, the crowd quiets, and Professor E. Franklin Frazier begins his introduction to Project Awareness. He explains its purposes and its hopes. He then introduces Project Awareness's first debaters. I can't clearly see any of the participants on the stage, which is the major trade-off for choosing a seat in the back near the exit. I see one tall dark figure shaking hands with an even taller dark figure. Bayard Rustin is the first speaker. When he begins to speak, the pitch of his voice startles me. It is high and almost grating in its tone. But he's very gracious. He notes the positive contributions of the Nation of Islam in helping many poor Negroes learn the benefits of middle class virtues. And he agrees with many points of Malcolm's analysis of America's treatment of black people. But then he contends that Malcolm's solution is no solution and that he presents no adequate program.

"The Nation of Islam proposes that a Black State should be formed to be run by Black people, of Black, and for Black people. But where is this black state to come from?" He accuses the Black Muslims of fantasizing a utopian society and that his plan to help develop small Black businesses is no basis for improving the economic picture for all Black people. "If you don't have an adequate program, and if you don't rely on progressive allies, you throw yourself open to being utilized by people who have no interest in what we are doing. The Muslim movement basically fails to see the real problem. The problem cannot be stated as Black against white, but rather as man's injustice to man. Any movement that starts out by blocking out the best minds many of which are white as well as black is doomed to failure. Change requires power and power requires allies. You can't get allies if you avoid all contact with whites." Then it is Malcolm's turn. All I can see is this tall bespectacled brown man who moves slowly, gracefully to the mike. He starts with the traditional Islamic greeting, "Salaam aleikum." The traditional response is bellowed back to him from the center of the auditorium, "Wa aleikum as salaam." The responsive shout sends a surge of adrenaline through my body. As he speaks, I am surprised by a quality of warmth in his voice even as he sends volley after volley of condemnation against white people and America. He reminds the audience that before they were anything else—American, Republican, Democrat—they were Black. With each statement, the crowd roars. I'm startled. Malcolm has barely begun and the crowd seems to be with him. The previous Spring I had written a paper in one of my sociology classes on the Black Muslims, so I think I know what's coming. I imagine that whites will be characterized as incorrigible devils. I'm close. Malcolm accuses the American white man as being the greatest racists, killers, and liars on the planet, and he's only getting started. With each indictment, the audience erupts with a great enthusiastic roar of approval. I'm in shock. I contemplate leaping from my chair to beat a hasty retreat to the exit. Malcolm continues:

"We who are followers of the Honorable Elijah Mohammed do not make a choice between integration and segregation. Segregation, as we are taught by the Honorable Elijah Mohammed, is that which is forced upon inferiors by superiors. Separation is done voluntarily by two equals. When you find an all-white school they don't call it a segregated school, they call it a separate school. When you find an all-Negro school, they call it a segregated school because it was set up by the white man. If it was an all-black school that had been set up by the black man with a curricula put in the schools by the black man himself, they would call it a separate school. But because the Negro schools in Harlem have been set up by the white man himself, on an inferior basis, with inferior teachers, in inferior buildings, black people who are defenseless, who are harmless, and because of your indoctrination and brain washing are brainless and senseless, have no intellect whatsoever of their own where they can think for themselves. It is because America has taken millions of black people from the East, from their own culture, from their own civilization, and brought them here and stripped them, and brought them down to the level of an animal, then turned around and taught them that they were savages in the jungle, cannibals eating people, when they were caught and brought here. This is supposed to justify the American white man's treatment of these people. It's like taking a horse, putting him in a cage, tying him up and putting another horse on the outside, and then telling everybody that the horse in the cage can't run as fast as the one outside, and this is what you have done to the American Negro. You have brought us here and stripped us of everything we once had. You stripped us of our culture, you stripped us of our language, you stripped us of our God, our religion, our background. You cut off all our roots, our old ties we once had with our kind in the East. And after stripping us of our roots, and destroying us as a people, making us become dead as a people, mentally and otherwise, then you point the finger of scorn at us and tell the world we're not ready for freedom; we're not qualified for freedom.

It is for this reason that God is bringing America to its knees. It is for this reason that God is going to judge America. It is for this reason that America is doomed, and it is for this reason we who follow the Honorable Elijah Muhammad feel that our only hope is not integration with a doomed society but separation from a doomed society." Now people are standing at their seats and cheering wildly.

"South Africa practices what it preaches. Russia practices what it preaches. It's a dictatorship. It doesn't preach freedom. South Africa doesn't preach freedom. Russia doesn't call itself the leader of the free world. It's America that looks upon herself and represents herself as the leader of the free world while she has 20 million black people here who aren't even citizens. How can you and your government and your governmental leaders stand up in the United Nations and point the finger at South Africa for practicing what it preaches. It preaches apartheid and it practices apartheid. It preached the inferiority of the races and it practices the inferiority of the races, whereas you preach one thing and practice another thing. You say that this is the land of equality and 20 million of your black citizens, so-called black citizens, don't have equality. You say this is the land of freedom and 20 million black people don't have freedom. You say this is a land of justice and 20 million black people here don't have justice. And the government from the Supreme Court, the Senate, and the Congress and the President, all of them combined are not able to bring about any change in the attitude of white America toward black America." The audience's cheers grow louder. And I grow more fearful. Toward the end of his talk, Malcolm suggests that, "A Black state should be constructed with territory in the continental United States and that America owes this to Black people as reparations for 300 plus years of brutalizing slavery. Then the Black man can take care of his own by creating businesses by black people for black people. But if you try and keep us here against our will and enforce segregation upon us, you are going to have violence throughout the country. You are going to have it whether you like it or not." The walls of Crampton auditorium reverberate with the thunderous cheers and applause of the audience. This overwhelms me. I enter a zone of non-thinking, which I often do when I experience or imagine an unbearable threat.

During the rebuttal, Rustin seems up to the task, despite the unequal cheers he received. "My opponent says that the United States owes Black people territory making up the area of nine American states. And I say he can have Mississippi, Alabama, Georgia, the Carolinas...." The rest of his countdown is drowned out by laughter. I relax a little. Bayard seems to be scoring real points with the audience. He also ridicules Malcolm's small business plan for Negro advancement. "The Black Muslims have put forth no concrete program except speaking on 125th Street. I think he is leading Negroes down a primrose path and he does this by playing on your emotions." Malcolm's rebuttal is also spirited. "If the black man has spending power of $20 billion as the government economists say they do, we feel that the black man's spending 20 billion dollars a year not setting up any businesses, not creating any industries, not creating any job opportunities for his own kind, he's not in a moral position to point the finger today at the white man, and tell the white man that he's discriminating against him for not giving him a job in factories that he himself set up. If a black man has 20 billion dollars and those-so-called Negro leaders are such geniuses that they can integrate white restaurants, and integrate white factories, and force themselves into endeavors the white man has set up, they should use this same ingenuity to show the black people how to pool their wealth and set up something of our own. Then they won't have to force our way into his anymore.

Rustin also says that all we do is speak on 125th street. We don't waste our time on 125th street. But you can reach more people in the street who want a change than you can in bourgeois society, the bourgeoisie church and the bourgeoisie circles. Our program is directed toward the man in the street. So we spend our time in the street. What we do with that man, instead of trying to change the white man to make him accept us, we can change the mind of the black man and make him accept himself." More thunderous applause and howling cheers!

When the debate is over, I sit dumbfounded, demoralized, and depressed. The students' cheers for Malcolm continue to echo inside my head long after the debate has ended. I can't understand why Malcolm X's diatribe has such appeal. Oh, I understand the anger, the bitterness and sense of betrayal that Negroes feel about their treatment in this country. Whenever I attempt to imagine myself experiencing the tiniest bit of the brutality and humiliation that Negroes have experienced for the past three centuries, it sets my hair on fire. My meager attempt at empathy induces unbearable rage within me, and I want to kill the first honky I see. Anyone who does not feel rage at such barbaric treatment must be dead inside. What I can't understand is the students' apparent enthusiasm for Malcolm X's remedies. Complete separation from whites? A Black state within the United States? From my perspective, Rustin ripped this nonsense to shreds. Yet here is a large portion of the 1500 attendees clapping, hooting, and hollering for the Black Muslim minister's dystopian analysis of America and utopian solutions to the Negroes' dilemma. I know intellectually that a race war is a preposterous fear, yet that fear crowds out all other thoughts. The worry spigot turns on again. Will an anti-white fervor begin to appear first in the eyes of my classmates then later in their actions? Will a general race war break out all across America? I can't deny Malcolm X's charisma or the considerable truth in his analysis of the treatment of Negroes by whites. But a race war would be disastrous for Negroes and whites and for America. I need to know what Brandon and the other members of NAG think about this debate and about the solutions proposed by Malcolm X.

Chapter 17.
Brandon's story

My paranoia now is in full bloom. When I walk on campus en route to my classes in Douglass Hall, I keep my eyes downward. I don't want to see hostile black faces. Occasionally, I look up and peek for a second into the eyes of a student in search of Malcolmized hostility. Rarely do I see anything that even approximates anger or hostility. But I expect it nonetheless. Mostly I see indifference or eyes that say, "Why are you staring at me?" I want very much to talk to Brandon. I want to know his reactions to the debate, and maybe he can help me understand the boisterous enthusiasm for Malcolm X. As I'm walking toward Douglass Hall, I see Brandon coming out of the building. I dash toward him yelling, "Hey, Brandon. BRANDON!" The sight of a white boy running toward him smiling while screeching out his name is so unusual that Brandon doubles over in laughter. "Hey, Izzy. Where's the riot?" I quickly stop and laugh at Brandon's laughter and wonder what I must have looked like. "You got a minute? I want to ask you about the debate."

"Cool, Jack. What d'ya want to know?"

"Who do you think won?"

"No question about it, Malcolm won, rhetorically, and emotionally."

I'm appalled. "But what about the substance of their arguments. Malcolm's in La La Land as I think Rustin made clear. His solutions make no sense."

"Say what? Malcolm was brilliant and clearly won the debate. Tell you the truth we were surprised. Everybody in NAG fully expected that Bayard's arguments for integration would win over the audience. But you were there. You saw. You heard."

"Yes, I was there. I saw and heard, and now I fear. Yeah, Malcolm was charismatic, but his ideas terrify me."

"Look, he didn't convert me or anybody else in NAG, but Malcolm taught me something at that debate. I mean his theological worldview is alien to my democratic socialist perspective as is his solution of racial separation. You have to understand, Izzy, that for the past couple of years I've been exposed to the hope, the optimism, and the real problems facing black people. I've experienced Southern black culture and the culture of Howard's Black Bourgeoisie. I've endured the hell of a Mississippi prison farm and walked the gauntlet of many a picket line in the country of hate. And I'm still a secular socialist. But what Malcolm showed me the other night in Crampton Auditorium is the raw power that exists within our collective blackness." I begin to feel a panicky chill slithering down my back. The sound of the phrase "collective blackness" feels like a prison door separating me off from a people I have come to admire, and whose quest for dignity and respect I have made my own. I see Brandon on the other side of the door, waving goodbye, and a cold premonition of painful catastrophe comes over me that will soon sadden and anger not just me, but the country as a whole. I try to sweep this image under the rug of my conscious preoccupations. "I understand what you are saying, Brandon," (although I don't), "But surely you can't believe that Negroes in America can obtain justice and economic opportunity without white allies. Isn't that what Bayard said?"

'Democratization and socialization the Negro cannot do alone.' Civil rights is not just about Negroes getting the rights, respect, and dignity due them, it's also about making America a better country, a country that lives up to its stated ideals." Brandon's eyes go wide, and I can see he's doing his best to restrain his anger. His cheeks fill with air, which he then pushes from one cheek to the other.

"Listen Izzy, you need to understand something. I came to this country from Barbados. There and throughout the Caribbean my black face is in the majority. There we hold our black heads high. Then I come to New York and I begin to feel something different about the way black people are treated in America. Disdain and disrespect are even more prominent here in DC and in the surrounding areas of Virginia and Maryland. But it was only when I went on the Freedom Rides that I got a mouthful of all the putrefying poisons of white supremacy. I heard what happened to Desirie, Izzy, and I'm really sorry, man." "Thanks, Brandon, what happened to her is horrible." "I know it is. How's she doing now?"

"She's mending physically. I'm not sure how she's doing emotionally. She's been keeping her distance from me because of my skin color. Ain't that ironic?"

"Maybe to you, Izzy, but that's what we darker skin folk have had to deal with for centuries. If you've got time, I'd like to tell you another story. " "I've got time," I said cautiously, wondering what Brandon will lay on me now.

"Poor Desirie was battered in Aniston and that was horrible with the Klan fire-bombing the bus and all, but it got much worse in Montgomery and Birmingham. Did you know that Jim Farmer was about to call off the Freedom rides because of the brutal treatment the Riders received in Birmingham at the hands of the Klan? Farmer was terrified by the prospect of having the possible, if not probable, deaths of many young people on his conscience. The brutality was blessed by the Birmingham police. They had disappeared from the bus station for about 15 minutes to allow the Klan to crack open some Freedom Rider heads. The police are mostly Klan members anyhow. A lotta blood was spilled at the Birmingham Bus station, yes there was. Well, we got a call from Diane Nash who is a committed sister in the Nashville SNCC contingent. She was persuasive in her argument that we can't just stop the Freedom Rides. If we do, that's a solid message to the racists that might makes right; and that all they have to do is to mobilize overwhelming violence and the freedom fighters will fold like a Bedouin tent. She said that we can't let that happen, so she organized another group of freedom riders from Nashville and she wanted to know if NAG would send some volunteers. Our group left a week after Diane called, and we were the first ones to test the trains. We flew to New Orleans and then we got on the Illinois Central en route to Jackson, Mississippi. Just like at the bus stations, a mob was waiting for us at the train station. Now I'd seen hostile crowds before in Virginia and Maryland but nothing like this. These honkies were yelling, spitting, throwing cans and lit cigarettes at us. Man they were even fighting each other to get at us. One little old white man tried to get up from his wheelchair so that he could take a swing at me. I couldn't believe how contorted his face was with hatred and rage. He was shaking so bad that when he finally hit me, it was no blow at all. However, some younger honkies got in some serious licks. When we arrived in Jackson, we promptly entered the white waiting room. And we were just as promptly arrested. We kept mouthing off at the cops. No matter what they did to us we remained nonviolent. You see, Izzy, we were nonviolent, but we were not gonna be pacifist." Brandon laughs at a private memory, and then continues. "Here was SNCC's strategy. We wouldn't accept bail if we went to jail. The Jail, No Bail slogan would result in our filling the jails of Mississippi. I heard that over 400 freedom activists ended up in jail by the time the Freedom Rides were stopped, including "Yours Truly". I first landed in the Hinds County Jail. And do you know what those Mississippi Honky motherfuckers did? Uh, sorry about that Izzy."

"No, no, that's quite alright. I agree; they were honky motherfuckers. Go on."

Brandon faintly smiles and continues. "They wanted to avoid the negative international publicity that broke upon the heads of the Alabama segregationists, but they couldn't afford to let the Freedom Riders openly defy their Jim Crow laws and escape without some serious damage done to them. But after Alabama, the 'good white citizens' could not be seen doing the damage. Instead the police tried to collude with a dozen of the toughest Black prisoners, that's right, Jack, the Black prisoners, the lifers and long-termers with violent records, and attempted to bribe them. Here's the deal they offered these long-termers: An easier time in prison, reduced sentences, and maybe a little cash if they beat up the Freedom Riders. Brandon then began to imitate the Honky MFs. "Heah's yore chance to whip some Yankee haids, no questions asked." And boy, were those crackers surprised when these righteous brothers said no. The courage that these brothers showed in saying no, even though they knew exactly how totally at the mercy of the penal system they were, made me cry. When the number of prisoners got unwieldy, the Freedom Riders and their supporters were segregated from the general population of black prisoners. At night, we all sang freedom songs, which united us and enraged the crackers in charge. We could even hear the female freedom Riders singing over in the women's unit. Then the brothers above us began singing their work and prison songs. Even the white Freedom Riders were singing. The head honchos were unnerved by this defiance and so the threats began. First they threatened to deny us the mess cart if we didn't stop singing. This meant no gum, sodas, and snacks. No big deal, except for the cigarettes. Many of the Freedom Riders were chain-smokers. For them this was a real crisis. However, the brothers upstairs solved the crisis. They let down a bag on a string. We put in our orders and the money and down came the cigs. The smoking and singing went on. I had a week of this before we were told that we would be movin' to Parchman Penitentiary. Okay, that scared me. Parchman was reputed to be the most brutal prison in the South. And I knew that meant we were going to one of the worst hellholes in the country and that we would be tortured. It was after midnight when they came for us. We were herded into trucks. The doors were locked and we were driven away in complete darkness. When we arrived at dawn, there was just enough light to see barbed wire stretching far into the distance and armed guards with shotguns. Beyond the guards and inside the fence, we could see a complex of boxy wooden and concrete buildings. And beyond them, nothing but dark, flat Mississippi delta. We were taken to the basement of a long low brick building. We were made to strip and stand nude while waiting to be processed. The off-duty guards were shouting crude comments and cackling. They seemed to have a fixation about genitals, a preoccupation with size. They burned us with cattle prods. You could actually see smoke and smell skin burning. The man in charge of the processing was a massive, red-faced cigar-smoking cracker in cowboy boots who strutted about shouting orders and threats. His name was Deputy Nosyt. They told us that in order to protect us from the other prisoners, we were going to be locked up in maximum security. We followed the fat-ass Deputy Nosyt, who we began to call 'Deputy Noshit, down the dingy corridors to a group of cells. We had to shower and shave off any facial hair. We were given as clothing a flimsy tee shirt and a pair of boxer shorts. No shoes or socks. We were then placed two in a cell, which was a six by nine feet concrete and windowless box with two steel racks for bunks, a sink, and a commode. The only time we left the cell was for a weekly shower." Brandon pauses for a moment as the memories continue to flood his brain, and it looked to me as if he were trying to achieve editorial control over them. Or it could have just been the pain I am feeling from my over-active empathy for the horror experienced by Brandon and the other Freedom Riders. He must have picked up the anguish in my face because he continues in a lighter vein.

"Now just because we were in lockdown 24/7 that did not mean this was a situation of unrelenting horror. No way, Jack. Our group possessed such a range of ideologies, religious belief, political commitment and backgrounds, age and experience that we had the most amazing discussions and debates. But the common denominator that we all shared was moral fortitude." Then Brandon's expression changes presumably due to a more painful memory coming in. "During our second day there, we began singing our freedom songs. In marches Noshit: 'Y' all gon' ha' to stop that singing. We ain't having none of that shit heah.' The next time he shows up, 'Ah'm warning you. You gonna lose yore mattresses.' Even with the thin mattresses you felt the sharp edges of steel when you tried to sleep. We didn't stop. In came Noshit for the mattresses with a bunch of guards. My cellmate and I would not give ours up. They snatched mine out from under me dumping me on the floor. My cellmate wrapped himself around his mattress. A guard pulled him into the corridor, but couldn't pry the mattress loose. The guard and my cellmate wrestled with the mattress for a few minutes. The guard finally yells "Awright, go git 'em, Dusty." A short, muscular prisoner jumped on Frank and started pounding him. After only a minute of this, he got the mattress. What a humiliating scene it was, Izzy, Dusty was black. At first I was upset with Dusty even though I knew the brother didn't have a choice. He seemed to enjoy his work too much. Frank defended him. 'what you talking about,?' I said to him. 'He like to take yo head off.'

'Hey, he coulda messed me up something terrible, man. But I could feel him pulling up. Besides, I know it hurt him worse than it hurt me. Every time he hit me, Dusty started crying, man. That's why I gave him the fucking mattress.' After lunch, the preachers in our group started praying and singing hymns. But Noshit wasn't having any of that either. The preachers insisted that they were going to praise their God. Noshit replied, 'Wal, tell you whut. Y'all can sing yore hearts out to Jesus, but yore asses belong to me.' He slammed the door behind him. The preachers started up again with renewed fervor. Then guards showed up with the fire hose. They hosed us all down. Someone hollered, 'Hallellujah! He washing away our sins. Next time, bring some soap.'" I'm so engrossed in Brandon's story that I lost sight of the fact that we have been standing in front of Douglass Hall the whole time. His story conjured up in me such fearful and horrific images that I'm exhausted. "Brandon, can we sit a minute?"

"Sure, Izzy. Shall we find our table at the Student Union?"

"That would help." As we make our way to Miner Hall, I ask Brandon how he could possibly endure such barbaric treatment. "Wait, it gets worse! Noshit introduced Frank and me to a form of torture that I had never heard of. They called them wrist breakers. It was essentially a small vise. The pain was excruciating. If you tried to ignore the pain, they'd twist it in such a way that you would feel your bones about to break. The pain would make you flip over, Jack. And if they continued to twist, the agony was so great you'd find yourself rolling over on the floor." I don't know how much more I can listen to this horror, but Brandon keeps on.

"When it was my turn, I had convinced myself that I would not let them flip me. After I had flipped a couple of times, Noshit asks if I had had enough. I just stared at him. He flipped me again. 'Enough yet?' I lay on that floor and started singing a movement song: 'I'm going to tell God how you treat me, one of these days.' The entire row joined in."

We take a break and grab some coffee. When we return to our table, Brandon continues. "If the wrist breaker affair was a kind of victory, the next event was a ridiculous defeat. One of the white members of our group, who was a committed Gandhian, began a hunger strike. Frank and I were in passionate agreement—no hunger strike. We needed our energy to deal with all the whup-ass that the jailors were laying on us. Generally the other NAG folk were opposed to the hunger strike. The ministers, pacifists, and Gandhians were for it. Through group pressure those of us against the strike finally caved. Frank and I were the last holdouts. The thought that finally sunk us was that we would be the only ones in the group eating. That thought was morally repellent to both of us. The next morning, we told the trustees to take the food back. Our jailors were puzzled. They'd never encountered a move like this. Noshit told them to leave the food, but no one touched it.

Then supper came and the food, which had always been disgusting, suddenly was much more appealing. Fried chicken, peas, greens and corn bread still steaming and butter. The food was placed in the slot in the door where we could see and smell it. We had to endure the smells because the penalty for knocking over the trays was solitary confinement in the hole. We wouldn't eat it though. The pigs responded by bringing us even better food--Roast beef, mashed potatoes, pecan pie. After a couple of days, we all had severe stomach pains. Now we started fighting with each other over the wisdom of the hunger strike. The arguments got louder and more contentious. This went on for several days. Then on the fourth day, Frank leaped out, pointing and shouting. 'Look, look, that one's empty. I don't know who, but someone just ate. I don't care who it was , but Frank Wade's gonna be second.' Me and James Farmer held out for another day. But before I started eating, I had something to say to the group. 'Friends, most of you don't know me. My name is Brandon Blackwell. I'm in with Frank Wade. We are the two youngest freedom fighters in here. Now I'm young and pretty, but I will be fighting for our people's freedom until the day I die, so there's no doubt that I'll land in jail again.   I bet many of you will too. So remember my name. Because if we're ever in jail again and any of you even mentions the words hunger and strike, I'm gonna denounce you properly. I'll be at the front of the line to denounce you. You can tell everybody that. That if they are ever in ail with Brandon Blackwell, never ever mention anything about any hunger strike.'" We both start laughing. "Yeah, now I can laugh about it; but at the time, it was no laughing matter," Brandon says, shaking his head vigorously. "Of course, now that the strike was over, the food reverted to its formerly disgusting smell and taste.

Shortly after the strike ended, we learned that CORE had made a deal that we were all to be released, and all Freedom Riders were required to leave the state immediately. A number of us were opposed, but to no avail. Even though we were willing to stay and keep the jails filled, we were so excited to finally get out of Parchman and leave behind the 100 daily humiliations and acts of brutality that we all were subjected to."

"Brandon, I just can't believe it." His eyes widen with shock. "You don't believe me?"

"No, I course I believe you. I can't believe that this kind of barbarity goes on in the United States."

"Oh Izzy, you've been brainwashed, just like all the other flag-wavers in this country. You've been at Howard for how long?"

"This is my third year."

"Your third year. Come on, you must know by now how this country treats black people. How can you possibly hold on to your fantasy idea that this country is the epitome of Truth, Justice, and the American Way?" As he says this, he flexes his muscles in mimicry of Superman. "Anyway, Izzy, the reason I told you that story about my jail time in Mississippi is to help you understand why Malcolm's oratory grabbed such a hold on me and on so many black people in the audience. America keeps giving black people the message that we are not wanted in this country. And if we want to be here, then we have to eat the white man's shit and then thank him for it while we wipe his ass. And while I can't buy Malcolm's separate state for Blacks, I am becoming convinced that black people have to stand together, work together, and progress together. I know some people are gonna accuse me of being anti-white, but that ain't accurate. The truth is that I am pro-Black. When Malcolm said that before every other way in which we may identify ourselves, American, Democrat, Republican… we are Black, that audience in Crampton, black people from Africa, from the Caribbean and from the good ole US of A felt free to recognize their oneness, to give loud affirmation to something they were being educated to suppress and deny: our collective blackness."

I look at Brandon and I can see the pride he feels, the sense of wholeness in his blackness. And for the first time I can feel the emotional undertow of Malcolm's speech, something that my fear of rejection as a white person prevented me from hearing. It's important to belong and to experience the shared fate of a people. Your people! More important yet was to stand and fight together in order to be treated with respect and dignity. This was no different than what I had been taught since childhood, that Jews should stick together and fight together for their rights. Since childhood, I have heard the half-serious joke that the evaluation of any world event begins with the question, "Is it good for the Jews?" I now can hear Brandon voicing the same question, "Is it good for the Blacks?" At the same time, I feel rejected, cast aside because of my whiteness. I had agreed—and still agree- with Rustin that this fight, while primarily focused on Negroes and their rights, is about much more. It's about whether America can ever live up to its professed ideals that under the law all men are created equal and that they share equal rights. And whether it's possible for whites and blacks to live together and work together to create a more perfect America.

"Well, later Izzy, I gotta meet up with some NAG folk." I watch Brandon's jaunty, rhythmic movements as he walks away. In my mind's ear, I hear the hiss of envy. Brandon knows who he is and he knows his purpose in life. He's a committed activist fighting for the rights of his people. In my mind's eye, I see myself shrink by comparison. Who and what am I?

When I get into one of my periodic funks, I always head for the basketball court. At the time, it's the best therapy I know. I'm happy to see that the outdoor court at the Takoma Playground is empty, and I can try and give my B-Ball creativity full reign. I fake out imaginary defenders and drive to the hole. And when I'm ready to let my "J" fly, I send the softly spinning orb through its netted destination...from 15, 20, and 25 feet. The sound of the ball swishing through the net is my greatest reward. And with each successful flight of the net-fluttering ball, I feel a bolus of self-esteem injecting into my spiritual veins. After a 20-minute intense workout, I sit on the bench by the side of the court and reflect on my conversation with Brandon. I wrestle with the fact that Brandon and I share the same goal but for different reasons. We both want to see Negroes receive their long overdue rights and be treated with respect in America. But he identifies with his people, dark skin people. For him, it really is about what's good for the blacks. I want the world to make sense.

I cannot articulate why this feels like a difference of cavernous proportions, but it does. And this difference bears directly on the question of whether I should join NAG. I have great admiration and respect for the members that I have encountered so far. They are smart, brave, and committed activists, and I know that their cause is just. But I distrust their zeal and fear where it will take us. I'm terrified that joining NAG would be a lethal decision. I don't want to die for a lost cause. On the other hand, I have been greatly impressed with the student movement and what it has already achieved in a little less than two short years. What a gift that this generation of students is giving to future generations—the destruction of white supremacy, Jim Crow Laws and American Apartheid. And I could be a part of this gift. What greater use could I make of my young life? My mind keeps bouncing from one image to the other, from Izzy dead to Izzy proud. I cannot know the final outcome of the civil rights struggle and, not knowing, I have to choose. So I do what I often do when trying to choose between two serious directions in which I could take my life. I shoot a basketball. I tell myself that if I make three consecutive jump shots from 22 feet, I will join NAG. Any miss and I'll decline the honor. The first two shots are true. They touch nothing but net. I tell myself that if I really want to join, I will make the last shot. If I don't make the shot then I really don't want to join. I lift myself into the air and let the ball fly in a perfect arc with perfect form. Convinced that the ball is going into the hoop, I pull my hand away a little too soon and instead of a swish, the ball begins to roll around the rim. It makes several rotations before it seems to catapult off to the side in a hideous replay of my failed shot in overtime of the Interhigh Playoffs a few years back. It seems strange that I take this outcome to be an inexorable sign of my decision. But the decision is final. I call Brandon and tell him that I'm not going to join NAG, and I will regret that decision for the rest of my life.

Chapter 18.
Black like Me?

I spend the next week in a truly delicious funk. Pay attention in my classes? Forget about it! The sound of my professors' voices during their windy lectures resembles the barely interpretable static-altered voices on a police radio. At work, I let the kids at the playground do whatever they want. I might have been physically present, but mentally and emotionally, I'm in the land of self-pityville. During the weekend, whenever Adam is out of our room, I lie in bed listening to every sad doo-wop song I can find on the radio. And to add a little sophistication to my pity party, I find among my brother's LPs, the truly depressing music of the French classical composer Marin Marais. I constantly berate myself for not having the balls to become a civil rights activist. After all I believe in the cause. Why did I tell Brandon no? Over and over, I flagellate myself with questions and accusations of a deficient manhood. When I finally have exhausted my lexicon of self-deprecating epithets, the realization kicks in that I lack the passion to become an activist. I am not sure whether that is because I lack sufficient rebelliousness in my soul, or that I think it's just too damn difficult to challenge the perniciously racist social mores of our beloved "Land of the free."

On a chilly November morning I wake up with a very heavy feeling. Remnants of a disturbing dream are popping in and out of consciousness. It has something to do with becoming black. I drag my sleep-mugged body into the shower and allow myself to enjoy the warm comforting cascade of water. I remember John Howard Griffin's book, Black Like Me, in which he chose to have his skin darkened so that he could live as a Negro in the South. In the dream I had, I suddenly become black, and it 's not of my choosing. The same terrible humiliations that happened to Griffin happen to me. How ridiculous, I think, as I laugh at my dream. I stand in front of the mirror and dry myself off. As the steam-fogged mirror clears, I see something unexpected in my reflection. My face seems much browner than

I remember; browner, in fact, than any tan I have ever had. The rest of my body reflects back a darkening tone, not as dark as my face, but clearly darker than it's ever been. I assume that this is a sleep-induced hallucination. I turn away from the mirror and forcefully slap my cheeks—all four of them—hoping that I will wake up. When I turn once again to face the mirror, I see the same brown reflection. A full blast of Heebie Jeebies seizes my body and I let out with a scream. I throw a towel around me and run into the kitchen screaming, "Ma, I'm turning black! I'm turning black!"

"Why are you yelling, Izzy? Look at you. You're white as snow. What craziness is this?" I shake my head vigorously. "Look at me and look in the mirror, here. Can't you see? I'm already chocolate."

"Don't be such a meshuganah, Izzy. You're seeing things. Go lie down, you'll feel better." That is my mother's omnipresent remedy for everything. It's her sole bubbemayseh. Whether it's a hangnail or a hemorrhoid, it's always, "Go lie down, you'll feel better." Seeing that I'm getting nowhere with my mother, I call out to my brother. "Adam, come look at me, I'm turning into a Negro!" My brother storms in from our room angry and frustrated. In the background, I can hear the sounds of Tchaikovsky's Marche Slave, and I know he's in the middle of cataloguing his humongous record collection. He does not like to be disturbed when in the middle of such pedestrian, clerical tasks. Even angry, I recognize that he has a handsome face, a face I resent because it has everything that mine lacks, a straight nose, wavy black hair, enviably straight teeth, and an appealing smile. "What is it now, Izzy? Why are you interrupting me?"

"Look Adam, I'm turning black."

"Aw for Christ's sake, Izzy, you're crazy. You have the same pasty color you always have. Whatd'ya mean you're turning black?"

"That's what I see when I look in the mirror. My face is a deep chocolate color."

"You're nuts. I bet its wishful thinking. I think you want to be black. Going to Howard is changing you. You're so impressionable, Izzy; it should surprise no one that you have black on the brain."

"Why would I want to be a member of another despised minority? Being Jewish is enough of a problem."

"Yeah, and you're about as good a Negro as you are a Jew."

"Aw you're no help." I push past him and go back into the bathroom and slam the door. Again I look in the mirror and again I see my chocolate colored reflection staring back at me. By now, I've calmed down enough to contemplate the catastrophic. What if I were black? Maybe I should try and embrace it. I tried to imitate the cool confident walk of black men. As I watch this performance in the mirror, my attempt at being cool comes off like a person walking on one leg that is a half a foot shorter than the other. Disastrous! Now I begin to dance, trying my best to "blacken" my every dance move. This is better. I already know that some black people think I dance pretty well. I'm feeling better already. As I continue to dance for my brown reflection, I notice that I have a hard-on. I'm feeling sexy and loving the way I feel. No shame, just free. My moves are looser, more emphatic. I start waving my arms over my head in a circular pattern Free my sexy soul! I yell as my whole body whirls in a circle. As I whirl and whirl, I'm enveloped by a joyful and peaceful feeling, which is quickly interrupted by a searing pain. I have slammed my erect penis into the base of the bathroom sink. Owwoooh, I howl. My brother Adam thinks I'm singing the doo-wop songs he detests and registers his complaint by banging forcefully on the wall that separates our room from the bathroom. That shuts me up. I try not to yell as I wait for my painfully throbbing member to calm down. Then I hear laughter. It's a laugh I have never heard before, high pitched and seemingly with a black accent. "Hee, hee, hee, hee, hee." I can't tell where it's coming from.

"Why you trying t'be a brothah?" Where did that come from? I hear this voice, my voice, but I know I haven't said what I hear.

"Why you trying t'be a brothah?" the voice demands again. It seems to be coming from the mirror. I look at my brown reflection, which has a large grin on its face. The laughter continues, but the pitch has shifted downward by two octaves, "Heh, heh, heh," and it begins to speak again. This time I see his lips move. "You neva gonna be a brothah, ya dig? You a jive-ass honky trying t'be a brothah. I'm hippin ya, man." This really upsets me. I can't let this charge go unanswered. "Now you listen here you, whoever you are, you brown version of me. I am not a jive-ass honky. "

"Oh yeah you are. You jivin' me right now, wid all yo' sposed empady fo' de struggle uh de brothah. As long as you ain't one, you fine. What it is, Honky! Look at ya'. You be shittin' yo' pants lookin' at me. You be actin' likes de wo'ld's comin' t'an end if ya be a brothah."

"Look I don't know where you came from, but my heart's in the right place. I just want to find out why so many white people hate your black ass." The reflection loves this. "Haw Haw Haw,". "Oh my God! I'm so sorry I said that." By now my brown reflection is shaking and swaying he was laughing so hard. "Oh yeah. Right On! You sho' nuff"'s some pure-hearted Honky, ain't ya?" There's a banging on the bathroom door. "Izzy? What's going on in there? Who the hell are you talking to? I can't concentrate with all that yapping going on in there." After all these years, my brother's anger still frightens me. "Uh, n'nothing , Adam, I'm just rehearsing a talk I have to give in one of my classes." "Well, keep it down, please. I need to work. I know you're alone in there, but that doesn't mean you have to play with yourself." I hear him laughing to himself, pleased with his own witty banter.

There's quiet in the bathroom, but only momentarily. My brown reflection continues to stare at me with an expression of reproach. Then he starts up again.

"You think cuz ya' likes doo-wop and play hoopball dat you some kind of brothah. You think cuz' ya' chose t'go t'Howard University, you a brothah. Shee-it, ya' ain't no brothah." I'm tempted to scream out my protest, but I see in my mind's eye my brother's angry face. Instead I whisper.

"Listen, I never said I wanted to be a brother. I want to understand what the Negro has experienced and how this race problem came to be. Most of all, I want to know why I have all this crap in my head about Negroes."

"Ain't this a shame, dis be wo'se dan ah' thought. You wanna be some Liberal." I frown at my reflection. The truth of his words wakes me to the reality that I'm talking to myself. But why am I seeing a brown me. "Who are you?" I ask.

"Why, I'm de truth behind yo' pretenshuns.," he says with a wide grin. If ya' wanna be a brothah, you''d gone on de Freedom Rides. If ya' wanna be some brothah, you''d be out on de picket lines, o' waaay down Soud heppin' de folks t'destroy segregashun. But ya' dun didn't go, did ya' Honky?"

"Damn you. I didn't. "

"See whut ah' mean—de truth behind yo' pretensions." I can't stand to look at that brown face anymore, and I quickly leave the bathroom.

I'm so shaken by this encounter with my brown reflection that I have to find a way to purge the image from my mind. The only antidote is basketball. I spend the next hour trying to jump higher, shoot straighter, and move quicker with the ball than ever before. My workout completely banishes the brown reflection and anesthetizes me from all feelings of guilt for not dedicating myself to the cause of civil rights. A renewed passion for playing college basketball replaces my desire to become a civil rights activist.

I'm excited when the first day of basketball practice begins. But something doesn't feel right. Whee's gone and so is Linc and George Brown. With Walter Harrison and myself being the only two returning letterman, we will have to develop a new chemistry with a basically all-new team. Two new guards joined the team to challenge me, Peter Grant and Clayborne Hill. Both are good shooters, but neither is an excellent point guard. Since I also favor the shooting guard spot, one of us will end up as the point guard as a consolation prize. Point guards do most of the passing to other players and relatively little scoring, while the shooting guards do just that—shoot the ball.

When St. Paul University travels up from Virginia to play us in early December, Coach chooses Clay to be the point, and Peter and I are deemed the shooting guards. However, the ball rarely shows up in my direction. Clay feeds Peter and Walter full course meals plus dessert. Me he puts on a starvation diet. Peter leads us with 22 points and I have three. Our first half lead disappears and St. Paul ends up crushing us, 85-66. I'm not happy and I express my unhappiness in the locker room after the game. "Hey Clay, have I offended you," I ask sarcastically. He picks right up on my unhappiness and he apparently knows why. "Look, White, every time I look in your direction, you and your St. Paul defender looked like the two of you were sharing his uniform." Everyone in the locker room howls with laughter. That makes me even madder. "Bullshit, Hill, I was open most of the time. But you acted like I was the Invisible Man."

"White men look that way to me. Y'all look like ghosts."

"Well, I ain't no ghost."

Hill then changes his tune, and begins to act like a subservient slave. With obsequious servile movements, and in a high pitched voice reminiscent of the "Lightening" character on the Amos and Andy TV show, he says, "Oh ah's sorry little white massa. Next game, I make's sure I hand's yo the ball." Now he's bugging his eyes out and scratching his head, he adds, "Maybe, I's hands it to ya on a silver platter." My response to this ugly display is to ask him to stop being a putz. "Putz?" Hill exclaims. That's a Jewish word isn't it?" He then addresses everyone else in the locker room, "Did y'all know that we have a kike among us." I turn crimson and before I can stop myself, I retort, "If I'm a kike, then you must be a nigger." He leaps from the bench and is about to throttle me, but is grabbed by several of our teammates. Nobody can look me in the eye. Walter Harrison says in his very quiet way. "Aw Izzy, that was uncalled for."

"I know, Walter, and I'm terribly sorry. But Clay has no business calling me a kike."

"Two wrongs don't make a right, Izzy," Walter answers, his voice filled with dejection and disappointment. With great remorse I whine, "I know, I know! It just came out of me." I attempt to apologize to the remaining teammates in the locker room, "GUYS, I'M SORRY!" Several remain silent and continue getting dressed. A few mumble a form of forgiveness, "Tha's cool, Izzy." Clayborne won't even look at me, probably to keep himself from killing me.

I sit alone in the locker room for a long time thinking about what just happened. I can't believe I had used that word and with hostility. I remember what Linc and Whee Willie told me last year when the three of us talked about my ever saying the word nigger. Linc had said, "It's not skin color, Izzy,. It's history! Don't matter the context, the word nigger out of a white man's mouth brings nothing but pain and memories of pain." And Whee had added, "In every black man you meet, there is a scar as old as slavery and you best not pick at it. You can't see it, but by God it's there." Then I was talking about using the word as a sign of friendly belonging. When I insulted Clayborne, I sounded like every other white bigot I detested. I had come to Howard to rid myself of racist venom, and here it squirts out at the first sign of attack from a black man. I'm failing again.

If I thought Hill put me on a starvation diet during the St. Paul game, during our next game against Lincoln, he makes me feel like I was in solitary confinement. He does not pass the ball to me once. During the first half I don't mind. I think of the freeze out as penitence for my verbal crime. During the second half, however, I begin to get upset. After all, I'm playing in order to help the team win, and I'm supposed to do that by scoring. But the only time I score is when I take over the point guard job while Hill takes a breather on the bench, and I set up my own shot. Hill and Grant are sensational, however, and we win the game on the strength of their combined shooting skill.

Occasionally, I do learn from experience. Our next game against Hampton is to be our last game before the Christmas break. I beg the coach to let me play the point. Since no vocal opposition comes from either Hill or Grant, the coach is inclined to say yes. During the first half, I'm still functioning in penitent mode. I dutifully distribute the ball to my four teammates and rarely take a shot. Nonetheless, by halftime, we are leading by five points. I have accumulated six points on the strength of my foul shooting. Every time I drive the middle, defenders collapse on me, and I pass the ball off to a player on the wing. I do mean collapse; because in their attempts to slap the ball away from me, they invariably slap me. It's like running a gauntlet.

In the second half, I change tactics. Now I distribute the ball to me as well as my four teammates on the floor. And I'm hot. I'm making jump shots from everywhere—from the corner and the top of the key. I feign driving to the basket and hit two pull up jump shots as my opponent continues stumbling toward the basket. Coaches always say, "feed the hot hand", so I feed myself. My final shot is a pull up jump shot. But I have to extend myself as high as I can jump because my opponent isn't fooled.

Before I release the ball, I have to adjust its position to avoid my defender blocking it. That pulls my body out of its normal position. As I come down, I hear a pop; and I'm overtaken by a level of pain in my knee that I didn't know was possible for a human to feel. I lie sprawled out on the floor writhing in agony. I can faintly hear the cheers of the crowd because the ball apparently has successfully gone into the basket. I have scored my 19th and 20th point and have given our team a winning lead. I have also dislocated my kneecap. It has drifted to the right of my leg; and to my pain-altered vision, my kneecap now resembles a large tilting tumor sitting on my leg. As I'm carried off to the locker room, the crowd gives me a standing ovation. But one person (who stands out from all the rest) is standing holding her cheeks with horror in her eyes, a poignant contrast amidst the resounding cheers. It's Desirie. I weakly wave and smile in her direction, but I'm not sure if she sees me wave. The sight of her concern for me triggers the long dormant feelings I have for her. Now the pain of her loss returns and magnifies the pain of my physical injury. Once in the locker room, the team trainer has placed my leg in a splint. I will soon graduate to crutches. And for the next uncountable collection of days, I have one more pain to demoralize me even further. I now have to try and accept the inexorable reality that my college basketball career is over.

Christmas is not my holiday, but I love it anyway. It truly seems to be a season of good will. People seem nicer; and either because of or despite the rampant commercialism of the holiday, people are in a giving mood. But what really stands out for me is the music, particularly Handel's "Messiah". In my humble opinion there has been no greater piece of music ever written. I am not a religious person, but the music does inspire. Rumor has it, Handel wrote all 186,000 notes in 24 days. Amazing! And every Christmas day, I watch one of my favorite movies-the 1951 version of Dickens' "A Christmas Carol", starring the gifted British comedic actor, Alistair Sim. More than any other characterization of Ebenezer Scrooge I have ever seen, Sim truly captures the bitter, stingy man who fears being crushed by the world, and who therefore develops a mean and uncaring persona in defense. Then through the visitation of three Christmas spirits, he breaks through the defensive cover to reveal his jovial, good-hearted core. As I sit on the couch watching this movie for the umpteenth time, it occurs to me that the journey Scrooge takes is not unlike what I imagine a successful psychotherapy to be like. In my Introduction to Psychology class, we're learning about the different approaches to psychotherapy. The early psychoanalytic therapies that focused on peoples' defenses against their true nature actually stir my blood. Maybe psychology is for me. As I look back on my own life, I can point to so many events and relationships that I know have helped shape the person I have become. It seems to me at that moment that becoming a psychotherapist might be great fun, always interesting, and often rewarding when I can help a person get past their problems and begin to live a more satisfying life. During the rest of Christmas day at least, I feel a jolt of optimism over the prospect that I may yet snatch a successful career at Howard University from the jaws of confusion. I promise myself then and there that I'll spend the rest of my Christmas vacation reading anything that pertains to psychology and psychotherapy. My commitment to solitary reading lasts all of two days.

Chapter 19.
Negus With Attitude

Except for Christmas Day, the Holidays are barren. There is no love, no glory, no sense of connection to the university. And there's not much physical activity since I'm hobbling around on crutches. Two and a half years into my university experience, I'm still feeling alienated, lonely, and a failure. I have failed in my so-called love affair with Desirie; failed as a neophyte civil rights activist; and ultimately a failure in my career as a varsity basketball player. Even my new enthusiasm for psychology cannot quell the gloom that has come over me. In my "white" world, I fare little better. Except for The Three Miscreants my connections to my high school friends have seriously deteriorated. Most of them are at other colleges. Many are at nearby University of Maryland joining fraternities, having wild parties, getting laid. None of that is happening for me. Even James, Peter, and Bobby are developing lives independent of my everyday life. I still see them, but very infrequently.

On the Saturday after Christmas, I automatically dial the phone numbers of Peter, Bobby, and James. I urgently need to talk to someone. James is the only one who answers. I implore him to meet me somewhere so we can talk. An hour later, we're sitting across from one another at the Silver Spring Hot Shoppes ordering an early lunch. His raven–black flattop has had a recent mowing, which sharpens his already keen features: his prominent, high cheek bones, pointed nose, and piercing black eyes. It's only after we have both ordered our Mighty Mo's that James asks in his customarily dry manner, "What's going on, Izzy?" His expression suggests a combination of compassion and impatience. He seems to be bracing for another one of my patented monologues of self-deprecation. I put my head in my hands and begin to shake it. "Shit, James, I think I've made a terrible mistake. I shouldn't've gone to Howard." James sighs. "Why are saying this now?"

"Because, I'm a failure. I've failed at everything there." James shifts into irony mode.

"That's some failure. Your way is paid at college for the entire 4 years. You made the basketball team. Your grades aren't awful and you are biologically intact, since you didn't go South on the Freedom Rides where you surely would have been beaten to within an inch of your life. Like I said, some failure."

"You don't understand! I have retarded myself socially by going to a predominantly black school."

"You didn't seem to be doing so badly with Desirie. You've broken that taboo. Why haven't you met more black girls or made more male friends there?"

I have ratcheted up to a full whine. "I don't know, I don't know!" Apparently, I whined a little too loudly. When I look up, I see a half-a-dozen heads have turned in my direction, all with perplexed expressions. I look back at James and I see that the compassion that had been evident has now drained from his face and what is left is an expression of sheer exasperation. He takes a deep breath and then says, "Look, Izzy, I have an idea. Did you read a couple of weeks ago about Ernie Davis?" I brighten with curiosity. "Yes he won the Heisman Trophy and is the first Negro to do so. He's such a great back. He's going to the Cleveland Browns. With him and Jim Brown in that backfield, the Browns will be unstoppable."

"Yeah, well, I also heard a rumor that the Sammies let him into their fraternity."

"The Sammies?" I ask.

"You know, the Jewish Fraternity at Syracuse, Sigma Alpha Mu; hence Sammies."

"So what's that got to do with me?"

"Well, he's the first Negro to join a white fraternity. How about you being the first white to join a black fraternity at Howard?" My mind flashes to a conversation I had with my teammate, Hank Dobson, about Omega Psi Phi. "Izzy, I think you should really consider going on line with the Qs. If you show any interest, I think the Qs would be willing to break the color line for you." "Really?" I ask. "What do I have to do to become a pledge?"

"Well, first I have to run it by the Grand Basileus and he would have to run it by the membership committee."

"And if they approve me, then what?"

"You'd have to have your head shaved and fork over $200."

"Say what? Let me get this straight. In order to enter a line, I have to give you all my hair and more money than I possess. Hank, don't get me wrong, it would be an honor to be the first white member of Omega Psi Phi, but I can't afford it. Sorry man, I just can't do it."

"I guess that feels like you're being 'scalped' twice," Hank said with a chuckle. "But think about it, Izzy. Becoming a fraternity man, particularly a member of the Qs, would be the capstone of your education at Howard. You know, Omega Psi Phi represents the initials of the Greek phrase that means, 'Friendship is essential to the soul'. And we are dedicated to the Cardinal Principles of Manhood, Scholarship, Perseverance, and Uplift. In other words, Izzy, we will make a man out of you. " I thought he was asking me to join the Marines. "And you will make friends for life," he adds. "How about that? Pretty attractive, don't ya think?" I can clearly see through his eyes, how attractive being a fraternity man can be. But would that life fit me? "Hank, I'll think about it and let you know." I didn't know what else to say. Truth is, I want to join the Qs, but I guess I want my hair and my money more.

Neither one of us ever brought the subject up again.

I laugh at that memory but think that James is on to something. "You know James, you're right. Joining a fraternity may be just the oddball move for me to make for me to feel more connected to Howard. But I've never been the fraternity type. I've always tried to hang with people from every group, but never wanted to join any of them. But you know what? I need to do something. Thanks, James, you've been a big help." James grins at me. "Well, Roll over Beethoven and tell Tchaikovsky the news!"

We finish our Mighty Mo's and leave the Hot Shoppes, which is now bustling with its lunchtime crowd. James drops me back at my apartment and soon I am behind the closed door of my room deep in thought about which fraternity I should try and pledge. I want to avoid the three most prestigious frats on campus, the Kappas, the Alphas, and the Ques, because I know they all haze their pledges mercilessly. I'm afraid I wouldn't be able to stand such treatment; and I also fear that because I'm white, I might come in for worse treatment than the other pledges. Instead, I come to the not well thought through conclusion that a more obscure fraternity might be more open to my color and less prone to abusive hazing practices. I discover a fairly new fraternity that was formed at Howard in the last 10 years known as Beta Omicron Sigma Sigma. The acronym suggests their motif. They are the BOSS Men- The coolest of the cool. Following a tradition of several other fraternities, the founders of BOSS had no interest in joining an already existing organization. Like the Phi Beta Sigma founders, the founders of BOSS wanted to be a fraternity that shunned the bourgeois inclinations of the Alphas, Kappas, and the Omegas. On the first day of the new semester, I search for the BOSS fraternity house, which is located several blocks off campus. Its location is as obscure as the fraternity. It's on the Eastern edge of LeDroit

Park. Once a prime area of real estate for prominent black families, LeDroit Park's older middle class families vacated their homes to buy quality housing left in the wake of white flight to the suburbs. Houses there are now being filled with lower income occupants. The BOSSmen found an old Victorian house that is significantly run down, and they have put their own "cool" stamp on it.

On the grass fronting the house, there is a small sign with the Greek Letters Beta Omicron Sigma Sigma. They appear to be carved out of aged wood, which gives the feeling of a beach house. Under the letters is the fraternity's motto, "Home of the Brave and Land of the Cool". Hanging from the overhead that shades the porch are two ivory African masks.

I lift the heavy knocker shaped like a lion's head and let it drop. I do this three times in rapid succession. The sound it makes is reminiscent of the metallic thud on ancient horror movie mansion doors, a sound that made audiences fearful of the anticipated monsters or their makers who lurked within. A studious looking Negro opens the door and stares at me with silent incomprehension. He is a lean six- footer, with dark horn-rimmed glasses wearing a grey sweater with the Greek letters Beta, Omicron Sigma Sigma sewn onto it in orange. Ironically, these were my high school colors, and I immediately take that as a positive omen and begin to relax. "Hello, my name is Izzy White and I'm a Howard student who may be interested in joining your fraternity." My studious interlocutor's eyebrows shoot upward, and his eyes bug out with shock. "You say what, Honky?" Not quite the welcome I had expected. I become a little annoyed. "I want to speak to someone about joining your fraternity. " Horn rims struggles to keep from laughing in my face. "OK, I think you best talk to the Negus." Now it's my turn to stifle my laughter. "The what?

"The Negus," he repeats with emphasis. He sees my discomfort in repeating the word Negus and says for my edification, "Not Niggas. It's Negus."

"I assume that is the term for your leader?"

"Tha's right. The Ques have their Basileus, the Kappas, their Polemarch and we have our Negus. It's an Amharic term, which means King."

"Oh."

Without saying a word, Horn Rims extends his arm into the house beckoning me to enter. Once inside, he says, "Wait here and I will let the Negus know you are here. " Horn Rims then climbs the wide staircase. I look around the large living room, which creates a feeling of faded opulence. Heavy velvet maroon drape panels hang shabbily on either side of each window. Ecru-colored sheer panels cover the windows so some filtered light is able to come through. The living room is furnished with a large once plush maroon velvet couch with heavily carved mahogany legs.

Two wing side chairs covered in badly worn maroon and gold cut velvet flanked the 6' high cream-painted fireplace. Above the fireplace carved in aged wood is the Greek acronym for BOSS. Along the mantle are several African pieces made of bronze and brass. A large oriental rug is rolled up against one wall leaving open to full view the dark wood plank floor that has been dulled from use. A dark mahogany table is situated between the couch and side chairs. It's covered with empty beer cans and mangled pizza covers, apparently from a New Year's Eve party.

A few moments later, I see a tall, muscular dark man descending the stairs. He has the demeanor of a proud African chieftain. He's wearing the same grey sweater with orange Greek lettering as Horn Rims, but he is dressed in sharply creased black slacks instead of jeans. He stares at me severely and says, "I am the Negus of B.O.S.S., but I am better known as Lloyd Redmayne." He turns to point at Horn Rims who has been following him down the stairs. "And this is Colby Betterman, the Parliamentarian of B.O.S.S."

"Great to meet both of you," I say.

"And you are Izzy White?"

"That's right; Izzy White," I answer, trying to lighten the mood.

The Negus continues to stare at me coldly and suggests, "That is truly one weird name." His eyes widen and he doubles over with laughter. Colby Betterman does the same. This abrupt change in mood breaks down my own stiff demeanor and I laugh with them. The three of us continued to laugh for the next few minutes, and I already begin to feel like a BOSSman. My laughter seems to offend the Negus whose cold look has returned and who says in a stern voice, "What you laughing at?"

"I'm sorry, I-I uh," The Negus resumes his high-pitched laughter, his entire body shaking with mirth. "I'm just messing with ya, Izzy." I respond with a nervous laugh.

"You know Izzy," the Negus continues, "we're a little different kind of fraternity, so I better tell you about BOSS and see if you think it' ill be a good fit for you."

"Sure, that would be helpful."

"The fraternity got started about ten years ago when our three founders quit the pledge lines of the Alphas, the Kappas, and the Ques, respectively. They agreed that these fraternities try too hard to ape the white fraternities and are not a proper conduit for the development of black manhood. They just help to produce more members into the Black Bourgeoisie. Have you read that book, Izzy?"

"What book?"

"Black Bourgeoisie" by E. Franklin Frazier. You know he's the Chairman of Howard's Sociology Department."

"No I haven't. I've heard of it, but I haven't read it.

"The Professor's thesis is that the BBs want to differentiate themselves from the masses of poor Negroes. But they can't because of the total rejection we all feel from the white world. This rejection makes them feel inferior, and they try and compensate for this sense of inferiority by creating a world of make believe in order to manufacture their wished-for status in America. Originally, social distinctions among Negroes were based on family background and color snobbishness. Light-skinned mulattoes, who themselves were products of the rapes of slaves by their masters, thought they were better than their darker brothers and sisters. So they began to ape the upper class patterns of rich white folk. They do crazy shit like having cotillions and coming out parties for new debutants as if they were a super-rich upper class society. All this make-believe is heralded by the Negro Press, which makes a big deal about any so-called event of Negro High Society. All of the Rag-mags like Ebony and Jet constantly exaggerate the alleged achievements of the BBs. Seems like anytime a nigger shows up somewhere in a tuxedo, his picture appears in Jet." The Negus laughs at his little joke and continues.

"The main way Negroes try to differentiate themselves is by money. Members of so-called Negro society are not rich. They include members of the professions and men and women of business who have enough money to engage in conspicuous consumption. But they are by no means rich. Far from it! They mortgage their homes so that they can afford to buy vacation homes in upper class vacation spots such as Sag Harbor and Oak Bluffs. But even in those places they are allowed to buy only in small, gilded Black ghettos. The traditional fraternities and sororities play a significant role in grooming Black brothers and sisters for this misguided lifestyle. Their approach to life is fantasy-ridden; their values are hollow, and their psychic lives are spent in guilt, conflict, and low self-esteem."

I'm taken aback by his use of this offensive sobriquet for Black people in front of me, but I'm even more stunned by this withering critique of American Negroes. I have heard something like it before from those Howard students who originally hailed from the Caribbean, such as Brandon Blackwell and Winston McKenzie. It's beginning to dawn on me that there are a significant number of students at Howard who are rebelling against the black middle-class life style-the so-called Black Bourgeoisie. And I have to admit they seem to be making a pretty good case. The Negus continues: "Now BOSS desires to help create a different kind of Black man, one who is simultaneously idealistic and cool; one who believes in doing well by doing good. BOSS men are neither selfless nor selfish. We are both at the same time. Our actions help others even as we help ourselves. I know that may sound contradictory, but it's not. It is factual."

"That has some real appeal for me."

"Glad to hear it, Izzy," the Negus says off-handedly, apparently not glad at all to hear my interrupting him. "So we are about the repair of the American Negro male's socialization. The first step in that repair is to reconnect the black man with his true origins, Mama Africa." With that the Negus goes over to the mantle place where he begins to stroke a brass figure of the head of a regal looking African. " Come over here, Izzy, I want to show you something. We have been told the big lie by the Tarzan movies. We who originally hail from Africa are not savages. Our ancestors did not live in savage African communities. There have been numerous great African civilizations, Izzy. Centuries ago there were the great Empires of Ghana, Mali, Songhay and Benin. You see this mask here, Izzy. Look at this beautiful work of art. This is a commemorative brass head of an ancient king of Benin. Benin was a highly developed civilization that existed between the early 1300s to the late 1800s.

It was located in what is now southeastern Nigeria. They were great artists in brass, bronze and ivory." The shock of recognition stands my hair up. I had seen a very similar brass head at Henry Prescott's house when we both were in high school. I'm struck now, as I was then, by the beautifully formed features, the intricately beaded headdress, the fully formed lips and wide nostrils. I have never found these features beautiful before now. For the first time I see a beautiful woman who looks nothing like Elizabeth Taylor or Jean Simmons, or any other of the movie stars that had defined for me the only standard of beauty I had known. Desirie is so beautiful in her brownness, but her features tilt toward the keen features of white women. The more I stare at this brass figure, the more meaning it has for me. As I listen to the Negus expound with great pride the cloistered African past, I rummage through my memories of what I have thought and learned about Africa and its peoples. And I know that the Negus is right. We got nothing like this view of Africa from the Tarzan movies that gave us so much Saturday afternoon pleasure in the darkened movie theatres of our youth. I lament even more all of the misinformation I have been fed about Africans and about black people in general.

"This is exquisite," I exclaim.

"The reason I'm showing you this, Izzy, is to make it clear to you that we in B.O.S.S. believe that you cannot separate Black manhood from its African roots. We are not just Americans. We are African Americans. I hate the slave-based term Negro, but we are stuck with it until we can convince our brethren that the term African-American is the more accurate and therefore the more appropriate name for us."

"Then why would you even consider me?"

"A good question. Have a seat, Izzy," the Negus commands pointing to the velvet couch. Hey Colby, can you get us two cokes. You see, Izzy, even though we emphasize blackness and the unity and identity of black men, we also believe in brotherhood. In fact, it is our contention that once black men can accept their blackness and understand the significance of their rich African roots, they are in a better position to accept the white man as a brother. Another way of putting it is that we need to love ourselves before we can love our white brothers. As you probably know, Black people have bounced back and forth between two positions with respect to the white majority culture--integration, which has often meant giving up one's black identity, or separation which assumes that the only way black people can be Black and proud is to separate themselves from whites entirely. You are probably most familiar with the case for integration. Were you at the debate between Bayard Rustin and Malcolm X?

"Yes I was."

"So you know Malcolm and the Black Muslims want to create a black state within the United States. Earlier in the century Marcus Garvey and his United Negro Improvement Association wanted to encourage all American blacks to return to Africa. From our point of view neither makes much sense nor seems feasible. What we fervently hope is that we Black men can learn to value our roots, learn to love ourselves as Black men, and from this position of cultural strength reach out to our white brother. So Mr. Izzy White, our little white brother, we are reaching out to you."

"After hearing your story, I'm honored that you would even consider me. I'm definitely interested; but if I pledge, what can I expect? I mean what will happen?" Colby Betterman brings us two cokes in large slender glasses filled with crushed ice and garnished with a mint leaf. Such style I think. I flash on an image of our being two Southern Gentlemen sipping mint juleps on a sweltering summer day. The Negus takes a sip of his "coke julep", eyes me carefully, and returns to his pontifical style of speaking. "The pledge line has already begun, but it would be no problem fitting you in. Once the fraternity as a whole approves you, you will meet your pledge brothers. They are called Peons because they do all of the menial tasks that the BOSS brothers hate to do for themselves. So for the next three weeks, you will be a Peon for every BOSS brother. Now we are reasonable men so we don't overdo the bossing around. You'll see; it's not too bad. After that is Hell Week during which we will test your mettle. Now it's definitely not hazing. We don't do that. But it can be strenuous and somewhat challenging. I can already tell in the short time I've known you, Izzy, you will pass with flying colors." I'm not as convinced as the Negus about how I will fare during the next four weeks, but I decide to give it a try. When I take my leave of the fraternity house, I find that the weather has changed and not for the better. The brisk but sunny morning has given way to a freezing grey and rainy afternoon. I take the weather's deterioration as an opportunity to second-guess my decision to pledge BOSS. My sleep that night is frequently interrupted by dreams of predatory BOSS brothers making my life a living hell as a Peon. When I awaken, however, I remind myself that I have made a commitment to try toa join aa fraternity. So try I will. I receive a call that evening to inform me that the fraternity has approved of my becoming a Peon.

The next afternoon I return to the frat house to meet my five fellow Peons. Colby accompanies me into one of the back rooms of the fraternity house, which is furnished with the same eclectic combination of well-to-do days gone by and Africana. Apparently, all six Peons are to meet here after lunch every day (that we don't have an afternoon class) to do the bidding of any BOSS brother. Colby introduces me to my five line mates who sit around a well-worn mahogany table.

"Izzy, facing you on the far side of the table is John Clark. We call him Iron John because we believe he's the strongest cat on campus. John's a sophomore engineering major. On his right is Dex the Hex Dexter Gamble, a junior chemistry major. He creates chemical concoctions in the laboratory that he believes will put a spell on anyone who offends or mistreats him. To his right is Byron Frazier. Byron is an English major whose aspiration is to write the Great Black American Novel. Next to

Byron is Bill Gadfry who is affectionately known as Gadfly. He's the comedian of the group and, in fact, wants someday to be a stand-up comic. The last Peon here is Mel Gray. We call Mel, X-Ray, because he seems to have the rare ability of peering into men's souls." I knew X-Ray by sight because I had noticed him in my Introduction to Psychology class. He invariably looks at you with such intensity that it makes you wonder what he's trying to see. Like me, he has just become a psychology major. While everyone else gives me a cursory nod of greeting, X-Ray smiles at me in a way that suggests that we have a lot in common.

After I have been introduced to my line mates, Colby marches us into the living room where the Negus and the rest of the BOSS brothers are gathered. The Negus bellows "Welcome Peons," at which he breaks out into a malicious sounding cackle, and the rest of the fraternity cackles along with him. A group of the brothers all wearing gloves saunter toward us and stick a beanie on top of our heads. The Negus orders us to wear these beanies whenever we are in the presence of a BOSS brother. It isn't long before we all detect an unpleasant odor. In fact it's the unmistakable smell of urine. "Since you are now Peons," the Negus said, "these Peon caps in fact have been peed on by your big brothers by way of welcoming you to your new status. The BOSS brothers crack up at this, while the six of us cry in unison, "Aw shit man!"

"Now, now men," the Negus cautions, "This is your first test in becoming a Boss man and remember, you are not to remove these pre-treated caps in our presence as a sign of respect for your brothers-to-be. "

So that is the beginning of the three weeks preceding Hell Week. One of our major tasks is to clean up after the BOSS brothers. They purposely leave trash, half-eaten food, overturned cans and soda for us to clean up. Each of us is assigned specific times for bathroom clean-up duty. There they would leave the toilet bowl yellowed with urine with large, doubtfully human turds in copious quantities unflushed. Semendrenched sheets then must be washed and beds remade. And as we perform these housekeeping duties, we're subjected to constant verbal abuse. Every body part is commented upon and condemned or deemed insufficient in form and/or function. The three weeks preceding hell week are pretty hellish. At first the Peons feel like brothers-of-the damned and are unified in our common misery. But as time goes on, we begin to take our misery out on each other. We accuse one another of "shirking the shit" and therefore leaving more of it for others to clean. The main form of communication now is sniping at one another for real or imagined slights, insults, and other injustices. It reaches a point where we're fighting about how we are expressing our grievance to one another rather than the specific grievance itself. In fact, we often forget what the original grievance was about.

The exception to this every-man-for-himself griping that shakes the fraternity house walls is Mel and me. We have each other's back. If he begins to slack in his effort to be an adequate Peon, I help him out, cheer him up, and make him laugh. If I get down and disgusted about our duties or the verbal abuse we're getting from the Brothers, he's there to console, or calm me, or even to do some of my chores if I just can't hack it on a given day. As my confidence in my ever hacking it as a BOSS pledge sours, my gratitude and regard for Mel soars. My best guess is that Mel is feeling the same way about me.

The coup de grace in meaningless abuse comes with the shoes. Those 20 brothers must each own 10 pairs of shoes, and the Peons have to shine them all. None of us can imagine ever completing this tedious task. Whenever we finish shining one pair of shoes, there's always another pair waiting in a designated spot to be shined. By the middle of the third week I have had it. I start making noises about leaving the line.

Mel prevails upon me to meet for lunch at the cafeteria in the Student Union one blustery, cold January day. I arrive first and am therefore able to have the pleasure of viewing his arrival. He is a lanky, thin six-footer who moves with all the grace and elegance of a ballet dancer. Yet the walk is all rhythm and blues, smooth, sexy and cool. His dark chocolate skin color against his khaki shirt adds to his appeal. We both get in line and search for the edible lunch options. Since there are no BOSS Brothers around, we do not have to wear our peed-on caps, which would have made any option unpalatable. I settle for a bowl of chicken noodle soup and a roll.

Mel's explicit aim is to try and talk me out of quitting the line. "Look Izzy, Hell week begins next week and then we can cross over the burning sands and become BOSS men. You can last one more week can't you?" He stares at me with pleading, raven black eyes as if he's an about-to-be rejected lover fighting to save the relationship. He buys a large lunch, which he barely touches. "I'm not sure I can, Mel. What's the point of enduring all of this shit and abuse?"

"It's to make a man of you, to test your physical prowess, and it'll give you a taste of what the black man experiences at the hands of white people."

"So this is about racial revenge?"

"No Izzy, you're missing the point. It's about having you feel what we feel when we're subjected to 'all this shit and abuse,' as you put it. This is nothing compared to being thought of and treated as less than men every day by a large majority of white people in this country. Every black man who pledges a black fraternity gets a symbolic taste of what blacks have been through since slavery times. And a pledge's willingness to endure all this mistreatment and even physical violence by his brothers-to-be is his commitment to being reborn as a worthy black man and member of the fraternity. It's different in a white fraternity. In white fraternities, they're just fucking with you. There's no larger purpose to the bullshit that brothers subject their pledges to."

"Look Mel, I didn't come to Howard University to relive the black experience in America but rather to understand it. Where does this hatred and cruelty come from? How did White Supremacy become the norm of human relations between blacks and whites? Why does such an obvious deviation from any known religious ideal of how we should treat one another continue to be the norm? And how has such a perverted form of social relations shaped the black person's perspective on life."

"Izzy, you'll never be able to understand the black experience without experiencing some of that hatred and mistreatment. Here at least it is controlled and limited. Think about the anger you are feeling right now about your treatment by the BOSS Brothers. Imagine that you're not allowed to express it. What do you think happens to that anger you can't express? As Langston Hughes asks:

'Maybe it sags like a heavy load or does it explode?'

Or maybe it just poisons every cell of hope, every dream of being a man in America, like any other man, treated with respect and dignity. There are only a few ways to live with such anger. It may eventually explode, as Langston implies, or it may kill you from within. Or you find a way to use that anger to make you better, stronger, and more determined to succeed in this nigger-hating country even when the odds are so heavily weighted against you." As Mel talks, I watch how he moves his body, palms up imploring to be understood, head moving from side to side for emphasis, a sway in his torso revealing the power behind his words. It is a graceful ballet of passionate expression. And it moves me.

The next day I inform the Negus that I'm quitting the line. I tell him that this experience confirms something about myself that I already feared is true. I'm not the fraternity type. He tries very hard to reel me back in and repeatedly attempts to draw out my real reasons for quitting. I spare him my diatribe about the "non-hazing" behavior of the Brothers of BOSS, and about how disappointed I am by the gap between their idealistic aspirations and their actual treatment of the Peons. I saw nothing edifying or potentially redeeming about urine-soaked hats or the frequent assignments to the shit-bowl brigade. He finally relents and says he's sorry that it didn't work out. He is very gracious in wishing me well and that softens my anger towards him. For three weeks, I hear nothing from anyone associated with BOSS. I knew I would lose the friendship of all the other brothers, but I had been more hopeful about preserving my friendship with Mel. In early February, I hang around one afternoon after my classes to shoot hoops at the Quonset hut that serves as our gym. There he is shooting 18-foot jumpers around a ring of his own making. He isn't missing any.

Chapter 20.
"Honky-Nigga"

I watch Mel shoot for a few minutes before announcing my presence. He's so engrossed in his shooting he hasn't noticed me. "Mind if I join you?" I finally ask in an almost apologetic tone. He looks over and stares at me coldly for a moment. He then smiles weakly and says, "Sure Izzy." After I shoot around for a few minutes, I ask Mel if he would like to play Horse. Mel grins and answers with exaggerated enthusiasm, "Why sure, but let me introduce you to the way we play it way down South. It's the same game really, but we call it "Honky". I look at him in horror and ask, "You call it what?"

"Honky," he said. "I take a shot and if I make it, you have to try the same shot. If you miss it, then you get an "H" and so on, just like in Horse. "

"Why do you call it Honky?" Mel chuckles and says, "Oh that's just the way we black boys down South have some fun. But I tell you what. If it makes you feel better, we'll call our game Honky-Nigga. If you miss my shot, you get an H and so on, but if I miss one of your shots, I get an N and then an I and so on." We look at each other and burst out laughing at the same time. Mel begins by making three consecutive 18- foot jump shots. It's a beautiful sight. His form is perfect. He releases the ball at the top of his jump, perfect back spin, nothing but net. I make the first two, but my third shot rolls around the rim before falling off to the side. "H for you Honky," croons Mel, cackling as he moves to the next spot to shoot. His fourth shot goes half way down the hoop before popping out. From watching Mel shoot, I conclude that his range is limited to 18 to 20 feet. My sole advantage over him is that I can consistently make jump shots from 23 to 25 feet. I make my first shot and he subsequently misses it. "N for you... uh, uh... Mel". He cuts his eyes at me and then gives me a sly grin. Out comes an arsenal of fancy shots, right and left handed hooks, 15-foot jump shots that he purposely banks off the backboard, and one left-handed jump shot from about eight feet. Before I know it, I'm at HONK and he's only at NIG. Then he makes a fatal error. He tries to extend the range of his jump shot by launching one deep from the left wing 22 feet away from the basket. His shot looks like it's going through, but it bounces off the nearside rim. "Damn!" he mutters to himself. My next two shots are from 25 feet away. I hit them cleanly, but Mel misses them both. "You win," Mel says begrudgingly. "But it was close, NIGGA to HONK."

This loss only stimulates his competitive urge. A group of boisterous Intramural players come bounding into the gym at that moment. They see that we own the near half of the court. They wave to us and go to the far half and loudly begin to shoot around.

"OK, Izzy, enough of this Honky-Nigga-shit, let's go one on one. At first, I don't give it my all. Despite the skill Mel has shown me, I figure that since I played varsity and he didn't, I will have an easy time of it. Big mistake! Although I'm shooting well, he matches me shot for shot. Moreover, at 6 feet tall, he uses his height advantage to draw me under the basket where he can shoot over me. What really shocks me is the intensity with which he is playing. He doesn't just want to win he wants to crush me. I also discover that he is as quick as I am, if not quicker; and he has a variety of smooth and deceptive moves that frequently fool me. I quickly let go of the assumption that I'm going to win easily. I get my game face on, play like it was a college playoff game, and work as hard as I can to prevent my being embarrassed by this obviously very skilled and talented player. The group of Intramural players stop shooting and come to watch what must have appeared to them to be a grudge match. Mel wins 15-13. The group applauds Mel's winning shot from the corner. We're both dripping with sweat and decide we have had enough. We sit down on the small set of bleachers that reminds me of the ones we had at Coolidge High School.

"OK, Mel, you've been holding out on me. You've got some kind of game. You must have played high school ball. Spill man." Mel has a funny grin on his face. "Yeah, Izzy, I played. I was All-State out of Georgia. "Which high school?" I ask wondering if it could be possible. "Carver High School in Gainesville. Why?"

"I thought so. Then you must know Bob Kinnard."

"Sure I know him. He was our valedictorian. In fact, he's partly the reason that I'm here at Howard."

"Really! How so?"

"He convinced me that with an education at Howard, a Black man could go far. I didn't know this until I started hanging with Bob, but peoples down our way view Howard as the black Harvard. You see, my father works at a poultry-processing plant, and he's worked his ass off to make sure that I be the first member of my family to go to college. So I want to make it count."

"Didn't you get any basketball scholarships?"

Yeah, I was offered scholarships to two small black schools. But Bob convinced me that I would get a lousy education at these places. I got good grades at Carver, but Bob said we both needed the kind of education that only Howard could offer if we're gonna make it in the white man's world. You see, Howard has been recruiting bright but poorly prepared Negro students from the South and placing us in remedial English and math classes during our freshman year so that by the time we're sophomores, we'd be ready to do college-level work.

"OK, how come you didn't play for Howard? We sure could've used you."

"The main reason is I've got to concentrate on my studies. Howard's a challenge for me Izzy. Turns out, Bob was right. Our grades at Carver might've been tops, but we weren't prepared for the workload at Howard. Besides, no offense Izzy, but Howard could put together a better team from the stands then they had on the court." I could feel myself blushing. "You say what?"

"I know at least 8 guys who go to the games regularly who were All-State in high school. Like Bob and me, they come from schools that didn't prepare them for college. So they're busting their balls just trying to keep up. These are guys from Florida, Tennessee, Mississippi, Arkansas and the Carolinas. They' re big, strong and talented. I think Howard would easily win the CIAA championship if they played."

"If you say so, Mel." My voice oozes doubt. I'm having great difficulty accepting the truth of his claims.

"It's true Izzy. Everyone of them's a complete package. They all can score, rebound, and play D." I respond with cold silence. The truth hurts me and makes me a little angry. So I attack.

"How come I haven't heard from you since I got off line. I didn't expect I'd hear from any of the other pledge brothers, but I thought I'd hear from you."

"I know that hurt you Izzy and I'm sorry. But I was very disappointed and hurt too when you bailed. I needed time before I could even talk to you. "

"Come on, Mel, you know that BOSS is not a good fit for me. As hard as I tried, I couldn't buy into its bullshit goals. They're gonna make a man of me". I said this with all the mockery that I could muster. "I mean I'm not even black so how can I really fit the BOSS mold. They may not be interested in grooming the next generation of bougie Blacks, but BOSS's goals still are race-based. How can I connect to my nonexistent African past?"

"You're right Izzy the goals are bullshit, but that's not the point. Joining a frat is about making friends, life-long friends. The Negus's back-to-Africa rap is just another part of the crap you take when you're on line. It's supposed to make you feel bad and ignorant for not knowing anything about Africa. But Africa ain't my home. I'm from Georgia. What's Africa got to do with my life or my family's life, or for that matter the lives of the many generations before them since slavery began in this country? I joined BOSS not because I want to reconnect with my African roots, but because Gadfly was gonna join. He joined cause Dexter wanted to join. They're good guys, Izzy, and I'm sorry they won't be your brothers."

"I'm sorry too, Mel, but whatever I strive for has to make sense and joining BOSS no longer did. But I really hope that you and I can remain friends. I think we have a lot in common even if we aren't gonna be fraternity brothers."

"OK Izzy, even though you are not BOSS, let's go get something to eat."

"Great, but one other thing. Where does the term, Honky come from?"

"I don't know too much about it, but I do remember my grandfather telling me stories about the Wolof people in Senegal. He told me that we were Wolof, not that I gave a damn. Anyway, he said that Honky comes from the Wolof word, Honq, which means pink man. So Pink Man, are you ready to get some food?"

Over the next several weeks, I'm in a state of euphoria. I have finally made a friend at Howard, a black friend. I have felt so alienated from the school that I had given up on the prospect of developing any friendships at Howard. I was convinced that the achievement of zero friendships during the entire four years of my college sojourn would be its ultimate fruition. In fact, until I started hanging out with Mel X-Ray Gray, I hadn't realized how lonely and demoralized I have been. He appears to feel the same way. We spend a great deal of time together throughout the spring of 1962. We both have developed a nascent love of jazz, and on the weekends we would go to the Bohemian Caverns or to Jazzland to hear some of the top talent that played there.

Our relationship is going swimmingly until one day I get the bright idea of convincing Mel to meet my parents. I'm so euphoric about my new Black friend that I tell myself that it makes perfect sense for him to get a bird's eye view of my progenitors and my life on the white side. But as I pursue the matter, I begin to feel like a real estate agent representing both sides of a difficult sale. My father's initial response is less than enthusiastic. He jumps out of his chair and bellows, "You want to bring one of your Schwartzeh friends into my house? Over my dead body! I thought you were going to college to improve your mind not to lose it."

"Oh come on, Dad! Mel's a great guy. I think you'd like him if you give him a chance." My father bares his teeth and gives me a muffled growl. "Mom, do you think I'm crazy?" My mother nervously looks first at her husband and then at me. With a furrowed brow, she answers, "Of course not, dear. It's just that I don't want your father to get upset and say something that we'll all regret." Dad and I re-enter our perennial argument repeating a tactic prevalent in our previous debate over my attending Howard. He thrusts with his stereotype of the dirty worthless Negro, and I parry with my stereotype of the Black paragon of middle class virtues. After a few rounds of this, Mom's had enough. She whispers to me, "Go invite your friend and I'll talk to your father." I can't wait to tell Mel.

Suspecting that Mel might also resist my "let's all love one another" plan, I decide to invite him in person rather than on the phone. But my first sighting of Mel is not until the following Wednesday when, out of the corner of my eye, I notice him sitting in one of the reading rooms in Founders Library. He is dressed more like he is on a date than burning for an upcoming exam. In fact, he looks preppy in his blue and beige plaid shirt and black slacks. "Who's the lucky girl?" I ask as I sidle up noiselessly beside him. He is startled. He looks at my unexpected white face, recognizes me, frowns and then says, "Say what?"

"Who's the lucky girl?" I repeat.
"The only date I have, Izzy, is with the books. I have a major history exam tomorrow."

"Can I talk to you about something, Mel?"

"Will it take long? I really have to burn."

"It'll only take a minute." We step out into the corridor just outside the reading room. "OK, Izzy, what is so important?"

"I want you to come to brunch Sunday so you can meet my parents."

"Are you nuts? You want me to meet your parents after everything you've told me about your father's social attitudes? You might as well invite me to a Klan meeting."

"He's not that bad, Mel. Besides he'll be on his best behavior. Who knows? Maybe once he's introduced to your sparkling virtues his social attitudes may change."

"Yeah, and maybe then I'll be able to rent an apartment next door to yours."

"Ooh, that's a low blow."

"But it's true nonetheless that those two events share the same low probability."

"Look Mel, it's just one brunch."

"Let me think about it, Izzy. I'll let you know tomorrow. " The next day Mel calls me and says he'll come. I figure his curiosity trumped his fear. Whatever the reason, I'm ecstatic that he is willing to meet me on my home turf.

That night I had a dream that Mel had come to brunch as planned and my father was at his worst. Dad began with what I know he thought was a compliment. He "congratulated" Mel on appearing to be one of a rare species-a good nigger. Dad continued with a longish monologue that fully fleshed out his social attitudes with respect to Negroes. He told Mel that the best thing for niggers would be for all of them to return to Africa. But if they chose to stay in the good old US of A, they should work much harder at learning the superior habits of white people. First they need to learn how to speak English better. Then they need to learn a good trade, improve their work ethic, and sense of responsibility. Mel was so horrified that he lost the power of speech. The last image of the dream that I remember is the look of horror on Mel's face. I wake up in a cold sweat. I have to talk to Mel. I have to prepare him in case Dad acts anything like I saw in my dream.

"What's happenin', Izzy? Is the brunch off?"

"No, no, Mel. The brunch is still on. I just wanted to prepare you just in case my father does say the wrong thing. Now you won't have any problems with my mother and I'm 95% sure Dad will be pleasant. But it's that 5% that's bothering me. So if in the unlikely case that he says something offensive try not to take it personally."

"How should I take it, Izzy?"

"My dad has an 8th grade education so just try and brush it off to his lack of schooling ok?"

"It'll be fine, Izzy, I'm a big boy."

"That's great, Mel. So I'll see you Sunday morning at 10:30 in the lobby of Suburban Hill. You still have the directions?" "Yes, Izzy, I still have the directions."

At 10:30 sharp Sunday morning, I see Mel X-Ray Gray walking toward the front door of Suburban Hill Apartments. He is dressed in a Navy blue suit, white shirt and a skinny blue and white striped tie. Oh my God, I forgot to tell him to dress casual. Mel looks like he is going to church rather than to brunch. Then I thought maybe his garb is a plus and will help tranquilize my father's prejudices. We greet each other with a half hug and a handshake. "You look real sharp, Mr. Gray. Real sharp." As we take the eternal elevator ride to the third floor I remind him of the possibility that my father might pop off and inadvertently say something offensive. Again I ask him to try and not take it personally. I think I see his body tighten, but conclude I must be mistaken. In an effort to take his mind off what my father might say, I tell Mel that I'm sorry that he won't have a chance to meet my brother Adam. "He went with a friend to Baltimore to take in a mid-day classical concert." This information seemed to make him even more uptight.

When I introduce him to my parents, Pearl is her usual welcoming self. I am happy to discover that the jovial Mort White, rather than the angry one, has shown up. Nonetheless, Mel seems stuck in a rigid posture with a smile frozen on his face. He and I sit on the couch while my father sits in his favorite armchair. Mom is in the kitchen preparing brunch. My father looks at Mel and remains silent. He looks like he is trying to decide something. The longer the silence persists, the more uptight Mel seems. He sits straight as a board while looking warily at my father. Dad breaks the silence with this unexpected question: "What do you call a line of rabbits walking backwards?" Mel is so flabbergasted by the nature of the question he doesn't know how to answer. Finally he manages, "I don't know?" With a triumphant grin Dad replies, "A receding hare line." Mel and I look at each other and burst out laughing because my father's answer is so unexpected, and the joke is so hopelessly corny. Dad, however, is warmed by our apparent appreciation of his wit. He joins our laughter. The tension now is broken with the three of us laughing hysterically at Dad's silly joke. The commonplace conversation that follows relaxes us further. My father asks Mel what his father does for a living. "He works in a chicken processing plant in Gainesville, Georgia, where I'm from."

"Well, I'm a butcher so I guess me and your dad are in the same kind of business."

"I bet you two would like each other," Mel suggests. "You appear to have a lot in common." I thought for sure Dad would be upset at this comparison with a working class Negro, but he didn't flinch. Instead he asks Mel a lot of questions about his father's work and about life in Gainesville, Georgia. Much to my greater surprise, Dad easily shares with Mel the details of his own work and even some of his frustrations. "There's this one lady, Mrs. Katz, who comes into the market every other day to bust my balls about something."

"Mort!" My mother cries, "Watch your language!"

"Sorry Pearl," my father answers and then continues with his story. "Anyway, one day she's shopping for chicken. She must have looked at four different chickens before settling on one. So this one she wants to examine carefully. First she lifts a wing and sniffs; then she lifts the other wing and smells. Then she spreads the chicken legs apart and smells again. 'Mort,' she says, 'this chicken is no good. I want to see another one.' By this time I've had it with her and I say, "Mrs. Katz, could you pass a test like that?" Mel and I are laughing so hard we knock heads. Dad's laughing at our laughter. Mom is giggling but then adds, "Mort, that story is so old it's got a beard on it. OK boys it's time to eat."

Mom lays out our typical Sunday brunch Jew food on the side of the table closest to my father, the bagels, lox, cream cheese, tomatoes, onions and Chubs. On the side closest to Mel, she places scrambled eggs, bacon and toast. She does not want Mel to be embarrassed or go hungry if he doesn't like or want to try the Jew food. But I strongly nudge Mel to try the bagels and lox. He looks at the Jewish delicacies with the same expression I had when I first encountered chit'lin's. "I'll give the bagels and lox a try," Mel says with exaggerated enthusiasm. Mom makes him a sandwich with all of the accoutrements. Mel holds the alien sandwich in front of his face for an entire minute and then takes a healthy bite. After several chews, he nods his head approvingly and then reaches for the bacon and eggs. We eat in silence for awhile. My mother breaks the silence by asking Mel about his mother. Mel somberly replies, "She died three years ago." My mother is shocked and she gives her genuine condolences to Mel. "Thank you, Mrs. White. She was a great woman and I miss her terribly." I can tell that Mom feels guilty for bringing up his mother. She asks him no further questions.

Much to my astonishment, the rest of the brunch flows very smoothly. The four of us gab away as if we are old friends. When Mel gets ready to leave, my father says to him, "It's been a real pleasure meeting you, Mel," and I know he's being sincere. Mom too seemed to really like Mel. As he and I travel down to the lobby in the eternal elevator, Mel turns to me and says, "I could kick your ass, you dumb honky. Your parents are great. I wish you hadn't said anything beforehand and just let me find out for myself how your father would be with me. Instead you scared me to death with your premonitions of racial insults spewing out of your dad's mouth." I hesitate before responding to Mel's resentment. "You're right, Mel, and I'm terribly sorry. In trying to protect you, I made things worse."

"Yes, you did!" After we say our good-byes, I run up the stairs and back to my apartment. I am very eager to know what my father thought of Mel.

"You know, Izzy, I really like that Schwartzeh!"

Mel and I also play a lot of B-ball together even though we both soon realize that basketball is just a pretext for us to get together and talk. Our courtside revelations, discussions and debates become the highlight of our week. Both of us are currently taking Introduction to Psychology, a year- long course taught by Carolyn Payton, the best psychology professor in the department. We both love everything about psychology, but we are inclined to talk mostly about theories of normal and abnormal behavior and psychotherapy. I have fallen in love with the apparent precision of Skinnerian Behaviorism, while Mel is more excited by Freudian psychoanalysis.

As we're shooting jump shots, we pick up our debate from where we left off. "But Mel, we now possess a wonderful method for discovering the truth about human beings, the experimental method of science. Through precise observation and experimentation, we can learn verifiable facts about human behavior. Then we can develop methods to modify unwanted behavior. Behavior therapists are beginning to do that now."

"The problem is, Izzy, there is so much about human beings that you cannot directly see. We can't see the workings of a person's mind, his inner world. It's difficult enough to know our own mind. Not even science can shed light on another person's mind."

"Not directly, maybe, but by observing human behavior we can infer what people are thinking. Besides what's our alternative?"

"Let's start with our own minds. Through introspection we can learn a lot about ourselves. And because we are all more alike than different, we can make inferences about what people are thinking and feeling and why. Most importantly, we can't just rely on appearances. People deceive themselves and usually try and present themselves in a favorable light to others. We know people defend against revealing unacceptable attitudes. In fact, as Freud tells us, they hide these forbidden thoughts and wishes from themselves, not just from other people."

"Yes, and all of those internal factors you mention are virtually impossible to study scientifically. " Mel's eyes light up as he senses the core weakness in my argument.
"Well whose problem is that? Is it that our inner world is not important or is it that science is not yet able to study it?" We go on like this for over an hour, but I think we score more points with our jump shots than with our arguments. The truth of the matter is that I also love Freud and psychoanalysis. I introspect with a vengeance; and with each insight I uncover I feel a surging sense of power, the power to see beyond appearances, the power of a very special kind of knowledge. Mel, on the other hand, is playing to his strength. There is good reason for his fraternity brothers to refer to Mel as X-Ray. He has a natural gift for understanding what people mean but haven't said. He quickly grasps the feeling behind a person's words, particularly when the words are meant to conceal what a person is really feeling.

Our shared passion for psychology also has a dark side. Whenever we have a quiz or an exam, the first thing that Mel would do is to find me and ask how I did. He then compares his test score to mine and is visibly dismayed if his scores are lower than mine. It takes awhile for me to fully grasp the extent to which Mel is competing with me. At first, I assume that Mel is just a competitive guy and that academics is now something we can compete about in addition to basketball. But it eventually dawns on me that I have become the standard by which he judges himself. On the day of our final exam in Introduction to Psychology, Mel seems more agitated than ever. "What's the matter, Mel," I ask with genuine concern for him. "Nothing, Izzy," he answers with such tension in his voice that I can't discern whether he's angry or just nervous. I think it best to leave him be. After the exam, he leaves without saying a word to me. I fully expect that we will spend some time talking about the questions on the exam. That has been our routine. But he vanishes from the exam room, and I'm very hurt. In fact, I don't see or hear from Mel until we bump into each other in Douglas Hall where the grades for our courses are posted. Our final exam scores are listed as well as our course grades. "How did you do?" he asks with the same tension in his voice that I noticed at the final exam. "I got an A, Mel. How about you?" "I got an A too. But I mean how did you do on the final exam?"

"I got a 98, Mel." He explodes. "SHIT! I only got a 90." Mel is so agitated, he's turning in circles and stomping his feet. I don't understand his reaction. I attempt to pull him back into reality. "But Mel, we both got As in the course. Why are you so upset?"

"Goddammit, Izzy, it's barely an A. How'm I ever gonna make it as a psychologist in the white world. I'm gonna have to compete with the likes of you and all the other privileged white men out there. I'll never be able to get a job in psychology. Izzy, you don't have a clue about the advantages you have over every Black man who competes with you in the job market. You can't possibly understand what I have to deal with."

I'm so taken aback, that I'm rendered speechless. I can't believe the hostility pouring out of him, and that it's being directed at me. I feel like my best friend has just sucker-punched me in the gut. I want him to feel better. I want to reduce the distance that has suddenly sprung up between us. "But Mel, we both got As in the course. So my score is a little higher. So what. We both got As."

"Yeah, but you did better than I did. You always do better. There's no beating you, Izzy." There's just no beating you. " Mel starts crying. You're just superior, Izzy, and I'm inferior. No matter what I do, I'm inferior." Other students coming to look at their grades are staring at us with expressions of perplexed concern. I grab Mel and virtually drag him into an empty classroom. I push him into a chair and sit in another chair close by. "What's going on, Mel?" Mel waits a few minutes for the tears to stop and he can once again speak in a firm clear voice.

"Izzy, you just don't know. You just don't know what I've had to put up with all my fucking life. Growing up black in Georgia ain't no picnic. I could never tell a white person the truth about how I feel. I had to bow my head whenever I saw a white adult, and move out the way to let white people pass on the sidewalk. And if I dared to raise my voice to a white man, I would get a beating, either from the white man or from my father for being so stupid in talking back. And I couldn't just go into the front door of a movie theatre. Oh no; me and my Black friends had to climb up a fire escape to get to the balcony. You can't possibly know how it feels to bow and scrape and say Yassuh to all those sour-faced peckerwoods. Do you know how all this makes me feel, Izzy? Sometimes I'd see a white kid my age with these beautiful new textbooks, and I'd look at my raggedy-assed hand-me-down books and I would feel like NOTHING! You know, Izzy, that's what nigger really means. You're nothing! An inferior nothing! It don't matter who you are or what you've achieved. A black man with a mIllion dollars and a bunch of degrees by his name is still a nigger. You know, there are days when I look in the mirror and curse my blackness." I shiver at the memory of my hallucinatory black reflection.

"But Mel, you're telling me the truth about how you feel and ain't I a peckerwood?"

"No, Izzy, you're just white. You're neurotic as hell, but you are a kind person. I saw that kindness in your eyes the first time I met you. I said to myself, this is not your garden variety Honky."

"With friends like you, who needs therapists?" He gives me a weak smile.

"Mel, you're right. I can't imagine what you've been through, and I haven't lived under white apartheid, maybe a little gentile apartheid, but nothing like what you've experienced. But I sure understand your fear of white people because I'm afraid of black people."

"Then what the fuck are you doing at Howard?"

"Trying to understand it. Trying to cure it. You know my fear of Negroes cuts two ways. For the longest time, I've been afraid that some kind of contamination would happen if I get too close to black people. It's Negrophobia, that's what it is. But I'm also afraid of getting my ass kicked by a bunch of angry black kids." I told Mel the story about how my best friend Eddie and I were confronted by a bunch of "Block Boys" in the alley, and how we would have had our asses kicked if it hadn't been for an older black guy I had played basketball with on Canteen Night. He had recognized me and convinced the Block Boys to leave us alone. "And now Mel that I'm at Howard, I have a new fear-that the word nigga might come out of my mouth. You see I've grown up. Instead of fearing black adolescents, I now fear black college students. "

"No, Izzy, now you're afraid of yourself. You're just as afraid and paranoid as I am."
"That's right, Mel, this is what segregation and white apartheid produces, fear-based hatred."

"Ain't that right. Jim Crow makes Jim Crazy."

"I guess the difference is you feel inferior because you're black, and I feel inferior because I'm me."

"Comes to the same thing, Izzy. We both feel like nothing."

Maybe not quite nothing! When I see my grades, I discover that I've received all "As" for the second straight semester. This is good news and bad news. The good news is I've preserved my scholarship for my senior year and won't spend the summer worrying about money. The bad news is I felt the first comforting hug of superiority about my alleged intelligence. I have given up the fantasy that I am so talented a basketball player that every team in the National Basketball Association would surely come begging at my door to play for them. But now I imagine that not only am I smart enough to succeed in this life, but maybe I'm one of the smartest people alive. I've jumped on board a fast train at Inferiority, missed my stop at Smart Enough, and traveled all the way to Superiority.

Mel notices a change in my voice the next time he calls me. "What's happening Honky?" He says with a smile in his voice. "I will not dignify that question with a response, "I answer haughtily. Upon hearing this new Izzy persona, Mel's clearly perturbed. "Hey, what's up with you?"

"Why nothing, " I reply. "It's just that I do not want to be referred to by such an odious expression. After all, how would you like it if I referred to you as Nigga."

"What you say? You call me that all the time, and I know you mean it in a friendly way, and you know I mean the same thing when I call you Honky. What the hell's wrong with you today?"

"I shall endeavor to explain."

"Oh, wait a minute. I think I know what's going on with you. You got all "As" again, didn't you?"

"That is correct!"

"And now you think you're smarter than everybody."
"Indubitably!" I try to keep up my condescending demeanor, but in fact, my bubble has been burst by Mel X-Ray Gray's perceptiveness. The fact that he can see right through my arrogance and my ersatz professorial air both terrifies and relieves me. Mel just brushes it off as crazy white boy play-acting and decides not to give it any credence.

"Listen, Dr. Freud, the reason I'm calling you is to invite you to an end-of-the-year dance sponsored by B.O.S.S. I want you to take a second look at B.O.S.S."

"Aw Mel, you know how I feel about this..."

"Yeah, Yeah, I know how you feel, but I'm convinced you're making a mistake. You need us. You just don't know it yet. Besides I need you." I'm taken aback by his straightforward confession of his attachment to me, but I try not to show it. Instead, I nonchalantly say, "You've got me. What's B.O.S.S. got to do with our friendship?"

"Let's just say our friendship would be easier if you were a BOSS member."

"What does that mean?"

"Never mind that now. Will you come?" I'm a sucker for anyone pleading for my attention. "Alright, I'll come, but just to this dance. I'm not committing to the fraternity. I don't think I can."

Mel brightens. 'That's great, Izzy. The dance is this Saturday night, and it starts at 8 pm. See you then." After we hang up, I'm already regretting having said yes. I'm not exactly sure where Mel is coming from. He really seems to want to be friends, which gratifies me. He seems to be as excited about making a friend with a white boy as I am in having a black friend. But he left me with a mystery. I still do not understand why our friendship would be easier if I'm his fraternity brother. I don't see the connection. But go to the dance I will.

Lightening and thunderstorms accompany my ride down to the BOSS House. I take this as an inauspicious omen, but I keep trying to excommunicate this superstitious reasoning from my mind. These are the kinds of connections and conclusions that logic and scientific reasoning should banish from an intelligent and critically thinking mind. I find a parking spot that is almost a block away from the BOSS house. Despite the umbrella I have brought with me, the wind and the rain leave me wet and somewhat rumpled by the time I reach the door. I rap the Lion's head knocker with great force fearing that I will not be heard over the blaring music coming from within. Colby Betterman is wearing the same pair of horn-rimmed glasses as before. He smiles broadly and says, "Hey, Izzy, I'm glad you made it. Everybody's in the basement." I have never seen the basement before and I am amazed by its cavernous size. It easily accommodates the approximately 30 people within. The room is decorated with orange and grey festoons strung across the entire room. African masks are found on every available shelf. A BOSS member who looks familiar to me, but whose name I have forgotten, has set himself in one corner of the room as the self-appointed DJ. He is almost completely hidden by two stacks of 45-rpm records. As I survey the room, I hear Ike and Tina Turner's "It's Gonna Work Out Fine." Eight couples are undulating in time with the music. With silky rhythmic movements they all appear to be mimicking the sex act. One couple in particular catches my attention. The male partner is wearing a chartreuse suit, which on him looks exceedingly cool. I feel a pang of shame at the memory of laughing at some Black men who I have seen in the past in outfits of such shiny bright solid colors that they were blinding. But it's his movements that are familiar. X-Ray dances like the way he moves on the basketball court. I'm in awe of his wonderful dance moves: Smooth, swaying undulations, sudden explosive turns timed perfectly with his partner's moves. It seems as if they have danced together daily for years. The young woman has her back to me. Her movements in a tight basic black dress, which hug her curves tightly, are erotic and familiar. When the music stops. Mel X-Ray Gray comes rushing toward me with his dance partner. I'm paralyzed with shock. It's Desirie. She too is in shock and appears very nervous. Mel looks at Desirie then back at me and says with a big smile, "Izzy, I'd like you to meet my favorite cousin, Desirie Jackson." At the word cousin, I almost pee in my pants. I can't say a word. Desirie says it for us, "Ray, we know each other."

"You do?" Mel asks flabbergasted. "How do you know....Aw wait a minute. Ree, Izzy's the white boy you told me you met and that you liked but couldn't put up with his quirks?"

"That's right," she says blushing.

"What quirks?" I ask, reddening with embarrassment.

"We don't need to get into that now," Desirie answers in a snooty tone that really annoys me. I strike back. "As far as quirks are concerned, I defer to your superiority in that regard." We're now glaring at one another. Mel smirks at both of us. "I see that the two of you have a lot to talk about, so I will make a graceful exit." In a comedic crouch he slowly backs away from us as if he's making a deferential departure from a king and his queen.

Desirie is still angry with me when I say, "Let's dance."

"What?" She bellows in utter disbelief. I'm not to be deterred.

"Let's dance. Maybe we can communicate better on the dance floor." I grab her hand and gently, but firmly, guide her to a free area just as "Pretty Girls" by Eugene Church begins to play. I start with the Pony and quickly switch to the Slop and the Snap. She watches me for a moment and then decides to join me. Within seconds, we are dancing in perfect harmony. Her scowl turns into a smile; our discord dissolves into pure joy. A crowd gathers around us. First there is shock in seeing a white boy move the way I dance. But the people watching us are even more amazed to see an interracial couple dance so well together, so in tune with each other's moves. We then Cha-Cha to Chuck Jackson's "Any Day Now", switch back to the snap for "Shop Around" by Smokey Robinson and the Miracles. When Maxine Brown begins singing "All in my Mind", I hold out my arms for her to join me in a slow dance. She hesitates for a moment and then accedes to my request. She holds me at arm's length. By the time the record changes to Etta James singing At Last, we are cheek to cheek. A subtle lilac fragrance emanates from her and it makes me a little dizzy. I have never felt so happy. I gently kiss her cheek. Desirie is taken aback. "What are you doing, Izzy?"

"I'm trying to communicate with you. We don't do so well with words, so I thought I'd try with actions."

"And what exactly are you trying to communicate?"

"That I've missed you so much, and that I think I love you."

"Oh Izzy, what are you saying?" Desirie has such a forlorn look on her face that it makes me doubt that she could possibly feel the same way.

"Desirie, I can't stop thinking about you. I want to be with you day and night."
She surprises me. "Izzy, I want that too, but you know it's impossible. The world is just not ready for this."

"The world? Fuck the world. We'll make our own world."

"And if we ever have kids, Do you want to go through the pain of watching our children being scorned or even physically beaten because of how they look or because of a decision that they did not make?"

"You fear the world too much."

"With good reason. Look what happened to me on the Freedom Ride."
"But we can avoid the crazy bigots. We'll find a safe place and make a home together."

"Make a life together? Izzy, we hardly know each other."

"But that's exactly how I want to spend my life-getting to know you." I can hear desperation in my voice as I plead with Desirie to share my dream. In my mind, our union will be the triumph of love over bigotry. What could be more satisfying than for us to be together and at the same time to vanquish racism, our mutually hated foe? Tears begin to well up in her eyes. She believes that I don't take seriously enough the power and cruelty of our adversary. In her eyes, I am naïve about the world and about marriage. The more I plead, the more fearful she becomes. I finally allow myself to see the fear in her eyes and I just stop the pleading. "Let's dance," I say cheerfully, and she issues a heavy sigh of relief. The DJ put on "It's Twelve O'Clock", written and sung by our classmate, Van McCoy. The song grew out of a serenade that Van and his group The Starlighters gave students on the Howard campus. The chimes of the Founders Library clock tower that ring at midnight inspired the melody. I hold Desirie very close as if I will lose her forever after this night. Forgetting everything and everyone around me, I kiss her right there on the dance floor in front of all the would-be fraternity brothers that I have previously rejected. First she holds back, but then engages me in a long and deeply fulfilling kiss. Our tongues connect in a way that they never could through mere conversation. That kiss melts the last vestige of my Negrophobia. I'm kissing the woman I love. Until now, I believed that such happiness was unattainable. Now I know that together we can vanquish any foe, master any challenge, and endure any hardship. Unfortunately, I can see in Desirie's face that she remains unconvinced.

"OK, Desirie, let's not worry about the future. Let's focus on now. I want to see you as much as I can during the summer. What are your plans?"

"I won't be here this summer, Izzy. I have to make some money to pay for my senior year so I got a job in Oak Bluffs." I feel like my hair is on fire from jealousy.

"Are you going to see Carter Wyatt?" I ask as innocently as I can. Desirie frowns.

"Oh Izzy, you disappoint me. Carter broke my heart once. Do you think I'm going to give him another chance to break it again?" The electricity of shame seizes my entire body. "I'm sorry, Desirie. My feelings for you are turning me into a jealous fool." Desirie smiles and says, "I'll miss you too, but we'll be together again in the fall. Until then, let's write each other as much as possible, OK?"

"Sure, Desirie, let's write." I try to cover up how abandoned I feel.

"Well, I have to go now," Desirie announces quickly and gives me a quick kiss on the mouth.

As high as I felt when we kissed, I now feel as low as I have ever felt. I'm already dreading a summer's length of loneliness.

Chapter 21.
That's Heaven to Me

I am fortunate enough to acquire a summer job at the National Institute of Neurological Diseases and Blindness. I actually had never heard of NINDB until a friend alerted me to the opportunity for a job at one of the Institutes of the NIH. This is truly an odd job, but the money is good. It finally dawns on me that despite my continuing scholarship at Howard, I need to save money for graduate school. I've decided that I want to get a Ph.D. in psychology and help people with my brilliance and my compassion. Whereas in the past I had been afraid of tackling psychology because I had assumed that I needed to have the intelligence of a Sigmund Freud, I now fancy myself as Freud's second coming. After all, we are the same height, 5' 7". Okay, I'm actually a half-inch shorter, but how significant is that in the scheme of things. My desire to revise, update, and "clean up" the entirety of Freud's psychoanalytic theories seems entirely feasible to me. In addition, I aspire to be the best psychotherapist in the world. Why think small? That's what getting all "As" in two consecutive semesters will do to you.

The part of the NINDB where I work is not located on the main campus of the NIH. It is situated in a low-to-the-ground building in Silver Spring, Maryland, which resembles nothing so much as an enlarged pillbox. My position is a research assistant on a 13-year Birth Defects Study. This study is exploring any and all factors that might lead to birth defects in newborns. On our first day, Dr. Cellborn delightfully entertains us with an extended lecture on the reproductive process. Our beautiful lecturer is very tall and bespectacled. When she opens her mouth, she is surprisingly soft-spoken, given that her demeanor, clothes, glasses and hairstyle all give the impression of a demanding high school math teacher. In her lecture everything is covered from embryogenesis to the last stage of delivery. Who knew that dropping a baby is so complicated? There I meet my two fellow research assistants with whom I'll be spending most of my workday. They are both students at Wheaton College, a

Christian-oriented college with a clear evangelical mission located in Wheaton, Illinois. Clayton Fogmeister is 6 feet tall, blond and wiry. His face possesses a constant wry smile. He wears steel-rimmed glasses and is bright and religious, but not a fanatic. Elwood Plethysma is the same height as Clayton, but he has a dark flattop, wears black-rimmed glasses, and his expression is inexorably stony serious. He is an evangelical Christian par excellence who is fervently committed to Wheaton's evangelical goals. Everyone he meets he wants to bring to Jesus. When Dr. Cellborn talks about how certain forms of birth control do not affect the fertilized egg, but rather prevent the egg from implanting to the uterus, Elwood screeches out, "Baby Killers!" Everyone turns to look at Elwood. Unflustered by the horrified stares of the group Elwood continues with his impromptu sermon, "It's God's law to protect the unborn." An uncomfortable silence overtakes this temple of science. A few minutes later Dr. Cellborn continues, "Thank you Mr. Plethysma for your contribution, but we have a lot of information we need to impart. So would you mind withholding your comments until after I finish the briefing." Plethysma gives her a hard stare, but says nothing more. Fogmeister looks at me and rolls his eyes. We both try to keep our snickering as quiet as possible. My mind automatically harkens back to that ridiculous incident when I asked my mother how the process of reproduction can be prevented or terminated. I had humiliated myself the next day by blathering about "protection sold in bottles" to my junior high school chums when they in fact were discussing a protection racket run by one of the biggest and meanest kids in the school. Then it had been my turn to be snickered at. The memory makes me blush, and I immediately curtail my own derisive laughter.

Dr. Cellborn continues her briefing of the research assistant's job. We are to spend the majority of our eight-hour day reading the labor and delivery records of birthing mothers. These records are supposed to list everything that happens in the operating room during the birthing process, including the administration of anesthesia. Our job is to record the types and amounts of anesthesia that were administered. Over a dozen hospitals participated in this study, hospitals from Boston to Birmingham. After one day of doing this work, the conclusion among the research assistants is unanimous: BORING!! What a snooze fest. I think the salary is so good because one has to possess a special ability to remain awake while reading these tedious, poorly written documents. The only interesting part of this work is the stories of the often pre-teenage girls giving birth. Some of the mid-teens are delivering their third or fourth baby. The biographical sections give you a brief peek into the often-horrendous lives of the study patients. Many are giving birth to the offspring of raping relatives. These stories are so heart-wrenching that my emotions shuttle back and forth during the day between the aforementioned boredom and a despairing form of sadness.

Clay, Elwood, and I eat our brown-bag lunches together every day. Often, this is the most interesting hour of the day, because we get into melodramatic discussions about everything from current events to ancient philosophical questions regarding the meaning of life. In fact, we have transferred the obligatory college bull session to an NIH research lab. On a hot day in the middle of July when the air-conditioning is less than adequate, we make the mistake of beginning a discussion of religion. It begins innocently enough when Elwood asks me if I'm a believer. I see Clay shaking his head at Elwood and silently mouthing "no".

"A believer in what?" I ask.

"In Jesus Christ, the Lord and Savior of the world," Elwood replies with wide eyes and a voice that is loud and proud. His fervor makes me uneasy. I want to talk about religion about as much as I want to talk about cholera. In as tactful a voice as I can muster I say that I do not believe that Jesus is the Son of God. "Elwood, I'm Jewish." Worry lines form on Clay's brow, but not on Elwood's. "Aha!" Elwood bellows. "You should read Paul's letter to the Hebrews."

"I don't like reading other people's private mail." Elwood misses my joke and earnestly replies, "The letter is not private."

"And if I read this letter, what will it do for me?" My skepticism is leaking out through all my pores. "It will convince you of the superiority of the New Covenant to the Old Covenant, and it will introduce you to the person of Jesus who is three in one-God, Son, and Holy Spirit."

"It will, huh?"

"Yes, Jesus Christ is conceived by the Holy Spirit, born of the Virgin Mary, and is true God and true man." I look at Elwood as if he has just arrived from some alien planet and somehow has learned enough English to share his strange extraterrestrial beliefs. I attempt a gentle rebuttal. "Elwood, I don't want to show disrespect for your religious beliefs, but there is only one way in which the so-called New Covenant is superior to the Old Covenant. It's crazier! It's beyond me how anyone can believe in Jesus' virgin birth, resurrection, and all the other bizarre claims of the New Testament. The Old Covenant is crazy enough with its numerous fairy tales. Burning bushes and parting seas indeed." I end my rebuttal with a very satisfying harrumph. Elwood stares at me with eyes ablaze. "Unless you accept Jesus in your heart as your savior and redeemer, you're going to Hell, my friend!" He finally replies, his voice unable to disguise its venom. "You're the kind of person we're after," he continues. Clay interjects, "Not now, Elwood."

"Yes, now. Help me, Clay, we have a soul to save. Izzy, we're very concerned about your soul." My fear transmogrifies into sarcasm.

"Yeah, you and Torquemada." Clay laughs, but my reference to the Grand Inquisitor apparently goes over Elwood's head. "Izzy, you have no idea the peril your soul is in. You don't want to risk eternal damnation." Elwood seems genuinely frightened for my wellbeing. Sarcasm devolves into anger.

"Elwood, leave my soul alone. If you want to believe that nonsense, that's fine with me. Let me be with my non-belief. You don't see me evangelizing you to atheism, do you?"

"But Izzy, you're wrong and the price of your error is unbearable to me as it should be to you." It's all I can do to contain my parboiling rage. To contain it, I assume a haughty intellectual posture. "Here's the problem, Elwood. You think I'm wrong, and I think you're full of shit. But I'm quite willing to accept that you fervently believe in nonsense without hassling you about it. But you won't leave me be with my 'error' as you call it even if I'm willing to risk eternal damnation."

"But Izzy, it's my responsibility as a loving Christian to bring you to Christ." As the room begins to heat up from the failing air-conditioning, so does our rhetoric. Elwood's resolve increases, as does his viciousness. "Izzy, the problem with you Jews is that you refuse to admit that one of your own could be the Messiah, something you people have wished for and dreamed of for centuries. Jesus comes along, and you kill him. No wonder you're the most hated people on the planet." This is such a hideous statement that my rage implodes. I burst out laughing and return to sarcasm. "Hey Elwood, where's all the Christian love you evangelicals keep singing about? Any statement that begins with 'You Jews' and ends with 'the most hated people on the planet' doesn't sound a lot like love to me." Without missing a beat, Elwood replies, "We're taught to love the misguided."

"You know, Elwood, you're the worst evangelical salesman I've ever met." Clay, apparently thinking the same thing interrupts, "Izzy, what Elwood is trying to say__"

I cut him off. "I know what Elwood is trying to say. I've heard it hundreds of times before. 'You're right and I'm wrong.' What you don't understand is that evangelism by definition equals disrespect. What you're saying is that because I'm a Jew, I don't have any sense, any intelligence, any ability to discover the truth." Clay beats Elwood to the punch before the latter can insult me anymore. "That's not what he's saying,"

"Well, that's what I'm hearing." Now Elwood and I are both moving rapidly toward apoplexy. We are glaring at each other. Clay tries to intervene but neither Elwood nor I pay any attention to him. A few minutes of this staring contest seems to cool both of us down. In a more congenial tone Elwood begins again. "Let me tell you something, Izzy." His voice is now more triumphant than angry. "You may scoff at the evangelical movement now, but we have a plan." I look at him dubiously and ask, "What pray tell is that?"

"Evangelical Christianity will soon take over the country."

"What? What are you saying?" Elwood waves his hand through his flattop and says, "Yes, we will start with the elementary schools and convert as many children as possible. Then we'll move to the high schools and eventually we will infiltrate the colleges and build more Christian colleges like Wheaton. For example, two years ago, Arizona Christian University opened in Phoenix. In Tulsa, Oklahoma, Oral Roberts University is due to open next year. With our base firmly established in the schools at all levels, we will elect more and more evangelical Christians to school boards, state legislatures and then the U.S. Congress. And one day soon the President of the United States will be a born-again Christian. The entire country will come to Christ and our country will be saved." I look at Elwood in total disbelief. I don't know whether to laugh or to cry. I spontaneously give in to the former and burst into uncontrolled laughter. Clay looks very distressed while Elwood turns a shade of crimson that I don't think I have even seen before on a human face. I look over at Clay and ask him if he agrees with Elwood. "Not at all, Izzy," he replies. "What you have to understand is that Wheaton College has a very diverse student body. We tend to agree with the conservative theology of the place, but beyond that students hold a wide range of opinions and about politics and about how far to push the evangelical mission of the school. There are a few who agree with Elwood."

"Many more than you realize, Clay," Elwood aggressively adds. Clay ignores Elwood and continues, "I don't quite agree with your view, Izzy, that evangelism equals disrespect. I have a right to share my views and try and influence yours, just as you have a right to try and convince me that atheism is closer to the truth. Ain't that so?"

"Maybe. The problem is when it comes to religion, nobody knows for sure. All we have are beliefs. Just because you believe something doesn't make it so, and yet we kill each other because our beliefs are different. So doesn't it make sense to just agree that we should just respect that we hold different beliefs and let it be. From this perspective, evangelism is disrespect." Now Clay is getting excited. "It's not disrespect, Izzy, it's democracy. Isn't this what democracy is supposed to be about—ideas competing in the intellectual marketplace. If we succeed in convincing more people that our perspective contains more of the truth, then our ideas win the day."

"Yes, and the soft underbelly of democracy is that extremely undemocratic ideas can be democratically approved. I tell you guys what I've learned at Howard University about the Jim Crow laws in the South and their impact on the lives of Negro individuals and their families has made me ashamed of our democracy. I still have difficulty accepting the reality that the ancestors of many of my classmates were slaves." Clay stands up, looks out the window, and then turns to me and says, "But that just means that your ideas about equality have not yet won the day."

"But that's my point. In a country that professes to treat everyone equally, so many states by popular approval continue to discriminate against an entire group of Americans because of the color of their skin. That too is democracy in action." Elwood who has been struggling to get a word in finally takes advantage of the pause in our dialogue. "Democracy might be the best form of human government, but it is still man-made and therefore laced with sin. Only a return to Christ will guarantee the freedom and liberty of all people." I'm now ready to blow my top. "If that's the case, how come 11 am on Sunday is the most segregated hour of the week? Blacks are not allowed to attend white churches even though preachers in both are heaping praises on the same Christian God. Forgive me, but the hypocrisy of Christianity practiced in the Unites States boggles the mind." Our voices are raised to the point that it draws the attention of Dr. Cellborn. She rushes into our office visibly agitated. "Why aren't you young men working? Lunchtime is over. Your blathering can be heard along the entire corridor. A little less chatter and a lot more productivity from the three of you, please!"

The hot days of June become even hotter in July. Each day at work Elwood tells me a new story in his effort to convert me. One day it's Rabbi Saul's implosive conversion to a follower of Jesus. The next day is a spiel about "What's in it for the Jews to convert". On still another, I receive a tedious genealogical lecture tracing Jesus' connection to King David and therefore how important it is for Christians to show Jews the way. The week ended with an appeal for me to begin my alleged process of conversion by joining a congregation of Messianic Jews. This is the stepping-stone to becoming a full-fledged Christian. Each day I get angrier and Elwood more frustrated. I can't wait for the weekend to come.

I am so disappointed that Desirie has not kept her promise. She barely writes me once a week. So I retaliate by writing her only every other week. Most of the intervening days I bounce from anger to guilt. Then finally I get so pissed off that I am causing myself such anguish that I don't want to write her at all.

This weekend there is a monthly dance party at the Maryland National Guard Armory in Silver Spring. I round up the Miscreants—Peter, Bobby, and James—and the four of us set off for the Armory. I always have to laugh whenever we approach the Armory. Located near the intersection of Georgia and Wayne Avenues in downtown Silver Spring it looks like nothing so much as a medieval Gothic castle with its many turrets and segmentations. I feel like we're about to lay siege to the headquarters of a wicked Norman king. The racket that we hear within as we walk up to the castle entrance suggests that the war has started without us. Honking saxes, wailing bluesy voices, and the staccato beats of a variety of drums. And every three minutes or less we hear the booming voice of an army commander. But in reality it is not an army commander. It's Motor Mouth himself, the DJ du jour, subbing for Don Dillard, a radio disc jockey who against all odds introduced rock- and-roll to Washington area teenagers from WDON-AM his tiny radio station in Wheaton, Maryland.

We enter the cavernous hall of the Armory where several hundred teenagers are bopping away to At the Hop by Danny and the Juniors. At first I can't pick out anyone I know. It's like watching a choreographed riot. The four of us saunter around the perimeter of the hall. After a few minutes, Peter yells out, "Hey look, there's Sharon with that tool Larry B." Peter doesn't wait for a response from any of us. He begins to chortle and to point frantically into the middle of the hall. "There's Turdface. Aw he can't dance worth a shit." None of us is exactly sure where Peter is pointing, but we all laugh in agreement. Bobby spots a former girlfriend and groans, "Oh God, there's Carol with Steve Weinberg. I can't believe that she dumped my ass for him." "You best believe it," I say with a grin on my face. James sings, "Don't be cruel to a heart that's true." James' singing never fails to leave us with the silly giggles. The song ends and Motor Mouth begins his staccato rap about the great music that keeps coming. He assures us that "WE'RE GONNA ROCK N ROLL ALL NIGHT LONG. NOW HERE'S A SONG THAT MADE IT TO NO.1 LAST YEAR, ERNIE K. DOE AND MOTHER-IN-LAW." A deep voice intones Mother-in-law and the choreographed riot begins anew. A hundred hormone-charged males begin dancing with a hundred nubile females. One girl stands out for me. She's a copper-haired colleen with sparkling green eyes. She's wearing white pedal pushers and a Kelly green shirt tied in a knot

revealing her tantalizing midriff. She's tiny, perky and full of
energy. She bounces around the dance floor with a perennial
smile plastered on her punim. She is beautiful, curvaceous and
surprisingly well endowed for her size. I'm smitten. My friends
disappear from my world and I begin moving in her direction,
but hardly aware that I'm doing so. I must meet her, but my
mind goes blank. I have no idea what to say to her. I am
suddenly standing in front of her and her 6-foot tall dance
partner. As I conjure up an image of Desirie's disapproving face,
I almost walk away. Instead I stand and stare. Speech is now a
distant memory. "Uh...uh," I eventually offer. "Yes?" She asks.
Her smile grows even more incandescent. "Uh...,uh," I repeat.
Words have deserted me, but not song titles. I hear myself
singing...loudly, "It's obdacious!"

    "What are you saying? What is obdacious?" She says
trying to hold on to her smile.

    "The way I love you," I say rather than sing. I had
doubted it could ever happen, but her smile evaporates. Motor
Mouth croons out the name of the next song, I Only Have Eyes
for You by The Flamingoes. The green-eyed colleen maneuvers
her partner so that her back is facing me. I just stand there in the
middle of the dance floor with a hundred couples around me
slow dancing. All are tightly squeezed together. Some are
nibbling on necks; others are grabbing buttocks; still others are
getting acquainted with their partner's tongue. I find myself
staring at her shapely behind, and I shake myself out of my
reverie. "Listen, I'm sorry," I manage, "but I want to meet you
and I don't know how to approach you." She moves her partner
180 degrees and is now facing me.

    "Well, your singing stinks and is probably not your best
pick-up approach. Look, wait until this song is over and then I'll
talk to you. Meet me at the entrance."

    After the song ends I see her walking towards me. Again,
in my mind's eye, I see now Desirie's disappointed face. We

didn't say we couldn't date during our summer apart. I miss her terribly, but I need to have some fun to deal with my loneliness. She sees me standing with my hands in my pockets and her smile brightens. She sticks out her hand and says, "Hi, I'm Maureen McKenna." Her smile and her demeanor are so welcoming that my entire body relaxes. I easily respond, "And I'm Izzy White."

"Nice to meet you, Izzy. Would you like to dance?" From the first rollicking beat of Bobby Darin's Queen of the Hop I know I have found the ideal dance partner. She bounces when I bounce, rocks when I rock, and when I blacken my dance moves, she shows me complimentary moves of her own. She fits my dance style like the perennial glove. Next comes The Wanderer by Dion and the Belmonts. I start with the Pony, move into the Slop and finally start Snapping. Maureen follows me effortlessly until I get to the Snap which she does not know. While I Snap, she does the Frug. I Snap around her in a circle and she stands there shaking her hips. In quick succession she does the Frug, the Hitch Hike and the Swim. The hormonal males and their nubile partners stop their own dancing. They form a circle to watch us. Soon they are clapping to the beat of our dance moves. I feel as if I have entered another plane of existence. This is perfect happiness. I had believed that this feeling was the stuff of movie tales. But here it is, and I am awash in pure joy. There's a beautiful girl shaking her hips and smiling at me. The crowd begins to add cheers to their clapping. I do not realize until that moment that at least half of the hormonal males and their nubile partners know me. They begin to shout my name, "Go Izzy Go" "Look at that crazy man go," someone shouts. That spurs me on to work harder, to experiment with new moves. I grab Maureen and we return to the Jitterbug. We attempt more complex turns and shifts that I have ever tried before. Maureen does not miss a beat. Whatever I attempt she follows seamlessly. Out of the corner of my eye, I see the Three Miscreants looking on. James stares, Bobby smiles, and Peter looks astonished. He knows better than the others just how advanced my dancing has become. I can tell by his expression that he can't believe some of my moves and that someone can actually follow me. When the music stops, Maureen flings herself into my arms and exclaims, "Oh Izzy, you're wonderful!" She continues to hug me and seems reluctant to let me go. She finally breaks from the hug and just smiles at me. I bask in the warmth of her praise.

But much to my astonishment, Maureen says she's in love with me. My comfortable way of seeing the world is undermined. My body quakes with a new feeling, a new way of thinking about myself. . Maureen interrupts my reverie. "Izzy! Izzy, are you alright?"

"I'm fine." She pulls me onto the dance floor. "Come on, this is my favorite slow song." As the Flamingoes begin to sing, Lovers Never Say Goodbye, Maureen glues her body to mine and starts nibbling on my neck. Though I find the sensation strange I'm hoping for my first hickey. She moves her mouth to my cheek and eventually her lips are plastered on mine. She kisses me and I go wobbly. Although she is only five feet tall, she has the strength to pull me upright. "Are you OK, Izzy?" She says as she holds a hand over her mouth in an unsuccessful attempt to stifle her laughter.

On our first date we go to a forgettable movie, then to the Silver Spring Hot Shoppes for Mighty Moes and a milkshake, and eventually to Valley Street, the local lovers' lane. We make out for awhile, but spend more time talking about ourselves, what our lives have been like up to this point, and our hopes and dreams for the future. She tells me that, like her parents, she's a devout Catholic and that she attends Mass regularly. I learn that her father is a Fourth Degree member of the Knights of Columbus and that her mother originally wanted to be a nun until she met Maureen's father at one of the first ever USO dances. They were married six months later. Maureen is the oldest of six children. She also thought about becoming a nun, but knows that she doesn't have the discipline for the rigors of the religious life. This family is seriously Catholic.

"Do you go to Mass every day?" I ask.

"No silly. Not every day, but every Sunday morning. We go as a family, me my five brothers and sisters and my parents. Do you go to church?"

"Church?" I reply horrified. "I don't even go to synagogue." Maureen looks puzzled.

"Izzy, why are you talking about synagogues? You're not Jewish."

"Oh yes I am!"

"OH IZZY!" Her voice turns whiney and her disappointment is obvious. Her hands fly up to her cheeks and she stares out the car window. She keeps saying over and over, "Oh Izzy. What are we going to do?"

"What? I just said I was Jewish, not that I have the plague."

"You don't understand. Because of your religion, I can never marry you."

"Marry me? Maureen, we've just met."

"But Izzy, I know you're the one. I feel it in my whole body. You're my soul mate."
"Uh, Maureen, you don't know anything about me except that I can dance."

"But that's how I know. We dance together like we've known each other all our lives. And since we dance so well together, we'll do everything well together."

"I'm having trouble following your logic here."

"Izzy, my mother told me that you can tell how a man will be in the bedroom by the way he moves on the dance floor. We're going to have a wonderful sex life and make lots of babies. But to do that we have to get married, and I can't marry you because you're not Catholic. There's only one answer, Izzy."

"I'm happy to learn that there's an answer. What is it?"

"You have to convert to Catholicism."

"I have to what? You want me to leave one crazy religion for an even crazier one?"

"Oh Izzy, you have to. Our happiness depends on your converting." I feel the heebie-jeebies crawling up my spine. "Maureen, I think we should slow down and get to know one another. I mean I like you. I like you a lot, but we hardly know each other. Let's just have fun and see what happens, ok?" She smiles weakly and says ok.

She is able to comply with my request for the next two weeks. We see a lot of each other and have many wonderful evenings...free of religious debate. We go to the now-integrated Glen Echo Park and laugh ourselves silly. We dance until we were exhausted at the weekly Armory dances. We kiss our way through a couple of drive-in theatre movies and feel each other's erogenous zones in the dark of Valley Street. On one of those nights parked on Valley Street, when we were taking a break from our heavy breathing, Maureen snuggles close to me, lays her head in the crook of my arm, her copper hair spread across my chest, and suddenly says in almost a little girl voice, "Izzy, can I ask you a question?" I feel myself tensing up, but I try to be nonchalant. "Sure," I answer. "Why don't Jews believe in Jesus?"
"Oh Maureen," I say, my body stiffening in dismay. We both sit upright at the same time. "Izzy, I tried not to say anything, but I need to know. I need to know how I can convince you to become a Catholic."

"Maureen, Jews think of Jesus as a wise teacher, but he is not the Messiah. The Jewish Messiah is supposed to be a warrior who will free the Jews from Roman oppression, not some other-worldly mystic who promises pie in the sky and everlasting afterlife." Maureen blushes from my characterization of Christian salvation. "But you're wrong, Izzy. Jesus is the Messiah. We have the truth. Catholics have always had the truth for the last two thousand years. We could be so happy, Izzy, if you'd only allow yourself to accept the truth."

"Maureen, you think I'm wrong, and I think you're wrong. So where do we go from here?"

"I won't give up, Izzy. You will become a Catholic." I have no more words. I pull her to me and kiss her harder and more passionately than I ever have before. I let my hands roam all over her body. She begins to moan and in a breathy voice calls out my name and moans, "I want you." She grabs my hand and says, "Let's go in the back seat." I'm getting very nervous, but follow her command anyway. We hastily climb into the back seat of my car, and she starts removing our clothes. It dawns on me that she is set on us going "all the way". Now Desirie's image looks horrified and I hear her say, "Don't you dare!" Maureen starts unbuttoning my pants and I have the ludicrous thought that I'm going to lose my virginity without my say so. She is now wet and willing and eager for me to enter her. I hesitate for a moment as I remember the Coitus Interruptus Debacle with Shannon. I also remember how the image of Desirie, who had already rejected me, prevented me from going any further with Shannon. Miffed at the painful memory I tell myself, the hell with it. Desirie is probably gonna reject me again in September. I pull out a rubber that I have saved for a year. I pray that it's still good. She says, "No rubber." I say, "Yes rubber." But in the awkwardness of our position in the back seat, I have great difficulty getting it on. Finally, I miraculously manage to get the rubber on my penis and try to enter her. "No, not there," she says with exasperation. "Here, let me help you." She grabs my penis and guides it into the correct orifice. I move inside her cautiously at first and then I begin to thrust rapidly. We both are moaning loudly. Even with the rubber on, I do not last long and I feel myself coming. Desirie's image has now faded into oblivion. I yell, "Oh Jesus!" Maureen yells back, "Yes, yes, Jesus!" "Oh God!" I yell, and she yells, "Yes, yes, God! They're the same!" We climax together with a mutual howl. A moment later she's crying tears of joy and laughing at the same time. "I knew we would come together as Catholics." "What are you saying, Maureen?" I'm afraid of what I'm going to hear. Now she smiles her incandescent smile and says, "By making love like this, we have sealed our love for one another and for God. I heard you cry out, Oh Jesus, Oh God. That must mean you see that they're the same."

"No it doesn't. This is my first time and WOW!"

"You really believe in the trinity, Izzy, you just don't know it yet. Now there's no obstacle to our getting married." She's bouncing up and down in the back seat of my 1954 Plymouth and clapping her hands like a little child at her birthday party. "This is a mistake," I complain. "What do you mean a mistake?" Maureen looks as if she has been sucker-punched in the stomach. "We should never have made love. It's too soon and it's giving you the wrong impression."

"THE WRONG IMPRESSION," she screeches. "I've just given you my heart, my body, and soul and you've given me what—the wrong impression? Oh Izzy, how could you? I promise you two things, Izzy White. You will become a Catholic and my husband." We drive home in silence. I might be her choice for a future husband, but she neither says nor kisses me good night when she gets out of the car.

So that was July. Despite my prayers not to bother, I have two people in my life who are hounding me to do what I must in order to reserve my place in heaven. August is worse. Elwood Plethysma by day and Maureen McKenna by night were both vying for my soul. Elwood reads me passages from the New

Testament to entice me with the rewards that will come to He that believeth in me. Maureen regales me with stories about her father; what a devout Catholic he is and, therefore, what a wonderful man he is. She tells me how handsome he looks in full regalia during the Color Corps march on St. Patrick's Day—a black tuxedo, white gloves, a red white and blue baldric, a red cape and a blue naval chapeau with a white fringe on top. And she ends her story with the plaintive question, "Don't you want to be like him?" Her enticements, however, are not spiritual. After her stories, she kisses me, arouses me, and pleads with me to go to Mass with her. As the days go by, I think I'm falling in love with her even as I become convinced that our relationship is doomed.

One Sunday in the middle of August I am invited to Sunday dinner with her family. I had refused Maureen's umpteenth pleading for me to attend Mass with the family, but I do agree to show up at her house at 1 pm for their weekly ritual of coerced family time. There are many firsts for me associated with this Sunday dinner. This is my first time as a guest at an after church meal with a Christian family, particularly as the designated boyfriend. It is also my first time in a split-level home. It is disorienting to me to see that once you enter the main room of the house there are three short steps running down to a lower level and another three short steps running up to a higher level. For me, it feels like a house running away from itself. And it is my first time in a house in Wheaton, Maryland, a recently built suburb just north of Silver Spring. Throughout my childhood, Silver Spring was the only suburb in which I had spent any time. Three of the younger McKenna children greet me at the door full of laughter and questions. One of the girls shouts in a singsong voice, "Maureen's got a boyfriend." The rest of the McKenna family comes into the foyer area as soon as I enter. Everyone is smiling at me, everyone except Mr. McKenna. His greeting is a stone cold stare. Maureen pushes past her siblings, grabs me by the hand and drags me into the living room. Maureen's 12-year-old sister asks, "Do you and Maureen kiss?" Before I can answer, her youngest brother, Richard, exclaims,

"Eew Gross!" Maureen's mother smiles at me and graciously says, "Welcome to our home." Her graciousness puts me at ease. Maureen's other siblings are all talking at once, and I'm unable to make out what they are saying. Her father bellows, "Cut the noise kids. Sit down. It's time to eat."

My first faux pas occurs when I reach for the homemade biscuits while everyone else is getting ready to say grace. Mr. McKenna's look of disdain is almost enough to send my totally shamed being slinking out the door. "Not yet, Izzy," Mrs. McKenna says with a pitying smile and her hands folded in a prayerful steeple. Mr. McKenna intones in a deep baritone voice, "Bless us, O Lord, for these Thy gifts, which we are about to receive from Thy bounty. Through Christ our Lord we pray. Amen." After grace, all of the female members of the McKenna family go into the kitchen. A minute later they return in single file with ham, sweet yams, mashed potatoes, and Del Monte canned peas. I find it difficult to eat with eight people staring at me. I wonder what I'm doing wrong. Conversation remains at the level of polite small talk until Mr. McKenna asks out of nowhere, "Where do you go to church, Izzy?" "I don't go to church, sir." I reply. Now everyone, but Maureen who has her head down, looks at me with a horrified expression. "And why not?" an indignant Mr. McKenna asks. "Because I'm Jewish, sir" I answer feeling an attack of heebie-jeebies coming on. By this time, I feel like I'm sitting on a nest of bees. More looks of horror from the siblings. Maureen looks nervous, her mother looks at me with pity, and disdain returns to Mr. McKenna's face. He looks at me like I'm a turd that suddenly landed on his dinner table. He cuts his eyes at Maureen and says nothing more for the rest of the main meal. During dessert one of Maureen's brothers asks me where I go to school. When I say I go to Howard University, a primarily black school, Mr. McKenna suddenly rises from his chair and leaves the room. Maureen goes crimson, the siblings look frightened, and for the first time Mrs. McKenna is horrified. Shortly after dessert, I pull Maureen aside to tell her I'm leaving. She looks sad, but she understands. I announce to the group that I'm leaving, and in unison the siblings say, "Aw so soon?" I continue the game by offering my apologies. I tell Maureen I will call her later, and I make a hasty departure.

I wait several hours before calling Maureen because I need to get over the rage, humiliation, and general malaise I feel about Sunday Dinner at the McKenna's. When I feel calm enough, I call Maureen. She informs me that from now on we will have to conduct our relationship in secret because her father has forbidden her to see me. She has no intention of heeding his command. Instead, she plans to take our relationship into hiding. "What did he say?" I ask. "You don't want to know."

"What did he say? I will keep pestering you until you tell me."

"Oh Izzy, it's too horrible to repeat."

"What did he say? I want every word verbatim."

"He said, I can't date any nigger-loving kike; and as long as I'm living in his house, I can only date Catholic boys." The rage and humiliation come storming back. "I guess that's it," I say.

"No Izzy, that's not it. You're going to become a Catholic and then I will marry you."

"And what makes you think I want to have anything to do with your family?"

"Oh they'll come around. You'll see.

"I'm not so sure."

"Izzy, let's go out tomorrow and we can talk about it in person."

When I pick her up the next evening, she says, "Let's go to Valley Street."

"I thought we're going to talk."

"We are, but I want to make sure we have privacy." When we have parked on Valley Street, she starts kissing me all over. I'm aroused, but my heart is not in it. I tell her to stop, but she continues to try and entice me by kissing me and removing her clothes. I pull away from her. "Listen, Maureen, this won't work."

"You're not breaking up with me?" Her face is wide-eyed with shock.

"I think it's best," I answer as gently as I can. I watch her face crumple into tears.

"You can't do this to me, Izzy, not after all I have given you." She is sobbing uncontrollably now, and I can't think of anything consoling to say. I drive her home; and when we reach her house, she starts pleading with me not to leave her. "It's for the best," is all I have to offer her.

During the last week of August, I receive at least a dozen calls from Maureen. It's clear she has progressed from sadness to rage. During the first three or four calls, I listen to her scream out her anger and resentment. I take the full volley as penance for all the real and imaginary transgressions my mind constructs. By the fifth call I have had enough. I listen for a minute and then cut her off. With every call I descend into sadness and ruminate about the difficulties of romantic love. By the end of the week, her calls begin to trail off until she stops calling altogether. Now I only have one person who is still trying to convert me. I still have Elwood Plethysma to deal with.

When I arrive at work on the last Monday in August, Clay Fogmeister pulls me aside. He is smiling impishly as he says to me, "Izzy. I want to show you something." He is holding a piece of unlined paper with some kind of drawing on it. Now he is dancing around me and giggling. He hands me the paper and it is indeed a drawing of what is supposed to be heaven. There is one lone figure sitting on a puffy cloud with his head resting in the palm of one of his hands. The figure looks forlorn, apparent even through his thick, horned rim glasses. Clay has entitled his work of art, Elwood's Heaven. In anticipation of my own guffaws, Clay bursts out into high-pitched laughter. The message could not be clearer. Clay's critique of Elwood's evangelizing is that he will end up alone in his self-constructed heaven. Clay is not disappointed. The laughter pours out of me. Elwood enters the workroom, grim-faced and anxious. Clay crumples up his work of art with his hands behind his back. "What're you two up to?" Elwood asks, in a voice that clearly implies that he thinks something sinful is taking place. Clay and I say in unison, "Nothing." Elwood looks suspiciously first at me and then at Clay. "What are you up to, Elwood?" Clay asks. Clay looks at Elwood to see if our Evangelist-in-Residence is on to us. Apparently, he's not. In fact, he's now enthusiastically seeking my attention. "Izzy, I want to read you something." He pulls out his well-worn copy of The Holy Bible. "Oh, Elwood, not again," I complain. "Just listen, will you Izzy?" He thumbs through the New Testament looking for the passage he has chosen to read to me. He believes that he's finally found the key passage that will turn the lock in my closed mind. "OK, Elwood," I say in a voice that communicates surrender. Elwood finds the passage and now assumes the dignified posture of a preacher about to begin his weekly sermon: There is only one love that loves unconditionally—the love of the Divine. I look at Elwood questioningly. "That's it? No hellfire or brimstone?"

Elwood relaxes and pulls his chair close to mine. "That's a distortion of the Christian message. It's actually about love." I'm astonished. Elwood's entire demeanor is changed, and the message of love is incongruent with the fiery tenacity of his previous evangelizing. This sudden change or clarification of the evangelical message jolts me; and for the first time since I met

Elwood, I give serious thought to what he's saying. Something in it clicks for me, and I share my epiphany with Elwood and Clay. "You know guys I finally understand something about you, Christianity, and all those who are attracted to this message. We can imagine perfect, unconditional love, but we just can't live it....except in our imaginations." Clay looks a little miffed, but Elwood is infuriated. He rises from his chair, looks out the window of our pillbox office, mumbles something to himself, and then wheels around, points a finger at me and shouts, "IZZY, YOU ARE DOOMED TO PERDITION! I need a break from you, Izzy, but I'm never going to give up. You understand me? I'm never going to give up. Your soul is overripe for saving." Elwood doesn't speak to me for the rest of the day, and is barely cordial for the rest of our last week together. Clay, on the other hand, remains friendly, and in fact we have lunch together at a nearby Chinese restaurant on the last day of work. I invite Elwood, but he refuses. During the month of September, I'm inundated with materials on Christianity along with the notes that implore me to accept Jesus as my savior before it's too late.

Hell hath no fury like an evangelist scorned...And he never gives up.

Chapter 22.
Soul Pain

Tomorrow I begin my last year as a Howard student. So what do I choose to do on my last day of summer vacation? I'm reading the latest issue of Elwood's self-produced magazine entitled Fire and Brimstone. As usual, the magazine is replete with Elwood's own jeremiads on the increasing decadence of the modern world. There is more of hell in this magazine than of heaven, and I suspect that Elwood takes great pleasure in "knowing" that the unbeliever is hell-bound. There's nothing like the Schadenfreude of the self-righteous! At some point I read the phrase, "You are damned" one too many times and I throw the magazine against my bedroom wall in total exasperation. I hunger to go outside; but when I look out my window and I see waves of heat rising from the street, I know that remaining in my air-conditioned apartment is the better idea.

You might wonder what my attraction is to Elwood's magazine since I don't believe a word of what I read. I confess it is the total certainty with which he believes. I am so impressed, no, astonished by his sense of certainty. And I am trying to understand that mindset. In my admittedly limited experience, I have found that I can be certain of nothing. Maureen too was so certain that I would convert to Catholicism and marry her when neither event was ever within the realm of possibility. So certain are they of their own individual truth that they are unembarrassed by their failed attempts in evangelizing me. They both wanted me to Come to Jesus, and each tried to get me to the same place by truly idiosyncratic means. Elwood preached and Maureen "put out".

In truth I miss Maureen. I miss her smile, her perkiness, her soft, creamy, voluptuous body, and her enthusiasm for lovemaking. She was a feast for all my senses. I had not planned to lose my virginity that night; but when I did, it felt like it was torn away from me. The tearing away of my virginity forced out of me a cry of loss. As I am luxuriating in the image of our skin-on-skin encounter, my phone suddenly rings. I answer and hear a shrieking female voice on the other end. There is just enough "signal" for me to detect within the hysterical "noise" that Maureen is trying to communicate something to me of the greatest urgency. "Calm down, Maureen, " I say. "I can't understand you for all your screeching." I hear breathless sobbing. "I'm... I'm late," she says a little more calmly before she again begins her ear-piercing lamentation, "I'M LATE; DON'T YOU UNDERSTAND!" I still don't get it.

"Late for what? " I'M LATE WITH MY PERIOD," And her wailing recommences. Now it is my turn to screech.

"WHAT? YOU CAN'T BE! I USED A RUBBER!"

"AND HOW OLD WAS THAT RUBBER?" She asks in a voice awash in tears. The panic that I hear in her voice has no difficulty traveling from her brain to mine. "HOW LATE?" I ask, matching her wailing howl for howl. Through her sniffling, she softly says, "Two weeks."

"OH MY GOD WE'RE DOOMED!" I cry. In my mind's eye, I see every dream, every plan for a successful life that I have ever conjured dashed to splinters against the rocks of real life. "Maureen, I will be right back. I put the phone on the bed go into the bathroom and turn on the cold-water spigot. I splash my face and quickly wipe it with a towel. I look into the mirror and see a very young face staring back at me. You, a daddy? Impossible! I begin laughing hysterically until tears roll out of my eyes. Then the tears continue, but now I am crying. The tears stop and I give myself a hard rebuking stare. OK Izzy, let's be a man about this. "I'm back," I tell Maureen once I pick up the phone. She has stopped crying, but there is sheer panic in her voice. "WHAT ARE WE GONNA DO, IZZY? WHAT'RE WE GONNA DO?" Maureen asks in a shrieking whiney voice. I reply in as manly a voice I can muster, "You'll have to get rid of it."

"What do you mean I have to get rid of it? We did this together. So we decide together. Besides I'm Catholic and the idea of destroying a life makes me sick."

"Well, are you ready to be a mommy? Because I'm not ready to be a daddy."

"No, I'm too young to become a mother."

"Well then, what do you suggest we do?" The more we talk about the possibility of our becoming parents, the more difficult it becomes to believe that Maureen is not pregnant. "Oh Izzy, I think I'm gonna be sick. I'll be right back." A moment later, I hear faint sounds of retching and of a toilet flushing. Another moment passes and Maureen is back on the phone. It's as if she never left. She begins to cry again into the phone and says through her tears, "My parents will kick me out of the house. I'll have no place to go. Can I stay with you, Izzy?" This requests jolts me back to reality, and I realize we are getting ahead of ourselves. "Wait a minute Maureen, we don't even know for sure that you're pregnant." At this moment, our conversation produces its first intelligent idea. "Listen, I worked the whole summer with one of the world's leading authorities on human fertilization and reproduction, Dr. Fullmarks. Let me go talk to him. I'm sure he can give me the best information on the likelihood of your being pregnant and maybe some advice about what we should do." Maureen sounds relieved by the suggestion. "Oh Izzy, that's a wonderful idea. Call him right away."

"Maureen, its Sunday. I don't have his home number and nobody will be at work now. I'll call him first thing tomorrow morning."

"OK, Izzy. Call him as soon as you can tomorrow and call me after you speak with him."

I have no classes on Friday afternoon so I schedule a meeting with Dr. Fullmarks at 3 pm. As I enter his pristine laboratory—a startling contrast to the advancing state of putrefaction and decrepitude of the Howard U. Chem Lab--I see him bent over a microscope attempting to solve yet another mystery within the universe of the cell, I presume. He is the picture of the dedicated scientist, white lab coat, white fringes bookending a balding head, and large round-rim glasses. But when he turns to greet me, he gives me a beatific smile that reflects the true gentleness of the man. "Ah, Mr. White," he says with a warmth that surprises me. "It is so good to see you again so soon after the termination of your summer internship. I sensed the urgency in your message, but I am in the dark as to what can be so urgent in your young life."

"Disaster, Dr. Fullmarks. I am facing a disaster." Dr. Fullmarks motions for me to sit in a nearby chair and he pulls up another chair for himself. I look around at the stark whiteness of the laboratory and I feel momentarily like an inpatient in a psychiatric ward. The heebie jeebies begin to overtake me. "M' my girl-friend is two weeks late with her period."

"Ah, I see, and you think she is pregnant?"

"She thinks she's pregnant and she's managed to convince me."

"Well, tell me, Mr. White," Dr. Fullmarks asks with a piercing but kindly stare. "What is the current nature of your relationship?"

"That's what is so upsetting. We broke up two weeks ago. We made love once and she thought that meant I would convert to Catholicism in order for her to be able to marry me. I have no intention of converting to any religion, and marriage is a long way off for me. Anyway, Sunday night, I get this frantic call from Maureen crying that she's late. "

"Let me ask you Mr. White, during this one time you made love, did you use a condom?"

"Yes, but it was a year old. I've been carrying it around the whole time in case I found an opportunity to lose my virginity." Dr. Fullmarks begins to stroke his white goatee. "So this one time you made love with this girl was your first time?"

"That's right and I wasn't even planning to, but she insisted."

"Oh I see. So she held a gun to your head?"

"Well no, but she did grab my hand and pull me into the back seat of my car and began taking off her clothes and mine."

"Did the condom come off at any time?"

"No it didn't, and I remember taking it off myself afterwards and looking for holes."

A smile plays around Dr. Fullmarks' mouth. "It's always good to inspect one's handiwork. " Dr. Fullmarks chuckles to himself. I smile nervously. "Actually, Mr. White, what you are telling me is quite reassuring. Although condoms are not full proof, they are about 90 % effective. Your post-coital inspection may push the efficacy rating a little higher. Now when you combine that fact with another, the certainty that your girlfriend—Maureen is her name? -- is dealing with not just your rejection but also the destruction of her marital dream; those facts in conjunction suggest to me that the significant stress with which she is dealing is suppressing the appearance of her menses."

"Are you positive, Dr. Fullmarks?" I ask this with prayerful hands pleading for mercy from a deity. "I can't be absolutely certain, Mr. White, but if you wait one more week, the probability is very high that Maureen will get her period." When

I clasp him in a bear hug, he at first resists and then laughingly relents. "Oh thank you, thank you Dr. Fullmarks." I hold on to him tightly while I tearfully sing out my thanks. He gently separates himself from me. "Not at all, Mr. White. Not at all." I literally dash out of his lab and streak to my car.

As soon as I get home, I call Maureen and tell her the prognostication from my oracle. "Maureen, I think you can help matters by calming down and not worrying about it. I believe Dr. Fullmarks when he says that within seven days, you'll get your period." In a dejected voice, Maureen says, "OK, Izzy, if you trust him." I could hear that she doesn't trust the information I have just given her. In other words, she no longer trusts anything I say. Well, it wasn't seven days or ten, but a full 14 days later before Maureen got her period. Fourteen days and 15 nasty, tearful and desperate phone calls from Maureen. In those 15 phone calls, I receive a clear image of myself in Maureen's eyes: "Cad", "Gigolo", "User", "Manipulator", "Liar". But it is the last two epithets that really hurt: "Christ-Killer" and "Nigger-Lover." Painful, but clarifying! We could never be a couple.

In romantic relationships, the truth is always late.

After the tumultuous summer I have endured, I am happy to return to my classes at Howard. There, at least, professors are more interested in my mind than in my soul. I have finally left behind my two would-be soul-devourers: Elwood, the evangelical nudnik, and Maureen, my teenage succubus. Now I can focus on my new love: Psychology. I guess psychology has always been a secret obsession. I've always wanted to know what makes people tick; and like most people interested in psychology I first want to understand what makes me tick.

The first day I enter my class on abnormal psychology, I see Desirie. I tremble uncontrollably as I stare at her. She waves and smiles. I am surprised by how grateful I feel that she is smiling at me. I am even more surprised when my legs go wobbly. I laugh nervously and I am sure I look as goofy as I feel.

I wave at her like a five-year-old waving at a playmate. Then I suddenly feel such a fire in my loins that it is all I can do to restrain myself from grabbing her and kissing her passionately. She chooses to sit next to me in class and begins chatting away as if we have been in each other's lives every day for the past four years. I can't make out what she is saying because of the volume of sounds produced by my physiological responses to her nearness and her beauty. My heart sounds like a base drum and my stomach trumpets its borborygmi so loudly that I'm sure Desirie can hear it. If she does hear the rumbles of my stomach, she does not let on. The cacophony within tells me I'm helplessly in love with her. I finally hear her say, "Okay, I'll shut up now because here's Dr. Hicks."

Dr. Leslie Hicks is probably the most difficult faculty member at Howard to get to know. I think basically he is shy. He stands at the front of the class, 6 feet tall, thin with thinning hair and a cocoa-colored complexion, with a world-weary expression on his face, looking as if he would rather be getting a colonoscopy than having to face and teach us. He stands silently for the longest time before he finally says, "Welcome to Abnormal Psychology. The assigned textbook for this class is Robert White's The Abnormal Personality. But don't bother reading it. Just watch me, because I am the perfect example of an abnormal personality." This brings the house down. Five minutes go by before the laughter dies down. Anyone who is even superficially acquainted with Dr. Hicks knows he is speaking the unvarnished truth.

I couldn't believe how happy I am in the abnormal psychology class. The material is endlessly fascinating and every class I get to sit next to the young woman I truly love. After each class we have lunch together and talk about the information we have just absorbed and the humorous quirks of Dr. Hicks. Soon we begin to have study dates in Founders Library after which we go to the Kampus Korner for a bite to eat. Without uttering a word to one another about the status of our relationship, we are together again, a couple in love. We share a fascination with the different kinds of mental illness. Every time we read about a new disorder, we are both certain we have it. I am convinced that basically she is a manic-depressive because she blows so hot and cold. She is certain I am obsessive-compulsive. We have a great time making each other laugh as we spell out the various symptoms of the disorder we think the other possesses. She laughs at my tendency to line up my coins according to their different denominations, and I chuckle as I accuse her of being all happy and perky one minute and then down in the dumps the next. We each vociferously deny our assigned diagnosis. But this jocularity could easily slip into hurtful accusations. I become anxious when she accuses me of having a depressive personality, and she becomes depressed when I announce she is a very anxious person.

On a beautiful Sunday in early October, I take Desirie to one of my favorite spots in Rock Creek Park. As we walk, we hold hands and marvel at the coat of many colors of the season-turned leaves. Beams of Indian Summer sunlight break through the dense foliage of the Park. The beauty of the day and our surroundings comfort me and send my mood soaring. I stop and grab Desirie by her shoulders and kiss her with great passion. She kisses me back. Afterwards we smile at each other mirroring our now established feeling between us. Love is in the air of Rock Creek Park. We continue walking for a while and then Desirie stops me. She looks at me with an expression that seems to be a cross between admiration and sorrow. "You know, Izzy, I wish I had your self-confidence." This revelation astonishes me. "Are you kidding? I wish I had yours. I mean you went on the Freedom Rides and almost got yourself killed."

"Well, you would have gone if you had learned to control your anger."

"Yes and the only reason I had the strength to even try to do the training was because of you...because of how I feel about you. I didn't want to disappoint you."

"But you had the guts to come to Howard. Don't you realize how brave a decision that was?"

"Brave or odd. I'm not sure which. Listen, Desirie, I've fought a life-long battle against feelings of inferiority. I live in a slough of doubt. I second-guess every decision. And everyday, I lacerate my mind with questions about my intelligence, my abilities, my looks." Desirie squeezes my hand and looks into my eyes with such sympathy that I have to fight back the tears. She smiles at me through tears of her own. "I think I must see myself in you because I do the same thing. I don't think I'm very attractive."

"My God, Desirie! You're a beautiful young woman. And you've grown prettier since I met you four years ago."

"Oh Izzy, my nose is too wide."

"What do you mean? I love your nose. I reached over to kiss it and she pushes me away. "Don't, Izzy!" Her sympathetic smile of a moment ago is now gone and is replaced by an expression of hostile fear. A moment ago she looks at me with love; now she is looking at me as if I were the enemy. "Is this real, Izzy? I've got to know that you really care for me and that you're not just a college playboy looking for a piece of black ass?" I burst out laughing which seriously offends her. She turns her back on me and starts to walk away from me rapidly. "Desirie! Desirie!" I call after her. "I'm not laughing at you. I'm laughing about what you said. Me? A playboy? That's hilarious. I've only just lost my virginity this past summer." She turns and faces me and looks at me searchingly.

"Oh so you have another girlfriend?"

"No, Desirie. We broke up."

"So you got what you wanted from her and then dropped her like a bad habit!"

"It wasn't like that, Desirie, I swear!"

"Oh, Izzy, how could you?" Desirie starts walking away from me again. I catch her and grab her by the shoulders. "Would you please listen to me? I'll tell you the whole story. Let's sit here." We sit on a giant boulder on the bank of the creek, and I tell her how I met Maureen. What a great dance partner she was. How our infatuation grew. How she got the idea in her head that she would marry me only after I convert to Catholicism and that if I loved her I would convert. How a make-out session led to going all the way in the backseat of my car. How we broke up after I said I wouldn't convert. How she called me, terrified that she was pregnant. How my meeting went with Dr. Fullmarks. All the nasty things she said about me while she waited to get her period, which, thank the Lord she got. I conclude with, "We haven't spoken since she got her period." Desirie's face registers a kaleidoscope of emotions: a bolus of fear, a flash of anger, a scintilla of doubt, a look of horror, an incredulous smile, a burst of laughter and finally relief. "OK, Izzy, I guess you're not a playboy." She is laughing at herself for even imagining the possibility.

We walk for a long while until we find a bench. We sit silently and take in the stunning fall view that surrounds us. Words are few until Desirie somberly begins to speak. "You know, Izzy, what worries me is the gap between our worlds and our experiences. You have no idea what it's like to live under Jim Crow oppression; what it does to your perspective. In our culture, everything white is good and everything black is bad. Look at our language. Brown is associated with shit, dirt, and mud. Black is even worse. Black is evil. We fear the dark or the dark hearts of people. And a black mood is probably the most awful feeling a person can have. I've grown up doubting my looks, not just for personal reasons, but because the culture believes all black people are ugly. Blacks have been compared to apes, gorillas, and chimpanzees. Now look at me. Can't you see that I'm too dark. I've never been able to pass the paper bag test. My nose is too wide. My hair is nappy." Desirie covers her face with her hands and once again the tears flow. I can't let her self-deprecations go unchallenged. "Desirie, your hair has always been beautiful." "Let me finish, Izzy. You have no idea the work that goes into creating the illusion that I have straight hair-The hot irons; the harsh chemicals; the painful brushings. Men of all races do look at me, and in some way find me attractive I guess, but all they want is to fuck me, not to love me.

"But I love you, Desirie."

"How can you? You hardly know me. If you really knew me, you couldn't possibly love me."

"Why are you saying this? You're beautiful inside and out."

"How can you love this dark brown skin, this hair, this nose? And what's inside doesn't bear telling." Her lamentation does bring to my mind the memory of a black maid my parents briefly hired when I was five years old. Her very dark skin—darker than Desirie's-- made me think of dirt, and it took me a great while before I understood that when she held my hand, I would not automatically become dirty. Later that year, when I went through a TB scare, my parents blamed the maid. They assumed that she lived in a hovel and was therefore a likely carrier of tuberculosis bacteria. At that moment my self-hatred mirrors Desirie's own self-loathing, and I realize that we are both prisoners of some of the same painful, soul-devouring myths.

I don't know what to say to her or how to console her. I put my arms around her and just hold her while she cries. She finally looks at me with tears still streaming down her beautiful brown face and says, "Oh Izzy, I do want to love you, but I'm so frightened." I kiss her with all the force of my yearning. "Desirie, I want to make love to you. She smiles and rapidly nods her head. "But where Izzy? Where can we be together?"

"I don't know yet, but I'll find a place. " She grabs my hand and smiles at me again. "We better get back," she says. "We have an exam tomorrow morning in Abnormal Psych. She chuckles and says, "This has been some study date."

"Well, you know what they say about all work and no play."

"Yeah, well we didn't do either." We walk back to the parking lot and there are three other cars besides mine parked there. One looks oddly familiar. It's a 1959 Chevy Bel Air. It looks exactly like Bobby Kaplan's car, but it can't be. That would be too spooky. As we approach the car, it seems to be rocking back and forth. Funny sounds are issuing from the back seat. We hear heavy breathing, followed by moans and a familiar male voice singing out "Oh my God,"—a phrase that was painfully familiar to me. There is no doubt. Its Bobby and Judy. I tell Desirie who I think it is. We look at each other and [burst out laughing.] Desirie with wide eyes and a mock expression of anger says, "I hope you don't have that in mind for us. I ain't giving it up to you in the backseat of no damn car." We both laugh. As our laughter subsides, we notice that it has grown silent inside the car. Slowly, very slowly, the back window begins to open and we see a head rising up to look out the window. First I see the familiar flattop and then Bobby's full face with a sour expression. "Sheeyit. It can't be you, Izzy." Now he's laughing his high-pitched embarrassed laugh. I can barely glimpse Judy and the sheepish smile on her face. Bobby is bare-chested and Judy is holding up some clothing in front of her torso. In a phony formal tone, I say to Desirie, "Dear, I would like you to meet my very good friend, Bobby Kaplan and his inamorata, Judy Ginsburg. Bobby and Judy; this is Desirie Jackson. After hellos are said all around, Bobby says, "Be out in a minute." He rolls up the back window and holds a shirt against it while Judy presumably puts her clothes back on. Then he takes the shirt off the window and puts it on his bare torso. They get out of the car, pat themselves down and resume their introduction. At 5'4", Desirie towers over Judy who is barely 5 feet tall. Bobby is an inch taller than I am. "What are you doing here?" I ask Bobby. "Well, whatever it was, you two should try it," Bobby says with a devilish grin. Desirie's face takes on that utterly delightful crimson and brown color. And then she laughs. Her laughter drives my own, and soon we are all laughing. The conversation divides into two. Judy and Desirie are getting to know one another.. Judy, at first seems uncomfortable talking with Desirie. She's not sure what to say to a Black woman. But Desirie's natural charm draws her in. Bobby and I have moved a few feet away "The irony of the situation, Bobby," I tell him, "is that Desirie and I had just decided that we want to do what your doing, but not in a car. Where can we go?" Bobby again gives me his devilish grin. "You do know that I own and manage an apartment building around 16th and U. There's a room I can let you use." "Bobby, that's fantastic. Thank you, thank you."

"When do you need it for?"

"How about this Saturday night?" Bobby takes out a little black book and makes a note. "Done. How's eight o'clock."

"Great!" My enthusiasm is a little too vociferous and it stirs the girls' curiosity. Desirie asks, "What're you boys talking about?"

"Oh nothing," we both say not quite in unison. The stupid grins on our face give us away. "Why do boys always lie?" Judy asks Desirie, as she moves her index finger to her chin in a mock pose of thoughtfulness. Desirie replies, "Ain't it a shame! They just can't help themselves. Apparently, it makes no difference whether the boys are white or black. All boys lie to their girlfriends." I am about to launch into a serious protest, but when the girls heartily laugh and tell each other that I was about to prove their point, I shut-up.

It is only Tuesday and Saturday feels like forever in the future. I can barely contain my excitement. I can't believe it is finally going to happen. I'm going to make love to the woman I love and have desired since our junior year in high school. Yesterday, Desirie and I took our Abnormal Psych exam and found it very difficult to concentrate. With her sitting right beside me, the exam questions were overwhelmed by her presence, her perfume and her concentration-destroying smile. I'd look at the exam, then at her, then back at the exam. She was doing the same thing. It's a wonder that we weren't accused of cheating.

I am now in my German class and find myself writing Desirie's name over and over again in my notebook. Ich liebe dich, I write. Even in German the phrase beguiles me. Mel Gray who sits near me is watching me write his cousin's name over and over, and he is quietly laughing. "Aw man, you got it bad," he whispers. "You best believe it. I'm in love, Jack," I whisper back. Dr. Dittersdorf catches us whispering. "Herr Vhite," he bellows. "Vhy are you not writing down vhat I write on ze board?" I finally notice that he has written a phrase attributed to Goethe about the brotherhood of man. I had it on good authority that Goethe did not actually believe in the brotherhood of man. In fact, I believe he was anti-Semitic. So I had no interest in writing such dribble in my notebook. And I make the mistake of saying so. "Dr. Dittersdorf, I am now a senior in college," I say, "and I feel I am quite capable of deciding what I should write down or not." This came out in a haughtier tone than I wanted, but I am embarrassed by his reprimand. A chorus of Oooohs echoed in the classroom. Dr. Dittersdorf screams out, "YOU WRITE DOWN VHAT I WRITE OR I VILL DENOUNCE YOU TO THE DEAN. Another chorus of Oooohs ensues only this time louder. I have the urge to stand up, click my heels, give a straight-armed salute and yell out, "Ja, mein fuhrer." Instead, I meekly say, "Yessir," and start writing furiously. The room is now filled with the tittering of my classmates.

Saturday finally comes. It begins as a rainy autumn day that does nothing to quell my heebie-jeebies. I am filled with excitement, desire, doubt and terror. What if I mess this up? What if I'm so nervous I can't get it up? What if I'm too small for her? Maybe she's already been with some black guys with huge organs and she's gonna be so disappointed with my pitifully deficient prick. It is hard, hard work to fend off my self-doubts and reassure myself that everything's gonna work out fine... if I just let nature take its course.

I don't quite know what to do with myself. I have a ton of homework, but I have difficulty concentrating on any of it. Even abnormal psychology, which I usually find engrossing, cannot hold my attention. I call Bobby to make sure our plans are firm. Bobby reassures me that our room is "ready" and that he will meet us there around 8 p.m. tonight. Then I call Desirie to see how she is feeling. Is she sick? Has she changed her mind? Has she come to her senses? She's fine and can't wait to see me. I am to pick her up at 6 pm and we will get dinner in Chinatown and then go to Bobby's apartment. We hang up and I look at the clock and it is only 11 am. The hands of the clock turn into slugs and seem to move about as fast.

In the early afternoon, the weather begins to brighten up and so does my mood. I have in front of me two books by the psychoanalyst Erich Fromm, Escape From Freedom and the Art of Loving. Escape from Freedom is helping me to understand why it has been so difficult for me to be completely myself with others. Every time I want to be myself, I feel isolated from others and the crippling sense of loneliness I feel makes me want to fit in with whatever group I happen to be involved with at the moment. This often takes place without my being aware of it. Before I know it, I'm laughing at jokes I don't think are funny, or I remain silent when others offer preposterous ideas and beliefs as if they are certain truths. Removing one's self-defeating internal constraints can be as difficult as freeing oneself from external oppression. In fact, the two forms of oppression are related. Internal fears can lead us to oppress others and to avoid the responsibility of creating a free society. From The Art of Loving, I am learning that love is often confused with the "falling-in-love" feelings of romantic infatuation and sexual desire; that love is a decision, a commitment and that it is related to a broader capacity to love human beings in general.

Is that what I am doing? Falling in love with Desirie or have I made a decision to commit to her. I feel I want her. I need her. But do I love her in the Frommian sense of the word? The more I read of The Art of Loving, the calmer I feel. It dawns on me that "loving' Desirie does not mean I have to impress her with my non-existent love-making skills, with my performance. Making love is not something I do to her, but rather is something I share with her. This epiphany conflicts with everything I have been told about how to Do It with a woman. The idea of "sharing with" rather than "doing to" her sounds…well, more loving. But can I do it that way with Desirie? Can I share with her instead of performing for her?

When I pick Desirie up she looks ravishing; tan, fitted skirt, burnt orange sweater, gold loop earings. In my eyes, she's the personification of autumn beauty. I want to make love to her right then and there, but I remember her prohibition on automobile assignations. I greet her with a passionate kiss. She responds in kind. "Mmmm, ain't we loose, tonight." She says this with a mischievous smile. "I'm hungry. Let's get something to eat."

"I'm hungry too," I say, leering at her. I see a flash of irritation on her face. "Izzy, would you please stop looking at me like I'm a piece of prime steak." I exaggerate my leer and make lip-smacking noises. She laughs and punches me in the shoulder and says in an exaggerated southern Negro accent "Go on now, you hound dog, and drive this car on out a here."

The Chinese food at the Far East is so luscious in aroma and taste that it serves to heighten my desire for Desirie. I am growing more confident that the heebie-jeebies will not seize me later and turn our love tryst into a disaster. I am able to park on 16th street between T and U Streets. We are just a little south of Bobby's apartment house. We find the three-story brick townhouse on the corner of 16th and Carolina Streets. The building had been recently painted a light grey that make it stand out from the other brown brick townhouses nearby. Bobby's building has one other distinguishing feature. It is the only townhouse that has windows on the side.

Bobby opens the door and gives us both a knowing, salacious grin. "Come in, come in, said the spider to the fly." When Bobby turns his back, Desirie rolls her eyes at me. He gives us a brief tour of the house. The downstairs rooms have 12-foot ceilings that made each room seem cavernous. The three bedrooms had been turned into studio apartments on the second and third floors. There is a common bathroom on each of the two upper floors. Bobby leads us to one of the bedrooms that is not currently rented. "You kiddies have fun now," Bobby says as he pretends to twist an imaginary handlebar mustache. He closes the door; and as he walks away we hear him making the sounds of faux diabolical laughter, "Bwa ha, ha, ha, ha!" Desirie looks at me and says with some disdain in her voice, "Izzy, your friend's a little weird."

"Yes, but at heart, he's lovable."

"You did bring protection, didn't you, Izzy?" The heebie-jeebies electrifies my entire body. "OH MY GOD! I FORGOT A RUBBER." Desirie stares at me in horror. "Oh Izzy, how could you?" She sits on the bed and holds her face in her hands. I sit beside her and try and hold her, but she shakes me off. "I am so sorry, Desirie." She continues to hold her face while she slowly shakes her head back and forth. I notice on the nightstand, just beyond her, a little box wrapped in a bow. And there's a little note attached that says For Izzy. I open the box and I find a condom. I can hardly believe that it really is a condom. I pick it up and I see that underneath the Trojan packaging, there is another note that simply says, For your screwing pleasure. I burst out into loud, manic laughter. I scream out, "Santa Claus lives!"

"What is it, Izzy? What are you saying?"

"Look, Desirie, Bobby left a rubber for me. He knew I would forget to bring one. Isn't he amazing?"

"Why are white boys so weird?" Desirie asks rhetorically.

"Let's not bring race into it. Bobby would be a little weird in any color." I hold up the condom for Desirie to see it. "But, as you can see, his heart's in the right place."

Desirie laughs and says, "I don't think that is where the rubber is supposed to go. Besides, I'm not talking about Bobby."

"Oh ho ho, aren't you the sassy one." I take her in my arms and kiss her slowly, then more forcefully. "Wait, Izzy. Let's get undressed and get into bed. OK?"

"Of course," I reply. I watch her retreat to a darkened corner of the room. "Izzy, would you mind turning around. I'm feeling a little shy with you."

"No problem." I turn around and begin undressing. I can feel the beginning of heebie-jeebies trying to take over my body. But I remind myself that I was about to be with, touch, feel, and love the woman that I have desired for so long. This thought relaxes me and melts the heebie-jeebies in its tracks. "OK, Izzy. You can turn around." I am only halfway undressed, but I turn around to see the most beautiful sight in my life. Desirie stands shyly in a diaphanous white nightgown that completely reveals a rich, dark chocolate-colored perfectly formed female body.

Desirie's coloring is so rich that it dispels any thought that might bubble up from my fetid racist unconscious. I see no hint of dirt or mud. I fear no oozing of any Negro miasma ebbing onto me. There was nothing repellent in this figure of exquisite beauty. "Desirie, you are beyond beautiful." Desirie is embarrassed and she quickly jumps under the covers. "Get into bed, Izzy," she commands. I do as she asks. I am not even flustered by the full erection that I already have. But I catch her staring at it. "I've never seen a white one before." "I don't think it's very different than a black penis; maybe smaller."

"Oh Izzy, don't bring that hang-up in here. Not now. You're not that small and besides it doesn't really matter. Not to me at least." She leans over and gently takes hold of my penis and begins to lick the shaft. She places her mouth on the head and begins to swirl her tongue. Within a matter of seconds, the sensations overwhelm me. "Oh, Oh God, Desirie, I'm coming." The milk of creation bursts forth on to the bed. I am crestfallen. "Oh Desirie, I am so sorry. I couldn't help it. I so much want to please you." She places her hand over my mouth and tries to calm me. "Shh, don't worry, Izzy, we have all night. I'm already happy to be with you this way. You know I've wanted you for as long as you say you've desired me. I've been so afraid... of the consequences; of what people might think; of what you might think. My worst fear is that you'll have your way with me and then conclude I must be a slut. Then you'll leave me, and my reputation in ruins. I hate this male logic and find it incomprehensible."

"I don't think that way, Desirie. I'm in love with you. Leave you? I'm terrified that you'll leave me; that I won't measure up." I begin kissing her face, her neck, and her ears. She begins to moan. I want to tour her entire body with my mouth. I kiss her breasts and her moans grow louder. But as I move toward her pubic area, she stops me. "No Izzy, not there; not yet." I begin to get hard again and want to quickly enter her. "Not yet, Izzy. Touch me here." She grabs my hand and leads it towards her clitoris. I try to be gentle in my stroking. She is becoming more aroused and her wetness begins to cover my fingers. A few moments later, she says, "Now Izzy, now." I try to enter her and I make the same mistake I made with Maureen. I miss the entrance. "Ow!" She cries. She grabs my penis and guides me in. The embarrassment almost makes me lose my erection. She prevents that with her body's undulations, and I begin to catch the rhythm of her movements and respond with complimentary movements of my own. I meet her breath for breath, moan for moan, cry for cry. Soon I lose the sense of whose voice is crying. I feel completely merged with her. We begin to move faster and faster toward one another, more urgently, both of us desperate for a release. We come together with a mutual cry of joy. I am not sure, but I think I hear the faint sound of applause from another room. I look at Desirie with great love and gratitude. She seems to be mirroring my expression. Her tear-laden smile warms me at my core. Our joy is so great it hurts. This is a revelation for me-- that joy and pain can be so closely linked. And in this merger of body and spirit, joy and pain, someone has finally captured my soul.

As we leave Bobby's apartment, we sing out in unison, "We're leaving." The only response we get is joint laughter-Bobby's high-pitched giggle and from the unknown female, a conspiratorial cackle. On the drive home, I occasionally steal a glance at Desirie. Each time I catch her looking at me and we crack up laughing. I don't think it is possible for me to be any higher or to feel any happier. I've just made love to the woman I truly love; the woman I want to be my life partner. And the gleam in her eye tells me she wants the same thing.

Desirie and I sit in my car parked in front of her dorm for the longest time. We just hold on to one another not wanting this life-changing night to end. The thought of separating is unbearable, as if parting would open up a massive wound inside each of us. I have never felt so close to anyone before. Desirie, finally, slowly, painfully pulls away from me. "I really have to go in, Izzy. If I bust curfew again, there'll be hell to pay."

"I know. But I can't let you go," I reply. I'm feeling the wound already. She pulls away completely and gathers her things together. She looks at me tenderly, quickly kisses my cheek and exits the car. Once outside the car, she turns and says, "I love you, Izzy White," and begins running toward the entrance.

I roll down my window and yell after her, "I love you too, Desirie Jackson."

As I'm driving home, an old song by Hank Ballard and the Midnighters keep repeating in my mind. Soon I'm singing at the top of lungs, "That Woman".

Chapter 23.
Jump Shot Redux

On a dreary afternoon late in October, I find myself obsessing about the possibility of nuclear war. This new terror arose in me when President Kennedy announced that the Soviets have placed Intermediate-Range Ballistic Missiles with nuclear warheads in Cuba. These missiles, according to the Washington Post, have a range of up to 3,000 miles. In other words, they could land on virtually any part of the United States. Of course, if the Soviets were ever to lob a few missiles in our direction, we would have to reply in kind. It's not rocket science to deduce that the possibility of world-ending nuclear war is a very real one. Well, I guess it is rocket science, but you catch my drift. I haven't slept well since the President's speech. I keep thinking about all those drills from the past when all American school children had to dive under their desks to protect themselves from the inevitable Atom Bomb. In our nuclear world diving under anything won't help much. Ever since the speech I have been rapidly cycling in and out of paralyzing states of terror. In calmer moments I wonder if there will be a world left in which to live. While in one of these terrorized states, my phone rings. I don't answer it right away, because I mistake the ring for the alarm bells going off inside my head. When I can finally discern that the bells I'm hearing are actually the rings of a telephone, I answer. "Hello?" I almost scream out. "Izzy, are you alright? It's Mel Gray." It took me a moment to focus.

"Mel who?"

"Mel Gray...from Howard."

"Oh Mel. Of course! I'm so sorry. I'm worrying about the missiles and was in the middle of an anxiety attack when you called."

"Missiles? What missiles?" I'm pissed that Mel has not joined me in worrying about the fate of the world. "The missiles!

The ones the Russians have installed in Cuba. A nuclear war is about to destroy us." I hear Mel chuckling.

"Izzy, is there nothing you don't worry about?"

"Mel! I can't believe you're so blase about missiles that are just 90 miles from Miami." Trying to ignore my hysteria, Mel changes the subject.

" Let me tell you why I called. The Negus has asked me to ask you to play with our intramural basketball team." This information is so perplexing that I entirely forget about missiles in Cuba. "The Negus asked you to call me?"

"Yes, he sho enuf did, Mistah Izzy," Mel replies. I ignore his imitation of the character 'Lightning' from the old Amos and Andy TV show. We had argued about the racist nature of the show. "He wants me to play B-Ball for Boss?"

"That's right. He wants you to be balling for Boss". We both laugh at his double entendre. "When does the season start?"

"In about 3 weeks," Mel says. Forlornly I ask, "I guess the games are played in the Quonset hut?"

"They sho enuf is, Mistah Izzy," Mel replies with a cackle.

"Will you cut that crap, Mel. We settled that argument awhile back if I recall."

"You were settled. I'm still unsettled. I can't believe you can't see how racist that show was."

"And as I said, I'm not sure the show represented anything, but these were gifted actors who created genuinely funny characters." With some pique, Mel says, "You still have a lot to learn, white boy."

"I'm sure I do. We can take up the argument again, if you like, during basketball practice at the Hut."

The thought of playing organized basketball again got my heart racing. I had never made my peace with the way my collegiate career had come to an end. Although my injury healed, my confidence didn't. Now I'm being offered another chance to shine, playing the game I love more than any other. When I show up at the Quonset Hut for our first practice, I see several players who don't look familiar. They don't look like any of the Boss fraternity brothers that I remember seeing at the frat house. When I ask Mel about it, he tells me in a whispered aside that I'm not the only ringer who'll be playing for the Boss team this year. Mel drags me over to a huge muscle-bound dark-skinned, so-called new Boss Pledge. He is six feet six and weighs about 240 pounds. "Izzy, this is Roscoe Barnes. We call him Bad Ass. His name says it all. You don't want to drive to the hole if he's in the vicinity because he'll make you eat the basketball. Bad Ass was an all-state center from Florida, and he led his high school team to the state championship two years ago. He led them in scoring, rebounds and blocked shots. "How you doing, Bad-Ass?" I ask him as nonchalantly as I can. He looks down at me. His eyes go wide for a moment and then resume their normal, cold stare. "I be cool. How you be? You that little white boy who played varsity a year or so ago?"

"That's me." I'm relieved that he recognizes me. I sense that otherwise he would not have been cool with having me as a teammate. I look around and see 10 to 12 guys shooting about a half dozen basketballs. The sound of bouncing balls brings back the memory of my first varsity practice in the Hut two years before. That funky sound always makes me think of a group of fans whomping the floor with rubber hoses. Mel takes me over to another ringer, Walter "Eagle" Holloway, who is consistently draining 20-foot jump shots from the corner when he isn't displaying some nifty moves to the basket. Walter is a thin, lanky, 6-foot, three-inch all-state forward from Pearl High School in Nashville, Tennessee. He's nicknamed "Eagle" because of his ability to "fly" to the basket. I watch in disbelief as Eagle practices his patented move. He starts in the corner, fakes left, takes one step right before gliding the rest of the way to the basket. The only Boss brother that I recognize is the first one I ever met--Colby Betterman. He is the guy who let me in on my first trip to the Boss house. I'm told that he is 6'2", but the way he jumps, he plays like he's 6'5". He doesn't shoot as well as the rest of us, but is a beast on the boards, despite his lean frame.

Despite our heavy school schedules, we are able to get in several practices before our first game with the Kappas. Howard's Intramural Basketball program is organized into different leagues. There is the Professional School League, the Fraternity League, The Frosh League, and the Independents League. League winners engage in a playoff leading to a championship game. After Mel and I have several arguments over who would play point guard and who would be the shooting guard, we agree to alternate in those two respective roles. With Bad Ass and Colby controlling the boards and Eagle shooting from the corner and driving to the basket, we know we have a strong team. Most of my teammates are in better shape than I am. Mel thinks we have the speed and mobility to play an up tempo game and he argues for that. I don't object; but by the middle of each practice, I have my tongue hanging out as I try to keep up with my teammates' pace. So in my first game against the Kappa's, I rapidly cycle from the game to the bench. I can only last about 5 minutes at a stretch before I need a blow. The Kappas have some talent but most of their players had spent time on the Howard football team. They are a muscle-bound group that wants to physically intimidate us. But they have no one to compete with Bad Ass Barnes who physically punishes the Kappa defenders as much as they punish him. I spend most of the game at point guard because my jump shot has to readjust to the weird dimensions of the Hut. I only make two out of ten jump shots. To make up for my shooting deficiencies, I keep feeding Mel, Bad Ass, and Eagle. They each score 20 points on jump shots and moves to the basket. Our passing is sharp and routinely leaves a man open for an easy shot. Final score-Boss 72, Kappa 59.

As my jump shot becomes more accurate, Boss's scoring increases. We score 80 points against the Alphas for a fairly easy win. There are no games during the upcoming Christmas holidays, so we have to wait until the New Year until we have a chance to improve on our two wins and no losses record.

Unlike previous years, Desirie and I see a lot of one another during the Christmas holidays. A day after Christmas, Desirie tells me that Mel is hosting a Christmas party at his Aunt's house, and she wants me to go with her. I say, "Sure. "What's Mel's Aunt like?"

"She's a very successful woman who's not hurting for bucks. She owns a house on Blagden Avenue. Have you ever heard of the Negro Gold Coast?"

"Of course," I reply.

"Well, wait until you see her house. About ten years ago, she relocated to DC from Georgia wanting to work as a beautician. Through hard work and some lucky breaks, she now owns several beauty salons in DC, one not very far from Howard University."

"I can't wait to meet her."

The following Saturday we arrive at Mel's Aunt's house a little late. Desirie seems very agitated and I assume it is because of our tardiness. She literally pulls me into the house. The house is a beautiful four-bedroom brick colonial with large rooms and high ceilings. I am astonished by the spaciousness of the place, as I was a few years before with the size of Henry Prescott's house. I remind myself that the stereotype that all Negroes are poor and live in hovels must be consigned to the dustbin of white supremacist demagoguery. A huge Christmas tree stands in the far corner of the large living room. The luminous tree decorations lend a festive glow to the entire room, which is now filled with the smiles and chatter of a dozen party guests. In the background we can hear Clyde McPhatter and the Drifters singing their up-tempo, bluesy version of White Christmas. Mel comes over to greet Desirie and me. "You two sure make an outstanding couple," Mel says with a bit too much cutting sarcasm for my taste. But I ignore my irritation and try to be pleasant "Yes, we do 'standing out' very well, don't we?" I reply. Mel shepherds us around the room to introduce us to a number of people we do not know. He leaves us in the company of BOSS brother, Colby Betterman and his dazzlingly attractive girlfriend, Maria Starnes, a raven-haired, sandy complexioned, green-eyed beauty. It takes the greatest restraint for anyone in that room to keep from gawking at her; until she opens her mouth. Maria is a Junior Fine Arts major at Howard with Academy Award aspirations and a painfully obvious affectation. Whenever she speaks she reaches an annoying level of pomposity in a very bad imitation of an Oxonian accent. Colby stands beside her grinning away as if he had just bagged the biggest fish ever. Maria is dominating the conversation with a monologue on her past and future acting achievements when we hear someone coming in the front door. Mel thought he had locked the door so he dashes to the foyer to see who has entered. It's his aunt who has returned early from an apparently unsuccessful dinner date. She looks around the room at the party guests; and when she sees me, her cold stare turns icy. She then looks at Mel and in a voice that no one in the spacious living room could fail to hear, she yells, "I TOLD YOU THAT WHITE PEOPE ARE NOT ALLOWED IN MY HOUSE! NOW YOU GET THAT PECKERWOOD OUT OF HERE!" With that she rockets herself upstairs. All eyes are on me. I turn beet red and feel like I could now comfortably fit into a thimble. Mel comes over to me crimson-faced and filled with apologies. This very brief taste of racial hatred directed at me hurts like hell. Consumed by shame and humiliation, I grab Desirie's hand and lead her toward the front door. To no one in particular, I say "Good-bye." The coup de grace of the evening, however, comes when I overhear Mel whisper to Desirie, "I told you that bringing Izzy was not a good idea." Out of the corner of my eye I see Desirie glaring at Mel. But she says nothing. Because she is upset, I am super-polite. I open the car door for her. Softly and gently, I ask her what's wrong. But she continues her silence for the next 15 minutes. The conversational void initially makes me nervous. But my angst soon turns into anger. To break the harrowing silence, I finally ask Desirie,

"What was that?"

"What was what?" She asks, glaring at me the same way she had looked at Mel only moments before.

"I heard what Mel said to you, and if looks could kill…"

"Leave it alone, Izzy."

"Leave what alone?"

"I don't want to talk about it." Now she can't even look at me. She's glaring out the window. "I know you're upset but I don't know why. I'm the one that was humiliated. I thought that my girlfriend might be sympathetic."

Instead of commiserating with me, Desirie is very quiet. "Desirie, I know you're upset about something, but I don't think it is because your alleged boyfriend has just been kicked out of somebody's house because of the color of his skin." Desirie can no longer remain quiet. She explodes: "Listen to you, Izzy. Everything is about you. You've just had a taste of what happens to Negroes everyday."

"Ok, so this is new to me and completely unexpected. I've never had this happen to me during my entire time at Howard. Aren't I entitled to feel bad about it?"

"Yes, you can feel bad about it Izzy, but it's hard for me to sympathize when this is the common fate of every Black person in this country. What happened to you tonight is nothing compared to the abuse that Black people experience every fucking day of our lives just because of the color of our skin." This last bit she says to mockingly hold a mirror up to my own words. "And we take it from people with the color of your skin. And that's what has me so upset. What am I doing with you, Izzy? What are we doing? The world's not ready for this—for us. Black people don't like it just as much as white people. You've been at Howard almost four years. Haven't you learned that yet? What chance do we really have in this world? We can't even marry in many of these great United States."

"So we won't live in any of those states. "

"You're missing the point, Izzy. Even if we could legally marry, what do you think would happen to our children?"

"Why are you so afraid, Desirie?"

"Aren't you? What do your parents think of our relationship? Are they happy about it? Are your friends happy, Izzy? I can tell you that no one on my side of the fence is happy. Not my parents, not my friends. Not even Mel."

This felt like a gut punch. "Mel? He's said nothing to me about it. I thought he was happy for us?"

"Well, he's not." A dark cloud of silence overcomes us both. When I drop her off at her dorm, she gives me no kiss, only a look of despair.

We have plans to go to a party that a friend of hers is giving on New Years Eve. Despite the tension, we agree to go. Through a series of tearful phone conversations, we also agree that we will table all conversations about the future and just enjoy what we have now. The future scares us both but for different reasons. She fears the implications and complications of an interracial marriage. I fear marriage and maybe even adulthood. When we share these revelations, we both can clearly see that anticipating the future poisons our present. We agree that we are both too young to even contemplate a permanent future together. "Let's just be college lovers and see what happens," she says. "RIGHT ON, MY SISTER!" I practically yell into the phone. Desirie laughs at my absurd affirmation and laughingly taunts me with my words; "So now we're brother and sister?" We both laugh and know that all is well. Once again we are each other's main squeeze.

One of the most difficult things for me to accept about my life is the fact that when one life endeavor thrives, another becomes difficult. When my basketball game is good, my love life stinks or my grades sink. If my love life prospers, my game suffers. And that's what begins to happen in the first month of 1963. Desirie and I are having the best time of our lives during the month of January. We see each other every day; we laugh a lot and even find the time and place for the occasional "roll in the hay". Even our fellow students are becoming comfortable with the idea that we are a couple. On the other hand, the accuracy of my jump shot for the next several intramural games is close to zero. We manage to win the three games we play in January against the Ques, the Phi Betas, and Alpha Phi Omega, the national service fraternity, but no thanks to my jump shot. I make two shots in each game and none of these except one is a jump shot. Bad Ass, Eagle, and Colby, however, dominate the backboards and Mel shoots the lights out of the gym in all three games. I know something is wrong, but can't figure out why this is happening. I content myself with the role of playmaker and distribute the ball to my teammates. But the jump shot has always been my bread and butter. There were times in high school when I felt I could score at will and I knew as soon as the ball left my hand that my shot was accurate. Even in college I occasionally had that feeling, one that has now totally deserted me. In February my problem continues. My accuracy begins to improve, but only slightly. We scrape by the Kappas. This time the score was 82-80 thanks to Mel's bank shot just as the final horn blows. We have a second easy game against Alpha Phi

Omega's, but then every team has an easy game against them. After winning seven games in a row, we are afflicted by the disease of overconfidence. In our second game against the "Ques" of Omega Psi Phi, we take our opponents too lightly. We had already beaten the Ques once even though they had several former Howard players. Taking a ten-point lead into the second half, we stop our potent running game. The slowed tempo is just what the Ques need to gradually reduce our lead. As the score gets closer, we start making mistakes and pointing fingers at one another. The fluid chemistry of our game disappears. I throw passes to areas where I expect my teammates to be and they are not there. Mel and Eagle complain to me about my errant passes. Bad Ass is upset because I'm not getting the ball to him enough. I complain because my teammates are not moving without the ball and our offense is sputtering. Because of our continuing sniping, we don't realize that the Ques have just taken the lead with only a minute left. I call time out. I call a play to set a screen for the Eagle, and he has the option of shooting from the corner or driving to the basket. Eagle is the only player on our team with a decent shooting percentage in the game. I bring the ball up to half court and feed it to Mel who fakes like he is going to drive to the hole. He passes the ball to Eagle hoping he will be open for a clear shot. Instead Eagle is double-teamed and can neither shoot nor drive. Mel moves over to help Eagle and is able to receive a pass from him. But with only a few seconds left in the game, Mel has no choice but to shoot a jump shot outside of his comfort range. The ball clangs off the rim, and the game is over. The Omega Psi Phi team is victorious, 80-78. In the beginning of March we have a successful return match with the Phi Betas. Boss and the Ques have identical records of 9 and 1 at the end of the regular scheduled games. During the single-elimination playoffs, we knock off the Alphas, and the Ques beat the Kappas. The long-awaited rubber match between Boss and the Ques is to be played on Friday.

At 3 am, Friday morning, I wakeup in a cold sweat. I've just dreamt that I am the soothsayer in the play Julius Caesar and I say the infamous line, "Beware the ides of March". I awake with such a heavy feeling. Today we play for the Fraternity League championship in Howard's Intramural Basketball program, and it is March 15th. Is this a bad omen or just a bad dream? Normally, I don't think of myself as a superstitious person, but I wanted to ward off all possible dangers to our championship chances. At 8 o'clock in the morning, I call Desirie. She's barely awake. "Why are you calling me so early, Izzy?" She says in a sleep-altered voice.

"Hi Hon," I respond in a super treacly voice. "I have a favor to ask, my dearest love."

"Izzy, what's the matter with you? You sound funny. What is it that you want?"

"Well, you know how I was telling you that when things are good in one part of my life, they stink in another?"

"Yeah, so?" Her voice switches from curious to suspicious.

"Well, I'm so happy with you and happy we're together." Desirie quickly picks up my drift. "You don't want me to come to the game today, do you?
"It's not that I don't want you to come, but I'm afraid that your presence will jinx me."

"Izzy, I'm going to use one of your words. Why do you have to be such a schmuck?"

"Desirie, I want you to come more than anything, but I'm just afraid…."

"You white weenie. I hope you and your fear will be very happy together, because I won't be at your wedding. And I won't come to your game."

"Aw, Desirie. Don't be mad," I say to a dial tone. She clearly does not want to hear anymore from me today.

The championship game with the Ques is close throughout. Neither team has more than a five-point lead. The Ques are led by former Howard star Mike Ingram, a 6'4" sharpshooter. He scores the first ten points for Omega Psi Phi. He's making jump shots from everywhere. My jump shot is falling today, thanks to the help of Bad Ass Barnes. We work the pick-and-roll play successfully at least six times during the first half. Bad Ass moves close to my defender to set a screen for me. If no other defender comes near me, I have an open jump shot. And like I say, I'm making these shots today. If however another defender moves toward me, Bad Ass rolls to the basket and I throw him the ball for an easy lay-up. The Ques seem to have no answer for this. Three times I make a jump shot and three times Bad Ass makes an easy layup. Mel's making his patented jump shot from the corner while our big boys are in a fierce battle under the backboards with the "trees" of Omega Psi Phi. At halftime we lead the game 42-40.

During the second half, the Ques make an adjustment and work their "switching" defense much better. Our pick-and-roll play is less successful. Neither Bad Ass nor I have an easy open shot. Because defenders are switching to cover Bad Ass on the pick-and-roll, Colby and Eagle are open on the wings. They provide a hefty amount of the scoring for us during the second half. Mel and I have to work very hard to get space enough to shoot our jump shots. Mike Ingram stays hot for the Ques and is now joined in the scoring by their seemingly unstoppable point guard, Randall Carr. Neither Mel nor I could cover him. When we try to cover him close, he drives right by us. If we give him any space at all, he makes his jump shot. The lead changes back and forth several times during the second half. With one minute left, the Ques are winning by two points and they have the ball. Mel is covering Carr and is able to knock the ball away. Mel gets the ball and dashes toward our basket. I see what's happening and race after the two them. Carr is very close to Mel and I am ten feet away. Mel fakes a layup and throws me a behind-the-back pass. I catch the ball and score an easy layup. The game is tied with 30 seconds left. The Ques are moving the ball around searching for an open man with the easiest shot. Eagle Holloway is overzealous in his defending and fouls the Ques center in the act of shooting. The center makes his first free throw but misses the second. Bad Ass gets the rebound, throws it to Mel on the left wing. As soon as I see the missed foul shot, I dash down the right side. Mel launches a 20-foot pass to me, and the lone Q defender charges toward me. With time running out, I shoot a jump shot from 22 feet, which touches nothing but net. The final score is Boss 81, Ques 80. We win the Fraternity League championship on my rediscovered jump shot. All of my teammates storm after me to congratulate me on my shot. Eight men, all bigger than I am, grab me, knock me to the ground, and damn near smother me with their weight and enthusiastic cheers.

I have completely forgotten that I had offended Desirie. I call her and excitedly share the news of our victory. She gives me an insipid expression of congratulations. Her underwhelming support brings me back to reality and I spend the next 30 minutes on the phone begging her forgiveness.

The Intramural Basketball Championship pitted the League champions against one another. We face the Jayhawks, the winner of the Independent league. The Med School team, the winner of the Professional league, plays the Frosh League representative, Drew Hall "A". With evenly distributed scoring among our first team players, we dispatch a feisty Jayhawk team. We come back from a ten- point deficit to win 85-81. The Med School has an easy time defeating Drew Hall "A" on the strength of Former Little All-America Howard star, Simon Johnson's 34 points.

For the first time in my life, I'm playing in a championship game. Desirie is so shocked that the Boss team has made it this far that before I can say anything, she informs me that she's coming to the game. I raise no objection because I want to avoid a repeat of my previous faux pas. To be honest, I don't know which will rattle my cage more—her being at the game or her anger at me if I forbid her to come.

During the first week of spring, we play the heavily favored Med School team for the Intramural championship. The Med School is led by Si Johnson, who was Howard's star guard some four or five years ago. Si can score from anywhere. He shoots well from the outside and possesses a repertoire of about 15 different ways to shoot the ball from just about any place on the court. Then add to his game an unstoppable hesitation move and you have a player who always gets himself open and who can shoot with two or three men guarding him at the same time. In the rare instance that he can't get a shot off, he passes to his big center, ironically named Ollie Short. Short is even taller than Bad Ass. Si Johnson has been averaging well over 30 points per game in the Intramural League, just as he did when he played for Howard. The Med school jump out to a quick lead and hold on to it during most of the first half. Even though I can clearly see Desirie sitting in the makeshift stands and can hear her cheering loudly, my jump shot is not affected. Toward the end of the first half Si Johnson and I are trading jump shots. We both make five in a row before I miss one. Almost on cue Johnson then misses his next shot. At the end of the half we reduce a 10-point lead to four.

For the first six or seven minutes of the second half, we get our offense in gear. Mel feeds me; I drive toward the basket and then dish the ball to Bad Ass. If Bad Ass is double-teamed, either Colby or Eagle is open for an easy layup. If our frontcourt players are well defended, Mel or I will be open for a jump shot. Our sharp passing assures that someone is open for an easy shot. We take an eight-point lead. Then every one of us goes stone cold. The way our shots are clanging off the rim, I think I am listening to the Anvil Chorus. With our offense grinding to an ignominious halt, Si Johnson takes over the game. He scores the next 12 points. The Med School's four-point lead continues until the final minute of the game. Mel makes a jump shot from 18 feet. On the very next play he steals the ball from the Med School point guard and passes the ball to me. I race to the basket as if I am going in for a layup, but instead I pull up for a 15-foot jump shot as time is running out. I watch the ball go on its merry-go-round, around and around the rim. I am transported back to that horrible moment in the High School City Basketball playoff game against McKinley Tech when I was in the exact same position watching the ball make its soul-crushing way round the rim and then out to the side of the basket. Once again, I watch the same despairing, repetitious end to a critically important game. As if it is genetically programmed to repeat itself, the ball rolls around and around and out to the side of the basket. We lose the championship game 86-84.

I am inconsolable. Even the warmth of Desirie's hugs and kisses fail to raise me from the depths of my despair. "Not again," I keep muttering in a barely audible voice. My teammates crowd around me patting me on my back and making supportive noises. "Tough luck, Izzy!" "You're all heart, Izzy!" "You laid it all out there, Izzy." Even Si Johnson comes by to say encouraging words and to congratulate me for being a battler. Desirie helps me out of the Hut as if I am a member of the walking wounded. She waits for me while I shower. In the shower, Mel and I stare at each other. I see a struggle of emotions playing out on his face, between sympathy and anger. Neither one of us says anything. But the anger I detect in Mel's face through the mist of the shower seems to have to do with more than just the loss of a game. I make a mental note that it is time for Mel and me to have a heart-to-heart.

When I meet Desirie outside, I still find speech difficult. A sprig of hope sprouts within me because I can smell spring in the glistening air. Silently, we make our way to the Student Union. We each order coffee and find our way to a secluded table. Desirie breaks the silence with the following encomium: "I'm sorry you missed that last shot, Izzy. You were so good throughout the whole game; and when you made those five jump shots in a row, even though I was there, I was convinced that the spell had been broken and you were going to win."

"Yeah, well, we didn't win."

"But you got your jump shot back. You made 7 out of 13 jump shots. That's something, isn't it, Izzy?" I smile at her with gratitude that she cares enough to count. But then the pall returns.

"But I missed the one that really counted. I let the team down."

"Oh Izzy, I know you feel awful, but you weren't the only one out there missing shots. You can't take the whole loss on your shoulders."

"Then why do I feel like such a failure?"

"This is you, Izzy. You minimize your accomplishments and over estimate your failures. I love you, Izzy, but you don't love yourself." I look at her with such a mixture of love, gratitude, and admiration. She really sees me.

"You seem to know me better than I know myself, Desirie?"

"Maybe I do, Izzy. Maybe I do."

Chapter 24.

Not In Our House

In our Abnormal Psychology class, we are studying the depressive personality, and the more I learn about its nature and causes, the more uncomfortable I become. So far this semester, I have seen myself clearly in the descriptions of every mental disorder we've covered. But the characteristics of the depressive personality seem to represent my own unique mental X-ray. The abstract characteristics presented here open a floodgate of memories of grey days and greyer moods, of sights when all color has been drained from every natural object of beauty, as if the flora and fauna of the world have been attacked and exsanguinated by a psychic vampire. While I am ruminating over my latest mental illness, I feel a note slipping into my hand. It's from Desirie. In a beautiful hand, replete with curlicues, she writes Let's talk after class. I have something very important to tell you.

After class we walk hand in hand out of Douglass Hall and into a brilliant spring day. The touch of her hand and the warmth of the long-awaited spring sunlight allow me to shed my melancholia like an annual skin. All the colors of the world are bright in my mind, and I conclude perhaps I am not a depressive personality after all.

We sit on the stone bench beside the campus sundial. I'm all ears eager to hear what she intimated is so important for her to tell me. The day is unusually warm and Desirie has unbuttoned her overcoat revealing a resplendent forest green sweater and a lighter green skirt. She has on black heels, and I am struck once again by how many Howard coeds wear heels to class. I've never even worn a tie in my almost four years here. Desirie is giving me her super serious look, which says that my unwavering attention is demanded. "Izzy, do you know about the new men's gymnasium that's being built on campus?"

"Of course, I'm really sad that I won't be able to play in it. I always hated the Hut."

"But do you know who's building that gym?"

"No, why?"

"Segregated unions, that's who!"

"Desirie, what are you talking about?"

"I'm not kidding. Four of the unions in which the construction workers belong have a total of three Negro workers among them. Needless to say, they discourage Black applicants to their unions."

"How did the three get in?"

"I have no idea, Izzy, but that's not the point. For all intents and purposes, these unions are segregated, and their white workers are building a gym on the campus of a primarily Negro university?"

"That's disgusting," I say with genuine anger. Desirie's eyes grow wide with rage. "You're damned right it's disgusting. That's what I want to talk to you about. The Liberal Arts Student Council is organizing a student protest against those unions and I want you to come with me to the demonstration."

"When is it?"

"Next Friday. Will you come?"

"Let me think about it Desirie. By the way, what kind of unions are we talking about?"

"Oh Izzy, I think you're avoiding a decision. What difference does it make which unions are involved. None of them should be segregated."

"I agree. I'm just curious. By the way, I haven't said I wouldn't go." Desirie puts her hands on her head and begins shaking it. "Izzy, you drive me crazy!" Shaking her head again in capitulation, she says, "I think there's a plumbers' union, uh...uh electrical workers' union, a sheet metal union, and a steamfitters' union. There. Are you happy? I feel like I have to pass an exam with you."

"A Plus, my darling!" My jocular grading does not charm her at all.

She sneers at me and says with exquisite mockery "And you're being 'A Putz', my darling." As she's saying this, she moves her head from side to side. I burst out laughing at her use of a Yiddish obscenity with a Negro accent.

"What's so funny?" she asks. She looks like she's ready to punch me.

"Nothing. I need a day to think about it."

"What's to think about?"

"Desirie, just give me a day."

That afternoon, I take myself to a basketball court where I often did my best thinking. Even though I think my basketball career is over, I practice my weak spots: Dribbling and shooting with the left hand; the cross-over dribble; the step-back jump-shot. I knew I should go to the demonstration with Desirie. It felt right; it wasn't particularly dangerous; and it would make her very happy. But would I be going just to be what she wanted me to be? I'm not sure. The Civil Rights Movement is a passion we share although I've been a little short on action. And whatever successes we help bring about would not only create a better world for people in general, but also a better world for us; a safer world in which we can be together. My choice is complicated by Mel's attitude toward my relationship with Desirie. Anything that brings Desirie and me closer threatens my friendship with Mel. Greedy me, I want both people in my life.

A further complication is that I can see that whatever postgraduate plans Desirie might have had, they are being supplanted by her new quest of becoming a full-time civil rights activist. And I sense she wants me by her side in this quest. But the more I think about joining her, the more I feel that something is not quite right. It's like a new suit that binds and itches and must be removed after a short period of time. But I look sharp in this suit and Desirie couldn't be happier. She squeals with joy when I tell her that I will join her in the student protest.

It's a perfect day for a protest. In fact this entire week has been a golden gift of warmth and light, and everyone in the Yard is in a good mood. Desirie finds me at the Sun Dial, which is fast becoming "our spot" on campus. She looks sharp in tight jeans and white shirt. In my eyes, the flowing curves of her body stand in sharp contrast to the basic angularity of the Upper Quadrangle. My brain, heart and private parts snap to attention at such a ravishing sight. She greets me with a wide grin and a passionate kiss on the mouth. Her joy eliminates all concern that she ordinarily would have about such a public display of interracial affection. My self-consciousness melts in the heat of this intimate contact. After we return to the reality of the emerging crowd of student protesters, I see Mel walking toward us. He is wearing the same blue and white Howard sweatshirt that I am. He is scowling at me, and I believe he has seen us kissing. "Hi Mel. What's happenin'?" My nervousness sends my greeting over the top in both loudness and enthusiasm. He responds with a barely audible "I'm cool man." To Desirie, however, he is much warmer. "What's happening Cuz?" He says with laughter in his voice. Desirie picks up immediately on the muted tension between Mel and me. In an effort to forge a truce, she says, "I'm so happy to be here today with my two favorite men." This makes Mel even more morose. He cuts his eyes at me and seems genuinely shocked that I have shown up for the protest. "Why are you here, Izzy?" Mel says this with a coldness that deeply pains me. I reply with hostility in my voice. "The same as you, Mel, to protest injustice."

"This ain't your fight, Izzy." In my most pompous voice, I reply, "I beg to differ."

Desirie has had enough. "OK, guys, let's move over closer to the stage. I want to hear the speaker." By this time a sizeable crowd has gathered around the makeshift stage that has been built near the new Fine Arts Building. A few students are holding up signs. "Desegregate the Construction Unions," reads one sign. Another reads "For shame, Lily White Unions are Building Howard's New Gym". A third reads "Down with Gym Crow". These signs will appear in a picket line in front of the Administration Building on 6th Street that is scheduled after the speaker's remarks.

As we approach the stage, we run into some of Mel's BOSS fraternity brothers, a few of Desirie's friends from Delta Sigma Theta, and a couple of the guys we played against in intramural basketball. The general atmosphere of bonhomie dissolves the tension between Mel and me. Someone in the crowd begins to sing and the crowd soon joins him with proud voices and rhythmic clapping.

"Old Gym Crow is dying
Freedom'll soon be flying.
Old Gym Crow's a sinner
Freedom gonna be the winner.
When Old Gym Crow is gone
Freedom will have won."

With each repetition of the chant, the mood of the burgeoning crowd grows increasingly festive. The collective sound of the swaying group surges louder and higher. We no longer can hear ourselves speak even in close quarters so we join the chant. We punctuate each syllable with a raised fist. It seems more like a rock concert than a student protest. Brandon Blackwell appears on the stage. His dark skin sparkles in the warming sunlight. His dazzling smile, alabaster against an ebony background, and clearly visible from any point in the yard, also warms us. He has both arms out with palms facing the ground. He lowers his hands by small increments, indicating by this eloquent sign language that he wants the crowd to become silent. Just as incrementally we reduce our noise to a muffle and then to silence. He picks up a bullhorn and begins to announce the featured speaker of the day. "Fellow students, it gives me great pleasure to introduce our former classmate and one of the stalwarts of the on-going civil rights revolution, Antoine Hart." In unison, the crowd goes "AHHHHH" as an onomatopoetic tribute to the initials of one of Howard's most popular civil rights activists. We all know that Brandon and AH spent time together in a Nashville jail for picketing a segregated movie theatre. The two of them had famously jawboned a drunk white guard armed with a shotgun into an anxiety attack.

Antoine Hart is not a big man. He is well under six-feet tall. He is caramel-colored, dressed in a tan sport jacket, dark brown slacks, a skinny tan and rust-colored tie swinging loosely on a white shirt. Last year he had spent time in a Louisiana jail on a bogus charge of criminal anarchy just for trying to meet with students at a local Baton Rouge Negro college. He had received calls from Brandon and other NAG members telling him that there is an important protest taking place right on his old campus. When Antoine heard about the absurdity of Howard University officials agreeing to allow segregated unions to participate in the building of the new men's gym, he did not hesitate. He readily agreed to speak at that protest. Antoine takes the bullhorn from Brandon, looks at it as if he is studying the teeth of a prized horse, and then turns to the crowd and bellows out in a strong and clearly audible baritone voice, "I don't need this thing." He hands the bullhorn back to Brandon who laughs and gives Antoine a high five. We let out with a roar of approval. Antoine surveys the crowd for a long minute and then begins, "Hello New Negroes." Our cheering grows louder and then shifts to a breathy response to Antoine Hart's salutation, "Hello AHHHH". Antoine laughs. "I call you New Negroes because we're through shucking and jiving." We respond with more thunderous cheering.

"You know, last year I spent more than 60 rotten days in a Louisiana jail for what they called 'criminal anarchy', can you believe that?" We all give out a deafening boo. "Just because I wanted to do exactly what I'm doing here, talk to students. SNCC wants to mobilize students--black and white--from all over the country to join in the broader civil rights movement. While most of the action thus far has taken place in the South, the denial of Negro rights and our human dignity is a national problem. We need volunteers all across the country for this struggle, a struggle that we will win because of our passion, our focus, and our nonviolent tactics." Our cheering begins again. Someone in the crowd cries out, "Preach it, AH!" Someone else says, "Amen to that." The cheering seems to animate Antoine even more and his body roams about the makeshift stage. He punctuates his words with an upward punch of his fist. His voice takes on the tone of a preacher. Another person in the crowd bellows "Take us to church, AH!"

"Now since I left Howard and since I became a field secretary for SNCC, my focus has been on the travails of the Negro in the South, particularly in Louisiana and Mississippi. But when I got the call from Brandon and he informed me of the mind-boggling mess that's going on right here at my old campus, I had to come and speak. Now I ask you, what could have possessed Howard's administration to tolerate segregated unions in the construction of the University's new men's gymnasium?"

"They crazy as bedbugs," someone in the crowd loudly opines.

"Jive turkeys!" Yells another. Still another barks out, "A bunch of Uncle Toms. Tha's what they be." Antoine knows he has us now. "And it's a damn shame!"

"What's a shame, AHHHH?" We ask in unison.

"When highly educated Negro officials kow-tow to their white masters. Ain't this a shame?"

"Right on, AHHHH. It's a damn shame."

"When the President of this University allows a new University building to be built by segregated unions. Ain't this a shame?"

We roar in response. "It's a shame."

"Now I do have some sympathy for the powers that be at Howard, because so much of the University budget is determined by a congressional committee that is made up of a bunch of Southern redneck racists. So you see, in large part, the University is one collective sharecropper whose souls and livelihood are owned by a new group of southern white masters. And you know that's a DAMN shame!" We let out with an unrestrained joyful cheer. "The white racist has always had his way of holding down the Black man. The whips of slavery gave way to the paucity of the sharecropper's wages. The sharecropper's financial misery was increased many times over by Jim Crow Laws that eviscerated so much of the Black man's soul. And the poisonous cloud of white apartheid continues to snuff out the life possibilities of little black children all over this country. But no more."

"Tell it like it is, AH," someone in the crowd yells out. "Not this time! And not in our house!" We let out with a prolonged, deafening shout of praise for this truth teller. As our collective shout continues, we jump up and down, thrusting our fists in the air repeating the preacher's last phrase, "NOT IN OUR HOUSE! NOT IN OUR HOUSE!" AH implores us to quiet down so he may continue. "We will not allow segregated unions to build on our campus!" AH points to us and we instinctively know to respond with, "NOT IN OUR HOUSE!"

"Gym Crow laws no longer apply!"

"NOT IN OUR HOUSE!"

"We will no longer be second class citizens!"

"NOT IN OUR HOUSE!"

"Nor will we allow ourselves to be mistreated or disrespected!"

"NOT IN OUR HOUSE!"

"The Anglo-Saxons have had their day. They'll not rule us for much longer!"

"NOT IN OUR HOUSE!" Desirie and Mel glance at me with a big grin on their faces.

"Don't look at me," I say. "I'm Jewish-American." The two of them double over in laughter. The call and response goes on for the next 10 minutes. When we reach a fevered pitch, AH concludes with "Now let's go tell the Howard University administrators! And what are we going to tell them?"

"NOT IN OUR HOUSE!" We march over to the Administration building chanting over and over, "NOT IN OUR HOUSE!"

A crowd of about 100 students spontaneously form a single file line and march toward the Administration Building, shouting all the while, "NOT IN OUR HOUSE." Windows begin to open in every classroom in Douglass Hall, and a few moments later students pour out of Howard's main classroom building and join the marchers. In fact, there are so many students that the sidewalk cannot hold them all. Students pour into 6th Street effectively blocking all traffic that tries to navigate the road separating Douglass Hall from the Administration Building. Car horns accompany the chant. Two Metropolitan Police cars attempt to make their way toward the Administration Building, but are blocked by cars in front of them. Two cops get out of their cars and start walking toward the students. One is white, the other Black. Someone in the crowd yells out, "At least the Pig Force is integrated!" The crowd roars with laughter. With difficulty the two policemen reach the front of the Administration Building. The two of them stand on the top of three steps that front the entrance. The white cop looks as if he just swallowed a lemon. The Black cop begins to speak through a bullhorn. "Now I know you all're upset, and I don't deny that you have a reason to be upset, but this crowd is gonna have to disperse. You're creating a public hazard." A crescendo of boos rains down on his head. Antoine Hart stands just below the policeman with his own bullhorn. He yells out, "We ain't leaving until we hear from President Nabrit that some action will be taken to rectify this unconscionable discrimination."

"You tell 'em, AH," someone yells out. Thus commences the battle of the bullhorns. The Black policeman ups the anti. "If you do not disperse, we will have to apply whatever force is necessary until you comply." More boos. "We're not moving until we hear from the President," replies AH. Great cheers break out whenever AH returns his defiant reply. As the bullhorns battle, the white policeman calls for backups. After several more bullhorn exchanges, we can see a large contingent of the Metropolitan Police Department moving toward us. AH bellows out, "Hold your ground!" The brave men in blue are prepared for a riot, and AH tries to psych up the crowd to become a human barricade. The police move slowly towards us with raised Billie clubs glinting in the sunlight, and their riot shields covering virtually their entire bodies. Just before the flash point is reached, President Nabrit appears on the steps of the Administration Building. He takes the bullhorn from the Black policeman. He's grinning from ear to ear. "I have great news," he begins. "I have just received a copy of a letter Labor Secretary Wirtz has sent to the Administrator of the General Services Administration. The letter states that contractors and unions involved in the building of Howard's new gymnasium are required to comply with the non-discrimination clause in the construction contract." We erupt with cheers. When the cheers die down, Nabrit continues, "If they refuse to comply within 10 days, Secretary Wirtz will ask the Justice Department to enforce compliance." Our cheers grow louder. "Secretary Wirtz's letter continues to say that he is now convinced that persuasion alone will not produce the action required." Our cheers are now deafening. "Victory in our house," AH yells through the bullhorn. And that becomes our new chant. "Victory in our house!" We spontaneously begin to disperse as the two policemen with their faces frozen in an expression of astonishment watch us unclog the street.

Once back in the Yard, Desirie excitedly says to me, "You see, Izzy, direct action works. The students can be powerful if we remain organized, unified, and we continue to challenge the power structure. Jim Crow will fold like a house of cards if we are persistent. I've decided that's what I want to do, and Izzy, I want you to join me. Let's put our plans to go to graduate school on hold and be civil rights activists for the next couple of years." My body fills up with the heebie-jeebies. "Whoa, Desirie. That's asking a lot."

"I know it is, Izzy, but think about it. It could be the most important decision you'll make in your life." I know she's right. This would be the most important decision in my life so far and a "no" is just as terrifying as a "yes".

With an unmovable frown on his face, Mel has been witnessing this conversation. "Desirie," he says, "Why don't you stop hounding him. Can't you see that he doesn't want to do it. He can't think past himself and his goals. Justice for Negroes is okay as a part time hobby, but it's nothing that he willing to commit his life to." With faux empathy, he continues. "And I can understand his not wanting to not give up on his goals. After all, the Jews have gotten their freedom." I blush a deep red. That comment cuts me deeply. Desirie sees the rising tension between us and jumps in. "Cut it out, Mel. That was uncalled for."

"Seriously, Desirie, have you ever thought about why Izzy wants to be with you? Do you think he really loves you? It's all about him, to prove to himself and the world that he's a great liberal."

"How do you know this, Mel?" Desirie replies with tears in her eyes. "How do you really know what's inside him?"

"I know white people. I'll grant you Izzy's heart is better than most, but he can't possibly see you beyond your black skin. You're not a full flesh and blood human being to white people. You represent some image they possess of Black women. Mostly it's about sexual conquest and sexual fulfillment. You're the black whore who's gonna satisfy every lustful fantasy that their fetid imagination has concocted. And that their frigid white women will never be able to satisfy! Desirie starts to cry. She looks at me imploringly and asks, "Is it true, Izzy? Is that how you think of me?" "Of course not, Desirie! In fact, I'm very much in love with you." She manages a smile through translucent tears. "Maybe in the beginning----"

"AH HA!" Mel pounces.

"Let me finish, Mel. Maybe in the beginning I thought: Wouldn't it be amazing if a Negro girl were attracted to me, not because of my ego, but because of my hope that this would be proof that Negroes and whites could love each other. And to be perfectly honest, I hoped that my feelings for Desirie would cure me of my Negrophobia. And by the way it has!"

"Well good for you, Izzy. I'm so happy for you." My body is seized with shame as I try and absorb Mel's sarcasm. Mel continues to slay me with a thousand cuts. He slashes at my idealism by claiming to have unearthed its selfish origins; he demeans my Jewish identity by somehow equating me with Jewish liquor storeowners who exploit the alcoholic vulnerabilities of their ghetto customers. Worst of all he continues to claim that my feelings for Desirie are not real and that he will do everything in his power to keep me from hurting her. Desirie can no longer stand our arguing over her, and she dashes away toward Founders Library. Her sobbing is audible almost to the steps of the library. Mel and I disconsolately look at her until she disappears within the confines of the library. When we can no longer see her, we turn toward each other and just glare. A painfully long minute passes without either one of us saying a word. Then we turn and go our separate ways.

Chapter 25.

The End of the Beginning

I watch in uncomprehending horror. The May 3rd
evening news begins with a report from Birmingham, Alabama,
where dozens of Black teenagers are marching toward a set of
barricades erected by the Birmingham police. These teenagers
walk in the direction of a set of powerful fire hoses aimed at
them. At "Bull" Connor's order, the hoses are turned on and their
power is difficult to fully grasp. One little girl, apparently around
8 years old, is literally rolled back down the street from which
she had begun her march. A group of teenagers are pinned
against the wall unable to avoid the hoses' violent spray. Despite
their awful force, the hoses fail to quash the protest. In fact, this
shameful display of official power arouses the crowd even more.
Bricks and broken bottles are hurled at the police who now
move toward the crowd of teenage demonstrators with a pack of
leaping, yapping, growling German shepherds barely contained
on their leashes. The ear-piercing screams of the crowd of dark-
skinned victims are unbearable. I along with the entire nation, I
imagine, get to see a German shepherd with its teeth sunk into
the side of a teenage boy, biting, tearing, and turning its head
from side to side in an effort to remove a hunk of flesh from its
victim. I am nauseated by the sight of government-sanctioned
fangs and fire hoses unleashed upon a group of young people
who are marching to obtain the same rights that every white
person enjoys in our so-called Land of the Free. I am perplexed,
increasingly demoralized, and profoundly befuddled. How can
this happen in America, the alleged leader and model of free
nations? But the question is quickly answered when I remind
myself of all that I have learned in the past four years at Howard
about race relations in America and its odious provenance. I am
watching the dead Confederacy come to life again to fight once
more to preserve the hateful bulwark of its society—the
oppression of dark-skinned people. Yes, in my mind, I know how
and why this is happening, but to see with my own eyes this
revolting display of official hatred of one group of American

citizens for another makes me cringe with disgust---Disgust with Alabama, with the South, with white people, with my feelings of powerlessness, and ultimately with myself. For a moment I think maybe I am making a mistake by not joining Desirie in the civil rights struggle. Could there be any more important work right now? It seems obvious that I should join the woman I love in this worthy fight. Yet something holds me back. Is it fear for my life? And what if I do die? There would be much posthumous praise heaped upon the head of this heroic martyr who sacrificed his life for such an honorable cause. Of course it would be praise I would never hear. And the way racist southerners have been treating white protestors, my period of heroic struggle could be awfully short. I realize that I want a longer lifespan in which to make whatever contribution I am going to make in this life. The truth of the matter has already been proven—I would make a lousy civil rights protestor. I am incapable of learning the discipline of nonviolence; and when push literally comes to shove, I would feel compelled, not unlike the German shepherds, to sink my teeth into the hides of haters-- only in self-defense of course. I urgently want to connect with Mel and Desirie. I am worried that the Birmingham Massacre has destroyed my relationships with the two of them.

On the third ring, a lethargic voice answers the phone, "Yeah?"

"Hi Mel. It's Izzy."

"What you want white boy?" I pick up on the depressive timbre in Mel's voice and know immediately that he too has watched the horrific scene in Birmingham.

"Look Mel, I know you are not terribly fond of white people right now, but you know that ain't me."

"Really? How can I be sure?" Sarcastically, he adds, "Y'all look alike to me. What's worse is y'all act alike."

"Right. That's why James Peck got his head broken in Birmingham because he was a white Freedom Rider." The conversation is heating up and now Mel's voice possesses no trace of its previous lethargy. "Well, if that white man can join the struggle, why can't you?" Now I get angry. "Oh come on, Mel, Peck is a trained and seasoned activist. He took part in the earlier freedom rides back in the 1940s. And he's a conscientious objector. His whole life has been about the nonviolent struggle for civil rights and freedom for the oppressed." There is a long pause and then Mel finally asks, "So why you calling, Izzy?" I didn't want to just come out and beg him not to hate me because of what the racists in Birmingham did. Instead, I try to turn him into my counselor. "I have a dilemma. I don't know whether I should postpone graduate school and fight for civil rights with you and Desirie." Another long pause. "I guess you watched the news too, Izzy. " The edge in Mel's voice disturbs me. "It was horrible," I reply. "Yes it is, Izzy, and after watching that obscenity, I'm convinced that there're two reasons why you shouldn't go with us." Deflated, I ask what the reasons are.

"If you go, you will be killed. I am convinced of that. And I told you before it's not your fight."

"Mel, why do you keep pushing me away. Look, no one is really free unless we're all free." I say this with undisguised anger. "Oh I see that you're now parroting our history professor," Mel says with a contemptuous laugh. "But I believe it. This is everyone's fight."

"Then what's the dilemma? Why aren't you jumping right in?" Before I can answer, Mel answers for me. "I'll tell you why it's such a dilemma for you. You're a very idealistic person, Izzy, but it's the idea that you love: Truth, Justice, and the American Way. And I don't trust the love of an abstract idea. I don't trust it, because in the day-to-day struggle, the sweat, pain, and grit it takes to wage this fight is beyond you. I'm convinced that when the going gets tough, you gonna get going, Izzy... in the opposite direction."

"So you can read my mind now Mel? He chuckles. "They don't call me X-Ray Grey for nothing." I reflexively laugh back. "As long as we're speaking truth to one another, let me tell you that another part of my dilemma is you."

"What d'ya mean by that?" I take a deep breath before I can spell it out.

"I want your friendship, Mel, and your opposition to me and Desirie being together frankly stymies me. You know how much I love your cousin..."

"No, Izzy, I don't know that! Here again, I think you love the idea of being with a Black girl and that she seems to have some feelings for you. I think you bathe in your own self-reflection as a tolerant liberal."

"I know. You said that before. So I guess you also think that I hang around with the likes of you because it proves that I'm a great liberal?"

"If the shoe fits, Izzy."

"Jesus, Mel, I thought we're further along than that."

"Look, Izzy, you don't really know her or me for that matter. You two come from different worlds. It can never work, not in today's America. And I don't want to see her hurt. She's already had her heart broken once, and she almost didn't recover. I could kill that bright-skinned motherfucker. He was so color-struck that he crapped all over Desirie."

"Yeah, she told me about Carter, but she said it was his mother who thought she was too dark for her son."

"Then he's just a punk-ass Mama's boy."

"OK, but what's that got to do with me? Look, Mel, I desperately want your friendship, but you keep rejecting it. What can I do to get us passed this impasse?" Mel is silent for a moment. "I don't know Izzy. Sometimes I look at you and I think you're the best friend that I never had. I see how hard you work to be my friend. But when I feel myself moving toward you, I feel like I'm somehow betraying my people. I don't know. It's hard to explain. I just know that no matter how much I love you, if a race war were to break out--and it seems like one will soon--I know deep within me which side I would be on; and I would have no problem blowing your head off." I stare at the phone in absolute amazement. "Mel! What are you saying?"

"I'm sorry, Izzy, but that's how I feel. I know you're basically a good guy, but you are one of them; and I would rather die shooting white people than be killed by one of my own because I either opposed my people or stood on the sidelines."

"So let me get this straight. You would kill the closest thing you've ever had to a best friend out of a sense of loyalty to your 'people'?"

"Tha's right my white brother. Dig ya later."

I am dumbfounded and sad….and lonely as I absorb the fact that he has hung up on me.. I realize that despite his homicidal fantasy and his occasional anti-Semitic outbursts that I still want Mel as a friend. I hear myself saying, You mean more to me than I ever could have imagined my Black brother.

The next day, I arrange to have lunch with Desirie. We both have some time on our hands so we decide to drive to Chinatown for lunch. We find a secluded table at the China Doll restaurant. The place is strangely un-crowded for a weekday lunch hour. But I am happy because I need privacy for what I expect to be a difficult conversation with the love of my life. We sit down and Desirie looks at me with a nervous smile on her face. She knows that I am about to give her my decision on whether I am going to join her in a life of civil rights activism, and she is dreading the likelihood of my saying no. In a misguided effort to soften the blow, I begin to tell her how much I enjoyed being with her at last month's demonstration. As soon as I see her eyes brightening up with hopeful anticipation, I know I've made a mistake. "I can see how exhilarating and meaningful direct action can be, Desirie, and I know there's a strong part of me that wants to join you in this work, in this adventure...."

Excitedly, her voice rises as she interrupts and asks, "Then you'll do it?"

"Hear me out, honey. You know I'm committed to equal rights for Negroes, and you know how much I've come to hate segregation and white supremacy." She nods her head first with enthusiasm and then with caution. "I hear a 'but' coming," she says. I nod in agreement. "But, number one, I don't have your passion; and I realized that if I do it, I am doing it for you, just to be with you, to be the person you want me to be." Her eyes well up with tears, but she continues to listen intently to my apologia. "I would do almost anything for you, Desirie, but the one thing that I cannot do is to be something I'm not. No matter how much I want you, to be with you and be the person you need, I can't. It kills me to say it, but I just can't. I can't bear to lose you, but I know I am. I know it sounds silly to say, but I must give you up in order to save me. If I were to say yes today, I would destroy something vital in me, and in all truth I would then become useless to you." Desirie fixes her eyes on mine for a long moment. Her pleading expression swiftly changes to a stone cold stare.

"You know, Izzy, maybe Mel's right. This is not your fight. We Negroes must do this for ourselves. We appreciate your support and your sympathy, but we have to do this." She says without feeling, "Izzy, I loved you terribly." Her use of the past tense crushes me. "But now," she continues, "I see that we are different and we're moving in different directions in our lives." My response to her pulling away from me makes me blush. "So we're breaking up?" I can't believe that at this very delicate and painful moment that I can be such a ninny. In a disgusted tone, Desirie says, "No, bright boy, you're breaking up with me." I look at her dumbfounded, which she finds unbearable. Shaking her head in disbelief, she says. "Listen, Izzy, I gotta go."

I watch her walk away in total disbelief. What have I done?" I've never felt this way about any girl and I'm giving her up. And for what? Some precious notion of authenticity? What's wrong with me? You know how they say that just before you die, your entire life flashes by in your mind's eye. All of the great times that Desirie and I had together rush through my brain and then...nothing except despair and self-loathing. Could dying be any worse?

For me the merry month of May is one of cauterizing sadness. I cry an ocean of tears, and the more I cry the less I feel. By the last week of May, I am completely numb. Now all events and their significance—good or bad-- wash off me like water off a mallard's back. I learn that I have aced all my finals, will graduate eighth in my class, and will soon be off to graduate school at the University of Illinois reputed to have one of the best graduate psychology programs in the country. But all of this good news has the same effect on me as the terrible news that continues to ooze out of Birmingham. On the 11th there are bomb attacks on a local motel where many of the protest leaders are staying, and another on the parsonage of Martin Luther King's brother. This leads to a riot that brings a large battalion of state troopers armed with submachine guns, and the ensuing confrontation results in at least 50 people wounded. Nothing touches or penetrates me. The misery of numbness is accentuated by the fact that Desirie has not spoken to me since our lunch at the China Doll. Being alive but "dead" is not new to me, but now feels more intense than ever before. By the end of May, I can no longer stand it. Without any willful intervention on my part, the tears reappear, a flood of unrelenting sorrow. Although I have promised myself that I would not call her, I find myself dialing her number on a grey Sunday during the Memorial Day weekend. I do not expect to get her. In fact, I fantasize that she is having a wonderful time in some beach-like setting with another man. When she answers the phone, I try to strangle my fantasy-induced tears. Her noncommittal hello feels like a beam of sunlight soothing every sore spot in my soul. "D'Desirie? It's Izzy."

"Izzy?" Desirie says excitedly. She allows a slit of enthusiasm to open and then quickly close. "What do you want, Izzy?" She says flatly. I want to tell her that I take it all back. That I want to be with her always and that I'll go wherever she goes and fight whatever battle she fights. But instead of noble apologia, I choose maudlin drivel. "I just wanted to hear your voice."

"Why are you calling? We're broken-up." Forlornly, I reply, "Yeah, I know, but it's so hard."

"Well, you're making it harder, Izzy. You don't think it's hard for me?"

"Desirie, I know that we can't be together, but can't we be together one last time?"

"You're just a horndog, Izzy?"

"It's not just about sex. I want to be close to you one last time."

"Oh, it's a goodbye fuck you want?"

"Damn, Desirie, why do you have to piss on everything I say?"

"Because I'm pissed off at you. Look, Izzy, I think I know you better than you do yourself, and I know you're making a terrible mistake. And your mistake is my heartbreak."

"You may be right, Desirie, but I can only go with my gut. For me to postpone or more likely give up grad school and join you in the Struggle just doesn't feel right. I know for sure that I don't want to be a professional activist. And you do. I know that and I accept that; and given that we seem to be on two very different paths in our lives, I don't know how we can be together." Apparently wearying of the argument, Desirie agrees to a final meeting. "Where?"

"The only place I know where we can have any privacy is Bobby's place. You know, where we were before."

"I used to think that being with a white boy meant that we'd go to fancy restaurants and maybe spend a night at the Shoreham Hotel. Instead, I get the Fleabag Hilton."

"Oh come on. It's not that bad." I can hear her breathing in a way I know to mean that she is concentrating hard on making a decision. "Okay, Izzy, when?"

"How about Saturday? In fact, how about I pick you up at 6 and we'll have dinner first? "

"No Izzy, no dinner. Pick me up at 7:30."

"Seven thirty, then, I'll be at your door."

The next evening Bobby Levine and I meet at the Silver Spring Hot Shoppes. We each order a Mighty Moe and a coke. As we wait for our food, I very cautiously broach the subject of "borrowing" a bedroom at his apartment building near 16th and U Streets. "Again?" He bellowed. "Can't you find another place to get laid?"

"Actually no. That's why I'm asking. Listen, this will be the last time and you won't even have to spring for the rubber." He laughed his high-pitched laugh of incredulity. "The last time my ass."

"Seriously. Desirie and I are breaking up."

"So this is a good-bye fuck."

"Those were exactly her words. I prefer the term swan song."

"You sure it's not a rabbit duet?" Bobby laughs profusely at his word play.

"Very funny." My sour response provokes even more high-pitched laughter. It finally registers that I'm not laughing and he says, "OK, when?" I throw my fist in the air and scream out, "Yes!" Several diners turn in their seats to gawk disapprovingly at me. "Saturday night, around 8?" I ask in a voice now reduced to a conspiratorial whisper. "Fine, Bobby replies with his customary smirk. "Now you owe me two"

"Two what?"

"That's for me to know and for you to find out."

"Oh God, I'm not sure I want to know."

I pick Desirie up at 7:30 sharp. I know it's corny, but she really is a vision of loveliness. She is wearing skin-tight blue shorts and those chocolate extremities emanating from the bottom of her shorts are putting me in an incredibly agitated state. Her breasts push tightly against her pale grey tee shirt. Her welcoming smile is suffused with sadness. Bobby has given us a different room. This one is much nicer than the last and more formally decorated with aging mahogany furniture. For a second I think we are in the great room of a men's club whose grandeur had faded long ago. I move toward Desirie to kiss her, but she gently pushes me away. With the same sad smile on her face, she looks at me directly and begins to undress. Staring back, I do the same. Our previous shyness has completely disappeared. We stand naked in front of one another. I am so aroused I want to just leap upon her. I'm so enthralled with her beauty that I find it hard to believe there was ever a time when the sight of a brown body turned me off. Still standing, we kiss. I can wait no longer. I guide her to the bed and carefully lay her down. She places the rubber on my penis quickly and with consummate skill. I fit my loins to her and try to enter her. With a rubber on, my member is blinder than usual, and again, I hit the wrong spot. "Ow," Desirie cries, "that white pole can't see shit." We both burst out laughing. "I'm embarrassed to ask you again to help me find Nirvana."

"I've never heard it called that before. Here, I'll guide you in." She takes hold of my penis and gently moves it to the correct orifice. I glide along this beautiful chocolate river, confident as a seasoned river pilot, and as content as a baby in its mother's arms. We move slowly at first and then with a speed that feels out of both our control. At our mutual crescendo, we both scream with joy and relief. Bobby is right. A rabbit duet after all!

Afterwards, I stand up and Desirie notices that I have a half erect but naked penis. "Izzy where's your rubber?" She says with genuine fear. "I'I don't know." I look on the floor and under the bed, while Desirie frantically searches the sheets. Out of the corner of my eye, I see something hanging between Desirie's legs. She looks as if she is giving birth to a very small alien creature. Semen is pouring out the open end of the wrinkled condom on to the bed. She finally notices what is happening and quickly extricates the semen-smeared "afterbirth" from her body. I double over with laughter. But Desirie's face is fixed in ...terror. "Oh Izzy, what if I get pregnant?"

"You won't. All of the semen is leaking out now."

"But you don't know for sure."

"I don't know anything for sure, but the chances are slim." I get back on the bed and wrap my arms around her. I kiss her passionately and we both are quickly aroused again. Breathless, she manages to ask if I have another rubber. I don't and am seized by a swamp of confusing feelings: Anger, panic, disappointment, and humiliation. I begin to frantically search the room for perhaps a left-behind condom, hoping against hope that Bobby has repeated his generosity. Now that I'm in a panic, Desirie is sitting on the bed with her hand cupped across her mouth, laughing long and hard. But there on a dark dresser in the darkest corner of the room is another little box with another little condom. Underneath the condom is a note from Bobby, which simply says, "Now you owe me two."

Now that I'm properly sheathed, we begin again. We make love like we have known each other forever. As she gently moans, I feel myself falling into a whirlpool, which spirals downward into some unknown place. I tighten momentarily out of fear, but then let go hoping that wherever I land I will be safe. I thrust and she thrusts back harder and faster and takes me to a higher speed. With my cheek sealed to hers, we come together. I feel tears running down the side of my face and I don't know if they are hers or mine. I pull my cheek from hers to look at her and see that she is now sobbing. "Oh Izzy, how can you leave me? I love you so much!" Our unity is shattered. I sit up and look at her sobbing, and I feel helpless to alter the departing trajectory of our lives. I feel the full force of my decision now, and the sights and sounds of two hearts breaking render me speechless. I want to say something, words of comfort or explanation that will ease her pain, but no words come. Until this moment, Desirie was the one person I could say anything to, open my heart to.

Now, it's as if the plugs have been ripped out of our private switchboard. The sight of her imploring eyes is unbearable. I turn my back to her and dress without saying a word. Now I hear an angry voice exclaim, "Damn you, Izzy, take me home."

We drive to Desirie's apartment in silence. She is too angry to speak, and I don't know what to say. I park in front of her apartment building and words continue to fail us. We look into each other's eyes searching for an improbable solution to our dilemma. "Well Izzy," she says, finally, "you had your goodbye fuck."

"For Christ's sakes, Desirie, don't say that. Fucking is not what we did. The word hardly captures the love in our love-making and you know it!"

"What difference does it make? We're breaking up." Speechless again, I say nothing.
"Aren't you gonna say anything?" Desirie asks plaintively. Her sadness corrodes my coherence and I search desperately for something comforting, useful, healing to say. All I can manage is, "Desirie, I love you more than I thought possible and I will miss you terribly." Before I can see her face completely crumble in sorrow, she turns her back to me and opens the car door. "Have a nice life, Izzy." She slams the car door and runs into her apartment building. As I watch her disappear, a sense of emptiness overtakes me. Even though I am the one who initiated the break-up, I feel bereft. For the thousandth time, I am sitting in my car in front of the house of a girl I love balling my eyes out.

Howard University's 95th Commencement takes place on a hot Friday afternoon in early June. The ceremony is being held in the Yard with the speaker's platform located at the entrance to Douglas Hall. During the Procession, I am already roasting in my academic robes. We march to our seats in alphabetical order. Because of the distance between Jackson and White, I don't even manage a glimpse of Desirie. After the Invocation and a musical number by the University Band and Choir, President Nabrit's brother, who is President of a Black university in Houston, begins the Commencement Address. Unfortunately, it is a tedious, pompous bore from start to finish, and my mind has no choice but to escape into the nebulous realm of my reveries. I want to discover in my musings a multi-faceted gem of meaning, significance, and purpose. After all, in another hour I will be a full-fledged college graduate, and I should know by now who I am, what my path in life is to be and what I have learned in my four years at Howard. But my reveries are jumbled, involving quick flashes on some of the emotion-charged experiences I had at Howard. On my freshman year's daily hitchhiking trip to school with drivers from all walks of life, I witnessed their ubiquitous regression from generous human benefactor to prurient racist voyeur into the sexual anatomy and characteristics of Black men and women. Next I see myself in a sea of Black students entering the Rankin Chapel for Freshman Orientation, feeling alienated, vulnerable and overwhelmed by my Negrophobia. I see my chemistry lab partner's acid-stained hands offering me a powdered donut, and I'm having an anxiety attack out of fear that such intimacy will engulf me with Negritude. I remember the shock I felt when I encountered Negro students who were not only my intellectual equal, but who were also superior, in intelligence, education and attainment. No one in my white world prepared me for such a "counter-intuitive" discovery. I recall the struggle to make the Howard varsity basketball team and how during the entire season I alternated between feeling like a white token and feeling so Black that I had concluded it was alright to call my new friends on the team that weird and wonderful term of endearment—nigger. I recollect the initial thrill I felt in intellectual pursuits. I came to love learning passionately and eventually fell in love with psychology. And psychology is providing answers to human mysteries that have caused me great befuddlement and angst. It was not long before I knew I was committed to the profession. Yet another image focuses on the few intimate friendships that I have made during my time at Howard. These allowed my empathic antennae to absorb on several levels the pain, joy, anger, frustration, and marvelous achievements that arose from the three and a half century experience of being a Black person in America. I conclude perhaps self-righteously, but accurately nonetheless, that no white person can really understand what it means to be Black without immersing oneself imaginatively into the multifaceted Black experience. And yet those friendships also taught me that despite culturally generated differences, people are people with all the same faults, foibles, and heroic tendencies that make up the human comedy. Next I focus on my flirtation with becoming a civil rights activist and my constant struggle between fear and exhilaration, disillusionment and hope. Then there is Desirie who I love even more than psychology, but apparently not enough to commit my whole life and being to her. I flash on many of the wonderful conversations we had and the love we made and gave one another. I am deep in one of those skin-on-skin recollections when I faintly begin to hear the Hallelujah Chorus, which lets me know that the Commencement Address is over. My reveries end as well. During the subsequent Conferring of Degrees, I automatically stand up to get a better look when Desirie Jackson's name is called. The surrounding laughter makes me aware that I'm the only one standing. I sit my mortified ass down.

After the ceremony, I join my parents and brother who are all smiles. My brother claps me on my back. My father is taking pictures while my mother hugs me tightly. She appears to be afraid to let me go as if I were leaving forever. For a brief moment, I see Desirie with her parents and siblings, but she does not see me. I wrestle with myself over the idea of going up to her to congratulate her. But I know that what I really want from her is forgiveness and a pledge of her continued love. I therefore remain rooted with my family by the sundial.

Chapter 26.

Blowing in the Wind

Throughout the summer of 1963, there has been a great deal of publicity about the upcoming March on Washington For Jobs and Freedom. Publicity is probably not the right word. Hysteria is more accurate. The entire city is besieged by an overwhelming fear of a pending race riot. The week before the March newspaper columnists and TV commentators predicted that a racial Armageddon was about to descend upon the "Capital of the Free World". It got so bad that I was afraid to mention my interest in going to the March alone to any of my friends or family. If you think my father fearfully fought the idea of my attending Howard four years ago, he's now apoplectic about my attending the March. Even my mother rushed in to share her anxious premonitions. "Izzy, I'm so afraid that you'll be killed in that March. Please don't go!"

"I have to, Ma. I made a promise?"

"A promise? Who did you promise?"

"I promised myself."

"So you've never broken a promise before? I rather you live than you be so honorable."

"Nothing will happen to me, Ma."

"How do you know this? You have a crystal ball?"

"Ma, it's gonna be a peaceful march. My mother shakes her head and walks to the kitchen mumbling, "My son the oracle." My father is sitting in the adjacent dining area trying to eat his breakfast. "Mort," my mother implores," "Talk to your son."

"Aw for Christ's sakes, Pearl, can't a man eat his breakfast in peace?"

My father yells from his seat, "Izzy, don't be such a meshuganah. It's crazy for you to go to that March. Don't you realize that you and all the other naïve students are being manipulated by the Communist Party."

"Aw Dad, there ya go again."

"It's true. J. Edgar Hoover has the proof. "

"I'm sorry, Dad, but you're full of shit." His eyes begin to bug out in fear and anger. He rises and with both hands on the table he yells even louder. "YOU LISTEN TO ME YOU LITTLE PUTZ. YOU'VE GOT TO LEARN THAT IN THIS WORLD NOBODY REALLY GIVES A SHIT ABOUT YOU EXCEPT YOUR FAMILY." I can't take it anymore. I turn my back on both my parents and head for the door. "Bye Mom, bye Dad. I hope to see you tonight." As I walk in the corridor toward the stairway, I can hear my parents arguing about which one of them should have stopped me.

Because I know that it will be impossible to drive my car all the way to the Washington Monument Grounds, I park my car at the Eastern Avenue District Line and take the Federal Triangle bus to get within striking distance of my destination. I long for the recently retired streetcars that would have taken me right to Constitution Avenue. I arrive at the Washington Monument around 9 AM and see a smattering of people sitting on the grass waiting for some signal for the March to begin. I hear a voice ask over a loudspeaker, "Has anyone seen Lena Horne, because she is supposed to perform shortly." There are so few people so far that I begin to worry, and there is no one that I know. Within the next hour, however, more and more people show up, and I can see a train of buses lining up at a pre-ordained bus stop. A woman in a white dress with a blue sash comes up to me asks me to sign a pledge card that commits me to working toward the achievement of "social peace through social justice." Soon the grass by the Monument seems to be completely covered with marchers who collectively have brought a large variety of protest signs. There are red-letter signs on a white field combined with white letters on a red field that say We March For Integrated Schools Now! We Demand Decent Housing Now. We Demand Voting Rights Now! I see a union sign that says Civil Rights plus Employment equals Freedom. The pace of the burgeoning crowds picks up rapidly. Before long the grassy area of the Monument and Constitution Avenue is filled with people and signs. Just as I slip into feelings of loneliness and alienation I hear a familiar refrain, "Hey white boy!" In the blinding sunlight I see five tall dark shadows walking toward me. It's Courtney Cartwright and his friends Claudine, David, Vincent and James. "Hey Courtney, you're a sight for sore eyes, and I mean that literally." In my effort to discern the shadows, the sun hurts my eyes. There are greetings all around. "What's happenin', White. I'm surprised to see you here."

"Why? Aren't we on the same page when it comes to human rights?"

"But this March is about Negro rights."

"Same thing," I opine. James laughs and asks, "When did you become Colored?"

"When I tell people I just graduated from Howard, they all think I must be Colored."

"Me too," says Vince. I've seen you play B-Ball and dance. No white boy I know moves like that."

"They say that imitation is the sincerest form of flattery." Claudine weighs in. "Do you still dance, Izzy?"

"Whenever I hear the music." This makes everyone chuckle. "How are you Claudine?"

"Look Izzy, this is how I am." She holds out her left hand, which is sparkling from her dazzling diamond ring. "Me and Courtney are gonna get married."

"Whoa, that's exciting. When?"

"In two weeks, Izzy. And after a weekend honeymoon in the Bahamas, I start working on a Masters in Social Work."

"Where, Claudine?" "Here, Izzy, at Howard."

"And you, Courtney. What are you up to?"

"I got an apprentice type job at an architectural firm downtown."

"Wow, you guys are starting a brand new life. That's great!"

"How about you, Izzy?"

"I'm going for my Ph.D. in Psychology at the University of Illinois. In fact, I leave for Champaign-Urbana in a week."

"That's so great, Izzy. You'll be a great head-shrinker," Claudine says with a wide smile. I have to chuckle at that. "Well, to tell you the truth, I'd rather expand minds than shrink heads." Vincent says, "Hey I see people gathering at the Ellipse. I think there's gonna be music. Let's go." The six of us head toward the Ellipse with hundreds of other marchers. We see more colorful signs: We Demand an End to Bias Now. UAW Says Jobs and Freedom For Every American. Now we hear music—Joan Baez singing "Oh Freedom". Then, Odetta sings "I'm On My Way." We hear the voices of the Marchers watching the singers as well as those coming from all up and down Constitution Avenue. After a few songs, we notice that there are people marching up Constitution Avenue, and we think the March is beginning.

Further up the avenue I see two very unexpected signs: BOSS for Jobs and Freedom; BOSS Demands the End of White Supremacy. I try to see who's carrying the signs, but their bodies are blocked by the crush of people. As the spacing of the marchers changes, I see the Negus of BOSS. He has on a multi-colored African shirt and a matching hat. And now it's clear that Colby Betterman is carrying one of the signs. Next to him is Mel Gray carrying the second sign. Eight other BOSS brothers are with them. In a few moments, we catch up with them. I introduce Courtney and his friends to the brothers of BOSS. Courtney and the Negus are about the same height, but while Courtney is loose and lanky, the Negus is ramrod straight. The Negus' entire demeanor is Africa Proud. Tentatively, I say hello to the Negus. "That's a beautiful shirt. What do you call it?" It's called a Dashiki, which derives from a Yoruba word for shirt. And my cap is called a Kufi. My question, however, provokes a monologue from the Negus about the importance for Black people to re-engage with their African roots. The Negus addresses Courtney and his friends as a group.

"I hope you folks are in touch with your African lineage because Black people don't really know who they are unless they reacquaint themselves with their place of physical and spiritual origin. You know my birth name is Lloyd Redmayne, but I am thinking of changing it. I don't buy that shit of Malcolm's of putting an X after your name, but I haven't come up with an Africanized name that feels right." Courtney eyes the Negus questioningly trying to decide if the Negus is serious or play-acting a roots man. Courtney decides to take him seriously and replies, "I'm not sure about that Lloyd. Africa is a very different place than here, and I'm not sure what relevance it has for me or my family. I'm an American not an African. Out of the corner of my eye I see Mel Gray slowly and surreptitiously nodding his head. I also see the anger in the Negus' eyes. "Well, Mr. Cartwright, you must be one of those soulless Bougie Negroes who thinks he can make it in the white man's world."

"You think you know me Mr. Redmayne, but you don't know me. Where do you get off stereotyping me?" Claudine becomes agitated and intervenes. "Boys, boys, calm down. We're all on the same side here. We're marching for our rights. Isn't that why we're here? The Negus says, "I'm here to fight for the dignity of Afro-Americans. I think Black people need to unite and demand our rights, not beg for them. And this March is the first sign I've seen of the Black Masses beginning to do just that. Why are you here, Mr. White?" I am startled by the Negus's question. I thought I was observing an argument between the Negus and Courtney. "I mean I ask you this because this is really not your fight, is it Izzy?" I didn't realize how angry he has been with me for de-pledging BOSS until now. "I think it is. Negro rights are human rights." The Negus purses his lips and says, "The notion of human rights seems pretty abstract to me, Izzy, but what we Black people are fighting for comes from the lived experience of our people, from the cultural degradation, blood, and lives of our ancestors. We have been raped physically and spiritually by the white man for over 300 years, and as a result, we have lost touch with the sources of our strength and of our manhood."

"You sound just like Malcolm." The Negus smiles and says, "Malcolm is not wrong in his analysis, only in his proposed solutions. And even those are not uniformly bad. His call for a Black State within the United States of course is nonsense." Courtney then jumps in with "You challenged Izzy about why he's here, how about you? Given your Black Nationalist views, why are you here?"

"Because demanding your rights is an act of manhood: and even though I believe prospects are slim that we will fully obtain them in this country that believes in democracy for the pale, it is necessary for us to make the attempt." Courtney responds, "I understand what you are saying, but my view is that race is a social fiction and should not be given such a place of prominence in our thinking. We are all Americans and all are entitled to the same God-given rights.

Now mind you, this intellectual debate is taking place as we are marching toward the Lincoln Memorial with signs and banners brightly waving and the sound of music hovering over us all. It seems as if hundreds of thousands of Black and white people were taking a holiday promenade down a major avenue of one of the most elegant parts of the city. As the debate between the Negus and Courtney rages on I hear someone near me sounding out an unusual syncopated beat with his mouth. Drawn by the sound, I eventually find the acappella drummer, and I discover that it is Rick Bee Bop Frazier who I haven't seen in a couple of years. "Hey Bee Bop, what're you beating out?"

"It's a Joe Morello's drum solo from Brubeck's Take Five album. Ya dig, man? Hey, Izzy, is that you? I'm so glad you're at this March man. It's so boss to see white brothers and sisters joining their Black brothers and sisters at a march for jobs and freedom."

"Man, it's been awhile since I've seen you, Bee Bop. What've you been up to?"

"I graduated, like you, my pale brother. I got a degree in Fine Arts. I've decided to make music my life. It's the only language I speak well. Besides, do you know that in the arts there is not the same kind of racial hatred as in other professions? I routinely jam with brothers of all hues, and the only criterion for eligibility is that you have to be good at what you do. That's a world I can live in."

"So what's next for you?"

"I got a part-time job in a music store, which allows me plenty of time to work on my drumming and play with several different jazz groups at various clubs in DC. And you Izzy?

"Grad school; University of Illinois."

"That's great, Iz. I always knew you were heavy."

By now we are adjacent to the Reflecting Pool. Bee Bop addresses the group and says, "My feets need to chill, people. Let's go stick our dogs in the Pool." Everyone loves this idea. A few moments later our entire group has their feet in the Reflecting Pool along with several hundred other marchers. From here we are able to see the speakers' stand at the Lincoln Memorial. Because of the loudspeakers set up at the Ellipse, we can hear Peter, Paul, and Mary singing Blowing in the Wind. In the middle of the song, its author, Bob Dylan, joins the three troubadours.

As tears pool in my eyes I see the same thing happening to everyone in our group. Even the Negus's cheek is tear-stained, and his habitually icy demeanor thaws in the warming profundity of Dylan's words. Despite our differences our shared tears tell the same story. We all lament the brutal treatment accorded dark-skinned people in our country, and we all share the same idealistic goal-that all people should treat our fellow Americans with respect. We must acknowledge that every American has the same rights. It may not be cool to say it, but that is what this march is about. We see each other's tears and know we are forever united by this goal.

With the addition of the BOSS brothers we have become a largish group. We all get out our brown bags and have our lunch. Our conversation turns to speculation about the prospects of an improved football season for the woeful Washington Redskins. Claudine groans, "Oh brother!" And pulls out a book. Hope springs eternal because several of us thought the Redskins were going to improve over their five win season the year before. Their record of 5-7-2 was a significant improvement over the 1961 season in which they won only one game while accumulating 12 losses and one tie. Some are convinced that they will even do better in the coming year. Others thought that unless the Redskins dump their coach, Bill McPeak, they would permanently remain in the bottom half of the Eastern Conference of the NFL. Ever the skeptic, Lloyd Redmayne suggests, "The only reason that the Redskins improved at all is because their racist owner, George Marshall, finally got a black player in Bobby Mitchell. And that brother tore up and down the field, blowing by all defenders and scoring more touchdowns for the Redskins then they have seen since the 1930s. They got to get rid of their owner as well as get a new coach. In my lifetime, I would like to see a Black coach and a Black quarterback, but that ain't gonna happen, not with the Redskins."

"Amen to that," says Courtney, happy to find something he and the Negus can agree on. David suggests that we find another team to root for because the Redskins will always cause you heartburn. "I'm getting heartburn just listening to you cynics badmouth my team. They're gonna win a championship one day," I predict.

"Yeah and the USA will have a Black President one day," says James shaking his head in disbelief. That tears it. We all laugh uncontrollably for several minutes until we simultaneously complain of belly pain. Lloyd Redmayne is laughing so hard he damned near falls into the Reflecting Pool. Colby reels him in just in time. But in the process, Colby loses his balance and falls face first into the Pool. Now the laughter becomes so hard and prolonged, the belly pain is almost unbearable. As Colby pulls himself up, the Negus can barely get the words out between his guffaws. "Hey Colby, don't you know that swimming is not allowed in the Reflecting Pool." Still caught up in the giggles, Bee Bop chooses this moment to give me half of his powdered doughnut. Without thinking about it, I take a bite. I suddenly remember my panic attack when Courtney offered me the same treat in Chemistry Lab. This sets me back into laughter, and I am in such pain that I am rolling round on the grass. Bee Bop looks totally confused. "What did I do?" he asks me. This makes me laugh even more. When I can finally compose myself, I tell him that he has just reminded me that I am cured of my Negrophobia. "Aw Izzy, you are one strange white cat." I tell the group the story and Courtney turns crimson. He says, "You know I wondered for the longest time why you were so hesitant to take a bite out of that doughnut. I thought you were worried about the acid stains on my hand. But that made no sense because you had just as much acid on your hands."

"And I was too embarrassed to tell you what I was really worried about. I was absolutely terrified of becoming nigrafied."

"Oh yeah, Izzy, ain't nothing worse than being nigrafied," says, Lloyd. Once again we engage in a group guffaw. The nearby marchers are beginning to look a little perturbed at what must have seen to them to be a pack of hyenas yucking it up.

It's approaching two o'clock when the speeches are to begin, and all of us are feeling the heat. Even though I have lived in DC all my life, it still surprises me how intense the August heat can become. The high humidity increases our suffering because it feels like we're breathing with a wet rag over our faces.

Claudine is waving an ineffective fan that she has retrieved from her purse. "You know what, boys, we need to find some shade. Let's head for the trees on the side of the Memorial. We all agree and start heading for our new destination. As we walk among the sea of signs I see one that rivets my attention: We Seek in 1963 the Freedom that was Promised in 1863. It is truly sad to realize that it has been 100 years since the Emancipation Proclamation and Negroes are still treated so hideously in the so-called "Land of the Free".

Off to the right side of the Lincoln Memorial, I see two familiar faces holding signs. It was Archie Green, the card shark I met at the Student Union my freshman year.

With him is Archie's best friend, Rayford Dixon. Archie is holding up a sign that says No U.S. Dough to Help Jim Crow Grow. I laughed to myself as I remembered the student protest at Howard against segregated unions contracted to build the new Burr Gymnasium. Ray Dixon's sign says We March for Jobs For All/ A Decent Pay Now. "Hey Archie, Ray, what the hell are you guys doing here?" They both look at me and didn't immediately recognize me. They were in shock to have their attendance at the March questioned by some unknown white boy. "Who the fuck are you?" a perturbed Archie Green says to me. His uncomprehending eyes looked me up and down in fear. "It's me, Izzy, Izzy White. We met a few years back at the Student Union. You and Ray asked me the same question about my attending Howard. " Ray is the first to recognize me. Oh yeah, I dig ya now. Hey Archie, don't you remember, you did your Black survival rap for this white cat after you cleaned out a group of fellow students in a card game. Archie scratches his goatee and looks at me again with greater intensity until recognition comes. "Well, I'll be damned. What's happenin', Izzy? What the hell are you doing here?"

"The same as you. Supporting a good cause. But I have the virtue of consistency. I told you guys four years ago that I was sympathetic to the cause. You, however, thought that any political or direct action was to quote you, 'A fucking waste of time'."

"Yes, well that was before the sit-ins, before I learned about NAG and SNCC and the power of the student movement. Much to my surprise, I learned that direct action was dangerous, exciting, life threatening, and ultimately effective. In fact, I found that hassling racist peckerwoods was more fun than getting rich playing cards." And Ray interjects, "Like I told you before, the issue is power. And when I saw what the student movement has produced in the last four years, I'm convinced that we can bury Jim Crow once and for all. What about you, Izzy? What are your plans?"

"I've been amazed by what has been accomplished and depressed by the horror of the racist resistance. And I now know that I can only root from the sidelines. I don't have the balls to become a full time activist. So I'm off to grad school in two weeks." Courtney jumps into the discussion, "But Izzy, you're here at the biggest march ever for Negro rights. You're braver than you think."

"Maybe, but I never bought into the hysteria surrounding the March. I've always passed the hysteria off to mass Negrophobia." Lloyd Redmayne adds, "You're right about that, Izzy. And the hysteria starts at the top. The President is shitting his pants right now because he's afraid that when you get a large group of niggers together, you know a riot's gonna happen. That's why he wants all the niggers out of town before sundown. Don't you know the Army is hiding somewhere around the Memorial just waiting for us Jiggaboos to get out of hand? "

"But I see a lot of white people in the crowd."

"Worse yet. Everybody expects Negroes to turn on the whites in the crowd and start an interracial riot right here on the grounds of the Lincoln Memorial." Lloyd throws a fake jab at me. 'Take that, Izzy Whiteman," the Negus says as he begins his dance of laughter. We all laugh at Lloyd's parody. Vince announces that the speeches are about to begin. Dick Gregory is at the microphone and he says, "The last time I've seen so many black people was in a Birmingham jail." I look around at what seemed a half-a-million people laughing at Gregory's line. People stretched from the Lincoln Memorial all the way back to the Washington Monument.

The Star Spangled Banner is sung, and then Archbishop O'Boyle gives the invocation. A. Philip Randolph, the Organizer of the March, begins the speeches:

"We are gathered here today for the largest demonstration in the history of this nation. Let the nation and the world know the meaning of our numbers."

Contradicting the critics of the March, he continues that we are not a pressure group or mob. "We are the advance guard of a massive moral revolution for jobs and freedom. " Thundering applause accompanies loud yells and whistles. Toward the end of his remarks, he adds "The March on

Washington is not the climax of our struggle, but a new beginning not only for the Negro but for all Americans who thirst for freedom and a better life." His remarks fill me with a rare moment of happiness and self-contentment that I pushed myself to attend this historical event.

The sun has become so intense that it affects our concentration. In search of shade, we all agree to continue our sojourn toward the more heavily treed area almost behind the Memorial. As we do, we hear the Opera singer, Marion Anderson, who 25 years before had been denied the right to sing at the DAR Constitution Hall because of her color. She is singing He's Got the Whole World in His Hands. At one shady expanse we see a group of NAG members and with them are Desirie and Michael White. Michael had been the first person I met at Howard who prophesied to me that "a change is gonna come". After an extended round of introductions, Michael White grabs me and says, "You see, Izzy, a change is underway. You remember when I told you it was coming? Well, by God, it's here! It's here, Izzy, and I sill can't believe my own words and my own eyes. " "You were right, Michael. I didn't really understand what you originally meant. But now I do, Michael, now I do. We clap each other on the back. In my enthusiasm, I grab Desirie's hand and give her the warmest of greeting. In return I am met with a very cool hello. So many people, so many signs, I can hardly see anything. Some marchers have climbed the trees in order to see what's going on. John Lewis, The Chairman of SNCC is the next speaker. Lewis was tough on President Kennedy's Civil Rights Bill that is currently before Congress. But I am more taken by his critique of Congress and his call for a social revolution.

My friends let us not forget that we are involved in a serious social revolution. By and large, American politics is dominated by politicians who build their careers on immoral compromises and ally themselves with open forms of political, economic, and social exploitation.

And his response to Congressional failure:

"If we do not get meaningful legislation of this Congress, the time will come when we will not confine our marching to Washington.

We will march through the South, through the streets of Jackson, through the streets of Cambridge, through the streets of Birmingham.

But we will march with the spirit of love and with the spirit of dignity that we have shown here today. By the force of our demands, our determination and our numbers, we shall splinter the desegregated South into a thousand pieces and put them back together in the image of God and democracy. We must say, "Wake up America. Wake up!!!"

The members of NAG who are with us are hooting and hollering their applause and support. Phil Workman whispers to me, "You should hear what he was originally gonna say. But Randolph talked him into cutting his more inflammatory metaphors."

"Like what, Phil?" He is shushed into silence so I never learn what Lewis had to cut.

Lewis's speech affirms the core belief of everyone there. Yes it's a fight for Negro rights, but more importantly it's a fight for the democratic ideal. Everyone's freedom is yoked to that of Negroes. There are so many shouts of "Amen", "You tell 'em", and "Preach it Rev. Lewis" that I think the collective mood can reach no greater heights. Our group is so high that we can barely absorb what the next group of speakers has to say. But I am so gratified to hear that the next speaker, a white Walter Reuther President of the UAW and CIO, tells the capacious crowd that Negroes should not be patient about obtaining their rights, rights guaranteed by the Constitution. I surprise myself when I let out with a very loud "DAMN STRAIGHT." Claudine laughs and says, "Izzy, I swear you must have Black blood in your family."

"Claudine, today I am Black, white, yellow, red and every other color that exists in the citizenry of the United States of America. This has been a great day so far."

After the consummate joy of the last two speeches and the emotional high that accompanied them, I am drained. I zone out. I can take in no more. And that is too bad because I really wanted to hear James Farmer of CORE, Whitney Young of the National Urban League and Roy Wilkins of the NAACP. The next voice I'm aware of is that of Gospel singer, Mahalia Jackson, singing "I've been 'buked and I've been scorned". The only other time I have ever heard such a soulful, passionate lamentation was when I heard the opera singer Richard Tucker sing "Kol Nidre". I look around at the group of people who I have accompanied to this moment, and, like me, they seem to be awakening from a prolonged sleep drawn to this voice of tears and pain. Our attention is riveted, our eyes moist, and our hearts riven with shared pain, pain that has nothing to do with color. Every human being who is alive this day knows the pain of being scorned, rebuked, and mistreated. There seems to be no escape from the malevolence of other human beings who look, act, think, and believe differently. And now comes Rev. Martin Luther King. Before A. Philip Randolph finishes his introduction a quarter of a million of us erupt into sustained applause for, in Randolph's words, "the leader of a moral revolution". I had heard some of his speeches before and was already enthralled by his moving metaphors. I am not disappointed today.

But one hundred years later, the Negro still is not free.
"One hundred years later, the life of the Negro is still sadly crippled by the manacles of segregation and the chains of discrimination."

From the multitude come the myriad sounds of affirmation. I rise up and throw my fist in the air. A few moments later King pleads:

"It would be fatal for the nation to overlook the urgency of the moment. This sweltering summer of the Negro's legitimate discontent..."

Mel Gray wipes his face and says, "Amen to that!"
"...will not pass until there is the invigorating autumn of freedom and equality. Nineteen sixty-three is not an end, but a beginning. And those who hope that the Negro needed to blow off steam and will now be content will have a rude awakening if the nation returns to business as usual. And there will be neither rest or tranquility in America until the Negro is granted his citizenship rights. The whirlwinds of revolt will continue to shake the foundations of our nation until the bright day of justice emerges."

We all stand up and join in the thunderous applause that overtakes the entire area of the Mall.

"The marvelous new militancy which has engulfed the Negro community must not lead us to a distrust of all white people, for many of our white brothers, as evidenced by their presence here today, have come to realize that their destiny is tied up with our destiny. And they have come to realize that their freedom is inextricably bound with our freedom."

I jump to my feet again and yell out "Yes!" But I notice that I am conspicuously alone.

King begins to describe his dream. And with each element of the dream, the crowd's mood rises.

"It is a dream deeply rooted in the American dream. I have a dream that one day this nation will rise up and live out the true meaning of its creed: 'We hold these truths to be self-evident, that all men are created equal.'

I have a dream that my four little children will one day live in a nation where they will not be judged by the color of their skin but by the content of their character.

I have a dream today.

I have a dream that one day every valley shall be exalted, and every hill and mountain shall be made low, the rough places will be made plain, and the crooked places will be made straight, "and the glory of the Lord shall be revealed and all flesh shall see it together."

Now everyone around me stands up and cheers and I silently remain seated. The atheist in me keeps me rooted to the ground.

And then comes his finale which leaves us all in high sprits, great hope, and emotional ecstasy:

"But not only that:

Let freedom ring from Stone Mountain of Georgia.
Let freedom ring from Lookout Mountain of Tennessee.
Let freedom ring from every hill and molehill of Mississippi
From every mountainside, let freedom ring.

And when this happens, and when we allow freedom ring, when we let it ring from every village and every hamlet, from every state and every city, we will be able to speed up
that day when all of God's children, black men and white men,
Jews and Gentiles, Protestants and Catholics, will be able to
Join hands and sing in the words of the old Negro spiritual:

Free at last! Free at last!
Thank God, Almighty, we are free at last!"

We all look at one another and no one is able to speak. King's words touch a very private place in each of us. His refrain of "I have a dream today" tells me dreams are the necessary prerequisite to action. And his dream is one I share: That one day everyone will grasp the necessity of viewing others as worthy of respect; that beyond all of the artificial categories of rank, status, class, race and religion, we are all made from the same fallible clay. His dream clarifies for me what I truly believe, who I really am. That is the unexpected gift of my time at Howard. Until this moment I had thought the phrase "To thine own self be true" was little more than a Shakespearian aphorism. I had searched for so much during my four years at Howard, the cure for my phobia, a special girl, validation of my quest to play college basketball, a career path; but I found the one thing I never expected to find—me, a self to be true to.

We remain speechless as everyone in our accidental group looks deeply into one another's eyes for a seemingly endless interval. Then we give one another a final goodbye hug. The group disperses in every direction, but two remain--Mel and Desirie.

"Well, Mel, I guess this is it. I doubt if I will see you again before I leave for Illinois."

"Izzy, I wish you the best."

"So I guess we can remain friends." In a gentle mocking tone, I add. "Your conditions have been met. Desirie and I are not together either actually or romantically." Desirie scowls at me, and Mel objects.

"Aw Izzy, don't...." I interrupt him. "I'm just messing with you, Mel. Didn't your X-Ray pick that up?"

"Nah, I'm too damn nervous about saying goodbye." With that, he grabs me in an intense bear hug. I return the embrace and beg him to please stay in touch.

"I never would neglect my best friend, Izzy. " I blush from this . "And now I'm gonna give you two a moment alone." Smiling sweetly, Desirie puts her hand on my cheek. "Izzy, you're such a sweet putz, and I'm going to miss you terribly." I laugh at her "yiddishkeit". The doleful pain begins in my chest as I study—perhaps for the last time—Desirie's beautiful brown face, her luminous smile, and her lust-seeding body. One by one my erogenous zones that she had so gently brought to life say a silent goodbye to her.

"Izzy, I hate to admit it, but you were right. As much as I loved you and still love you, we are not right for one another. We come from such different worlds, and our lives seem to be heading in different directions. I know that I have tried to make you something you're not. But that was only because the thought of losing you is so hard to bear."

"I know, Desirie. I wanted very much to be what you wanted, but as hard as I tried I'd get to a certain point and get lost. I no longer felt like me. It was very confusing because I know we want the same thing, but for different reasons. "

"Just because we are passionate about each other and we share some basic beliefs about Negro and human rights does not mean we can succeed in making a life together. Besides we're too young to get married. We're still trying to figure out who we are, and unless we know that, we have no chance of succeeding as life partners."

"I know you're right, but I want to be together with you. I can't bear to lose that. It's so good with us."

"You're just a horny white man, Izzy."

"If so, I'm horny just for you. I don't want to sleep with anybody else."

"That won't last long," Desirie says with a chuckle. But then she sees the sadness that comes over me, and she shifts out of her glibness. "Look, Izzy, it's been wonderful to be close to you that way, but we have to move on. I sincerely want us both to each find another partner who will be just as fulfilling." The thought of her with another man shuts down my ability to speak. "Listen, I have to go. I wish a wonderful life for you, Izzy." With that, she gives me a soft kiss on my lips. When I try to extend the kiss to a more passionate level, she pushes me away. "No, Izzy!" Then more softly, "Goodbye." She turns and walks toward the Reflecting Pool. I can barely see Mel standing by the pool waiting for her. As I watch her grow smaller in size, I look around to see the dissipating crowd going back to their shuttles, buses and cars. Soon the sign-littered grassways and the multitude of paper wrappings blowing in the wind like the idea of change itself are the only evidence left of today's momentous event, the largest and possibly the most morally portentous march ever held in the Nation's capital. I walk over to the Lincoln Memorial, stand in front of it just staring at the magnificent sculpture of a rare human being. I stand here for the longest time wondering what "The Great Emancipator" would have thought of this march and its large interracial turnout. I think he would be amazed by the turnout, but appalled to discover that our country is still so flummoxed by the racial divide and still fighting over the freedom of Black people. Despite the portents of positive change, the miasma of white supremacy is still poisoning the fragile growth of racial harmony. As if the statue were real, I say aloud "Yep, Mr. Lincoln, same old shit."

Acknowledgements

Many people contributed to the creation of this book beginning with my teammates and fellow students from long ago days at Howard University. They unknowingly contributed to the formation of my memories; and these have served as the fuel for the unfolding story of Izzy White? The novel was well served by the contemporary assistance tendered by several dear friends and colleagues who read early drafts. Dr. Paul Wachtel gave me a wealth of suggestions, criticisms, and creative advice. Dr. Kathryn Fentress also provided some excellent suggestions for improvement. Other friends and colleagues who read the novel and gave me sage advice include Dr. Mark Frankel, Joanne Gottheil, Scott Stossel (himself a wonderful editor and writer), Suzanne Payne, a Howard classmate and now dear friend, and my son and daughter-in-law, Neal and Emily Weiner. Other classmates gave me wonderful historical information about basketball and fraternity life at Howard; they include Wendell Boyd and Marshall Ishler. My nephew, Forest Rothchild, not only read the novel, but also helped this "computer dinosaur" prepare the manuscript for conversion into an Ebook. He also has constructed my new website. My gratitude for his efforts is boundless. Finally, words fail to do justice to the magnitude of love, support, and commitment that my soul mate, Annette, gave to this project. She served in several roles in producing the novel. She was a wonderful copy-editor, a supportive but challenging sounding board, and a sensitive and insightful "typical reader". She uncovered many false notes that found their way into the early drafts of the novel. In addition, she was an amazing hope peddler during those terrible moments when I thought I was wasting my time. Despite all this support, I am the lone culprit for any errors of fact, questionable writing, and dubious story making found within.

Made in the USA
Charleston, SC
12 February 2016